TASTES L

"We have been tracing [...] said the patrolman Hory.

"Why?" I asked. He had [...] height, palms empty and [...] rod weaving a pattern of threat directly before my eyes.

Hory, the rod in one hand, searched in the front of his tunic and produced a tangler. It flicked out from the tube to loop about my wrists, bringing them tightly together.

"Why?" he echoed. "Because I now know who you are. You gave yourself away, or that beast of yours did, when he had you bring out the ring." Hory kicked out and Eet's motionless body rolled over. I tried desperately to reach him through mind touch but met nothing. Once before I had believed him dead: now the evidence of my eyes assured me that was true.

"You are Murdoc Jern and your father was a notorious Guildman," Hory continued. "Your father was killed for information he had, probably about"—with the rod Hory indicated the ring—"that. You ought to have known you could not stand up against the Guild. Or did you believe that with that beast of yours you could do it? We will get the truth out of you with a reader-helm—"

"When and if you get me to a patrol base!" I said.

"Oh, I think that now there will be no chance of your escaping." Still facing me with the weld rod, Hory stooped and picked up Eet, a long string of furred body, by the hind legs. "This goes into cold storage. The lab will want to see it. And you shall go into another kind of storage, until you are needed."

Eet swung, a pitiful pendulum, from Hory's hand. I looked at Eet's body and my hate was no longer hot but cold, clear and deadly in me. And because I did look at Eet at that moment I saw my chance. For Eet came to life, twisting up to bury needle-sharp teeth in the hand which held him. And as Hory yelled in pain and surprise, I charged.

Baen Books
by Andre Norton

SEARCH FOR THE STAR STONES

ANDRE NORTON

SEARCH FOR THE STAR STONES

This is a work of fiction. All the characters and events portrayed in this book are fictional, and any resemblance to real people or incidents is purely coincidental.

A Baen Book

Baen Publishing Enterprises
P.O. Box 1403
Riverdale, NY 10471
www.baen.com

ISBN 13: 0-978-4391-3337-8

Cover art by Bob Eggleton

First Baen paperback printing, February 2010

Distributed by Simon & Schuster
1230 Avenue of the Americas
New York, NY 10020

Library of Congress Cataloging-in-Publication Data:
2008027067

Printed in the United States of America

10 9 8 7 6 5 4 3 2 1

CONTENTS

THE ZERO
STONE

For A. M. Lightner,
who was the "Godmother" for Eet

ONE

The dark was so thick in this stinking alley that a man might well put out his hand and catch shadows, pull them here or there, as if they were curtain stuff. Yet I could not quarrel with the fact that this world had no moon and that only its stars spotted the night sky, nor that the men of Koonga City did not set torchlights on any but the main ways of that den of disaster.

Here the acrid smells were almost as thick and strong as the dark, and under my boots the slime coating the uneven stone pavement was a further risk. While my fear urged me to run, prudence argued that I take only careful step after step, pausing to feel out the way before me. My only guide was an uncertain memory of a city I had known for only ten days, and those not dedicated to the study of geography. Somewhere ahead, if I was lucky, very, very lucky, there was a door. And on that door was set the head of a godling known to the men of this planet. In the night the eyes of that head would blaze with welcoming light, because behind the door were torches, carefully tended to burn the night through. And if a man being hunted through these streets and lanes for any reason, even fresh blood spilt before half the city for witness, could lay hand upon the latch below those blazing eyes, lift it, to enter the hall beyond, he had sanctuary from all hunters.

My outstretched fingers to the left slid along sweating stone, picking up a foul burden of stickiness as they passed. I had the laser in my right hand. It might buy me moments, a few of them, if I were cornered here, but only a few. And I was panting with the effort that had brought me so far, bewildered by the beginning of this nightmare which had certainly not been of my making, nor of Vondar's.

Vondar—resolutely I squeezed him from my thoughts. There had been no chance for him, not from the moment the four Green Robes had walked so quietly into the taproom, set up their spin wheel (all men there going white or gray of face as they watched those quiet, assured movements), and touched the wheel into life. The deadly arrow which tipped it whirled fatefully to point out, when it came to rest, he who would be an acceptable sacrifice to the demon they so propitiated.

We had sat there as if bound—which indeed we had been, in a sense, by the customs of this damnable world. Any man striving to withdraw after that arrow moved would have died, quickly, at the hands of his nearest neighbor. For there was no escape from this lottery. So we had sat there, but not in any fear, as it was not usual that an off-worlder be chosen by the Green Robes. They were not minded to have difficulty thereafter from the Patrol, or from powers beyond their own skies, being shrewd enough to know that a god may be great on his own world, and nothing under the weight of an unbeliever's iron fist, when that fist swung down from the stars.

Vondar had even leaned forward a little, studying the faces of those about us with that curiosity of his. He was as satisfied as he ever was, having done good business that day, filled himself with as fine a dinner as these barbarians knew how to prepare, and having gained a lead to a new source of lalor crystals.

Also, had he not unmasked the tricks of Hamzar, who had tried to foist on us a lalor of six carats weight but with a heart flaw? Vondar had triangulated the gem neatly and then pointed that such damage could not be polished out, and that the crystal which might have made Hamzar's fortune with a less expert buyer was an inferior stone in truth, worth only the price of an extra laser charge.

A laser charge—My fingers crooked tighter about my weapon. I would willingly exchange now a whole bag of lalors for another charge waiting at my belt. A man's life is ever worth, at least to him, more than the fabled Treasure of Jaccard.

So Vondar had watched the natives in the tavern, and they had watched the spinning arrow of death. Then that arrow had wavered to a halt—pointing at no man directly, but to the narrow space which existed between Vondar's shoulder and mine as we sat side by side. And Vondar had smiled then, saying:

"It would seem that their demon is somewhat undecided this night, Murdoc." He spoke in Basic, but there were probably those there who understood his words.

Even then he did not fear, or reach for a weapon—
though I had never known Vondar to be less than alert.
No man can follow the life of a gem buyer from planet
to planet without having eyes all around his head, a ready
laser, and a nose ever sniffing for the taint of danger.

If the demon had been undecided, his followers were
not. They came for us. From the long sleeves of their
robes suddenly appeared the bind cords used on prisoners they dragged to their lord's lair. I took the first of
those Green Robes, beaming across the table top, which
left the wood scorched and smoking. Vondar moved, but
a fraction too late. As the Free Traders say, his luck
spaced, for the man to his left sprang at him, slamming
him back against the wall, pinning his hand out of reach
of his weapon. They were all yammering at us now, the
Green Robes halting, content to let others take the risk
in pulling us down.

I caught a second man reaching for Vondar. But the
one already struggling with him I dared not ray, lest I
get my master too. Then I heard Vondar cry out, the
sound speedily smothered in a rush of blood from his
lips. We had been forced apart in the struggle and now,
as I slipped along the wall, trying to get beam sight on
the Green Robes, my shoulders met no solid surface. I
stumbled back and out, through a side door into the
street.

It was then that I ran, heedlessly at first, then dodging
into a deep doorway for a moment. I could hear the hunt
behind me. From such hunting there was little hope of
escape, for they were between me and the space port.
For a long moment I huddled in that doorway, seeing
no possible future beyond a fight to the end.

What fleeting scrap of memory was triggered then, I
did not know. But I thought of the sanctuary past which

Hamzar had taken us, three—four—days earlier. His story concerning it flashed into my mind, though at that instant I could not be sure in which direction that very thin hope of safety might lie.

I tried to push panic to the back of my mind, picture instead the street before me and how it ran in relation to the city. Training has saved many a man in such straits, and training came to my aid now. For memory had been fostered in me by stiff schooling. I was not the son and pupil of Hywel Jern for naught.

Thus and thus—I recalled the running of the streets, and thought I had some faint chance of following them. There was this, also—those who hunted me would deem they had all the advantages, that they need only keep between me and the space port and I would be easy prey, caught deep in the maze of their unfamiliar city.

I slipped from the shadow of the door and began a weaving which took me, not in the direction they would believe I would be desperately seeking, but veering from it north and west. And so I had come into this alley, slipping and scraping through its noisome muck.

My only guides were two, and to see one I had to look back to the tower of the port. Its light was strong and clear across this dark-skyed world. Keeping it ever at my right, I took it for a reverse signal. The other I could only catch glimpses of now and again as I scuttled from one shadowed space to the next. It was the watchtower of Koonga, standing tall to give warning against the sudden attacks of the barbarian sea rovers who raided down from the north in the lean seasons of the Great Cold.

The alley ended in a wall. I leaped to catch its crest, my laser held between my teeth. On the top I perched, looking about me, until I decided that the wall would now form my path. It continued to run along behind the buildings, offering none too wide a footing, but keeping me well above ground level. There were dim lights in the back windows of these upper stories, and from one to the next, they served me as beacons.

When I paused now and then to listen, I could hear the murmur of the hunters. They were spreading out from the main streets, into some of the alleys. But they did so cautiously, and I believed they did not face too happily a quarry who might be ready to loose a laser beam from the dark. Time was on their side, for with the coming of dawn, were I still away from the sanctuary, I could be readily picked out of any native gathering by my clothing alone. I wore a modified form of crew dress, suited to the seasoned space traveler, designed for ease on many different worlds, though not keeping to the uniform coloring of a crewman.

Vondar had favored a dull olive-green for our overtunics, the breast of his worked with the device of a master gemologist. Mine had the same, modified by an apprentice's two bars. Our boots were magnet-plated for ship wear, and our under garment was of one piece, like a working crewman's. In this world of long, fringed overrobes and twisted, colored headdresses, I would be very noticeable indeed. There was one small change I could make; I did so now, balancing precariously on my wall perch, once more holding the laser between my teeth as I loosed the seam seal and pulled off my overtunic with its bold blazoning. I rammed it into as small a ball as I could and teetered dangerously over a scrap of garden to push it into a fork of branches on a thorn bush. Then I crept along the wall top for the distance of four more houses until I came to the end at the rise of another building. From there I had a choice of leaps—down into a garden, or into the maw of another alley. I would have chosen the alley had I not frozen tight against the house wall at a sound from its depths. Something moved there, but certainly no number of men.

There was the sucking sound of a foot, or feet, lifted out of the slime, and I even thought I could hear the hiss of breathing. Whoever crept there was not moving with the openness of those who quested on my trail.

My hands had been braced against the house wall and now my fingers fell into holes there. I explored by touch and knew that I had come upon one of those geometric patterns which decorated the walls of more important buildings, some parts being intaglio and others projecting. As I felt above me, higher and higher, I began to believe that the pattern might extend clear to the roof and offer me a third way out.

Once more I crouched and this time I unsealed my boots, fastening them to the back of my belt. Then I climbed, after pausing for a long moment to listen to sounds below. They were farther away now, near the mouth of the alley.

Again my schooling came to my aid and I pulled myself up those sharply etched hand and toe holds until I swung over an ornamental parapet, past bold encrustations of demon faces set to frighten off the evil powers of natural forces.

The roof onto which I dropped sloped inward to a middle opening which gave down three floors to a center court with a core pool, into which rain water would feed during the spring storms. It was purposely smoothed to aid in that transfer of rain to reservoir, so I crept beside the parapet, my hands anchoring me from one spike of the wall to the next. But I did so with speed, for even in the dark I could see that now I was only a little away from my goal.

From this height I could see also the space port. There were two ships there, one a passenger-cum-trader, on which that very morning Vondar had taken passage for us. It was as far from me now as if half the Dark Dragon curled between. They would know that we had bought passage on it and would keep it cordoned. The other, farther away, was a Free Trader. And, while no one normally interfered with one of those or its crew, I could make no claim on it for protection. Even if I reached sanctuary, what further hope would I have? I pushed aside that fear and turned to examine the immediate prospect of getting to the doorway. Now I would have to descend the outer face of the building into a lighted street. There were more bands of decoration and I had little doubt they would make me a ladder, if I could go unsighted. However, torches flamed in brackets along that way, and compared with the back streets through which I had fled, this was as light as a concourse on one of the inner planets.

Few men were abroad so late with legal reason. And I heard no sounds to suggest that the hunt had spread this far. They must rather be patrolling near the field. I had come this far; there was no retreat now. Giving a last searching glance below, I slipped between two of the ornaments and began the descent.

From hold to hold, feeling for those below, trusting to the strength in my fingers and wrists, I worked my way down. I had passed the top story when I came upon a window, my feet thudding home on its jutting sill. I balanced there, my hands on either side, my face to the dark interior. And then I was near startled into letting go my grasp by a shrill scream from within.

I was not conscious of making the first few drops of my continued flight down the wall. There was a second scream and a third. How soon would the household be aroused, or attention raised in the street? Finally I let go, fell in a roll. Then, not even stopping to put on my boots, I ran as I had not run before, without looking back to see what fury I had roused.

Along the house walls, sprinting from one patch of shadow to the next, I dashed. Now I could hear cries behind. At the least, the screamer had aroused members of her own household. But there came a street corner and—memory had served me right! I could sight the bright eyes of the godling on the door. I ran with open mouth, sucking in quick breaths, my boots still fastened to my belt and knocking against my hips, the laser in my hand. On and on—and always I feared to see someone step into the open between me and the face with the blazing eyes. But there was no halting and with a last burst of speed I hit against the portal, my fingers scrabbling for the ring below the head. With a jerk I pulled it. For a second or two the door, contrary to promise, seemed to resist my efforts. Then it gave, and I stumbled into a hall where stood the torches which gave light to the beacon eyes.

I had forgotten the door as I wavered on, intent only on getting inside, away from the rising clamor in the street. Then I tripped and fell forward on my knees. Somehow I squirmed around, the laser ready. Already the door was swinging shut, shutting off a scene of running men, light gleaming on the bared blades they held.

Breathing hard, I watched the door shut by itself, and then was content to sit there for a space. I had not realized how great the strain of my flight had been until this island of safety held me. It was good simply to sit on the floor of that passage and know I need not run.

Finally I roused enough to draw my boots on and look about me. Hamzar's tale of sanctuary had not gone beyond the few facts of the face on the door and the guarantee that no malefactor could be taken from within. I had expected some type of temple to lie behind such a story. But I was not in the court of any fane now, only in a narrow hall with no doors. Very close to me stood a stone rack in which were set two oil-soaked torches, blazing steadily to form the beacon of the door eyes.

I got to my feet and rounded that barrier, waiting for a challenge from whoever tended those night lights. With my back to their flames I saw only more corridor, unbroken, shadows at its far end which could veil anything. With some caution I advanced.

Unlike the glimpses I had had into the various other temples of Koonga, these walls were unpainted, being only the native yellow stone such as cobbled the wider streets. The same stone formed the wide blocks of the floor, and as far as I could see, the ceiling as well.

They were worn in places underfoot, as if from centuries of use. Also here and there on the floor were dark splotches following no pattern, which suggested unpleasantly that some of those who had come this way earlier might have suffered hurts during their flight, and that there had been no effort to clean away such traces.

I reached the end of the corridor and discovered it made a sharp turn to the right, one which was not visible until one reached it. To the left was only wall. That new way, being out of the path of the torches, was almost as dark as the alleys. I tried to pierce its dusk, wishing I had a beamer. Finally I turned the laser on lowest energy, sending a white pencil which scored the stained blocks of the flooring, but gave me light.

The new passage was only about four paces long. Then I was in a square box of a room and the laser beam touched upon an unlighted torch in a wall bracket. That blazed and I switched off the weapon, blinking. I might have been in a room furnished by one of the cheaper inns. Against the far wall was a basin of stone, into which trickled a small runnel of water, the overflow channeled back into the surface of the wall again.

There was a bedframe fitted with a netting of cords, a matting of dried and faintly aromatic leaves laid over it. Not a comfortable bed, but enough to keep one's bones from aching too much. There were two stools, a small guesting table set between them. They bore none of the customary carving, but were plain, however smoothed by long use.

In the wall opposite the bed was a niche in which sat a flagon of dull metal, a small basket, and a bell. But there were no doors to the room. And I could see no other exit save the corridor along which I had come. It began to impress me that this vaunted sanctuary was close to a prison, if the trapped dare not venture forth again.

I forced the torch out of its wall hold and carried it about, searching the walls, the ceiling, the floor, to find no break. At last I wedged it back into place. The bell by the flagon next held my attention and I picked it up. A bell suggested signaling. Perhaps it would bring me an explainer—or an explanation. I rang it with as much force as I could get into a snap of the wrist. For so large a bell, it gave forth a very muted tinkle, though I tried it several times, waiting between each for an answer. That did not come, until at last I slammed it back into the niche and went to sit on the bed.

When the delayed answer to my impatient summons came, it was startling enough to bring me to my feet, laser drawn. For a voice spoke out of the air seemingly only a few feet away.

"To Noskald you have come, in His Shadow abide—for the waning of four torches."

It was a moment before I realized that that voice had not used the lisping speech of Koonga, but Basic. Then they must know me for an off-worlder!

"Who are you?" My own words echoed hollowly as that voice had not. "Let me see you!"

Silence only. I spoke again, first promising awards if my plight was told at the port, or if they would give me help in reaching it. Then I threatened, speaking of the ill which came when off-worlders were harmed—though I guessed that perhaps they were shrewd enough to know how hollow those threats were. There was no answer—no sign I was even heard. It could have been a recording which addressed me. And who the guardians here were I did not know either—a priesthood? Then they might be akin to the Green Robes and so would do me no favors, save those forced upon them by custom.

At last I curled into the bed and slept—and dreamed—very vivid dreams which were not fancies spun by the unconscious mind, but memories out of the past. So, as it is said a dying man sometimes does, I relived much of my life, which had not been so long in years.

My beginnings were overshadowed by another—Hywel Jern—who, in his time, had had a name to be reckoned with on more than one planet—and who could speak with authority in places where even the Patrol must walk with cat-soft feet, fearing to start what would take death and blood to finish.

My father had a past as murky as the shallow inlets of Hawaki after autumn storms. I do not think that any man save himself knew the whole of it; certainly we did not. For years after his death I still came across hints, bits and pieces, which each time opened another door, to show me yet another Hywel Jern. Even when I was young, at times when a coup of more than ordinary cleverness warmed whatever organ served him as a heart, he launched into a tale which was perhaps born out of his own adventuring, though he spoke always of some other man as the actor in it. Always this story was a lesson aimed at impressing upon his listeners some point of bargaining, or of action in crisis. And all his tales made more of things than of people, who were only incidental, being the owners or obtainers of objects of beauty or rarity.

Until he was close to fifty planet years old, he was prime assessor to the Veep Estampha, a sector boss of the Thieves' Guild. My father never tried to hide this association; in fact it was a matter of pride to him. Since he seemed to have an inborn talent, which he fostered by constant study, for the valuing of unusual loot, he was a valuable man, ranking well above the general core of that illegal combine. However, he appeared to have lacked ambition to climb higher, or else he simply had an astute desire to remain alive and not a target of the ambition of others.

Then Estampha met a rootless Borer plant, which someone with ambition secreted in his private collection of exotic blooms, and came to an abrupt finish. My father withdrew prudently and at once from the resulting scramble for power. Instead he bought out of the Guild and migrated to Angkor.

For a while, I believe, he lived very quietly. But during that period he was studying both the planet and the openings for a lucrative business. It was a sparsely settled world on the pioneer level, not one which at that time attracted the attention of those with wealth, nor of the Guild. But perhaps my father had already heard rumors of what was to come.

Within a space of time he paid court to a native woman whose father operated a small hock-lock for pawning, as well as a trading post, near the only space port. Shortly after his marriage the father-in-law died of an off-world fever, a plague ship having made a crash landing before it could be warned off. The fever also decimated most of the port authorities. But Hywel Jern and his wife proved immune and carried on some of the official duties at this time, which entrenched them firmly when the plague had run its course and the government was restored.

Then, some five years later, the Vultorian star cluster was brought into cross-stellar trade by the Fortuna Combine, and Angkor suddenly came to life as a shipping port of exchange. My father's business prospered, though he did not expand the original hock-lock.

With his many off-world contacts, both legal and illegal, he did well, but to outward appearances, only in a modest way. All spacers sooner or later lay hands on portable treasures or curiosities. To have a buyer who asked no questions and paid promptly was all they wanted at any port where the gaming tables and other planetside amusements separated them too fast from flight pay.

This quiet prosperity lasted for years, and appeared to be all my father wanted.

TWO

If Hywel Jern had contracted his marriage for reasons of convenience, it was a stable one. There were children: myself, Faskel, and Darina. My father took little interest in his daughter, but he early bent more than a little energy to the training of Faskel and me; not that Faskel showed any great promise along the lines Hywel Jern thought important.

It was the custom for us to assemble at a large table in an inner room (we lived over and behind the shop) for the evening meal. And at that time my father would bring out and pass around some item from his stock, first asking an opinion of it—its value, age, nature. Gems were a passion with him and we were forced to learn them as other children might scan book tapes for general knowledge. To my father's satisfaction I proved an apt pupil. In time he centered most of his instruction on me, since Faskel, either because he could not, or because he stubbornly would not learn, again and again made some mistake which sent our father into one of his cold and silent withdrawals.

I never saw Hywel Jern lose his temper, but his cold displeasure was not to be courted. It was not so much that I feared such censure as that I was really fascinated and interested in what he had to teach. Before I was out of childhood I was allowed to judge the pledges in the shop. And whenever one of the gem merchants who visited my father from time to time came, I was displayed as a star pupil.

So through the years our house became one divided, my mother, Faskel, and Darina on one side, my father and I on the other. And our contact—or mine—with other children of the port was limited, my father drawing me more and more into the shop to learn his old trade of valuing. Some strange and beautiful things passed through our hands in those days. Part were sold openly, others remained in his lockboxes, to be offered in private transactions, and of those I did not see all.

There were things from alien ruins and tombs, made before the time that our species burst into space; there were pieces looted from empires which had vanished into the dust of history so long past that even their planets had been buried. And there were others new from the workshops of the inner systems, where all the creative art of a jeweler is unleashed to catch the eye of a Veep with a bottomless purse.

My father liked the old pieces the most. Sometimes he would hold a necklet, or a bracelet (which by its form had never been meant to encircle a human wrist) and speculate about who had worn it and the civilization from which it had come. And he demanded of those who brought him such trinkets as clear a history of their discovery as he could obtain, putting on tapes all he could learn.

I think that these tapes in themselves might have proven a rich treasure house for seekers of strange knowledge, and I have wondered since if Faskel ever suspected their worth and used them so. Perhaps he did, for in some ways he proved to be more shrewd than my father.

In one of our round-table meetings after an evening meal my father produced such an alien curiosity. He did not pass it from hand to hand as was his wont, but laid it on the well-polished board of dead-black creel wood and sat staring at it as if he were one of the fakirs from the dry lands seeking to read a housewife's future in a polished seed pod.

It was a ring, or at least it followed that form. But the band must have been made for a finger close to the size of two of ours laid together. The metal was dull, pitted, as if from great age.

Its claw setting held a stone bigger than my thumbnail, in proper proportion to the band. And it was as dull and unappealing as the metal, colorless, no sparkle or hint of life in it. Also, the longer one studied it, the more the idea grew in mind that this was the corpse of something which might have once had life and beauty but was long since dead. I had, at that first viewing, a disinclination to touch it, though I was always avid to examine these bits and pieces my father used for our instruction.

"Out of another tomb? I wish you would not bring these corpse ornaments to the table!" My mother spoke more sharply than was usual. At that time it struck me odd that she, whom I thought immune to imaginative fancies, had also so quickly associated the ring with death.

My father did not raise his eyes from the ring. Rather he spoke to Faskel in the voice he used when he would be answered, and at once.

"What make you of this?"

My brother put out his hand as if to touch the ring and then jerked it back again. "A ring—too large to wear. Maybe a temple offering."

To that my father made no comment. Instead he said to Darina:

"And you see what?"

"It is cold—so cold—" My sister's thin voice trailed off, and then she pushed away from the table. "I do not like it."

"And you?" My father turned to me at last.

Temple offering it might have been, fashioned larger than life to fit on the finger of some god or goddess. I had seen such things pass through my father's hands before. And some of them had had that about them which gave one a queasy feeling upon touching. But if any god had worn this—No, I did not believe it had been made for such a purpose. Darina was also right. It evoked a sensation of cold, as well as of death. However, the more I studied it, the more it fascinated me. I wanted to touch, yet I feared. And it seemed to me that my feeling reflected something about the ring which made it more than any other gem I had seen, though it was now but age-pitted metal set with a lifeless stone.

"I do not know—save that it is—or was—a thing of power!" And my certainty of that fact was such that I spoke more loudly than I had meant to, so my final word rang through the room.

"Where did it come from?" Faskel asked quickly, hunching forward again and putting out his hand as if to lay it over ring and stone, though his fingers only hovered above it. In that moment I had the thought that he who did take it firmly would be following the custom of gem dealers: to close hand about a jewel was to accept an offered bargain. But if that were so, Faskel did not quite dare to accept such a challenge, for he drew back his hand a second time.

"From space," my father returned.

There *are* gems out of space—primitive peoples pay high sums to own them. What forms them we are not quite sure even yet. The accepted theory is that they are produced when bits of meteor of the proper metallic composition pass through the blaze of a planet's atmosphere. It was the fad for a while to make space Captains' rings out of these tektites. I have seen several such, centuries old, which must have been worn by the first space venturers. But this gem, if gem it really was, bore no resemblance to those, for it was not dark green, black, or brown, but a colorless crystal, dulled as if sand had pitted the surface deeply.

"It does not look like a tektite—" I ventured.

My father shook his head. "It was not formed in space, not that I know of—it was found there." He leaned back in his chair and took up his cup of folgar tea, sipping absent-mindedly as he continued to stare at the ring. "A curious tale—"

"We expect Councilor Sands and his lady—" my mother interrupted abruptly, as if she knew the tale and wanted not to hear it again. "The hour grows late." She started to gather our cups, then raised her hands to clap for Staffla, our serving maid.

"A curious tale," my father repeated as if he had not heard her at all. And such was his hold over his household that she did not summon Staffla, but sat, moving a little uneasily, plainly unhappy.

"But a true one—of that I am sure," my father continued. "This was brought in today by the first officer of the *Astra*. They had a grid failure in mid-passage and had to come out of hyper for repairs. Their luck continued bad, for they had a holing from a meteor pebble. It was necessary then to patch the hull as well." He was telling this badly, not as he usually spun such stories, but more as one who would keep strictly to facts, and those were meager. "Kjor was doing the patch job when he saw it—a floater—He beamed out on his stay line and brought it in—a body in a suit. Not"—my father hesitated—"of any species he knew. And it had been there a long time. It wore this over its suit glove." He pointed to the ring.

Over the glove of a space suit—the strangeness of that indeed made one wonder. The gloves are supple enough; they have to be if a man wears them in outer space for ship repair, or while exploring a planet deadly to his species. But why would anyone want to wear an ornament over such a glove? I must have asked that aloud for my father answered:

"Why indeed? Certainly not for any reason of show. Therefore—this had importance, vast importance, to him who wore it. Enough that I would like to know it better."

"There are tests," Faskel observed.

"This is a gem stone, unknown to me, and twelve on the Mohs scale—"

"A diamond is ten—"

"And a Javsite eleven," my father returned. "Heretofore that was the measuring rod. This is something beyond our present knowledge."

"The Institute—" began my mother, but my father put out his hand and cupped the ring in it, hiding it from sight. So hidden, he restored it to a small bag and slipped that into his inner tunic pocket.

"This is not to be spoken of!" he ordered sharply. And from that moment on we would not speak of it, as he well knew. He had trained us very well. But neither did he send it to the Institute, nor, I was sure, did he seek any other official information concerning it. But that he studied and tested it by all methods known, and they were not a few, that I also learned.

I became used to seeing him in his small laboratory, at his desk, the ring on a square of black cloth before him, staring down at it as if by the very strength of his will he would extract its secret. If it had ever had any beauty, time and the drift through space had destroyed that, and what was left was an enigma but no blazing treasure.

The mystery haunted me also, and from time to time my father would speak of various theories he had formed concerning it. He was firmly convinced that it was not meant to be an ornament, but that it had served its wearer in some manner. And he kept its possession a secret.

From the day my father had taken over the shop, he had set into its walls various hiding places. And later, upon enlarging the rooms, he had built in more such pockets. The majority of these were known to the whole family, and would answer to hand pressure from any of us. But there were a few he showed only to me. And one of these, in the laboratory, held the ring. My father altered the seal there to answer only to our two thumbs, and he had me seal and unseal it several times before he was satisfied.

Then he waved me to sit down opposite him.

"Vondar Ustle arrives tomorrow," he began abruptly. "He will bring an apprentice warrant with him. When he leaves, you go with him—"

I could not believe my hearing. As eldest son, apprenticeship, save to my father, was not for me. If anyone went to serve another master it would be Faskel. But before I could raise a question, my father went on with as much explanation as I was ever to get from him.

"Vondar is a master gemologist, though he chooses to travel rather than set up an establishment on any one planet. There is no better teacher in the galaxy. I have good reason to be sure of that. Listen well, Murdoc—this shop is not for you. You have a talent, and a man who does not develop his talent is a man who ever eats dry oat-cake while before him sits a rich meat dish, a man who chooses a zircon when he need only reach out his hand to pick up a diamond. Leave this shop to Faskel—"

"But he—"

My father smiled thinly. "No, he is not one who has a great eye for what is to be seen, beyond a fat purse and the value in credits. A shopkeeper is a shopkeeper, and you are not meant for such. I have waited a long time for a man such as Ustle, one on whom I can depend to be the teacher you must have. In my day I was known as a master at valuing, but I served in murky ways. You must walk free of such ties, and you can gain such freedom only by cutting loose now from the very name you carry on Angkor. Also—you must see more than one world, walk other planets, if you are to be all that you can be. It is known that planetary magnetic fields can influence human behavior, some ebb and flow in them producing changes in the brain. Alertness and sensibility are stimulated by these changes; memory can be fostered the brighter, ideas incited. I want what you can learn from Ustle during the next five planet years."

"Something to do with the space stone—?"

He nodded. "I can no longer go seeking knowledge, but you who have a mind link unto mine are not rooted. Before I die I want to know what that ring holds, and what it did or can do for the man who wears it!"

Once more he got up and brought out the ring bag, removed the band with its dull stone, and turned it about in his fingers.

"There was an old superstition once believed in by our species," he said slowly, "that we left impressions of ourselves on material things we had owned, providing those objects were closely tied into our destinies. Here—" Of a sudden he tossed the ring at me. I was unprepared, but I caught it, almost on reflex, out of the air. For all the months we had had it under this roof, that was the first time I had held it.

The metal was cold, with a gritty surface. And it seemed to me, as it rested in my palm, the cold grew stronger, so that my skin tingled with it. But I lifted it to eye level and peered at the stone. The clouded surface was as gritty as the band. If it had ever held fire in its heart, that was long since quenched or clouded over. I wondered briefly if it could be detached from that rough setting and recut, to regain the life it had lost. But knew also that my father would never attempt to do that. Nor,

I decided, could I. As it was, the mystery was all. It was not the ring itself but what lay behind it that was of importance. And now my father's plans for me also made sense—I would be the seeker for a solution to our mystery.

So I became Ustle's apprentice. And my father proved right; such an instructor is seldom found. My master might have made several fortunes had he wished to root on one of the luxury worlds, set up as a designer and merchant. But to him the quest for the perfect stone was far more meaningful than selling it. He did design— usually during our voyages his mind and his fingers were busy, turning out patterns which other, less talented men were eager to buy when he wanted to offer them. But his passion was exploration of the secrets of new-found worlds, doing his own bargaining with natives for uncut stones not far from where·they were first unearthed.

He laughed at the frauds he uncovered—the lesser stones soaked in herbs or chemicals to make them more resemble the precious, the gems treated by heat to change their color. He taught me odd ways to impress native sellers so that they respected one's wisdom and brought out the better rather than the worse. Such things as that a human hair stretched across real jade will not burn, even though you set match to it.

Planet time is reckoned in years, space time less easily. A man who makes many voyages does not age as quickly as the earth-bound. I do not know how old Vondar was, but if he were judged by his store of knowledge, he must have outstripped my father. We went far from Angkor, but in time we returned to it. Only I had no crumb, not even infinitesimally small, to offer my father on the history of the space ring.

I had not been more than a day under our own roof when I knew that all was not well there. Faskel was older. When I looked upon him and then upon my own face in my mother's well-polished mirror, I would have said he was the elder by birth. Also he was more assertive, taking over the role of my father's assistant, making decisions even within my father's hearing. And Hywel Jern did not lift even an eyebrow in correction of his presumption.

My sister was married. Her dowry had been enough to bring her the son of a Councilor, to my mother's great content. Though she had vanished from the house as if she had never lived, "my daughter, the Councilor's son's lady" was so ever on my mother's lips as to make of my sister a haunting ghost.

Of this household I was no longer a well-fitting part. Though Faskel masked for the most part his displeasure at my return, he became more and more officious in conducting the business when I was present—though I did nothing to confirm his suspicions that I had returned to supersede him. Once I had thought the shop all important, but off world so many doors had opened to me that now it seemed a very dull way to spend one's days, and I wondered that my father could have chosen it.

He roused himself to ask questions about my journeying, so I spent most of my time in his inner office retelling, not without some satisfaction, all I had learned. Though now and then a crisp comment reduced my self-esteem and sent me into confusion, for he made it clear that much of this he already knew.

However, after my first burst of enthusiasm, it became increasingly clear that if my father listened, he heard, or strove to hear, more than my spate of words. Behind his interest—and it was interest; in that I was not deceived—lurked some preoccupation which was not concerned with me or my discoveries. Nor did he mention the space ring, and I too had a strange reluctance to introduce the subject. Not once did he bring out that treasure to brood over it as he had in the past.

It was not until I had been four days home—it was the eve of First Landing Day when the high festival of the year was about to begin—that the shadow which I sensed on the household drew closer. Like all shops, we would remain closed during the festival. It was customary for families to entertain kinfolk and friends, making up parties to go from home to home. My mother spoke pridefully at the table that night of our going to Darina's and being included with them in the Councilor's own group for a pleasure cruise on the river in his own barge.

But when she had done, my father shook his head. He would, he announced, stay home. I had never seen my mother angry, though of late years she might have grown more assertive, stand against my father's pronouncements. But this time her anger exploded, and she stated that that choice might be his, but that the rest of us should go. To this he nodded and so I found that indeed I was absorbed in what seemed to me a very boring party. My mother beamed and nursed another dream, for Faskel was ever by the side of the Councilor's niece—though it appeared to me that that lady shared her smiles with several young men and that the portion of them which fell to my brother were not particularly warm. As for me, I escorted my mother, and perhaps pleasured her a little by the fact that I was traveled and that once or twice the Councilor singled me out to ask of off-world matters.

As the barge slipped down the river, there grew a kind of impatience in me, and I kept thinking of my father and who he might be seeing in the locked shop. For he had hinted to me that he stayed there, not only because of boredom, but because he had a definite reason for wishing the house to be empty that day so that he might meet with someone.

There had always been visitors whom my father had not made known to his family, some of them using darkness for a cloak, entering and leaving without their faces being seen. That he trafficked in things of uncertain history must have been known to the authorities. But no man ever spoke out against him. For the Thieves' Guild has a long arm and they move to protect one who is of service to them. My father may have outwardly retired from their Veep councils, but did a man *ever* retire from the Guild? Rumor said no.

Only there had been something in my father's attitude this time which made me uneasy, as if he both wished for and feared whatever meeting was to take place. And the more I thought on his manner, the more I decided that fear—if one could term it fear—had been uppermost. Perhaps, as my father had suggested, my travel had heightened in me a sensitivity which the rest of the family did not share.

At any rate I excused myself before sunset with the lame explanation that I must meet with Vondar, though my mother did not believe me. And I summoned one of the small boats for hire, ordering the oarsman to make good time back to port. Only so thronged were the waterways that our speed was no more than a weary crawl, and I discovered myself sitting tensely, willing us forward, my hands gripped tightly together.

Again, on landing, I found the streets crowded, and worked my way with impatient thrusting, which earned me some harsh words, splashes of scented water. The shop front was closed even as we had left it, and I went through the narrow garden at the back.

As my hand fell upon the door lock, the thumb against the print which would release it, I felt, as a blow, the full force of all the unease which had plagued me. It was dark and cool in the family rooms. I stopped by the door which gave upon the shop to listen, thinking that if my father still entertained his mysterious caller, he would not thank me to burst in upon them. But there was no sound, and when I rapped upon the door to the office, it echoed hollowly.

When I pushed, the door gave only a little, and I was forced to exert pressure of shoulder to force my way in. Then I heard the rasp of wood against stone, and saw that my father's desk, overturned, blocked my entrance. I thrust desperately and was in a wildly upset room.

In his chair sat my father, the ropes which held him upright stained with his blood. His eyes glared at me fiercely in denial of what had come to him. But that denial was the glare of a dead man. All else was overturned, some boxes smashed to bits as if the searcher, not finding what he sought, had wrecked the inanimate in his temper.

There are many beliefs in many worlds concerning the end of life and what may lie thereafter. How can any man deny that some of them may be true? We have no proof one way or another. My father was dead when I came to him, and dead by violence. But perhaps it was his will, his need for revenge, or to communicate, which hung on in that room. For I knew, as if he had indeed spoken, what lay at the roots of this.

So I passed him and found that inconspicuous bit of carving on the wall. To that I set my thumb as he had taught me. The small space opened, but not easily; it might have been some time since it was last bared. I took out the bag, feeling through it the form of the ring. That I drew forth and held before my father as if he could still see and know that I had it. And I promised him that what he had sought, I would seek too, and that perhaps so I would find those who had slain him. For this I was sure of, that the ring held the key to his death.

But this was not the last of the shocks and losses which were to come to me on Angkor. For after the authorities had come and the family had gathered and been questioned, she whom I had always called mother turned on me and said, in a high, fast voice, as if she dared not be interrupted:

"Faskel is master here. For he is blood and bone of me, heir to my father who was lord here before Hywel Jern came. And so will I swear before the Council."

That she favored Faskel I had always known, but there was a chill in her words now that I did not understand. She continued, making the reason plain.

"You are only a duty child, Murdoc. Though, mark me true, I have never made the less of you in this house because of that. And no one can say that I have!"

A duty child—one of those embryos shipped from a populous world to a frontier planet in order to vary the stock, by law assigned to some family to be raised and nurtured as their own. There were many such in the early settlement of any world. But I had never thought much about them. It did not greatly matter to me that I was not of her blood. But that I was not the son of Hywel—that I hated! I think she read this in my eyes, for she shrank from me. But she need not have feared any trouble, for I turned and went from that room, and that house, and later from Angkor. All I took with me was my heritage—the ring out of space.

THREE

The torch which had been in the room of the sanctuary when first I entered was sputtering to the end as I woke. What had the voice said? For the space of four torches I could shelter there. I looked at the floor. There were three more torches lying ready. Now I got up to force the dying one from its hold, light another in its place.

But after four torches—what? Would I be thrust out into the streets of Koonga again? At intervals I questioned the walls of the room, but no answer came. Twice I searched again, seeking some cunningly hidden exit. There was a building frustration within me. I had passed part of a night here, by my timekeeper, and some of the day thereafter. The four torches, I calculated roughly, would cover perhaps three days. But long before that the ship on which Vondar and I had passage would lift.

Nor would its Captain worry if we did not claim those passages. Once planetside, passengers were strictly on their own. A Captain would take steps to rescue a member of his closely knit crew, for the ship unit became as tightly welded as a family or clan, but strangers he would not aid.

What chance had I left? Was I under observation? How would the keepers of this place know when their torches were exhausted? Or had they through the years fallen into such routine that they could judge approximately? And what was their purpose? What did they get out of this service? A temple would accept a gift for a god. And to me this sanctuary continued to suggest a religious establishment.

I lay down again on the bed, rolled so that I faced the wall and that my breast was hidden from the room. My hands moved stealthily, for I had to believe that there was a watcher. If I could not hold to that hope, I had nothing left. Two pockets in my safe-belt. Between thumb and forefinger rolled the sleekness of the gems I carried. I palmed them and lay still, letting them believe I slept.

Vondar had had the best of our stock already locked in the safe of the ship. Eventually those should reach the storehouse of the jeweler to whom they had been consigned, there to wait for one who would never claim them.

What I carried were inferior stones, or so reckoned on inner planets. Only here two of them might well present a temptation to any watcher. Both were fruits of my own trading—one a carved crystal in the form of a small demonic head, with rubies inset for eyes, fang teeth of yellow sapphires, a weird, small curiosity. The very force

of the carving might make it attractive on this world. The
other was a thumb-sized "soothing stone" of red jade,
one of those pieces the men of Gambool carry to finger
while they talk business. There is a sensuous satisfaction
in the handling of such a piece, and perhaps they are
wise in their choice of this tension relaxer.

How much is a life worth? I could empty my safe-
belt—but I knew I must reserve a second payment if my
plan was to succeed. And I had chosen as best I could.
Now I rolled over and sat up. The light of the new torch
was brighter than the old.

The guesting table—I looked at it. Then I crossed the
room to sit on one of its flanking stools, lay the stones
on its surface. I did not raise my voice in any demand
this time but tried to be as one bargaining in the market place.

"It is said that for all things there is a price," I began
as if I spoke to someone who sat on the other stool to
my right. "There are those who sell, and those who wish
to buy. I am a stranger in your land, upon your world of
Tanth. By no fault of my own I find myself a hunted
man. My friend and master is dead, slain also for no
fault—for since when have the Green Robes ever before
chosen one not of their belief to satisfy their master? Is
it not said the unwilling sacrifice is the lesser one and
not pleasing to the power to which it is sped?

"It is true that I have killed, but only to defend myself.
I am willing to offer blood price if that is required of
me. But—remember, I am from off world, and so cannot
be bound by the laws of your land unless I willfully and
willingly break them by intent—answering only to my
own authority for all else."

Did anyone hear me? Was Tanth so removed from
the civilized worlds that the Confederation's authority

could be flouted? What would priests of a local god care for a rule based light-years away? Nor could I flatter myself that Vondar's death would set any fleets in motion to demand answers from Tanth's inhabitants. Like the Free Traders, we accepted risks when we traveled the far star lanes.

"Blood price will I pay," I repeated, fighting my mounting tension, willing my voice to remain even and low. I opened my hand and allowed the fingering piece to lie in the open. "This is a gem of virtue. He who holds it while thinking of or speaking on matters of import will discover his temper remains calm, his mind clear—" I wrapped my tongue in the rolling formality of the native speech, using the wording common to men of substance. In such little things sometimes there is great influence.

"To this gem of power"—I allowed the carved crystal to be seen now, the leering face uppermost—"I will add this talisman. As one can see, it bears the face of Umphal—" (Which it did not, having come from another world, where that nightmare demon was unknown. But it was enough like the effigies of Umphal I had seen here to pass.) "Set such on a frontlet and what fear need a man longer have of the grimace of the red-eyed power. For seeing his *own* face, Umphal will flee—is that not so? Thus doubly do I pay blood price, with a stone which gives men wisdom, and one which promises protection from that which rides the night north winds."

Trying to keep out of mind the thought that I might be speaking only to unhearing walls, that there were no eyes which watched, I spoke again:

"There is a Free Trader planeted at your port. For my blood price I ask only speech with her Captain."

Then I sat in silence, watching the two gems on the table, straining to hear the slightest sound which might reveal I did have a listener. I could not believe that after a period of time within this room sanctuary ended and that the desperate souls who came here had no other recourse.

I could not be sure—a click—had I heard a click? Dared I believe that I had heard such a sound? It had come from behind me. I waited a long moment and then arose and went to the niche, as if to drink from the flagon there. In the small basket beside that lay something which had not been there before—a flat cake. Once more I picked up that tantalizing bell and was about to ring it when the basket caught my attention. It had been shoved forward, leaving marks in the dust. By the look of those the stone behind it had slid out.

Certainly I had not been mistaken in my hearing of that click. There *was* an opening in the wall and I had been observed through it. They had furnished me with food. The cake was crumbly and smelled of coarse cheese, as it had been split open and smeared with that. To off-world taste it was unpleasant, but I ate it. Hunger can conquer much.

Waiting is the hardest test to which one can be put, and waiting was now mine. The torch had burned down and I was about to set another in its place when, without warning, a man appeared in the doorway through which I had first come. Though I went for my laser, he had me covered before my hand touched its butt.

"Steady on!" He spoke Basic, coming a step or two farther into the room. I saw a ship's tunic with the insignia of Cargo Master on the collar. "Keep your hands in plain sight."

He was an off-worlder, and his uniform was that of a Free Trader. I drew a deep breath. In so much had my plea carried.

"You have a proposition—" He eyed me narrowly, with little cordiality. "Speak your piece." There was a snap of urgency to that as if he were there against his will with danger breathing hot upon him.

"I want passage out." I cut my answer to that bare statement.

He had backed around so that his shoulders were at the wall—and faced me warily. A Cargo Master of a Free Trader needs must be more than a merchant. He does not grow fat and sleek, and slow of reflex, no matter if he is not a fighting man—officially—but a trader.

"With half the city to tear you down should you step upon the street?" he countered. Still his laser was aimed at my middle. There was no softening for my plight to be read on his face. The Free Traders are clansmen, with their ship their home. I was not of his brood.

"Tell me, Cargo Master"—I did not approach him, and now I must be a master bargainer indeed if I was to win my life—"what have you heard of me?"

"That you spat upon one priest, slew another—"

"I am a gem trader, late apprentice to Vondar Ustle—you have heard that name?"

"I have heard. He travels far. What of it? Does that make your crime the less here in Koonga?"

"There was no crime." How could I make the truth so plain he would believe me? "Do you think a man thrusts a rod into a yaeger-wasp nest and turns it deliberately, when he is in his right mind? We were in a tavern—the Sign of the Mottled Corby. Our business here was done, we had passage on the *Voyringer*. Then the Green Robes came in and set up that infernal spinning arrow of theirs. We thought we were in no danger, being off-worlders. When it stopped I swear it pointed between the two of us. Then the Robes moved in to take us—"

"Why?" I saw the disbelief in his eyes. "They do not play such games with off-worlders."

"As we thought also, Cargo Master. Yet they did. And Vondar was knifed down when he tried to resist. I burned a priest and was near enough to the door to get free. I had heard of this sanctuary—so—"

"Tell me—what was Vondar Ustle's hallmark? And it I have seen, I warn you." That shot from his lips as a ray might have from his laser.

"A half-moon wrought in opal with the signet, between its horns, a Gryphon's head in firestones." I made prompt reply, though I wondered what this Free Trader would know of a master gemologist's mark, which he would display for identification only to an equal in rank.

He nodded and slipped his laser into its holster. "What enemy did Ustle make here?"

That thought had plagued me also since I had had the time within this hole to think. For it was reasonable that, were a desire for revenge strong enough, my master might have been set up for such a kill. Though their demon was supposed to select his prey by chance alone, without aid from his servant priests, rumor suggested that he sometimes had assistance of mortal means, that a suitable gift to his shrine could produce a sacrifice which would please more than just the Green Robes and their lord. But there had been no clash with any local power. We had visited Hamzar, inspected his wares and purchased what Vondar thought good, exchanged trade gossip with him. There had been one visit to the nomads' market and some dickering for uncut crystals out of the salt deserts, but both sides had been pleased with the deal. I could see no local tie-up with any trouble. And now, though I would have given much to be able to produce such a neat solution, I had to admit the truth.

"It need not have been of Tanth at all," the Cargo Master replied. And he watched me as if I could then supply name and reason. A moment later, he continued. "Some strokes are aimed from longer distances. But—if you wish to take knife-oath for your master later, that is your affair. Always supposing you do come out alive. Now, what do you want of us? You say passage off world—how?"

"How would you do it?" I countered. "I will pay well to lift in your ship, and for passage to the nearest planet with a second-stage port. And do not tell me"—now I dared push a little; I could lose nothing by it, for my whole chance hung on the slenderest of threads—"that you cannot get me forth if you wish. The will of the Free Traders is too well known."

"We care for our own. You are not one of us."

"You care for your cargo also. Then accept me as cargo—a profitable cargo."

He suddenly smiled. "Cargo, is it?" Then his smile vanished and his eyes narrowed as he regarded me, as if by that gaze he could indeed transform me into a box or bale, to be stored in the hold of his ship. "You talk of profit?" he began, brisk again. "What sort of profit and how much?"

I turned away and sought my safe-belt. Then I showed him what I held and it took fire in the torchlight. Profit of a half year's careful trading on my own—two of them matched as closely as anyone could hope to find—Eyes of Kelem. They were gold, and scarlet, with flecks of green deep in them. And if you looked upon them long, the color flowed. Not a fortune, no. But, offered in the proper market, worth a whole voyage for a trader who was only average lucky most of the time. They were my best and I knew he guessed that.

He did not try to bargain, or belittle my offering. Whether he did indeed have some half sympathy for my plight, I do not know. But he looked at the stones and then to me, nodding, holding forth his hand and closing it over them in a manner which showed that he knew the rules of our trade also. Free Traders are alert to any cargo and deal in many things.

"Come!"

I followed him out of that room, leaving my offering behind me on the guesting table. For I was satisfied that they had kept their part of the bargain. We were again in the hall where the torches blazed behind the face, but these were now quenched and I saw through the holes the light of day. The Cargo Master stooped and picked up a bundle lying there, shaking it out to show me a worn uniform tunic and the cap of a crewman.

"Put them on."

I laughed, feeling a little lightheaded. "It would seem you came prepared," I said as I pulled the tunic over my head and shoulders, sealed it at collar and belt. It was small for me, but not too much so.

"I was—" He hesitated. "The news is loud. Ustle was known to our Captain. When the message came through he was enough interested to send me."

The set of his jaw told me that that was all I would get out of him on the subject. But I was the more heartened by this evidence that he had come prepared to get me out—though I would still have liked to go through the door weapon in hand.

We were not, however, to go that way, for the Free Trader walked briskly to the wall on our left, slapped his hand against it. Though that touch could not have moved the heavy stone, it swung inward, disclosing another narrow way, and he stepped confidently into that, leaving me to follow. When the stone swung back behind us, we were left in a thick dark, reminding me unpleasantly of the alleys through which I had earlier fled.

It was a very narrow passage, our shoulders brushing wall on either side. I bumped into my guide, who had stopped short. There was a click and then a blaze of bright light.

"Come!" He reached out a hand to pull me after him. I blinked and screwed up my eyes against the assault of that brilliant sun. We were in another alley, piled along the wall with containers of refuse. Things scuttled in the slime under our boots and my guide swore roundly as he kicked out at something which hissed at him. Six strides, as long and fast as we could make them, brought us into another and much cleaner byway. I had to fight my desire to run, or to look about me for attackers. It was necessary to put on the cloak of unconcern and match my pace to the Cargo Master's.

Then we were through the gates of the port. As I had thought, the *Voyringer* had lifted and only the trader remained, fins down, on the blast-scorched ground. The Cargo Master caught at my sleeve.

"Trouble—maybe—"

But I had already sighted that blaze of bright robes around the ship. There was a reception committee waiting. Perhaps just on the general principle that a hunted off-worlder would make for the only ship left.

"Drunk—you're an off-ship drunk!" The Cargo Master hissed at me in a sound much like that made by the alley scavenger. "This ought to do it!" I saw the blow coming, but I was totally unprepared to dodge it. A blast of pain spread from my jaw, and I must have gone down and out in the same moment, for there my memories of Tanth come to an abrupt stop.

There was a tap-tapping of jeweler's hammers in my skull, setting tighter and tighter a brazen band about my brain. I could not lift a hand to stop that torment. Then liquid splashed over me and I drew a choking gasp of air, which seemed to subdue for the moment the worst of the hammering. I opened my eyes.

A face hung over me, two faces, one very close, the other blurry and at a greater distance. The close one was furred, with pricked, tasseled ears, green-gold eyes. It opened a black-lipped mouth and I looked into a wedge-shaped space set with fangs, and a curling, rough-surfaced tongue. It was a small face—

Now the larger approached and I tried to focus on it. Space-tanned, with close-cropped hair, for the rest the face of any crewman, ageless and now expressionless.

I heard words—"Well, so you are back with us—"

Back? Back where? Memory stirred sluggishly—back in the cell of the sanctuary? No! I tried to sit up and my head whirled so that I was sick. But as ungentle hands thrust me flat again, I felt something else which could never have vibrated through Koongan walls—I was not only aboard a ship, but we were in flight. And the vast flood of relief which followed that realization carried me back into a limbo which was half unconsciousness, half sleep.

So I found myself aboard the *Vestris,* though the first days in her were not the usual spent by a passenger. The Cargo Master had indeed knocked me out to carry me aboard as his drunken assistant. But it would seem I was of less hardy structure than those his fists had dealt with heretofore, and I continued semiconscious for a longer space than the medico liked. When I was again fully aware of my surroundings, I lay in a cramped cubby off the medico's cabin, used by the seriously ill. It was some time before I had my interview with Captain Isuran. Like all Free Traders, he was ship-born, ship-bred, of a type growing more and more apart from planet-orientated men. All the Free Traders I had known before had been only casual acquaintances, and I found myself oddly ill at ease with these in such close quarters. I told him my story and he listened. And he asked who had wanted Vondar Ustle dead, but that I could not tell him. That there had been some tie in the past between my master and this Captain, I was sure. But Isuran did not explain and I dared not ask questions. It was enough that he would take me to another world, one on which I could contact sources who had known me as Vondar's assistant.

I had some time to meditate upon the future, for space travel is sheer monotony once one is off world. The crewmen develop hobbies to occupy mind and hand. For me there was nothing but my thoughts. And they were not so pleasant I cared to dwell long upon them.

Ustle had had contacts on many worlds, and I thought one or two might be willing to give me a chance at a planetside job. But, though I knew gems as a buyer, I was no designer, nor did I want a settled existence. I had tasted too deeply of Vondar's way of life. My safe-belt was very light now. And I would have to reach a second-stage port to tap past resources for expense money. Also—my savings were limited. I could not keep on as we had done alone. And there were very few, if any, Vondar Ustles in search of apprentices.

Also—what had been behind Vondar's death? That it was planned and not by the Green Robes alone, I had come to accept. But, though I tried—sifting memories—I could not bring to mind a single happening which would plant so deep a reason for someone to wish him dead. And perhaps not only him, for the Green Robes had moved in on both of us.

This was the second time death had abruptly come so close to me. I thought again of my father, or of him I would always think of as my father, for he had treated me as of his own flesh and blood and had settled for me (knowing as he must have how matters would go after his death) a future he thought would be the best. Who had been his visitor that day? And the space ring—my hand sought the last and deepest pocket of my safe-belt. I did not unseal it, only felt through it the shape of the band and that lusterless stone. Was I right that this was what my father's killer had sought? If so—could it also be—? I did not see how this could have followed us to Tanth. All the property on the bodies of their victims belonged to the Green Robes and were offered to their dread demon. No one but their order would have had the ring had I fallen prey to them.

I had a handful of facts and could go on endlessly building many surmises, without ever being sure that any were close to the truth. Although in the meanwhile I must seek some way of earning my living, I would, in time, have to learn what lay behind Vondar's killing. For I had such ties with him as would indeed demand the equivalent of the Free Traders' knife-oath.

But I was still far from the solution of my twin problems when the *Vestris* prepared for a landing, not on the planet at which I aimed, but on a lesser world. Cargo

Master Ostrend briefed me as to their reasons for the landfall. It was a lushly overgrown land, over-warm, too, to our tastes, with a nonhuman, batrachian-evolved native race. What those had to barter was a substance strained and fermented from certain plants, medicinal in nature. What the *Vestris* gave in return was seed shellfish, to be loosed in beds, considered a great delicacy.

"You might be interested in these." Ostrend took from his lockbox three objects and set them out on the top of his swing desk.

They were a pinkish purple in shade, and each was a tiny figure. I brought out my jeweler's lens to study them closer. Figures they were, as weirdly grotesque as any of the demons dreamed up by the imaginations of the artists of Tanth. They seemed to be fashioned of nacre, though not carved. I had not seen their like before. They were oddities which might appeal to collectors of the curious.

"There is a planter of shellfish beds—Salmscar. He has been experimenting with some of the mutated crustaceans. That's what keeps our trade going here; the things mutate so quickly that they cannot be bred true past about the second year. He plants tiny metallic 'seeds' in the mutants and in about three or four years gets these. Just a hobby with him. But you might do a spot of trading if you are interested."

I knew the Free Traders and their jealously guarded sources of items. If the mutant pearls had any value, Ostrend would not have made that suggestion. Unless, of course, he was either testing me or setting a trap—now I saw dangers standing to right and left. It was almost as if he were urging me to break their ship law. But I would not tell him so. A very small third mystery to add to the others. I expressed interest, which I did not have to feign, and did wonder what I had that I could offer for some of the things—not that I could use my few assets on a gamble, nor would I attempt any trade without full consent of my present shipmates.

FOUR

Since the ingrown community of the Free Traders was a closed clan and an outsider remained that, I was left very much to my own company, save for one member of the crew. The furry face which had hung so close to mine at my first awakening was one I was to see again and again. For Valcyr, the ship's cat, apparently decided that I was an object of interest second to none, and spent long periods of time crouched on bunk or floor of the cabin allotted to me, simply staring.

I was not used to companionship with animals and at first her attentions irked me, for I could not throw off the absurd feeling that behind those round, seldom-blinking eyes was a mind which marked my every move, sifting and assessing me and all I did. Yet in time I came to tolerate her, and finally, when it became apparent that the crew were not inclined, beyond a distant civility, to friendliness, I found myself talking to her for want of other conversation. For among themselves the Traders spoke a language of their own, unintelligible to me, so that any attempt to follow their speech was fruitless.

After my interview with Ostrend I returned to my cubby to discover Valcyr stretched on my berth taking her ease. She was a lithe and beautiful creature, her fur short and very thick, of a uniform silver-gray, save for her tail, where there were dark rings. She had moments when she displayed affection, and now she raised her head to rub against my hand, while from her throat rumbled a purr. Since such favors were rare, I was flattered enough to continue to stroke her while I considered the Cargo Master's suggestion.

We would planet on this world shortly, near a trading post where the men of the *Vestris* had been before. There were no cities, the natives being nomads by inclination, wandering in family-clan groups along the rivers from one marshy spot to the next. A few more civilized and enterprising clans had staked out semipermanent settlements near places where crustacean beds could be fostered. But these were no more than collections of flimsy reed-and-mud huts.

What I had brought to the *Vestris* had been carried on my person. Now I took inventory of my scanty possessions to see if I had anything at all which could serve as a trade item. The few small stones still in my safe-belt were not to be touched. Not that it was likely they would interest Salmscar. I regretted the packs abandoned at the inn on Tanth, the luggage gone with the freighter. But if one permitted regret for little, one might as well remember all the rest lost on Tanth. I had nothing to risk here. I said as much to Valcyr, and she yawned widely and set her teeth gently upon my hand to suggest she was no longer interested in being petted.

However, when we set down, I was ready enough to go planetside. The chance to get firm earth under one's feet is always acceptable to any traveler, unless he is as wedded to space as a crewman—and even crewmen must earth now and then.

What greeted our noses as we went down the outflung landing ramp was more than the scorch of burning from our fin-down—it was a stink of chemicals, enough to make one hold one's nose. Ostrend said the natives favored this section of hot springs and volcanic action, and now we could see rocks, water- and steam-worn into strange shapes. At intervals steam and vile smells burst through holes in the ground.

Beyond this tormented land was the bluish foliage of the marshes, while the various overflows from the caldron lands lapped on to feed a yellow river. The heat from the steam was almost stifling, the more so when combined with the chemical stench. We coughed and sputtered as we picked our way along a path, to find, on the banks of the river, the village we sought.

Ostrend stood there, his trade board between arm and hip, looking about in open puzzlement. After his description I had not expected to see much in the way of buildings. But certainly we looked now on what was not even the most primitive attempt at providing shelter, but rather an area of ruin and decay.

Mounds of ill-smelling reed stuff, with dried mud flaking off in great chunks, humped here and there. Among this litter nothing moved until a thing which was more leather-winged lizard than bird arose with a squawk and flapped awkwardly across the river. None of the traders pressed past Ostrend, but their heads swung from left to right and back again as if they were men suddenly suspicious of a trap.

The Cargo Master took from his belt a slender metal rod. Under his fingers it expanded longer and longer until he had a pole of double his own height. To the tip end he affixed a small pennon of bright yellow before he planted it fast in the soft mud of the riverbank. From comments, I gathered that, the village being deserted for some time by the signs, we could do no more than wait for the return of the natives—always providing that they were able to return. But since the visits of the *Vestris* were regular this could be expected to occur, again always excepting the fact that some disaster had not put an end to the established custom.

Captain Isuran, philosophical as a Free Trader must learn to be, was not happy. While his ship did not run on a tight schedule, yet time did set some barriers on each planeting. We could not wait too long before taking off. However, a failure to trade here would upset all plans and make necessary rearrangements to cover the losses caused by such an abortive stop.

Ostrend was in conference with the Captain for the hours that followed, while the rest of the crew speculated as to what might have happened, taking turns at sentry duty by the pennon. Since I was excluded from that, I allowed my own curiosity rein and explored, though not outside the limit wherein I could sight the sky-pointing nose of the ship.

Save for the novelty of the hot springs, and those soon palled, their heat and smell being more than anyone could take for long, there were few sights worth seeing.

The flying thing which had fled our entrance into the deserted village was the only living creature I had sighted. Even insect life here either was remarkably sparse, or for some reason shunned the vicinity of the ship. At last I squatted down by the side of one of the small streams which issued out of the section of hot pots and gushers, inspecting it for gravel. The gem hunter's preoccupation could grip me even here. But I saw nothing in the mess I scooped out and washed which held any promise.

There were some bits of a curiously dull black, which had the look of no mineral or the like, but of a kind of fuzzy burr. Yet when I separated them from the sand and stones with a stick, I discovered them to be extremely hard. Even pounding with a stone did not crush them, or even mar their velvety-seeming surface. I did not believe them seeds, or vegetable refuse, and my interest in them grew, until I had about a dozen laid in a row in the sun, being cautious at first not to touch them with my fingers. Nature provides some nasty traps on many planets. They had no beauty, and I did not think any value. But the contrast between their suggestion of softness to the eye, and their real hardness of surface was odd enough to make me gather up three for future examination. There are gems which must be "peeled," worked down in layers from their unattractive outer coatings or shells. One of little worth may so be turned into something of value. And I had some vague ideas that perhaps these might hide a surprise under that fuzzy surface, though I had neither the tools nor the skill needed for such a task.

As I knotted my choice into a square of seal-foam, Valcyr came walking, with that particular sure-footed daintiness of her species, along the bank of the small runlet. She progressed with nose to earth, almost as might a hound on a warm trail, and she was manifestly sniffing something which absorbed her attention.

Then she reached my line of rejected ovoids and nosed each avidly. To my limited human nostrils they had no scent, but it was plain they did for the cat. Squatting down, she began to lick the largest, having sniffed them all. Fearing for her, I tried to knock it out of reach, but a lightning swift slash from unsheathed claws, ears flattened to skull, and a low growl warned me off. Sucking my bloodied fingers, I withdrew. It was plain that Valcyr guarded what she considered a treasure of price and was not minded to have any interference.

Once I had withdrawn, she went back to her licking. Now and again she picked it up in her mouth to retreat a little way before she squatted down to return to her tongue-rasping exploration of the find.

"Any luck?" Ostrend's young assistant threw a long shadow past me as he came up.

"What are these? Have you seen them before?" I pointed to the fuzzy stones scattered about by Valcyr as she had made her examination and choice.

Chiswit sat on his heels to study them. "Never saw them before. In fact"—he looked up and about—"this whole stream is new here. Maybe one of the big mud-holes blew its top. Wait! Do you suppose that was what happened and there was gas? That could have driven out the Toads. They like the stink and the heat, but maybe they could not stand up to gas."

"Could be." But guesses about the disappearance of the natives, interesting as that might be, were not what I sought. I wanted information concerning the stones. If stones they were not, that was all I could term them. "You say you have never seen these. Was Valcyr with you when you planeted here last?"

"Yes. She has been ship's cat for a long time."

"And you never saw her do that before?" I pointed to where she now lay, the stone between her outstretched forepaws, her tongue working over and around it with absorbed concentration.

Chiswit stared. "No—what is she doing? Why, she's licking one of these things! Why did you let her—?" He scrambled to his feet and took two strides. Valcyr might not have seen him coming, but she seemed to sense a danger to her find. With it in her jaws, she was gone in a bound, heading away from the ship, weaving in and out among the twisted rocks.

We ran after her, but it was no use; she had disappeared—doubtless into some crevice where she could enjoy her find in peace. Chiswit turned on me with a demand as to why I had not earlier separated her from it. I showed him my bleeding hand and reported my failure. But the crewman was obviously upset and hunted through the rocky outcrops, calling and coaxing.

I did not believe that Valcyr was going to appear until she was ready, the independence of cats being their marked characteristic. But I trailed him, peering into each shallow, cavelike hole, rounding rocks in search.

We found her at last, lying on a small ledge under a deep overhang. Had it not been for the motion of her head as she swept the stone back and forth with her tongue, we might have missed her altogether, so close in color was her fur to the porous stone on which she lay. As Chiswit, speaking in a coaxing voice, went to his knees and held out his hand to her, she flattened her ears to her skull, hissed, and then gulped, and the stone vanished!

She could not have swallowed it! The one she had chosen had been the largest of those I had fished out of the stream, and it had been an ovoid far too big to descend her gullet. Only the fact remained that that was what had happened and we both had seen it. She crawled out of her crevice and sat licking her lips like a cat who has dined well. When Chiswit reached for her, she suffered him to pick her up, kneading paws on his arm as he carried her, purring loudly, her eyes half shut, with no signs that the swallowing of her find had done her harm, or choked her. Chiswit started at a swift trot for the ship, while I knelt to look at the ledge, still hoping that the stone might have rolled somewhere, unable to believe it was now inside Valcyr.

The gray rock of the ledge was bare. And had the stone rolled, it would lie now somewhere directly before me. But it did not. I even sifted the gravelly sand through my fingers, to produce nothing. Then I ran a forefinger over the ledge. There was a faint dampness, perhaps from Valcyr's saliva. But, in addition, something else, a tingling, almost a shock as I touched one point. The second time I put tip of finger to the same spot there was nothing but the damp, and that was drying fast.

"We saw her, I tell you! She swallowed a stone, a queer black stone—" Chiswit's voice rang down the corridor as I came along to the medico's quarters.

"You saw the ray report—nothing in her throat. She cannot have swallowed it, man. It probably rolled away and—"

"It did not, I looked," I said quietly as I came to the doorway.

Valcyr was in the medico's arms, purring ecstatically, her claws working in and out. She had the appearance of a cat very well pleased with herself and the world.

"Then it was not a stone, but something able to dissolve," he answered me assuredly.

I took out my improvised bag. "What do you call these? They are the same things she swallowed. I picked them out of a stream bed."

He placed Valcyr gently on the bunk and motioned me to lay the bag on his small laboratory table. In the ship's light the fuzziness of the stones was even more marked. He picked up a small instrument and touched the surface of the largest, then tried to scrape away some of the velvet. But the point of the knife slipped across the stone.

"I want a look at these." He was staring as intently as Valcyr had done.

"Why not?" He might not have the tools of a gemologist, but at least he could give me some report on their substance. His interest was triggered and I thought he would work to get to the bottom of the mystery. Then I looked at Valcyr. The surface of the table on which the stones lay was very close to her. Would she be as attracted to another as she had to her first choice? Instead, she drowsily stretched out full length, her purring growing fainter, as if she were already half asleep.

Since the size of the medico's quarters did not allow for spectators, Chiswit and I left him to his tests. But in the corridor the assistant Cargo Master asked:

"How big was that thing when she first picked it up?"

I measured off a space between two fingers. "They are all oval. She took the biggest one."

"But she could not have swallowed it, not if it was that size!"

"Then what happened to it?" I asked, trying to remember those few instants when we had last seen the stone. Had it been as large as I thought? Perhaps she had only nosed the one I believed she had picked, and had taken another. But I did not distrust my eyes that much. I was trained to know stones and their sizes. An apprentice to such a master as Vondar could judge a stone's size without taking it into his hand at all. True, this was something new. I had tried to crush one of those things between two rocks with no results.

"She licked it smaller," Chiswit continued. "It is a seed or some hardened gum—and she just kept licking at it—so finally it melted."

A reasonable explanation, but one my own tests would not allow me to accept. So—I had a paradox—Valcyr had swallowed what seemed to me a gem-hard stone, and one far too large to pass her gullet. Perhaps the medico would come up with an answer. I would have to wait for that.

On the second day the Captain broke out a small scout flitter, a one-man affair, but with range enough to explore the surrounding district. We could go on waiting here fruitlessly for months and he did not want to waste the time.

Ostrend took off in it and was gone two days. He returned with the disappointing news that not only had he not found the villagers, but that he had seen no natives at all. And that there appeared to be an unusual scarcity of all life along the river and its tributaries. A few of the flying things such as we had disturbed on the first day, and which were eaters of carrion, were all he sighted. For the rest, the planet, as far as his cruising range, was as bare as if any higher forms of life had never existed at all.

At that report the Free Traders held a conference, to which I was not a party, and it was decided that they would dump their now-worthless cargo of crustaceans into the usual river pens, as a sign of good faith should the natives ever return. They would also leave their trade flag flying as a symbol of their visit. But they would have to vary their future route in order to make up for the loss of trade here.

Which meant, I was curtly informed by Ostrend, that I was to continue my voyage on the *Vestris* for longer than planned. My first possible exit port had been that for which their medicinal cargo had been destined, and it would not now be visited. By space law I could not be summarily dumped on just any world, not when I had paid my passage, but must be carried to at least a second-stage port from which there was regular service. Now I would have to wait in boredom and impatience until we touched at such a place. And when that would be depended upon Ostrend's luck in picking up a cargo. He was continually with the Captain, going over taped trade reports, trying to find a way to make up for this failure.

As far as could be observed, Valcyr was none the worse for her extraordinary meal—not at first. And the medico's efforts to solve the mystery of the stones continued, until at last he came to the mess cabin, fatigue's dark shadows under his eyes, wearing a bewildered expression. He drew a half cup of boiling water, added a caff pill, and watched it bubble and brown in an absent way that suggested he saw something very different from that ordinary shipboard drink.

"A breakthrough, medico?" I asked.

His eyes focused as if he saw me for the first time. "I do not know. But—that thing is alive!"

"But—"

He nodded. "Yes—but—The reading is very low—resembling hibernation level. Nothing I have can open its shell, or whatever holds that germ of life. I'll tell you something else—" He paused to drink the full contents of his cup in one intake of liquid. "Valcyr is going to have kittens—or something—"

"The stone? But how—"

He shrugged. "Do not ask me. I know it is against all nature as I know it. She ate that thing, you both say she did. And now she is going to have a kitten—or something—"

"I'll tell you something else," he added as he drew a second portion of water. "I have rayed those stones into ash. And maybe I ought to do the same to the cat—"

"Why?"

This time he dropped two pills into the steaming cup. "Because if what I think is true, it is no kitten she is carrying. In fact it may be nothing we want aboard. I will keep an eye on her from now on. When her time comes—well, I can do what is best then." He took the second cup in a couple of gulps. When he left the mess cabin I saw that he turned to climb to the Captain's quarters.

One of the dreads of a trading ship is an unnatural life form loose on board. There are all kinds of horror tales about what has happened to ships unfortunate enough to pick up stowaways which later turned them into drifting charnel houses. That was the very reason Valcyr and her kind had their secure position on board ship. There were other safeguards, irradiation of suspect cargo by immunization rays and the like. But still, in spite of all precautions, sometimes the alien slipped in. If it was harmless it could prove a nuisance or even a new and amusing pet. But the chances were great that such uninvited guests would be inimical.

Traders are mainly immune to diseases of planets other than their native ones. Parallel but different roads of evolution performed this essential service. But they are not always immune to bites, stings, and attack from living creatures.

Now it seemed that Valcyr, meant to be the sentry at the gate, might well have unwittingly betrayed our fortress. She was kept in an improvised cage in the small sick bay. But the medico reported she did not protest imprisonment as she might have done normally. Instead she slept much of the time, rousing only to eat and drink. She did not resent his handling of her, but seemed happy and content. We all visited her, and speculation concerning the nature of what she was about to introduce among us was rife.

Ship time differs from planet time; we reckon it only artificially in days and nights because for so many centuries our species did live by sunrise and sunset and the flow of days. We were perhaps four weeks of such arbitrary time off the marsh planet when the medico broke into the off-watch rest cabin with the news that Valcyr had disappeared. In spite of his initial uneasiness, she had been so lethargic since we had upshipped that he had come to believe she would not fight confinement. Nor had she. But the fact remained that when he had taken her food and water, he had found the door swinging free and the occupant gone.

A ship's interior is limited, and one would think that there would be few places where a cat, small as she was, could hide. But when we started a search from the control room down to the sealed cargo hatches and then, mentally accusing one another of having been careless, retraced the same way in pairs, even in threes, we found no trace of our quarry.

We were in the corridor outside the mess cabin when Chiswit and Staffin, the junior engineer, both turned on the medico and accused him of doing away with Valcyr. Tempers were out of control by then and I had never realized how much the cat meant to these space voyagers until I heard the hot flow of anger in their tones. The medico denied their accusation just as vehemently, saying that he was well prepared to take measure for anything she might deliver, but that Valcyr would be safe. It was he who turned them all on me, snarling that I had allowed her to eat the stone in the first place, had even brought more of them on board.

What might have happened I do not know. But the Captain swung down the ladder and snapped orders. I was sent to my cabin, to remove temptation from his men, I suppose. And at that moment I was willing enough to go. In fact, when I closed the door behind me I thumbed the lock. For I had discovered in the last few minutes that that wild night of flight through Koonga City had left its mark—and that when I heard that note in the voices of the crewmen, I had instinctively reached for a weapon I did not wear.

I turned toward my bunk and froze. By the medico's reckoning Valcyr was still some time from the moment when she was to solve the mystery. Yet she lay now on my bunk. Where had she been during the search? I had looked in here twice, the others at least once, yet now she lay there as if she had rested so for hours. And she was licking again—a thing which lay limply by her side.

Though I was not familiar with kittens, I was sure that what Valcyr now cared for was not the normal young of her kind. It lay supine at its greatest length, head and tail outstretched. I could see the rise and fall of its side as it breathed with fast, fluttering breaths, so it was alive. But otherwise it looked dead. The body was covered with a black fuzz, close in appearance to the outward coating of the "stone." This was wiry and did not yield much to Valcyr's caressing tongue.

The neck was long, out of proportion, the head sharper of muzzle than seemed right, while the ears were only indicated by tiny upstanding tufts of hair. The legs were short, the tail again long, the underside and tip furless, rather as if it were covered with dark, tough skin. The paws, which it had drawn up and curled against its belly, were also furless, those in front resembling hands more than beast's paws.

No, I did not believe it was a kitten. But it looked very helpless as it lay there panting. And Valcyr's pride and concern for her strange child were very apparent. It was my duty to go and call the medico. But instead I sat down on the side of the bunk, leaving Valcyr good room, and watched her energetic washing of the changeling. What she had given birth to I could not guess, but somehow I thought it worth saving. And that was my first meeting with Eet.

FIVE

I found it increasingly hard to think of betraying Valcyr and her offspring to the crew. Because that was the feeling which I finally identified—that a disclosure of their presence would be a betrayal. And I who had never felt any strong emotion for an animal knew one now. I questioned myself, trying to discover why, and found no answer. But the fact remained that I could not call anyone, no more than if I were chained to the bunk, silenced by a gag.

The small creature stirred at last, raising its narrow head and turning it back and forth as if seeking something. But it did so blindly, for its eye slits were closed. Valcyr, purring, put out a foreleg and fondly drew it closer. But that head had swung around to face me, and I thought that, though the thing was so young, blind, and helpless, yet somehow it was aware of me, not in fear, but for a purpose. I tried to laugh at that.

Disturbed, I got up from the bunk and went to sit on a wall seat, my back half turned to those two. I strove to concentrate on my own difficulties. Since I could not hope now for an early release from the *Vestris*, or even be sure on which planet I would land, I must be prepared for a dubious future. Once more I ran my hand along my safe-belt, fingering each of the pitifully few bulges left in it. The last one of all—the space ring—

Hywel Jern had been killed for it; of that I was as certain as if I had witnessed the act. But—had our disaster on Tanth also stemmed from its possession? Why Vondar and not me, if that were true? Or was it necessary to make sure of us both, so that no awkward questions could later be raised by a survivor? Why—who—?

My father had had close ties with the Thieves' Guild, in spite of his retirement from their company. Any man in those ranks could and did make powerful enemies. But, I believed, his services had continued in part even after his settlement on Angkor.

I continued to rub the ring's shape through the stuff of the belt and my thoughts went round and round, presenting me with no solution. I do not know when it was that I had begun to notice an unusual degree of heat in the cabin. I had opened the sealing of my coverall, and felt the trickle of sweat drops down my cheek and chin. Now I raised my hand to swab those away and my eyes lit upon the skin across the back and fingers. Rising on that once-smooth surface were purplish blotches, swelling as might water-filled blisters.

I tried to rise, only to discover that my body was no longer under my control. And I was shivering. The extreme heat of moments earlier was now an inner cold. I knew a tearing nausea, but I could not vomit. I clawed open my clothing and saw that the blisters were thick also across my chest and upper arms.

"Help—" Had I croaked that, or only thought I had? Somehow I lurched up and pushed around the wall of the cabin, using its support to make my way to the small com on the wall. There I shook and wavered as I tried to press the alert button.

It was getting hard to see—in fact a thick fog curled up about me as if I were back in that world of geysers and steam. Had I been able to press the button? I leaned my forehead against the wall so that my lips were not too far from the com as I croaked my plea:

"Help—sick—"

I could no longer stay on my feet. Aiming myself at the bunk, I tottered forward, completely forgetting Valcyr. But as I crashed down I encountered no furry bodies. The bunk was empty and I lay on it shuddering.

Now I was back in the dank steam of the deserted planet, and that wreathed in scalding curls about me, so that I cried out in torment. Across seamed and stinking mud I ran, unable to sight my pursuers but knowing I was hunted. Once the mists parted and I saw them for an instant. They came laser in hand and all wore the same face, that of the medico Velos. But still I kept my stumbling feet and fled.

"They will kill—kill—kill—" The words rang across this evil world in a vast thundering. "They will kill you—you—you!"

I was lying once more on my bunk, shivering again. But the mist had disappeared and my sight was clear. And not only my sight but my mind. There was a whistling whisper—it came from the wall—out of the wall.

Once before I had heard words out of a wall—or the air. But that had been on Tanth in the sanctuary. And I was not there—but in a cabin on a Free Trader. In me was a vast urgency, a need to hear more of that whispering.

As I pulled myself up my covering slipped away. I was no longer clothed and my body was covered with purple blotches which were dried in scabs. Hideous! I was lightheaded when I moved, but somehow I got to the wall and the com set there. The light below it was on—it was open—and somewhere in the ship people were talking, close enough to the mike so that some of their speech was broadcast, though slurred. I tried to hear—

"—danger—seal up—cannot even space him—seal door—set down on moon—burn out the cabin—"

"—deliver him to—"

"No chance." The first speaker must have moved closer, for I heard him more clearly. "He is dead, or near enough not to matter. We are lucky so far, and we can take no chance of the infection spreading. Get rid of the plague evidence before we planet on any port. Do you want to be proclaimed a plague ship?"

"—held responsible—"

"Return their fee. Show them the picture tape from the cabin; one look at that ought to convince them that he was of no use. As for searching him—do you want the plague?"

"—not people to be easily satisfied—"

"Show them the tapes!" It was the medico talking, I was sure now. "Do not even open that cabin again until we can burn it out, and we go suited when we do that. On a dead moon where the infection cannot spread. Then we keep our mouths shut, and tightly. No one but *those* will be asking for him. As far as the rest, he is still back on

Tanth, or dead there. And there will be no questions asked for some time anyway—if ever. *Those* will see that his trail is muddled. We cannot deliver him now—we have a body and a sealed cabin—plague—"

That they were discussing me I had no doubts. Now that I was on my feet, the first giddiness had gone and I could think. Velos termed me dead, or near so, but at that moment I felt very much alive. And I had no mind to fall victim to the fate the speakers had in mind for me. If Velos had his way my cabin door would be welded closed from the outside, not to be opened again for fear of contagion. They would shut off the ventilation, all outlets, to confine the disease, and I would have a hard and lingering death. On the other hand it would appear that I had not engineered my own escape from Tanth. Why had I not been suspicious at how easily it had worked? I had been taken to be delivered elsewhere. And I nursed no doubts as to the nature of those to whom I would have been presented as if I were a piece of cargo.

What escape was left me?

"Outside—"

I turned my head too quickly and had to clutch at the frame of the bunk as my vertigo returned. There was a small dark patch there and it moved. I stared stupidly for a moment, until I could focus on it.

The creature I had last seen curled by Valcyr hunched beside my pillow. Now it seemed twice the size it had been at birth. Its eyes were well open and it looked at me intently. Seeing me stare in return, it reared its head, its long neck moving with reptilian sinuosity.

"Outside." Again that word formed in my mind, and I could only connect it with the animal. Somehow in my weak state of health such communication did not make me wonder.

"Outside, where?" I asked in a whisper, and then squeezed around to shut off the com. I had no desire to reveal my partial recovery to any possible listener.

"That—was—well—done. Outside—the—ship—" returned the thing backed against my rumpled pillow.

"That is open space—" I continued to carry on the conversation, convinced now that it was part of my fever. Perhaps the other words I had heard over the mike were also fever dreams—

"Not—so. You heard—they will kill—you. Smell their fear—it is a bad smell—all through this ship—" The narrow head raised higher and higher and I saw the nostrils expand as if the creature were indeed scenting the unusual in the flat air. "Go outside—quick—before they seal—the door. Take a suit—"

Wear a space suit—through the lock? I might live then as long as the air in the suit lasted. But that would only prolong life for a short time.

"They will search—not find—then come back—hide—" persisted my strange cabinmate.

A very wild plan with practically no chance of succeeding. But such is our clinging to life that I was ready to consider it. My cabin was not too far from the space lock, and the cubby storing the suits. On the other hand, the opening of that compartment would be instantly signaled to the bridge—and suppose we were in hyper—?

"Not so," cut in my companion. "Feel—"

It was right. The hum of a ship in hyper was absent. Rather I felt the vibration of a ship cruising in normal space.

"They seek—moon—dead world—to hide plague—or perhaps to meet others."

I pulled open a storage compartment. A coverall hung inside and I jerked it out, put it on. Wherever the fabric touched my scaling blotches they itched, but that was a minor discomfort when I had so much else to worry about. As I sealed the front opening, the creature on the bunk hunched together, quivered, leaped—landing on a small railed shelf level with my shoulder. I flinched and blinked.

Now that it was closer I could see it in detail. And it was indeed a weird mixture. Its fur was still the wiry black fuzz. The paws were naked skin. They were gray, white on the undersurfaces, and the fore ones were very like tiny hands. The head was reminiscent of a feline's, as was the body, except the limbs were too short in comparison with the length of the frame. Stiff whiskers bristled from the upper lip, but the ears were smaller than a cat's. The eyes were also out of proportion, being large and showing no pupils at all, only dark, slightly protruding orbs.

The whiplike tail was furred for its length in a ridge along the upper surface, but the tip and underparts were bare. Strange as it looked, it was not in any way repulsive, only different.

It stepped from the shelf to my body, settling itself around my neck, its hand-paws clinging to my right shoulder, so that its head was not far from my ear, its hind claws driven into the fabric over my upper left arm.

"Go—they come."

It was as sharp as an order and I found myself obeying. But before I left the cabin I received one more instruction.

"The air duct—feel inside."

The screen across it gave way easily to my first tug. I was so bemused now I followed instructions without question. Inside I found my safe-belt, which had been laid in the center of that tube, concealed from without. Automatically I searched its pockets by touch. My small resources were still mine.

"Quick!" That was reinforced with a sharp pinch from the hind claws.

I inched open the cabin door. The faint glow of the passage showed me it was empty. But I could hear the ring of boot plates on a ladder not too far away. I lurched for the suit locker. Suddenly it seemed my very thin chance was better than no chance at all!

The dreamlike quality of my actions continued to hold. I no longer, even with a small part of my brain, questioned the need to flee the interior of the ship, or whether any of this wild plan was feasible.

I regained a measure of strength and the more I walked the steadier I became. There was a fleeting satisfaction in disappointing Velos, who claimed I was dead or close to it.

The latch of the suit locker yielded to my tug and I slipped inside, pulling the door shut behind me. In one way I was favored, I saw as I glanced around that dim interior. The *Vestris* followed the general pattern of an exploring vessel—which was only logical, since a Free Trader often did discover new worlds.

There was another opening at the end of this space, giving entrance directly to the lock, saving time when one must suit or unsuit in leaving or entering the ship. I ran my hand along the rack of suits, striving to find one enough my size to be, if not comfortable, usable. Free Traders are now of a general physical type, slight of build. Had I not myself been thin and under height, I could not have squeezed into their protective covering. As it was, I was going to have a tight fit—a very tight one—so much so that I could not even buckle the safe-belt about my middle. Well, perhaps it could go over, if not under, the suit.

When we entered the locker my small companion swung down from its perch on my shoulders, and seemed almost to flow across the floor. It stopped before a clear-sided box and sat up on its haunches, using those hand-paws to feel along one edge in a way which argued intelligent purpose. Then the front of the box sprang open and it flashed in, to curl up. Mystified, I watched.

"Close this!" The imperative command ringing in my head brought me down on one knee, the suit making me clumsy.

I was not quite sure what the box was. Its clear front, metal sides and back were both protective and designed to give one visibility of the contents. There were hooks at the back, as if it were meant to hang from a support. I guessed that it had been fashioned to bring back specimens from a new-found world.

"Close it—hurry—they come! You will take me—so!"

The bright eyes turned up to mine, willing me. Yes, I could feel the force of the will. Again I obeyed.

My safe-belt could not be hooked over the suit. I hurriedly unsealed its pockets and shoveled their contents into a belt pouch—all save the space ring. That wide band of metal had once fitted over a space glove; perhaps it could again. And it did—snugly.

I strapped on the rest of the equipment, dimly aware of the suicidal folly of my plan. But the fact remained that were I to appear now anywhere in the ship I would probably be burned down without mercy. There is no fear quite like that of plague. With the carrying case containing my self-appointed company under my arm, I opened the door into the lock. My issuing out of the ship would activate alarms. But would they immediately believe that their quarry was seeking such a way out? Velos had reported me comatose. And I hoped they would cling to that thought.

The door of the hatch rolled back into place and I dogged it shut. Why not stay just where I was? Because there were inner controls and that door could still be opened from the corridor. They need only open it and beam a hole in my protective suit, then thrust me into space. A clean death as far as they were concerned, with little chance of my contaminating my slayers.

Even as I thought all this my hands were busy thumbing the release of the outer hatch, almost as if they worked independently of my orders. Then the warn light flashed and there was a rushing of air. I edged through, planting the magnetic plates of my boots on the surface skin of the ship.

I had traveled spacers for years. However, my acquaintance with such had been limited to the activities of a passenger. But now I had sense enough to keep my eyes on the ship under my feet, resolutely away from the void it sailed. I had fastened the box by a safety cord to my harness and that swung out, tugging at me, but not with force enough to break my magnetic hold on the ship.

Shuffling, not daring to break contact with the surface, I moved away from the hatch. I thought it would not be long before I was followed and the folly of what I had done struck me like a blow, breaking that dream state which had held me since the creature had first thrown its thoughts at my receptive mind.

If that *was* all real and not some fever dream, I had received telepathically those suggestions and orders. No man can laugh at the idea of esper powers, as the so-called enlightened once did. It has been established that they exist, but do so rarely, and erratically. However, I had never had any contact with such before, and was certain I had no "wild talent."

"Move!" That order rang as sharply in my head as the first communication had done. "Move—toward the nose—"

For the first time since our association had begun, I balked. In fact I could not have moved in any direction at that moment. I was frozen in such wild terror as I had never believed a man could experience and not go mad. For I had lost all prudence and looked away from the ship under me, out and up.

Words hammered in my mind, but I did not understand them. I knew nothing, saw nothing but that emptiness. Something jerked and tore at my harness. The creature was plunging about in its box. I could see its mouth open and close, its eyes no longer shining beads but fiery and bright. But I watched it with detachment, the terror of space holding me fast.

But it was while I watched the creature's frenzied movements inside that box that I also saw the closing of the hatch I had left open. And I think I screamed inside my helmet, the shrilling of my own voice deafening me. I was locked out here now, alone with nothingness!

Did I go a little mad? I am sure now that I did. I must get to the door, I must—I have no true recollection—did I hurl myself? What happened in those seconds of raw, mind-shattering panic? I have never known. But I was no longer rooted—the ship was there, and I was turning over and over, away from it, without any hope of aid—floating out into the eternal dark.

I think I fainted then—because there are blank spaces in my memory. True consciousness only returned with the sensation of being pulled, drawn. I had a moment or two of heartfelt relief. They had roped me, I was going back to the *Vestris*. Even if that meant I was going to certain death, I did not care. Quick death was an end to be sought in preference to this spinning in the void forever.

My shoulder, my arm, pain—a pulling pain which grew stronger. My right arm was stretched straight ahead of my body as if I pointed to some unseen goal. And on the glove blazed light, a light which fluctuated as if it were fed by energy which came in spurts. I followed that outstretched arm as a diver's body follows his upheld, water-cutting arms, and there was the strong, sinew-tormenting pull, as if my arm had become a rope drawing me to an anchorage.

Nor could I move my arm, or even my legs. I was frozen into this position—a human arrow aimed for a target which I could not guess. That I was aimed I did not doubt. There was no rope on me—no, I was swinging through the void following that light on my glove. My glove? No! The space ring on my finger!

That once-clouded stone was the beacon of light pulling me on and on. I could turn my head a little and see in the reflected glory of that light that I still towed the box with its furry occupant. But the creature was curled in a tight ball which rolled helplessly and I thought it was probably dead.

Where the *Vestris* might be I had no idea. There was a sense of speed about my present passage. And I could not turn my head very far to see what lay behind, above, or below.

Time ceased to have any meaning. I wavered back and forth between consciousness and black non-being. Only gradually did I become aware of approaching something. At last I could make out the outline of what once might have been a ship; at least the inner portion of that drifting mass might have been a ship. About it, like tiny satellites about a planet, were crowding bits of debris, grinding now and then against the hull, swinging out, but not to break away. And the ring was pulling me straight into that grinding! Caught by even a small fragment of that and I would be as dead as if a laser had cut me down.

Yet try to fight the pull as I did, I had no chance against the force drawing me on. My arm was numb, the joints seemingly locked in that position. I had ceased to be a man; I was only a means for the ring to reach whatever target it must find.

Inside the suit, my helpless body, that which was the thinking, feeling part of me, cowered and whimpered. I shut my eyes, unable to look upon what lay before me, and then was forced to open them again because hope refused to die. We were very close to the outer circle of debris, and I thought I could see a hole in the side of the derelict ship—either an open hatch or some other break.

It was, as far as I could guess, since my sight of it was limited by the mass of stuff about it, larger than the *Vestris*, perhaps closer to passenger liner. And its lines were not those of any ship I knew. Then—we were in the first wave of debris—

I waited for the crushing of those bits of jagged metal—until I saw that the floating stuff was parting before the beam of the stone, as if that had the power to cut a clear path. Hardly daring to believe that such would be the case, I watched. But it was true, a great lump dipped and bobbed and moved reluctantly away.

So we came to that dark doorway. I was sure it was a hatch, though there remained no evidence of any door. But the opening was too regular to be a mere hole. Into and through that dark arch the ring continued to pull me, lighting up dim walls. And then my beacon hand struck painfully against a solid surface, and continued to beat through no desire of mine, hammering upon the inner hatch of this long-dead ship as if demanding entrance. Finally my gloved flesh came to rest on that resisting surface as if it were welded there, while I struggled until my magnetized boots struck the floor and I could stand, my right hand pinned to the door, my feet anchored once again.

SIX

There was such an overwhelming relief in being shut in, out of the void, that for a space that was all I felt—until the knowledge that I was now caught in another trap dispelled my only too short sensation of safety. My hand was still fast against the door and I could not pull it loose. Rather, it dragged me further and further forward, until my whole body was flat to that surface, almost as if the strength of the attraction could ooze me through the age-worn metal itself. And a second wave of fear arose in me at the thought that I would be held so for all time, trapped in this hatchway.

The glow from the stone was no longer so bright as it had been. In these confined quarters it would have been blinding had its brilliance shown as it had in space. But it was still flickering. I struggled wildly against the hold, until I wilted, exhausted, held upright by my hand against the door.

As I hung there, staring dully at the light, my hand, and the door, a fact broke through my bemusement. The flickering was now more deliberate. Almost it followed a pattern—on, off, on, off, with varying intervals between flashes. The suit was insulated, of course, but where the palm of my glove met the substance of the door, a reddish stain was spreading. Even through that insulation I could feel a tingle of concentrated energy.

Again I sensed I was only a thing to be used by the stone, that I was its tool and not it mine. The tingle became pain, and finally agony, with nothing I could do to ease it. The red stain brightened and at last I saw dark lines crack open. As the agony grew, the door began to give way. It fell in broken shards from the frame and I was pulled on.

I caught only glimpses of corridors, for it seemed that the stone now sped to make up for the time lost in defeating the barrier at the hatch. I was twice pulled past breaks in the hull.

My journey ended in a section where there were strange shapes of machines—or I believed them to be machines. And this part of the ship seemed intact, undamaged by whatever had struck to finish its life. The stone whisked me around and through a maze of rods, cylinders, latticework, piping, coming at last to a box wherein I could see a tray. And set on that were black lumps. With a last spurt the stone once more plastered my hand to the viewplate of the box. It flared in a burst of dazzling light. And behind the plate I saw a small answering flicker from one of those lumps. But it was only a flicker and quickly gone. Then the glow of the stone died, too, and my hand fell limply to swing by my side, a dead weight. I was alone in the dark bowels of a long-dead ship.

I collapsed, to float, and then felt the bump of the box in which my companion traveled. How much air I had left in my suit tank I did not know, but I doubted whether it was enough to keep me living long. The stone had clearly led me to my death, not in a void where I would have spun forever, but in this tomb of blasted metal.

There is the ancient fear of my species of the dark and what may creep therein. I raised my left hand and fumbled with the button on the fore of my harness until the sharp ray of a beamer glowed, picking out the case of lumps which might once have been stones to rival that in the ring. There was, of course, no hope that I could find any compartment with air remaining, or any form of escape. But neither would I stay supine where I was, just waiting for suffocation to finish me.

My right arm was still useless. I took that hand with my left and wedged it into the front of my harness, keeping it across my chest. I would have cast off the box with the dead creature, only, when I looked down at that tightly curled body, to my vast amazement, I saw the head move, caught the gleam of eyes. So it had also survived our voyage to the derelict!

The magnetic plates on my boots allowed me to walk along the deck, though the slow spin of the ship made the deck become wall, or even ceiling. Finally I loosed the plates and pulled along by handholds.

All ships of my own time carried lifeboats, with directional finders which would locate the nearest planetary body and would then direct the boat there—though there was always a chance the survivors might be landed on a world inhospitable to human life. Perhaps this ship had a similar arrangement for the safety of passengers and crew. If so—and I could find one—though they might have all been used when the ship was first abandoned—I might still have a thin chance.

It is the nature of my species that we find it necessary to keep fighting for life until a last blow ends us. That inborn instinct drove me now.

The stone, I deduced, had brought me to the engine section of the ship. Whatever empowered it in space and acted as a homing device had drawn it straight to those burned-out bits in the box, once, perhaps, the motive power for the ship.

I pulled myself through the remains of the engine room. There might, I thought, be other energy sources in the lifeboats. They should be several decks higher, close to the crew and passenger quarters—always supposing this ship duplicated the general layout of those I knew.

I found no ladders, only wells which were cut through the levels. There were hints here and there that this vessel had never housed beings of my type. At the foot of the second well I hesitated. The ship rolled lazily; I might float through one of these—only my beamer showed no handholds to pull me along, and to be sucked in and then spin helplessly—At last I used my boot plates, walking up along walls which moved ever to make my head swim and induce a return of the vertigo which had been a symptom of my illness.

The next level had cabins, most of their doors open. I peered into one or two. There were shelves which might have been bunks, save that they were very short and narrow, and they were so uniform in the interior design I thought this must have been crew territory.

Once more I made a spin walk to the next level. There had been a carpet on the floor here and the cabins were larger. My beam illuminated a splash of color on the wall, focused on a picture or mural—queerly disjointed figures or objects, which my eyes could not follow, colors which hurt. Passenger territory. Now—along here I should find LB hatches.

There was something floating against the wall of the corridor. It seemed to lurch at me and I fended it off with aversion, refusing to look closely. Passenger or crewman, here was one who had not reached any LB. My touch sent it swirling back and away.

I had begun to think I was wrong in my hopes when I came to the first port and looked through its door into an empty socket. The LB had been launched, which meant live passengers had reached it. Some had escaped that long-ago wreck. And though the port was empty, it raised my flagging hopes.

The dial on my air tank had swung far toward red. I glanced at it once and then swiftly away. Better not to know how near I was to the end. Even were I able to find a usable LB and launch it, how long would it be before I reached a planet? If and if and if again—

Suddenly the numb arm across my breast twitched and pulled against the confining strap. I looked down. The stone shone. Was it answering once more a call from an installation similar to the one I had found in the engine room?

Though the pull tugged at my secured arm, it was not enough to jerk it free of the fastening. But it did provide a guide along this corridor. Past two more empty berths I traveled. Then my arm gave a hard jerk, which did tear it loose and bring its dead weight around to point to a surface now almost under me as the ship rolled. There was another hatch to an LB berth—but it was closed. Perhaps no one had reached it.

Again my glove went to that door, anchored me, and the light from the stone flared. But this time it did not burn through. The hatch cover rolled aside and I saw the projectile shape of an LB. Once more my arm dropped, but I pulled myself along with my left hand, pried at the hatch of the LB. It gave and I fell into its interior, bringing the box of the creature with me.

There was a flickering of light, not only from the stone, but on a panel at the nose end of the LB. There were hammock-like slings to take the bodies of passengers and one was close enough for me to clutch. I could feel a vibration through the small cabin. Whatever energized this LB was not dead—the thing had at least enough power to cruise out of its sling inside the skin of the parent ship. We shot forth with enough force to pin me down, and I blacked out.

"Air—"

I looked blearily about. The beamer still shone, now straight against a curving wall, to be reflected back dazzlingly into my eyes. Suddenly I realized that I was breathing in shuddering gasps, coughing a little. For the air I fought to draw into my lungs had a strange odor which irritated my nasal passages. On my shoulder was a furry burden, and a whiskered face was thrust close to mine, dark beads of eyes watching me intently.

"Air it is," I answered dreamily. More and more this had the cast of a weird nightmare. Logical, perhaps, after a fashion which nightmares seldom are, but certainly not believable. For now, however, I was content to lie half entangled in the hammock, rapidly breathing that disagreeable air.

When I turned my head a fraction I could see a board of controls. The numerous lights which had played so swiftly across it at my first entrance now were cut to three—one yellow-white, in the center and a little above the other two, one red, and the other a ghostly blue. I looked down at my hand. There was still a glint of light in the stone, showing beneath the clouded surface, and a faint tingling prickled in my hand.

At least I was still alive, I was free of the dead ship in an LB, and I had air to breathe even if it was not the air my lungs craved. It would seem my entrance into the projectile had activated its ancient mechanism.

If we were on course for the nearest planet, how long a voyage did we face? And what kind of a landing might we have to endure? I could breathe, but I would need food and water. There might be supplies—E-rations—on board. But could they still be used after all these years—or could a human body be nourished by them?

With my teeth I twisted free the latch which fastened my left glove, scraped that off, and freed my hand. Then I felt along my harness. These suits were meant to be worn planetside as well as for space repairs; they must have a supply of E-rations. My fingers fumbled over some loops of tools and found a seam-sealed pouch. It took me a few moments to pick that open.

I had not felt hunger before; now it was a pain devouring me. I brought the tube I had found up to eye level. It was more than I could manage to sit up or even raise my head higher, but the familiar markings on the tube were heartening. One moment to insert the end between my teeth, bite through, and then the semiliquid contents flooded my mouth and I swallowed greedily. I was close to the end of that bounty when I felt movement against my bared throat and remembered I was not alone.

It took a great deal of resolution to pinch tight that tube and hold it to the muzzle of the furred one. Its pointed teeth seized upon the container with the same avidity I must have shown, and I squeezed the tube slowly while it sucked with a vigor I could feel through the touching of its small body to mine.

There were three more tubes in my belt pouch. Each one, I knew, was intended to provide a day's rations, perhaps two if a man were hard pushed. Four days—maybe we could stretch that to eight. But the gamble was such as no sane man would have taken by choice.

I lay quietly until my strength began to return. The leaden weight of my right arm tingled a little, not from the action of the stone, but as if circulation returned. With that came a painful cramping. I forced myself to flex my fingers inside the glove, to raise and lower my forearm, setting my teeth against the hurt those exercises caused me.

In time my arm obeyed me as well as it had before the stone had taken over. I pulled myself up into a sitting position and gazed about the LB. There were six of the hammock slings, three on each wall, and I lay in the last to the right. None of them had been placed close enough to the control board for the occupant to reach it. This was true also of the regulation escape boats I knew. Their course tapes were set, so that if a badly injured man managed to reach one of them, it would serve without need for human manipulation.

Like the bunks I had seen in the ship, these hammocks, gauging by their size, were not intended for the human frame. And certainly the air still rasping my nose

and lungs was not normal. I wondered briefly if it held
some poisonous element which would in time finish me.
But if that were true there was nothing I could do
about it.

On the wall I traced outlines which I thought marked
storage compartments. Whether E-rations lay behind
those still—The dreamy state continued to hold me.
Though my strength returned to my body, it was as if I
watched all this from a distance and nothing really mattered. Once I raised my hand to look at it. Those dark
patches which had been the purple, swollen blisters, and
then scaling scabs, had rubbed off their rough surfaces
inside the glove. The skin beneath was shiny pink and
new.

Again the furred body moved and I felt the wiry hair
rasp against my neck. Then my companion moved out,
crawling down my body, reaching out a hand-paw to
catch at the webbing of the next hammock. It was a long
space to span, and at last the creature dug the claws of
its hind legs into the stuff of my suit, lunged forward,
and so was just able to grasp the edge of the web. With
sinuous dexterity it took firm hold and swung over to its
new position.

The hammock served it as a ladder and it climbed
agilely to one of the outlined lockers. Holding with a left
forepaw and both hind legs to its swaying anchorage, it
ran the other set of small gray fingers over the surface.
When it pressed or released, I could not tell, but a panel
swung open with such speed that the creature had to
duck to escape.

Behind were two tubes secured in a rack. Each had
something vaguely resembling a laser grip, and I thought

they might be weapons—or perhaps survival tools. Leaving that door aswing, the creature went methodically to the next. I was a little troubled as I watched it.

Even after our communication I had continued to think of my companion as an animal. It was clearly the offspring of Valcyr, strange though its begetting had been. I had heard of mutant animals able to communicate with man. But now it was brought home to me that whatever this creature was, it had intelligence above the level I had assigned it. And now I asked, my voice overloud in the small cabin:

"Who are you?"

Perhaps it would have been better to ask, "What are you?"

It paused, its forepaw still outstretched, its long neck twisting so that it could look straight at me. And for the first time I remembered I had awakened without my helmet, with the air reviving me. Surely I had not taken it off while unconscious—so—

"Eet."

A single word with a queer sound—if a word in one's mind may also register as a sound.

"Eet," I repeated aloud. "Do you mean you are Eet as I am Murdoc Jern, or Eet as I am a man?"

"I am Eet, myself, me—" If it understood my division of terms it was not interested. "I am Eet, returned—"

"Returned—how? From where?"

It settled back into the hammock, which swayed under its weight as light as it was, so that it must clutch at the webbing to keep its position.

"Returned to a body," it replied matter-of-factly. "The animal made me a body—different, but usable. Though perhaps it needs some altering. But that can come when there is time and the necessary nutriments."

"You mean you were a native, one of those we could not find? That because Valcyr ate that seed, you—" My thoughts jumped from one wild possibility to the next.

"I was not native to that world!" There was a snap to that, as if Eet resented the suggestion. "They did not have that in them which could make Eet a body. It was necessary to wait until the proper door was opened, the right covering prepared. The beast from the ship had what I needed—thus she was attracted to the seed and took inside her the core from which Eet could be born again—"

"Born again—from where?"

"From the time of hibernation." There was impatience now. "But that is past—it need not be considered. What is of importance in this hour is survival—mine— yours—"

"So I am important to you?" Why had it urged me out of the *Vestris*, saved me by removing my helmet in the LB? Did it need me in some way?

"It is true that we have need of one another. Life forms in partnership sometimes make a great one out of a lesser," Eet observed. "I have obtained a body which has some advantages, but it lacks bulk and strength, which you can supply. On the other hand, I have skills I am able to lend to your fight for life."

"And this partnership—it has some future goal?"

"That has yet to be revealed. Now we think of continuing to live, a matter of major importance."

"I agree to that. What are you hunting for?"

"What you have already imagined might be here, the food and drink intended to sustain those escaping in this small ship."

"If it is still here and has not dried to dust, or if it will feed us and not be poison." But I pulled myself up yet farther in the hammock and watched Eet claw open another locker.

This contained two canisters set in shock-absorbing bands. And though Eet wrestled with them, he could not free either. At last I dragged my weak-legged self from my hammock to the next and managed to pry the nearest canister from its hooks.

It had a nozzled tip. I gripped it between my knees and used one of the small tools from my harness to open it. Then I shook the can gently. There was the slosh of liquid inside. I sniffed, my mouth dry again as I thought of the wonderful chance that it might actually hold water. The semiliquid E-ration contained moisture but not really enough to allay thirst.

Its smell was pungent, but not unpleasant. What I held could be drink, or fuel, or anything. Another chance among all those I—we—had taken since we had left the *Vestris*.

"Drink or fuel, or what have you?" I stated the guesses to Eet, holding out the canister so that he, she, or it could sniff in turn.

"Drink!" was the decided answer.

"How can you be so sure?"

"You think I say so just because I wish it? No. This much have I in this body: what is harmful to it, that I shall know. This is good—drink it and see."

So authoritative was the command that I forgot it came from a small furred creature of unknown species. I put the nozzle to my lips and sucked. Then I almost spilled the container, for though the stuff which filled my mouth *was* liquid, it had a sour bite. Not wine as I knew it, but certainly not water either. Yet after I had swallowed inadvertently, my throat was cool and my mouth felt fresh, as if I had drunk my fill of some cool stream. I took another drink and then passed it to Eet, holding the container while it sucked. Thus we had our necessary moisture. But for food we were not so lucky. We found in another locker blocks of a pinkish stuff, dried and hard. Eet pronounced them dangerous, and if they were the E-rations of the LB, they were not for us.

He found some queerly shaped tools and another set of weapons, but that was all—except for a box, in the last compartment, that had various dials and two rods which could be pulled out from a place of safekeeping on its back. These extended, and between them there was a thin tissue which expanded to form a film. I judged it a com device—doubtless meant to beep a distress signal once the party aboard the LB made their landing. But those it might have summoned were long since vanished from this portion of the galaxy.

Since my species entered space we have known we were latecomers to the star lanes. There were other races who voyaged space, empires and confederations of many worlds which rose and fell, long before we knew the wheel and fire, and reached for metal to fashion sword and plow. We discover traces of them from time to time and there is a very brisk trade in antiques from such finds. The Zacathans, I believe, have archaeological records of at least three star empires, or alliances, all vanished before *they* pioneered space, and the Zacathans are the oldest people we have firsthand knowledge of, with a written history covering two million planet years! They are a long-lived race and prize knowledge above all else.

Even this LB, could we possibly by some fluke land on an inhabited planet, would bring me enough from its sale to set me up as a gem buyer. But the chance of that happening was so small as to be infinitesimal. I would settle gladly for any sort of a landing where the air was breathable and there was enough food and water to sustain life.

There was no reckoning time in the LB. I slept and so did Eet. We ate very sparingly, when we could no longer stand the demands of our bodies, and drank the liquid of the vanished voyagers. I tried to get more information out of Eet, but he stubbornly curled into a ball and would not answer. I say "he," for while he never stated his sex, if he had one, I came to think of him as male, and since he did not correct that assumption, I continued in it.

We had but half a tube of nourishment left when that white light on the board, so steady that it had ceased to interest us, flashed into yellow and there was a warning buzz along the walls. I hoped (or did I fear?) that this meant a landing. And I huddled back in the hammock, Eet sprawled flat against me, wondering how well we would set down in a craft ages old and powered by energy close to extinction.

SEVEN

We must have blacked out in shock following our entrance into the atmosphere, for when I was again conscious of my surroundings, we lay in a ship which no longer vibrated with life—though it swayed under my half-aware movements as if we were caught in a giant net and there was no stable earth under us. I screwed the helmet of the suit back into place and saw that Eet had been prudent enough to return to the box. Then I crawled, inch by inch, to the hatch, the LB slipping and shuddering under me in the most alarming way.

The inner catches on that were simple, devised for survivors who might have been injured and able to use only one hand. But when I tried to push it open there was resistance, and curls of white smoke trickled in. I had to fight the stubborn metal until I was able to wedge open a space wide enough to scramble through without tearing my precious suit.

There I was met by more puffs of thick smoke. I looked around for a stable foothold. The LB seemed to be sliding sideways and I had little time for choice. When it gave a convulsive tremble I jumped, into the smoke, and crashed through that veil into a mass of splintered and broken foliage, some of it afire.

A branch as thick as my wrist, with a broken end like a spear point, nearly impaled me. I caught it with both hands and hung for a moment, thrashing wildly with my feet for some hold. But it bent under my weight and I slid inexorably down it in spite of my struggles. I crashed on, down through more branches, bringing up at last on a wider one where my harness caught on a stub of mossed wood and I found a precarious landing. There was a heavy tearing a little ways away. I thought that perhaps the LB had gone down. I clung to the stub which had hooked me and drew a deep breath as I looked around.

The masses of leaves screening me in were a sickly yellowish-green, which here and there shaded to a brighter yellow, or a dull purplish-red. The branch under me was rough-barked, wide enough for two men to walk, and splotched with purple moss, in which grew spikes of scarlet crowned with cups which might be flowers, but which opened and shut as I watched with the rhythm of breathing or of a beating heart.

There was a great ragged hole overhead which marked more than my own descent, probably the entrance of the LB. But elsewhere the canopy of growth was thick and unbroken.

I drew the box containing Eet up beside me and saw that he was sitting on his haunches, looking about him with reptilian twists of his long neck, so that sometimes he appeared to turn his head completely around on his shoulders. There was a crashing which I did not really hear, but rather felt as a vibration through the shaking tree, and then a final thud which set my perch rocking under me. I judged that the LB had at last met the ground. The fact that so heavy a craft had taken so long to fall suggested two things—that this net of vegetation grew well above the ground, and that it was tough enough to catch the entering ship, cushion it for a space, delay its final landing.

The smoke was thickening, coming from above. If there was a fire blazing there, then a withdrawal was certainly in order. To outrun a forest blaze in my unwieldy suit was nigh impossible.

I got to my feet and edged along the limb, heading, I hoped, for the parent trunk. At least it grew wider and thicker ahead of me. There were other aerial growths besides the moss with the breathing cups. One barred my way very soon. The leaves were yellow, broad and fleshy, curving up so that those in the center formed a cup. And in that, water, or some colorless fluid, gathered. Above this leaf-enclosed pondlet was the first animate life I had seen.

A flying thing perhaps as large as my hand unfolded gauzy wings to flutter away. It had been so much the color of the leaves that it was invisible until it moved. Another creature raised a dripping snout and bared teeth from where it crouched on the other side of the cup. Like the flying thing, it was camouflaged, for its wattled, warty covering was like the rough bark of the tree limbs, and of the same dark color. But the fangs it showed suggested that it was carnivorous, and it was about the size of Valcyr, with long legs which were clawed, clearly meant to grip and hold, perhaps not only the aerial trails it followed but also some prey.

Nor did it have any fear of me, but stood its ground, fangs bared, its ugly head down, its shoulders hunched, as if it was about to spring.

To advance I must cross the outer leaves of the pool plant. And while my challenger was small, I did not underrate it for that reason. There had been no laser with the suit—after ship custom all arms were locker-stored during the flight. Most Free Traders carried only the non-lethal stunners anyway. But I did not even have one of those.

"Let it be." Eet's command rang in my head. "It will go—"

And go it did, with a suddenness which left me believing it had vanished like some illusion wrought by a Hymandian sand wizard. I saw a flash across the bark beyond the pool plant, and that was all that marked its going.

Cautiously I stepped onto the broad leaves. Their surfaces broke under my weight, and yellow stuff oozed up and about my boot soles, the leaves themselves turning dark, seeming to rot away at once, flaking in great shreds from the holes. More of the gauzy things took to the air, and the surface of the leaf pool was troubled as other small life arose to its surface and leaped into the air, to splash back, as my passing put an end to their world.

I slipped and slid, careful of every slime-coated step, until I reached the other side. My face was wet with sweat inside the helmet, and I was breathing slowly and with an effort. I had come to the end of my air supply, and whether it would mean death or no, I must open my helmet.

Squatting down on the limb, I clicked open the latches and breathed, half expecting to have the lungs seared out of me by that experiment. But, though the air was laden with smells, and many of those noxious as far as I was concerned, I thought the air less bad than that I had encountered in the LB.

I could hear now, and there were sounds in plenty. The buzzing of insects, sharp calls, and now and then a distant heavy thud, as if someone beat a huge drum and listened to its echoes dying gradually away. There was a rustling and a crackling, too. I could smell a stench which was certainly born of burning, though I did not see any movement of tree-dwelling things which would suggest that the inhabitants of these leafed heights were fleeing a fire.

Behind me the pool plant shriveled, its bruised leaves falling away in festering shreds. Now the inner petals or leaves which had cupped the water unclasped and a flood poured out, to cascade and then drip from the big limb into the mass of vegetation below, carrying with it wriggling, struggling things which had lived in it. The plant continued to die and rot until only a black blot remained on the limb, a most nauseating odor rising from it, making me move on.

The limb road grew wider and thicker. Now it was a running place for vines, which crossed it and looped around it, forming traps for the feet of the unwary. I continued to sweat as the muggy heat held me. And the suit became more and more of a burden. Too, I was hungry, and I remembered the drinker at the pool, wondering if I could turn hunter with any success.

"Out—!" Eet was economical with words now, but his meaning was plain. I put down his traveling box and opened it. He flashed out of its confines and stood poised on the limb, his head flicking from side to side.

"We must have food—" I remembered what he had said about being able to tell what was edible and what was not. The fact that on an alien planet practically all food might mean death to off-worlders was to the fore of my mind. We might have made a safe landing here only to starve in the midst of what was luxurious plenty for the natives.

"There—" He used his nose as a pointer, elongating his neck to emphasize his statement. What he had selected was an outgrowth on one of those serpentine vines. It rose like a stem, from which quivered some narrow pods, more flat than round. They shook and shivered as if they possessed some odd·life of their own. And I could not see why Eet thought them possible food. They appeared less likely than the cluster of ovoid berries, bursting with ripe pulp and juice, which hung from another stem not too far away.

I watched my companion harvest the pods with his forepaws. He stripped off their outer shells to uncover some small, far too small, purple seeds, which he ate, not with any appearance of relishing that diet, but as one would do a duty.

He did not fall into convulsions, or drop in a fatal coma, but methodically finished all the buttons he could strip out of their pods. Then he turned to me.

"These can be safely eaten, and without food you cannot go on."

I was still dubious. What might be good for my admittedly half-alien companion might not nourish me. But it was the only chance I had. And there was another cluster of the trembling pods not too far beyond my hand.

Slowly I drew the space stone from my gloved finger, stowed it away in a pocket on my harness, and then unsealed the gloves, allowing them to dangle from my wrists as I reached for the harvest.

Once more I saw the healing scars of the blisters. My flesh was pink and new-looking in unseemly splotches against the general brown of my skin. Though I was not as space-tanned as a crewman might be, my roving life had darkened my skin more than was normal for a planet dweller. But I was now spotted in what I was sure must be a disfiguring manner, though I could not see my face to judge. Until the blotches faded, if they ever did, I would be marked as undesirable to any off-worlder. Perhaps it was just as well we had not made landing at a port; one look at me and I would have been sent into indefinite quarantine.

Carefully I husked the pellets. They were larger than grains of hoswheat, hard and smooth to the touch. I raised them to my nose, but if they had any odor, it was slight enough to be overlaid by the general blast of smells all about us. Gingerly I mouthed several of them and chewed.

They seemed to have no discernible taste, but became a floury meal between my teeth. I found them dry, hard to swallow, but swallow I did. Then, since I had taken the first step and might as well go all the way, I harvested all within reach, chewing and swallowing, giving Eet another two clusters when he signified they would be acceptable.

I allowed us some small sips from the canister of liquid out of the ship, which I had made fast to my harness. That cleared the dry-as-dust feeling from my mouth tissues.

Eet had been moving impatiently back and forth along the branch as I ate, progressing in darting runs, pausing to peer and listen, then returning. Although it had been but a short time since his birth, he had all the assurance of an adult, as if he had achieved that status.

"We are well above ground." He came back to settle down near me. "It would be well to get to a lower level."

Perhaps as I had depended upon his instincts to find us food, so I should harken to him now. But the suit was clumsy to climb in, and I feared a false step where the vines were so entwined.

I crawled on hands and knees, testing each small space in advance. Thus I came to the point from which those vines spread, the giant trunk of the tree. And that bole was giant indeed. I believe that had it been hollow, it would have furnished room for an average dwelling on Angkor, while its height was beyond my reckoning. I wondered just how far it was to the surface of this vegetation-choked world—if the whole planet was covered by such trees.

Had it not been for the vines, I would have been marooned aloft, but their twists, slippery and unpromising as they looked, did afford a kind of looped stairway. I had two cords with hooked ends coiled in my harness—intended to anchor one during space repairs, though I had not discovered them in time to keep me on the *Vestris*. These I put to use now, hooking them to vines, lowering myself to the extent of the cord, loosing by tears to hook again. It was an exhausting form of progress, and I grew faint with the struggle. The muggy heat made it worse.

Finally I came to the jut of another wide branch, even larger than the one I had left. I dragged myself out on that, thankful to have reached such a small link with safety. The thick foliage made this a gloomy place, as if I were in a cave. And I thought that if I ever did reach the surface of the forest floor, it would be to discover that day was night under the sky-hiding canopy. Perhaps it was the tear made by the LB which allowed even this much light to filter through.

Those patches of moss with the breathing cups were not to be seen on this level. Instead there was a rough, spiky excrescence from which hung long drooping, thread-thin stems or tentacles. These exuded drops of sap or a similar substance. And the drops glowed faintly. They were, I believed, lures, attracting prey either by that phosphorescence, or by their scent. For I saw insects stuck to them, sometimes thrashing so hard to be free that the thread-stems whipped back and forth.

Eet halted beside me, but I could sense his impatience at the slowness of my descent. Unburdened by a suit, he could have already reached the ground. Now he kept urging me to go on. But if he had some special fear of this arboreal world, he did not share it with me. His attitude had grown more and more like that of an adult dealing with a child who must be cared for, and whose presence hinders and makes more difficult some demanding task.

Groaning, I began the descent again. Eet flashed by me and was gone with an ease I envied bitterly as I took up my crawl, hook, hold, free, hook, crawl. As the gloom increased I began to worry more about my handholds, about being able to see anchors for the hooks.

It was as if I had started at midday and was now well into evening. The only aid was that more and more of the vegetation appeared to have phosphorescent qualities and that the spike growths with lures became larger and larger, giving a wan light. This glow grew brighter as darkness advanced. Perhaps the dusk really was due to the passage of time, and planet night was nearly upon me.

The thought of that led me to greater efforts. I had no wish to be trapped in the dark, climbing down this endless vine staircase. So I passed without halting two other limbs which offered tempting resting places and kept doggedly on.

Since that creature which had drunk from the pool plant had vanished I had seen no life except insects. But there were those in plenty and they varied from crawlers on vine and bark to a myriad of flying things. Some of the largest of those were equipped with spectral light patches too. Their antennae, their wings, and other parts of their bodies glowed with color instead of the ghostly grayish illumination of the plants. I saw sparks of red, of blue, of a clear and brilliant green—almost as if small gems had taken wing and whirled about me.

I was sure it was night when I slipped over the last great loops of vine which arched out and away from the tree, and which carried me, as I clung to their now coarse-textured surfaces, down to the floor of the forest. I landed feet first on a soft sponge of decay, into which I sank almost knee-deep. And it was as dark as a moonless and starless night.

"Here!" Eet signaled. I was floundering, trying to get better footing in the muck. Now I faced around to the point from which that hail had come.

The roots of the vines stretched out about the monster bole of the tree, so that between them and the trunk was a space of utter dark, where none of the light plants grew. It seemed to me that my companion had taken refuge in there. Painfully I pulled loose from the sucking grip of the mold, using the vine stems as a lever, and then I edged between two of them into that hollow.

Save that we lacked light, and weapons, we had won to a half-safe refuge. I could not guess as to the types of creatures roaming the floor of the forest. But it is always better to assume the worst than to try for a safety which does not exist. And on most worlds the lesser life is tree borne, the greater to be found on the ground.

I half sat, half collapsed in that hollow, the spread of a tree root giving support to my back. I faced outward so that I could see anything moving beyond that screen of vine roots. And the longer I sat there, the more I was able to pick out, even in the dark.

In my harness was the beamer, yet I hesitated to flash it unless the need was great. For such a light might well attract attention we would desire most to avoid. I could sight some of the sparks of light marking flying creatures. And now there were others which did not wing through the air, but crawled the ground.

There were sounds in abundance. A dull intermittent piping began once I was settled. And later a snuffling drew near and then faded away again. I craved sleep, but fought it, my imagination only too ready to paint what might happen if I closed my eyes to a danger creeping or padding toward our flimsy refuge.

The beamer was in my hand, my finger on its button. Perhaps a sudden flash of light would dazzle a bold hunter and give us a chance of escape, were we cornered.

Eet climbed to what appeared to be his favorite resting place, my shoulders. His weight was more than I had remembered; he must be growing, and faster than I had known any animal cub or kitten to do so. I felt the rasp of his wire-harsh hair against my skin. Certainly Eet was no pet to be smoothed.

"Where do we go now?" I asked, not because I thought he could give me a good answer, but just for the comfort of communication with another who was not as alien as this place in which I crouched.

"At night—no place. This is as good as any to hide in." Again I read impatience in his reply.

"And with the morning?"

"In any direction. One is as good as another. This is, I think, a large forest."

"The LB crashed not too far away. Some of its survival tools—the weapons—if they still work—"

"Commendable. You are beginning to think again. Yes, the ship should be our first goal. But not our final one. I do not think any help will come seeking us here."

I found it harder and harder to fight sleep, and felt the tickle of Eet's fur as he settled himself more heavily across my shoulders and chest.

"Sleep if you wish," his thought snapped at me. "Treat your body ill and it will not obey you. We shall need obedient bodies and clear minds to face tomorrow—"

"And if some night prowler decides to scoop us out of this hole? I do not think it is any safer than a tark shell."

"That we shall face if it happens. I believe my warning senses are more acute than yours. There are some advantages, as I have said, to this particular body I now wear."

"Body you now wear—Tell me, Eet, what kind of a body is really yours?"

I had no answer, unless the solid wall which I sensed snapping down between our minds could be considered an answer. It left me with the feeling of one who has inadvertently insulted a companion. Apparently the last thing Eet wanted to disclose was the life he might or might not have had before Valcyr swallowed the stone on the swamp world.

But his arguments made sense; I could not go without sleep forever. And if he had those warnings which animals possess and which have long been blunted in my species, then he would be alerted long before I could hear or sense trouble on the way.

So I surrendered to sleep, leaning back against the tree root with the night of the strange world dark and heavy about me. And I did not dream—or if I did, I did not remember. But I was startled out of that slumber by Eet.

"—to the right—" A half-thought as sharp as a spear point striking into my brain roused me. I blinked, trying to come fully awake.

Then I could see it, a glimmering. I thought that the dusk in which I had fallen asleep was not nearly as thick now.

It stood, not on four feet, but as a biped on two, though hunched forward, either as if that stance were not entirely natural, or as if it were listening and peering suspiciously. Perhaps it could scent our alien odor. Yet the head was not turned in our direction.

Like the colored insects and the plants, it had a phosphorescence of its own. And the effect was startling, for the grayish areas of light did not cover it as a whole but made a pattern along its body. There was a large round one on the top of the skull, and then below that, where the eyebrows of a human might be located, two oval ones. The rest of the face was dark, but ridges of light ran along the outsides of the upper and lower limbs, and three large circles such as that which crowned the head ran in a line down the center of the body. For the rest I could see that the four limbs were much thicker than those lines of light, and that the body was roughly ovoid, the wider portion forming the shoulders.

It moved a little away from the vines where it had stood and now I perceived that it carried a club weapon. This it swung up and down in one quick blow, and I heard an ugly hollow sound, which marked the striking of a victim. The attacker reached down a long arm and gathered up a limp body. With its kill in one hand and the club in the other, it turned and was gone, bursting through the vines at a speed which almost matched that of the drinker from the pond plant.

It was certainly more than an animal, I decided. But how far up the ladder from primitive beginnings I could not guess. And it had been as big as a tall man, or even larger.

"We have company," I observed, and felt Eet move restlessly.

"It would be wisest to seek the LB," he returned. "If that is not too badly damaged—The day is coming now."

As I got to my knees to crawl out of our temporary shelter I wondered in which direction we should go. I certainly could not tell. And if Eet did no better we could pass within feet of the wrecked ship and perhaps never sight it. I had heard of men who wandered lost in circles in unfamiliar territory when they had no guides or compasses.

EIGHT

"Any suggestions as to how we *do* find the ship?" I asked Eet.

Without inquiring if I cared to be his mode of transportation, he had climbed to my shoulders. In this dank heat and with the weight of the suit pressing me down, his presence was a drag.

Eet's head waved back and forth, almost as if he could sniff out our path. There was a constant patter of drops from above. It might have been raining forever in the dusk of the forest—or rather, dripping from the condensation of moisture above.

No underbrush existed here, save for the parasitic plants, which apparently did not need sunlight and were rooted on tree or vine trunks. Most of these gleamed ghostily.

But there was no clear vista in any direction. The trunks of the tree giants stood well separated one from the other because of their size, the large and strong forcing their way to the light and sun, the weaker dying. However, every one bore a lacy coating of vines, those twined and twirled from their own rootings to make a choked maze.

Under the tree where we had seen the clubber make his kill we came upon a kind of path, maybe a game trail. It was tempting to turn into that easier way—tempting, but dangerous.

"Right!" Eet's head swung in that direction.

"How—?"

"Smell!" he rapped out. "Burning—hot metal—At least this body has some good points. Try right and walk softly."

"As I can," I snapped in return. Slogging through the soft muck of long-dead vegetation was not easy. The plated boots I wore sunk in at each step and I had to pull my way wearily through either sifting sand or glutinous mud. Yet I clung to the suit, unwieldy as it was for such travel, because it gave me a sense of security.

As usual Eet proved to be right. Light pierced the gloom ahead after we rounded two more of the giant tree boles and their attendant festoons of vine stems. In this dusk the brilliant, eye-dazzling shafts of sunlight made me stop short, blinking.

There was a mass of splintered limbs, torn and mangled vines. Smoke still arose in languid trails, the stench of burned vegetation as thick as gas. But so full of sap or moisture was that growth that the fire set by the crash of the LB had not spread, but been quickly smothered. The ship had rammed down on nose and side and was buried deep in the muck, the metal shell crumpled and rent in some places.

Across the forest hole its fall had torn, brilliantly hued insects darted or drifted, lighting to crawl over the still-oozing sap. I saw a scurry as some four-footed explorer crossed the burst hull. And, surveying that wreck, I was shaken by the closeness of our escape. What if we had not been able to scramble out before the LB had plunged from its first landing in the treetops?

Fighting my way over the mass of splintered, entangled, and half-burned debris about the ship was a slow and painful business. Eet had jumped from my shoulder and reached our goal with a couple of bounds, then raced along the sloping side.

"The hatch is buried," he reported. "But there is a a break here—not large enough for you—"

"But all right for you." I snapped apart a nasty trap of spiky, splintered limbs, pulled it away, then stepped out on a charred crust, my tread raising smoke and a bad smell.

I was just in time to see Eet vanish into the rent. From here the wreck looked even worse, and I believed that the inside of the cabin must be folded and pleated until there could be room there for no explorer larger than the mutant.

"A line—" came my companion's thought command. "Drop me a line—"

I clumped through the smoldering debris and wriggled close to the break, dropping one of the hooked lines I had used in my tree descent. A weight swung upon it and I hauled in slowly, the line jerking as if Eet steadied whatever it raised.

One of those things I had thought might be a weapon appeared, butt first. I grasped it eagerly. To have some arm available gave one a feeling of security. It did not fit comfortably in my palm and I guessed it had not been wrought for use by a human hand. There was no firing button such as one saw on laser or stunner, only a small lever difficult to finger. I pointed it at a ragged stub of limb projecting not too far away and drew back on that lever.

There was a weak flash, hardly more than a blink of light, but nothing else. Whatever charge the weapon had once operated upon had been exhausted. It was of no more use to us now than an awkwardly shaped club. And I said so to Eet.

He expressed no disappointment, but dived once more into the ship, while I dropped the line. In the end we assembled a motley collection of survival equipment. There was another canister of liquid, a sharp-bladed, foot-long tool which at least was still effective, for my practice swings at spikes cut those neatly through. Lastly there was a roll of fabric which could be folded into a small packet, or shaken out into a wide square, and which appeared to be moisture-resistant.

I had found among the shredded debris some more of those pods and had shelled their seeds into the canister we had already drained. We ate and drank before we decided in which direction to go.

There was no use in lingering by the wrecked ship. Had it been an LB of my own people, we could have set up a call signal and stayed hopefully nearby—though even then eventual rescue would have depended upon so many chance factors that we might never have been found. But we now had not even that slender tie with any predictable future.

"Where?" I asked as I made the fabric into a pack to lash to my harness. "Where—" And I added to myself, "Why?"

Eet scrambled up on the elevated end of the wreckage once again. His head turned and his nostrils expanded, as if he cast about for some scent as a guide. But as for me I could see no goal in this wilderness. We could continue to wander through the dusk under the trees until we died, and find no way out.

"Water—" His thought reached me. "A river—lake—If we can find such—"

A river meant an open highway of sorts—but leading where? And how were we going to find a river?

I had a sudden inspiration. "The game trail!"

Surely any animals large enough to beat that slot in the forest muck would need water. And a well-marked trail could lead to it.

Eet ran back along the battered tail of the wreck.

"An apt suggestion." He jumped to land heavily on my shoulder, nearly rocking me off balance. "To the left, no, more that way—" He used his forepaw to point. The path he indicated was not that which had been made by my blundering feet, but led off at a sharper angle to the left.

As we left the torn clearing, I glanced back. Eet's body somewhat masked it from view, but I saw that my dragging progress left very visible tracks. Anything with eyes could tail us. And what of the hunter with the club? Drawn to this break in the forest ceiling through curiosity, a native might well hunt us down.

"A contingency we cannot help. Therefore we can only be alert," Eet returned.

Alert he certainly was, and not to my comfort, he constantly changed his position. Too, since his weight was not inconsiderable, I was afraid of stumbling. The long knife from the LB allowed me to cut a path through the rim of debris beyond the burned space; then we were back in the dusky forest.

I would have been entirely lost as soon as the clearing was left behind, for we had to weave in and out to avoid the latticework of the vine roots. But Eet appeared to know just where we were going, sniffing at intervals and then directing me, until I almost fell into a sharp slot which marked the game trail. It had been so well used that it was cut more than a hand's breath below the surrounding surface soil. On it were prints of what might have been hoofs and paws, and even odder marks, overlaid one upon another.

We came in time to another opening, where one of the giant trees had crashed to its death, perhaps seasons earlier, taking with it the lesser growth, giving living room to bushes and shrubs. So riotously had these grown that they made a vast matted plug in the opening. There were things which might be flowers, wide of petal, with deep throats. But I saw a green tentacle whip from one of those gaping throats, seize upon a small, winged thing which had lit on a petal, and carry the victim, still struggling, back into the cavity. The petals were brilliant yellow, striped with a strident green, and the whole thing gave off a sickly odor which made me turn away my head.

The trail did not cut across this space, but skirted around the perimeter, almost three quarters of the circle, so that we re-entered the forest not far from where we had come out. And it was just before we went back into that gloom that I paused in slashing at a looping vine to examine a sign beside the trail which proved to me that we were not alone in walking it.

There was a clump of tall stalks, lacking leaves to their very tips. On each of these tips was a cluster of tiny, feathery dark-red fronds. Two of the stalks had been so recently severed that a watery substance still oozed from the clean cuts across their hollow stems. I leaned to see them the closer and there was no doubt. They had not been broken, but cut. I sliced another to prove it. In my hand the smooth stalk was supple, whipping, but from the cut lower portion the liquid welled.

"Fishing—"

"What—?" I began.

"Silence!" Eet was at his most arrogant. "Fishing—yes. Now take care. I cannot read much of this creature's mind. It is on a very low band—very low. It thinks mainly of food, and its thought processes are very slow and primitive. But it is traveling toward a body of water where it hopes to fish."

"The one with the club?"

"Unless there are two native species of primitive forms," conceded Eet, "this one is like that. As to its being the same, who knows? I think this is a route often used by its kind. It walks the trail with the confidence of a thing going a familiar road on which it has nothing to fear."

I did not share his confidence. For there was a thunderous crash not too far away. I threw myself, and incidentally Eet, toward the nearest tree, planted my back to it, and stood with that sap-stained knife ready. My field of vision was too limited. I could see nothing beyond the vines and the boles. But I tried to put my ears to service.

Nothing stirred. It had sounded as if one of those trees, which must have roots reaching to the very core of this world, had crashed. Crashed——? But the trees must eventually die. And having died and begun to rot, with the weight of the vines and parasites with which they were covered, would they not fall? As had the one which had made the second clearing? But what if the very one I had chosen as my backing would be the next? I moved away almost as fast as I had sought it.

I do not know how a thought can suggest laughter, but such a thought flowed from Eet. He was fast becoming, I decided, a less than perfect companion.

As if I were being punished for that, I caught one of my boots in a loop of root or vines and crashed as helplessly as the dead tree must have done. A thrust of irritation, sharp as any physical blow, struck me. Eet had leaped free in one of his flash reactions, and now sat a short distance away, his fangs bared, his whole stance expressing disgust.

"If you must clump about," he spat, "then at least lift your feet when you move them. But why do you continue to wear that burden of a useless overskin?"

Why indeed? I struggled to sit up. Inside the confines of the suit, my coverall was plastered to my body with sweat. I itched where I could not scratch, and I felt as if soaking in a bath for several days would not be enough to free me from the smelly burden of myself. Yet I clung to the suit as a shell animal might cling to its shell as a protection against the unknown.

I could never wear it into space again. When I examined it I could see tears which must have been inflicted during my descent of the tree. And the boots weighed my feet into a shuffle which could be dangerous in the muck. The harness which carried our very limited supplies could be adapted, but the suit itself—Eet was right.

It had no further use. Yet when my fingers went to the various seals and buckles, they moved reluctantly, and I had to fight down the strong need to hold to my shell.

However, as I discarded that husk and felt the cool wreath about my damp body, I had a sense of relief. When we moved on, I had a small pack on my back, my hands were free to swing the cutting knife, and I found I was no longer slipping and sliding. For the tough web packs worn inside space boots not only protected my feet from close contact with the muck, but gave me purchase. Now I longed for a pool or stream in which I could dunk my steaming body and get really clean—though any such exercise on a strange world would be utter folly, unless I could be very sure that the water in question had no inhabitants who might resent intrusion.

"Water—" Eet announced. His head swung from right to left and back again. "Water—much of it—also alien life—"

Scents crowded my nose. I could put name to no one of them. But I accepted Eet's reading. I slowed my pace. Underfoot the game trail was no longer so hard of surface, and the slots of the tracks in it were deeper sunk, more sharply marked. I made out one, superimposed on earlier prints, which was little larger than those I myself left. It was wedge-shaped, with indentations sharply printed in a fringe of points extending beyond the actual track.

I am certainly no tracker, nor have I hunted as a reader of trails. Though I had gone to frontier and primitive planets, it had been to visit villages, port trading posts. My acquaintance with any wilderness arts was close to zero.

But my guess was that whatever creature had so left his mark was large and heavy, as those indentations were deep and cleanly marked. And perhaps it was advancing at a deliberate pace.

"Water—" Eet repeated.

He need not have given that caution. The trail was mud now, holding no recognizable prints. There were here and there humps formed by harder portions of earth, and I jumped from one to the next where I could. In no time at all the mud was covered with a glaze of liquid out of which the trees and growth projected. And there were bits of refuse caught in tangles of vine roots, held there as high as my shoulder. It had the appearance of a land which had been flooded in the not too distant past, and which was now slowly drying off.

Puddles smelling of decay and bordered by patches of yellow slime showed between the trees, in hollows in the ground. And there were noisome odors in plenty. We passed a huddle of bones caught between exposed vine roots, and a narrow skull bared its teeth at us.

The puddles became pools and the pools linked into stagnant expanses of water. Here trees had been undermined, so that they leaned threateningly. And smaller ones that had been overthrown showed masses of upturned roots.

"Caution!"

Again I did not need Eet's warning. Perhaps his sense of smell was so assaulted by the stenches about that he had not sniffed that worker ahead until I had sighted him, her, or it.

On a tree trunk, which was not yet horizontal, but leaned at an angle out over the largest pond we had yet seen, lurked a creature. In this light it was easy to see. It was humanoid, save that a bristly hair grew in a stiff upright thatch on its head, in two heavy brows, down the outer sides of its arms and legs to wrists and ankles, and in round, shaggy patches, three of them, down its chest and middle.

Around its loins was a skirt or kilt of fringe, and encircling its thick neck was a thong on which were strung lumps of dull green alternating with red cylinders. A heavy-headed club had been wedged for safekeeping beside a stub of branch, as its owner was busy with an occupation demanding full attention.

A withe, which I recognized as one of the slender canes cut from the patch we had passed, had been bent into a hoop, one end extending for a handle. This was held firmly between the back feet of the worker, gripped tightly in huge claws. In its hands the native held a forked stick in which was imprisoned a wriggling black thing that fought so furiously and was in such constant motion I could not be certain of its nature.

Its struggles did it no good as the worker passed it back and forth across the hoop, from one side to the other, then from top to bottom and back again. A thread trailed from the end of that whipping body, to be caught on the frame of the hoop and joined to its fellows, forming a mesh. With a last pass of the captive, the workman appeared satisfied with the result. Then, with a sharp flip of his wrist, he sent the forked stick and its prisoner out into the pond. As soon as the stick hit water there was a turmoil into which stick and captive vanished, not to appear again.

The hoop holder now got to his feet, the net in one hand. He was taller than I by a head. While his arms and legs were thin, his barrel body suggested strength. His face was far from human, resembling more one of the demon masks of Tanth.

The eyes were deep-set under extravagantly bushy brows, so that while one believed them there, one did not see them. The nose was a fleshy tube, unattached save at its root, moving up and down and from side to side in perpetual quest. Below that appendage was a mouth, showing two protruding fangs and no real chin, the flesh, wattled in loose flaps, sweeping straight back from the lower set of teeth to join the throat.

Any traveler of the space lanes becomes inured to strange native races. There are the lizard-like Zacathans, the Trystians, who have avian ancestors, and others—batrachian, canine, and the like. But this weird face was repellent—at least to me—and I felt aversion.

When he reached the far end of the tree, which swayed under his weight, he moved with caution, trying each step before he put his full weight on it. Then he settled down, to lie full length, staring intently into the scummed water, the webbed hoop clasped in his left hand.

I did not dare yet to move. To skirt the edge of this lake meant coming into the sight of the fisherman, and I shrank from that. As I hesitated, Eet saying nothing though he watched the creature intently, the arm of the fisherman swept down and up again, scooping in his hoop a scaled thing about as long as my forearm.

He grabbed it out of the net, knocked it sharply against the tree trunk, and then knotted its limp length to a tie of his kilt.

"Go right—" Eet's thought came.

The fisherman was left-handed, his attention on that side. Right it was. I moved slowly, trying to put a screen of brush between us. But even when I was able to do so I felt no safer. It would be easy to become mired in a bog patch, and thus helpless prey for the club. My cutting knife was sharp but the native had the longer reach and knew this swamp. Also, to work any deeper into this flooded land and perhaps become lost in it was folly. And I said as much to Eet.

"I do not think this is a true swamp," he observed. "There are many signs of a great past flood. And a flood can be born of a river—"

"What is the advantage of a river—here?"

"Rivers are easier to follow than game trails. And there is this—civilizations are born on rivers. Do you presume to call yourself a trader and not know that? If this planet can boast any civilization, or if it is visited by traders from off world, you would find evidence of that along a major river. Especially where it meets a sea."

"Your knowledge is considerable," I observed. "And you certainly did not learn it all from Valcyr—"

Again I felt his irritation. "When it is necessary to learn, one learns. Knowledge is a never-emptied storehouse. And where else can one learn better of trade, traders, and their ways, then on such a ship as the *Vestris*? Her crew were born to that way of life and have a vast background of lore—"

"You must have spent some time reading their minds," I interrupted. "By the way, if you know so much—why *did* they take me off Tanth?" I did not really expect him to answer that, but he replied promptly.

"They were paid to do so. There was some plan there—I do not know its details, for they did not. But that went wrong and then they were approached and well paid to get you off planet and deliver you at Waystar—"

"Waystar! But—that's only a legend!"

If Eet could have snorted perhaps he would have produced such a sound.

"It must be a legend of substance. They were taking you there. Only they insisted upon following their regular schedule first. And when you took ril fever they decided prudence was in order. They would get rid of you lest you contaminate the rest. They would just not turn up at Waystar, but send a message to those who had arranged it all."

"You are a mine of information, Eet. And what was behind it—who wanted me so badly?"

"They knew only an agent. His name was Urdik and he was not of Tanth. Why you were wanted they did not know."

"I wonder why—"

"The stone in the ring—"

"That!" My hand went to the pouch where I carried it. "They knew about that?"

"I do not think so. They wanted something you or Vondar Ustle carried. It is of great importance and they have been searching for it for some time. But can you not say now that the ring is your most important possession?"

I clutched the bag closer. "Yes!"

Then, startled, I looked down at the pouch. It was moving in my hand, and there was heat. We had come into the open and there was daylight around, but I thought I could also detect a glow.

"It is coming alive again!"

"Use it then for a guide!" urged Eet.

I fumbled with the seal on the pouch, slipped the ring on my finger. But the band was so large it would have fallen off if I had not closed my fist. My hand, through no volition of mine, moved out, away from my body, to the right and ahead. It would seem that once more the stone used my flesh and bone as an indicator. And I turned to follow its guidance.

NINE

"We are followed," Eet informed me.

"The fisherman?"

"Or one of his kind." My companion did nothing to relieve my mind with that report. "But he is cautious—he fears—"

"What?" I demanded bitterly. "This knife is no adequate defense, except at close quarters. And I have no desire to stand up to him as might a Korkosan gladiator. I am no fighter, only a peaceful gem trader."

Eet disregarded most of my sour protest. "He fears death-from-a-distance. He has witnessed such—or knows of it."

Death from a distance? That could mean anything from a thrown spear or slingshot-propelled rock, to a laser beam, and all the grades of possible "civilization" in between.

"Just so." Eet had picked up my thought. "But—" I caught a suggestion of puzzlement. "I can read no more, only that he fears and so sniffs us prudently."

We holed up in a mass of drift thrust into a corner between two downed trees, eating from our supply of seeds, drinking from the ship's flask. The seeds might be nutritious, but they did not allay my need for something less monotonous. And I had seen none of them growing since we had come into the dripping country, so that I rationed carefully what we had. As I chewed my handful, I watched our back trail for any sign of a tracker.

I sighted him at last. He had gone down on one knee, his head almost touching the ground as that trunklike, mobile nose of his quivered and twisted above my tracks. If it was not the fisherman, it was one enough like him to be his twin.

After a long sniffing, he squatted back on his heels, his head raised, that trunk standing almost straight out from its roots as he turned his head slowly. I fully expected him to point directly at us, and I readied my knife desperately.

But there was no halt in that swing. If he did know where we were, he was cunning enough to guess we might be alert, and did not betray his discovery. I waited tensely for him to arise and charge, or to disappear into the brush in an attempt to circle around for an ambush.

"He does not know, he still seeks—" Eet said.

"But—if he sniffed out our trail, how could he miss scenting us now?"

"I do not know. Only that he still seeks. Also he is afraid. He does not like—"

"What?" I demanded when Eet paused.

"It is too hard, I cannot read. This one feels more than he thinks. One can read thoughts, and the cruder emotions. But his breed is new to me; I cannot gain more than surface impressions."

At any rate, though my trail led directly from where the sniffer now squatted, he made no attempt to advance. Whether I could leave the cover we had taken refuge in without attracting attention, I did not know.

Two trees, not the huge giants of the forest, but ones of respectable girth, had fallen so that their branched crowns met, their trunks lying at right angles. We were in the corner formed by the branched part, a screen of drift piled not too thickly between us and the native.

I saw that the branches were bleached, leafless, but matted together. Yet the stone pulled me toward them, as if it would have me go through that mass. I hunched down and began to saw away at the obstructions. Eet was there, his forepaws at work, snapping off smaller pieces, while I dug with the point of the knife in the soft earth under the heavier branches. We moved very slowly, pausing many times to survey the open ground between us and the sniffer. To my surprise, for I knew we were far from noiseless (in spite of our best efforts), he did not appear and Eet reported he had not moved.

It suddenly occurred to me, with a chill, what his purpose might be—that he was not alone, and that when his reinforcements moved into place there would be a charge after all.

"You are right." Eet was no comforter. "There is one, perhaps two more, coming—"

"Why did you not tell me?"

"Had it been necessary I would have. But why add to apprehension when a clear mind is needful? They are yet some distance away. It is a pity, but the day is almost gone. To them, I believe, night is no problem."

I did not put my thoughts into words; Eet could read them well enough anyway. "Are there any in front of us?" I bit back and curbed my anger.

"None within my sensing range. They do not like that direction. This one waits for the others' coming, not because he fears us, but because he fears where we head. His fear grows stronger as he waits."

"Then—let us get farther ahead—" I no longer tried to be so careful, but slashed at branches, cutting our way through the springy wall in quick blows.

"Well spoken," Eet agreed. "Always supposing we do not run from one danger into a greater one."

I made no reply to that, but hoped that Eet was reading my emotions and that they would scorch him. Beyond the trees were more of the scum-rimmed pools, fallen trunks. But the latter provided us with a road of sorts. The fisherman had been armed with nothing more lethal than a club, which he could not use at a distance. He knew we fled, and it seemed to me that speed was now in order.

With Eet back on my shoulders, his paw-hands gripping the ties of my pack, I sprang onto the nearest trunk and ran, leaping from one to the next, not in a straight line, but always in the direction the stone pointed me. For I could not help but hope that it would guide me to some installation, or ship, perhaps even a settlement of those who had owned the ring, even as it had brought us across space to the derelict. The great age of that ship, however, suggested I would find no living community.

We were out of the gloom. Not only had the flood cut a swath among the trees, but the secondary growth had been undermined and was scanty. Now I could see the sky overhead.

But that was full of clouds, and while it was still warm enough to make one pant when exercising, there was no sun. Insects buzzed about, so that at times I had to swing my hand before my face to clear my vision. But none bit my flesh. Perhaps I was so alien to their usual source of nourishment that they could not.

There was no sign of any pursuit, and Eet, though he had ceased to communicate when we began this dash, would, I believed, raise the warning if it were needed. I appeared to possess some importance to him, though his evasiveness concerning that bothered me.

Again pools began to link together, forcing me to make more and more detours from the direct path the stone indicated. I had no wish to splash through even the shallows of those evil-looking, bescummed floods. Who knew what might hide below their foul surfaces? Perhaps the insects did not find me tasty, but that did not mean other native life would be so fastidious.

I had no idea of the length of the planetary day, but it seemed to me now that the cloud blanket overhead did not account for all the lack of light and that this might be late afternoon. Before night we must find some safe place in which to hole up. If the natives were nocturnal, the advantage of any encounter would rest with them.

The water pushed me back, farther and farther to the right, while the tug of the stone was now left, straight into the watery region. Its pull became so acute and constant that I finally had to slip the loop from my hand and put it back in the pouch, lest it overbalance me into one of the very sinks I fought to skirt.

There was much evidence that not only had this lake been far larger in the not too far-distant past but it was still draining away in the very direction the ring pointed. It was hard going and from time to time I demanded of Eet reassurance that we were not being followed. But each time he reported all clear.

It was decidedly darker and I had yet found no possible place to lie up for the night. Too many tracks in the mud suggested that life, large life, crawled from pond to lake, came from the water and returned to it. And the size of some of those tracks was enough to make a man think twice, three, a dozen times, before settling down near their roadways.

I had passed the first of the outcrops before I really noticed them, so covered were they with dried mud which afforded anchorage to growing things. It was when I scrambled up on one to try for a better look at what might lie ahead that it dawned on me that they were not scattered without pattern but were set in a line which could not be that of nature alone.

My foot slipped on the surface and I slid forward, trying to stop my fall by digging the point of the knife well in. But the stone resisted my blade, which came away with an almost metallic sound, scraping off a huge patch of mud.

What I had uncovered was not rough stone, but a smooth surface which had been artificially finished. When I touched it I could not be sure it was stone at all. It had a sleekness, almost as if the rock had been fused into a glassy overcoat—though in places this was scaled and pitted.

In color it was dull green, veined with ocher strata. Yet it was not part of a wall, for the stones did not abut,

but had several paces distance between them. Perhaps there had once been some link of another material now vanished.

The outcrops ran in the direction the stone urged upon me, marching down to the lake, partially submerged near the shore, water lapping their crowns farther out, then entirely covered.

As I continued along the lake, now alert to any other evidence, I came across a second line of blocks, paralleling those swallowed by the water. These I took for a guide. They were certainly the remains of some large erection, ancient though they appeared. And as such they could well lead to a building, or even a ruin which would shelter us.

"Just so," Eet agreed. "But it would be well to hurry faster. Night will come soon under these clouds and I think a storm also. If more water feeds this lake—"

There was no need for him to underline his thought. I jumped from one of those blocks half buried in the muck to the next, listening for warning thunder (if storms on this planet were accompanied by such warnings) and fearing to feel the first drops of rain. The wind was growing stronger and it brought with it a low wailing which stopped me short until Eet's reassurance came:

"That is not the voice of a living thing—only sound—" He sniffed as thoroughly as the trunk-nosed native.

The blocks for the first time now were joined together, rising into a wall, and I dropped down to walk beside it. It soon topped my head. There were too many shadows in its overhang, so I edged into the open.

I would have climbed again after a while for a better look at the country ahead, but the tops of these blocks were not level. Instead they were crowned with projections, the original form of which could not be guessed, for they were eroded and worn to stubs which pricked from them at meaningless angles.

On this side of the wall the signs of flood ceased, except in some places where apparently waves had spilled over the top, in a few instances actually turning and twisting the mighty blocks of the coping over which they had beaten.

There were no trees here. We moved across an open space which gave footing only to brush that did not grow high. Where one of the waves had topped the wall, I saw that I walked on a coating of soil overlying pavement, some of which had the same fused look as the surface of the wall.

If I walked some road or courtyard, there was no other wall. The clouds were very thick and dark now, and the first pattering rain began. The wall was no protection, nor was there any other shelter in this sparsely grown land. I ran on, my tiring body having to be forced to that pace, both my pack and Eet weighing cruelly on me.

Then the wall beside which I jogged made a sharp turn left and ended in a three-sided enclosure. It had no roof, but those three sides were the best protection I had seen. We could stretch the shelter from the wreck over us to afford some cover. Also, I was not going to blunder on in the dark. So I darted into that enclosure, squatting down in the corner I judged easiest to defend. There we huddled, the covering draped over my head and shoulders, Eet in my lap, as the night and the storm closed down upon us.

But we were not quite in the dark. As I changed position I saw the faintest of glows from the pouch which held the stone, and when I pried open the top a fraction, there was a thin ray of light. Just as it had come alive before, so it was registering energy now. Was this ruin its goal? If so, had the LB led us directly to the home planet from which the derelict had lifted eons ago? Such a supposition could not be ruled out as fantastic. The LB could have been set on a homing device and the drifting ship might have met its fate soon after take-off. Unwittingly we might have made a full circle, returning the ring to the world on which it was fashioned. But the age of the stones at my back certainly argued that those who had dwelt here were long gone, that I had stumbled on traces of one of the Forerunner races, about whom we know so little and even the Zacathans can only speculate.

To spend a stormy night amid alien ruins of incalculable age was not my idea of a well-chosen pastime. My search for gems had taken me into many strange places, but then I had only been second to Vondar, leaning on his knowledge and experience. And earlier I had looked to my father, not only for physical protection, but for that teaching which would aid in survival.

As I crouched there with the rain drumming on the thin sheet which was my only roof, I was only partially aware of the night, the alien walls, the need for alertness. One part of my mind sought back down the years, to my father's first showing of the ring with the zero stone—for that was what he had once termed it, a challenge to his knowledge and curiosity.

It had been found on a suited body floating in space. Had that body been one of the crew of the derelict? And my father had died at the hands of someone who had then searched his office, the zero stone the prize the murderer sought.

Then Vondar Ustle and I had been entrapped at the inn on Tanth. And I could accept that that had not happened by a chance pointing of the selective arrow. It had been planned. Perhaps they had believed that, being off-worlders, we would resist the priests just as we had, and both be slain, as Vondar was. They could not have foreseen that I would break away and reach the sanctuary.

For the first time I resented my bargain with Ostrend. And the trader in me regretted the gems I had paid for a passage which had already been arranged by another. So—I was to have been transported to Waystar and turned over there to those paying for my rescue. For what purpose? Because I was my father's son, or his reputed son, and so might have possession of, or knowledge of, that very thing which now glowed faintly against my chest?

Again by chance I had escaped—the fever—a contagion picked up on Tanth, or on that unnamed world where the people had so mysteriously disappeared? That sickness which had so oddly struck just at the proper time—Oddly struck!

"Just so," Eet answered with his favorite words of agreement. "Just so. You alone of the crew sickening so—why did it take you so long to wonder about that?"

"But why? I know Valcyr picked my cabin to give birth—that must have been chance—"

"Was it?"

"But you could not have—" What if he could? As helpless as Eet's body had looked when I found Valcyr with him on the bunk, did that necessarily mean that his mind—?

"You are beginning to think," Eet replied approvingly. "There was a natural affinity operating between us even then. The crew of the ship were a close-knit clan. It was necessary for me to find one detached from that organization, one who could furnish me with what I needed most at that time, protection and transportation away from danger while I was in a weak state. Had I encountered them at a later period I would not have been so endangered. But I needed a partner—"

"So you made me ill!"

"A slight alteration of certain body fluids. No danger, though it appeared so." There was a complacency in his answer which for a moment made me want to hurl Eet out into the dark and whatever danger might lurk there.

"But you will not," he answered my not completely formulated thought. "It was not only a matter of expediency which made me choose to reveal myself to you. I spoke of natural affinities. There is a tie between us based on far more than temporary needs. As I have said, this body I now wear is not, perhaps, what I might have chosen for this particular phase of my existence. I have modified it as much as I can for now. Perhaps there will be other possible alterations in the future, given time and means. But I do have senses which aid you. Just as your bulk and strength do me. I believe you have already discovered some of the advantages of such a partnership.

"We are still far from any situation you may term safe. And our alliance is very necessary to both of us. Afterward we can choose whether to extend it."

That made sense—though I disliked admitting that this small furred body I could crush in my two hands contained a personality forceful enough to bring me easily to terms. I had had few close contacts with anyone in the past. My relationship with Hywel Jern had been that of pupil to teacher, junior officer to commander. And while Vondar Ustle was a man of easier temperament, far more outgoing than my father, the relationship had remained practically the same for me when I entered his service. Beyond that I had had no deep ties with any man or creature. But now I had been summarily adopted by Eet, and it appeared that my will did not enter into the agreement any more than it had with Hywel or Vondar—for it had been of their desire in both cases. But—my anger arose—I was not going to stand in the same relationship to *Eet!*

"They come!" Eet's warning shocked me out of my thoughts.

We had been so long without any contact with the natives that I had believed they had given up. If they moved in now, we might find our shelter a trap.

"How many and where?" Eet was right; in such a situation I must depend upon his senses.

"Three—" Eet took his time to answer. "And they are very hesitant. I think that this place represents danger to them. On the other hand—they are hungry."

For a second or so, that had no meaning for me. Then I stiffened. "You mean—?"

"We—or rather you—represent meat. Contact with such primitive minds is difficult. But I read hunger, kept in check mainly by fear. They have memory of danger here."

"But—by the signs we have seen, there is plenty of game here." I remembered the fresh tracks, the evidences of life we had seen in profusion, and how easy it had been for the fisherman to scoop out his prey.

"Just so. A puzzle as to why our trail would draw them past easier hunting." Eet did seem puzzled. "The reason, I cannot probe. Their minds are too alien, too primitive to read with any clarity. But they are aroused now past the limit of prudence. And they are most dangerous in the dark."

I fingered the beamer on my harness. If the creatures were mainly night hunters, a flash in their eyes could dazzle them for a moment. But my own folly in picking this hole with its towering walls about us might be the deciding factor—against us.

"It is not as bad as all that," Eet broke in. "There is a top to the wall—"

"Well above my reaching. But if you can climb it—climb!" I ordered.

I felt a sharp tug at one corner of the covering I had drawn over us.

"Let this free," Eet countered. "Climb I can, but perhaps we shall both be safe because of the fact that my claws are useful." He was out of my lap, dragging the cover behind him, though it was a burden which pulled his head to one side.

"Hold me up," he commanded then, "as high as you can reach, and take some of the weight of this thing!"

I obeyed, because I had no counterplan, and I had come, during our association, to give credit to Eet. I lifted his body, held it above my own head, and felt him catch hold, and draw himself up. Then I fed along the length of the shelter cloth, keeping its weight from pulling him back as he went. Suddenly it was still, no longer tugged.

"Tie the knife to it and let go—" Eet ordered.

Let my only weapon out of my hands? He was crazy! Yet even as my thoughts protested, another part of me set my hands busy knotting that tool-weapon to the end of the dangling cloth. I heard it, even through the storm, clang and rap against the stone as it was drawn aloft by Eet.

I faced around, to the open side of the enclosure. Though I did not have Eet's warning alert, I was sure that the aliens no longer hesitated, that they moved through the darkness. I pressed the button on the beamer, looking down the ray path.

They did indeed gather there, half crouched, their clubs ready in their fists. But as the light struck them full on, they blinked, blinded, their small mouths opening on thin, piping cries. The middle one dropped to his knees, his arm flung up to shield his hideous face from the light.

"Behind you—up!" Eet's mental cry was as loud as a shout might have been in my ear. I felt the brush of something at my shoulder, flung out my hand to ward it off, and touched the fabric of the shelter. My fingers closed about it and I tugged. But it did not fall; somewhere aloft it was anchored, to give me a possible ladder to safety.

Dared I turn my back upon the three the light still held prisoners? Yet how long could I continue to hold them so? I must chance it—

If only that improvised rope and whatever Eet had found aloft to anchor it would hold under my weight! But that was another chance I must take. I gave a short leap and caught the dangling folds with both hands, swung out a little to plant my feet against the wall, and climbed, or rather walked up that surface, the shelter my support.

TEN

I was not to escape so easily. There arose behind me a shrilling that topped the sound of the storm. Something thudded against the wall only inches from me, rebounding to the ground. I had kept the beamer switched on and the light jerked back and forth as I struggled to put distance between myself and the natives below. Perhaps that moving light misled them, or perhaps they were less adept with their clubs than we credited them with being. However, one hurled weapon grazed my leg and almost broke my hold on the fabric rope.

Fear alone gave me the strength to pull up on the rough crest of the wall. My leg was numb and I was afraid to trust my weight to it, so I dragged along like a broken-legged creature. The claws of the natives stuck in my mind. Those should aid them in gaining our perch.

Up here the wind and the rain buffeted us. I had not realized how much protection the walls had afforded below. I clung to the knobs and broken projections and pulled myself along, though I took time to switch off the beamer that I might not so brightly advertise our going.

"On, to your right now, and ahead—" Eet ordered.

I followed the line of the fabric to its end, found where the knife pinned it firmly into a crack between an eroded knob and the wall, paused long enough to worry it loose, and thrust that weapon into my harness.

To the right and ahead? The blasting of the storm was such that for some long moments I was not sure of the difference between right and left, having to think of my hands as guides. Eet's direction would apparently take me over the wall. Yet I was certain he did not mean us to descend again.

I discovered as I crawled on, dragging my aching leg, that here the wall was joined by another, leading off at a sharp angle in the direction Eet had indicated. It was slow and rough going, for the crest was as encumbered with humps, hollows, and stubs as the other had been. But at least they now served as anchorages against the wind and drive of rain.

The visibility was nil as far as I was concerned. I had to depend upon my sense of touch and Eet's guidance. Every moment I feared to hear the shrilling which would announce that the club holders were hard behind us.

The numbness in my leg was wearing off, leaving behind an ache which, when I barked that limb against one of the projections, made me yowl with pain. But I did not try to get to my feet. Crawling this uneven way seemed the safest.

We were heading out from the place where we had sheltered, directly into a dark unknown. Now I could hear, above the storm, not the shrilling of pursuers, but a roaring. And it was toward that that we headed.

At last I became so uneasy I paused in the lee of a large lump to use the beamer, sweeping the way before me. For a space the ray showed wall—then—nothing!

I swept the beam down, along the right-hand side of the wall. Water—raging water, beating its way around a vast tumble of rocks. As I sent the ray left, it caught the edge of something else, and I swiftly centered on that.

A rounded swell of mound? No, though it was patched with plants and moss which caught the light and held it, continuing to glow after the beam had passed. A curved object, taller than the wall at the highest point, stretching back and out into darkness where my beam could not reach.

The water which battered at the outer end of the wall washed it on one side, but apparently it was too securely rooted to be moved by that flood. I kept the ray playing on the portion nearest the wall, trying to calculate if I could cross to it. But that other surface, in spite of the growth of plants, suggested too smooth a landing, especially since my take-off room would be limited on this side.

"Well," I shot at Eet, "where do we go? On into the water? Or do we grow wings and head straight up?"

When he did not reply, I was suddenly afraid I had been left alone. Perhaps Eet, aware of his own ability to travel where I was a handicapped drag, had struck out for himself. Then his answer came, though I could not tell from what direction.

"To the ground, on the left. The water does not come this far. And the ship will give us shelter—"

"Ship?" Once more I swept the beamer ray, studied the mound. It could be a ship—yet it was not shaped like—

"Do you think there is only one pattern of ship? Even among your own people there are several."

He was right, of course. There is little resemblance between a slender Free Trader, meant to cut into planetary atmospheres, and a colonizer—so large it does not enter atmospheres at all, but uses ferry ships to load and unload passengers and supplies.

I edged to the left side of the wall. The nose of the vast object on the ground projected not far below. On that stood Eet, his wiry fur not in the least plastered down by the rain, his eyes pinpoints of light as the beam touched them. I swung over and allowed myself to drop, hoping I would be able to find secure footing.

Had I worn the magnetic boots, my feet might have clung. As it was, my fears were realized. I landed squarely enough, but skidded on, my hands and feet unable to find anchorage in the frail plants, tearing those out by their roots in thick wet pads as I went. I met the ground with a bump which drove most of the breath out of me. From my bruised leg there was such a stab of pain that I blacked out for a space. But the drip of water falling on and running down my face restored me.

Half of my body lay under the curve of the ship, if ship it was. But the rest of me was exposed to the storm. I scrabbled feebly with my fingers in the mud and somehow pulled back under the shelter.

There I huddled stupidly, not more than three-quarters conscious, without the energy or will to move again. The beamer had gone out and the dark closed in as completely as any of those monolithic walls I had been climbing.

"There is an opening—" Eet's words in my mind were only an irritation. I put my hands over my eyes and shook my head from side to side slowly, as if by that effort I could refuse communication. It was a call to action and I had no intention of obeying.

"Around here—there is an opening!" Eet was peremptory.

Stubbornly I looked to see where I was. My leg ached abominably and my exertions since we had landed on this inhospitable world had caught up with me. I was content to have it so. In fact, I thought dully, since that long period of boredom on the *Vestris*, I had not had a moment of rest.

Hunger gnawed at me with an ever-growing pain. There might be a few of the seeds rattling around in the container swinging from my pack, but I had no desire to mouth them. They were not food—Food was a platter of sizzling vorst steak, a mound of well-cooked lattress, beaten, creamed with otan oil and herbs; it was an omelet of trurax eggs sweetened just enough with a syrup of bargee buds; it was—

"An empty belly about to be gutted by the sniffers!" Eet rapped out. "They no longer sniff along the wall—they have found a way around it!"

A moment earlier I could not have moved, but Eet's words, whether by his will or not, projected a mental picture which acted on me as a whiplash might on a reluctant burden bearer. I moved, on my hands and knees still, but at what speed I could muster, under the overhang of the ship, around to where Eet waited.

When I tried to use the beamer there was no response. I supposed my fall had finished it. But somewhere above, Eet waited and gave directions. He had not found an open hatch, but rather a break in the fabric of the ship, and I climbed, using the edge of the rent to pull myself in. At last I lay on a slanting surface in a wan light.

That gleam came from a crowding of the plants which I had first seen in the forest. The shell of the ship might have been of an alloy which resisted the tearing claws of time. But here there must have been inner fittings which afforded rooting to the parasites as they rotted. The plants had grown and flourished, first on that, and then on the debris of their own ancestors, until the accumulated products of that cycle of life, death, decay, and life again had filled most of the open space. These broke off in huge, ill-smelling chunks which sifted to powder and arose in dust around me as I moved slowly and clumsily about.

The surface on which I half lay might be a floor, or the wall of the corridor. It was choked by plants, but those thinned out as one penetrated farther. I braced myself against the wall and looked back. I was certainly not as heavy of body as the sniffers and it had taken determined wriggling to enter. The opening my exertions had left would admit no more than one at a time, and that one only after a struggle. With the knife I could defend my new lair. We were out of the storm, and the wind was now but a muffled sighing.

Was this, I wondered suddenly, the goal to which the stone had been guiding us? If I explored farther into this disintegrating hulk would I come upon another long-deserted engine room with a box of dead stones?

I looked down at the pouch which held my strange guide. But that slight glow I had seen in the bog land was gone. When I brought out the ring it was as dull and lifeless as it had been before our venture in space.

"They sniff around—"

One of the glimmering plants guarding the rent shook and I made out the shadow of Eet crouched there, his neck outthrust at what seemed to me an impossible angle as he nosed into the night. "They sniff but also they fear. This is a place filled with fears for them."

"Maybe they will go then," I answered. The lassitude of moments earlier had again closed upon me. I was not sure that even if one of the natives tried to force his way in I could raise knife in defense.

"Two do—" Eet replied. "One remains. He waits underneath, but where he can watch this door. I think he is settling in for a siege."

"Let him—" I could not keep my eyes open. Such crushing fatigue was new to me. It was like being drugged. If I lay ready for the slayer's club, I could not help it. I was done.

If Eet tried to rouse me, it was in vain. Nor did I dream. Perhaps the dust of the plants, the crushing of their leaves, produced a narcotic which overcame me. When I finally did awake, light lay across my eyes and I blinked, dazzled. At least, I thought sluggishly, I was not killed in my sleep.

The refuse caused by my entrance into this lair was all about me. Plants torn from their roots were already decaying with strong smells. It was not their phosphorescence which gave the light, but day beyond. I began to crawl toward that more wholesome gleam as an escape from the evil-smelling mass holding me. But there was agitation at the jagged opening and Eet's body humped up, as if, small as he was, he would interpose that insignificant bulk between me and some danger.

"There are many now—waiting—" he warned.

"The sniffers?"

"Just so. Many—and they are always on watch."

I retreated crabwise from the light, The plants thinned and finally I reached a place relatively clean from their rooting.

"Another door—hole?"

"There are two," Eet replied promptly. "One is on the underside and too small for you. There can be no digging to enlarge it, for it is pressed against stone paving. I think it was once a hatch. The other is on the other side of the ship and they watch there also. They are showing more intelligence than I thought they possessed."

"Never underestimate your opponent." Those were not my words but ones I had heard often from Hywel Jern in the old days. I had not, I thought now, done much credit to his teaching.

"I do not understand what moves them." Eet sounded fretful, lacking in that assurance which could irritate one. "They have a fear of this place. That emotion is strong in them. Yet they stay here with great patience—waiting for us to come forth."

"Perhaps they did this once before—ran a quarry to earth, had it come out. You said they look upon me as meat. Yet the land abounds in other game—"

"Among some primitive races there is another belief." Eet had returned to his instructor role. "To eat of the body of a creature looked upon with superstitious awe or fear, is to imbibe the unusual quality of that prey. This may be such a case."

"Which could mean that they have seen men, or humanoids, before." I seized upon that as a small hope. "But they surely could not hold memories of the people who built those walls, this ship—the remains are too old.

And those are primitives, who normally do not remember events, save as vague legends, from one season to the next."

"Take your own advice," Eet made answer. "Do not judge all primitives alike. These may possess a form of memory more acute than any you have encountered before. Knowledge of events may even be handed down through a special body of trained 'rememberers.' "

He could be very right. Did those sniffers with their clubs, their near-to-animal look, treasure some tribal legend of a race which had once built here, had perhaps enslaved or mistreated their far-off ancestors—who had come to death in some fashion (perhaps at the hands of those same ancestors)? And now did they believe they had cornered one of the old masters and intend to have him out for the purpose of refreshing some inner strength?

"On the other hand," Eet continued, "there may have been landings of off-world ships, and you could be right in your first guess that men of your type have been hunted, killed, and their 'spirits' so absorbed by their slayers."

"All very interesting, but it does not get us out of here. Nor provide us with food, water, and the means of keeping alive while they cork us in here."

While I talked I brought out the two containers. The one with the seeds rattled faintly. But to my surprise the other was heavy and gurgled encouragingly.

Eet was amused. "Rain is water," he observed. "We had enough of that last night to fill a well-placed bottle."

Again he had put me to shame. I tested the contents for taste. The sharpness of the ship's liquid was still present, but much diluted. I sipped when I wanted to gulp, and then held it for him to do likewise, but he refused.

"There was much to drink last night. And this body does not need much moisture. That is one advantage in being small. But for food we do not fare so well—unless—" His neck went up to its full length. He was intently watching something which moved at the door rent. I could not make out the nature of the thing crawling in, nor did I have time to see it plainly before Eet sprang.

His feline ancestry went into that sharp attack. He bent his head and used his teeth, then came back to me dragging a body which dangled from his mouth, weighing down his head.

It was long and thin, with three legs on either side. The body was covered with plates of a horny substance, the head a round bead with four feathery antennae. Eet flipped it over to expose a segmented underside of a paler hue.

"Meat," he commented.

My stomach turned. I could not share his taste and I shook my head.

"Meat is meat." Eet was scornful of my squea-mishness. "This is a feeder on plants. Its shape may not be that of a creature you know, but its flesh is of a type you and I can assimilate and live upon."

"You live upon it," I said hurriedly. The longer I stud-ied that segmented insectile body, the less I wanted to discuss the matter. "I will stick to the seeds."

"Which are few and will not last long," Eet pointed out in deadly logic.

"Which may not last long, but while they do, I stick to them."

I averted my eyes and crawled a little away. Eet was a dainty eater. That, too, he took from his dam. But even though he was fastidious about the business, I had no desire to watch him.

My crawl brought me into a portion of the ancient corridor where I felt inequalities under me. I ran my hands over the surface and decided I had found a door and that the ship must lie on its side. I worked at the latch, if latch it was, trying to open it. There was always a chance that a small discovery might lead to a larger—even a way out past the sentries.

At last I could feel a slight give—then, with a suddenness which almost carried me with it, a plate gave way and fell with a clang, leaving my hands braced on the edge of a square space. I felt around carefully. It must be a door. But I could not explore below without light. Once more I clicked the beamer, but to no purpose. I glanced at the daylight coming from the rent. There was no way to introduce that to this point. But my eyes fastened on some of the plants which still grew unbroken above the level where I had crawled the night before. They were certainly very feeble torches, but they were better than nothing at all.

I crept past the busy Eet. The passageway was so full of debris at this point that I could not stand upright. And my badly bruised leg was a further hindrance. But I was able to jerk from their rooting two good-sized plants. With one in each hand I came back to the hole.

The phosphorescence was indeed very pale, but the longer I crouched with my back to the daylight, and held them over that dark drop, the more my eyes adjusted. And I was able to make out a few details.

At last I twined the dangling roots of the two together, and using those for a cord, I lowered the ball of plants into the dark. What I had uncovered was a cabin right enough. And as I examined it, allowing for the greater ruin and decay, I thought it twin to those I had seen in the derelict. There was nothing below to aid us, either as weapon or tool. But when I drew up my luminous plant ball, I had learned this much—with such a lamp I dared go deeper into the ship. For the darker the space into which it was thrust, the brighter by contrast became its glow.

With it again in hand I set about surveying the passage-way. Eet had said he had found only two other exits. But had he fully explored the ship? Suppose there was another hatch not jammed against the ground which we could force open to escape?

Leaving my improvised torch ball at the open cabin door, I climbed back to the rent to examine the rest of the plants. They were, judging by their stalks and leaf structure, of several different varieties. One, with long slender leaves parting into hair-fine sections, possessed a bulbous center which was particularly effective as a light-giver. I snapped off four of these. They were brittle and yielded easily to pressure. I knotted them together, using their fine leaves, and carried the mass in my hand as one might carry a bouquet of more fragrant and entrancing growths.

Eet had finished his meal and I found him sitting by my first torch, using a hand-paw to clean his face and whiskers, licking his fur in another entirely feline gesture.

"There is a division of corridor beyond. Which direction?" he asked, apparently willing to join in an expedition.

"There might be another hatch—"

"There is surely more than one for any ship," was his withering reply. "Right, or straight ahead?"

"Straight ahead," I said, choosing instantly. I did not have any idea how long my torch would last, and I had no desire to be caught by the dark in some inner maze.

But when we reached the crossway Eet had mentioned, he suddenly hissed and spat, his whip tail shooting up, his back arching, until he was a weird caricature of a cat.

What he had sighted was a shining trace along the wall. It was a little higher than my ankle at first, but ascended until it striped that surface at about shoulder height. I did not touch it. There was that about it which was so disgusting that I wanted no close contact. It was as if the slime which had ringed the dying lakes and ponds had here been used to draw a marker, fresh, as a warning.

"What is it?" So much had I come to depend upon Eet that I now asked that almost automatically.

"I do not know—except that it is nothing to be meddled with. And darkness is its choice of abode." I thought he seemed shaken as I had never seen him before.

"You must have been along here before, for you knew about this side passage. Was it here then?"

"No!" His denial was sharp. "I do not like it."

Nor did I. And the more I surveyed that sticky trail with its suggestion of utter foulness, the way it climbed the wall so that whatever made it might hang overhead—waiting—my imagination began to work. And in that moment I knew that only desperation worse than any I had faced so far would ever drive me to take that road deeper into a dark where such horrors might lurk.

I turned back, nor did it matter to me that Eet could read my mind and knew just what fears rode me. But I wondered if he cared, for he was streaking back along the passage as if some terror lashed also at his flanks.

ELEVEN

Our precipitous retreat was in itself so unnatural as to startle me when, back at the door rent, I paused to think. That the sight of a mere trail could so unnerve one was a disturbing thing. Eet caught my thought and answered:

"Perhaps that leaver of trails uses fear for a weapon. Or else it is so utterly alien to us that we are repelled. There are things on many worlds which cannot be contacted by another species, no matter how willing one is. However, I do not want to walk ways in which that prowls."

I edged forward on my belly, pushing before me, though my nose revolted, a small screen of debris. The air outside was bright with sunlight. I stared out longingly. For my kind were meant for the open day and not dark burrows and night's dusk. We were, a quick glance from side to side told me, close to the ground, and that was covered with patches of shaggy, yellowish grass. Between those were expanses of glassy surface which might mark ancient rocket blasts, as if this had been a port site.

For one or two heart-lifting moments I could believe that we were free, that no sentries lingered. Then I heard a shrilling, such as had been voiced the night before. But this was infinitely louder, since there was no storm. It hurt my ears with the pitch of its note. And it came from almost directly below me, so that I jerked back from the rent.

Eet's report reached me. "They are beneath, along the side. They wait for hunger, or perhaps what lurks in the depths of this wreck to drive us out to them."

"Perhaps they will lose patience." My hope was a forlorn one but I knew that the powers of concentration varied to a great degree, and intelligence had something to do with it. Intelligent purpose could teach patience which was unknown to those of lesser brain capacity.

"I think they have played this game, or heard of it played, before, with success." Eet refused to feed my hope. "There are too many factors of which we are not aware. For example—"

"For example—what?" I demanded when he hesitated.

"The stone led you here, did it not? But is it alive now?"

I freed the zero stone and held it out into the daylight. The gem was dead and murky. I turned it this way and that, hoping to awaken some response. Certainly it did not beckon us any deeper into the wreck. But as I inclined it outward, in the general direction of the rush of water along the other side of the ship, its condition suddenly altered. There was no bright flash, not even a glow to outshine the corridor plants, but there had been a small spark. Only now the width of the ship lay between us and the direction in which it pointed.

"There is one way." Eet set his hand-paws on my knee and stood with his nose almost touching the stone, as if it gave forth some scent he could trace. "I can get out of this hole, cross the ship above with that. I could perhaps trace it to its source."

I thought that he spoke the truth. Being small and wary, using the growths on the hull for cover, he could well do it. Though of what benefit such knowledge would be to us—

"All knowledge is of benefit," he countered.

I laughed without humor. "I sit waiting to be gathered up and put in some native's cooking pot and you speak of gaining knowledge! What good will it do a dead man?"

My thoughts probably did me no credit. It was true that a trap holding me was not one for Eet. He could leave at any moment he chose, with a good chance for freedom. In fact I did not know why he had remained as long as he had. But the zero stone—there was that in me which could not lightly surrender it, even for a space. I did not covet it, as one might covet some gem of beauty. It was rather that I was, in a manner I could not describe, tied to it, and had been ever since my father had first shown it to us. The more so since I had taken it from the hiding place he had devised for it.

To give it to Eet would be a breaking of ties I could not quite face. I turned the ring around and around, slipping its large circlet on and off my fingers, my thoughts disjointed, but mainly occupied with the fact that more than all else I did not want to remain here alone.

Eet said nothing more. I did not even sense that faint mind touch he maintained most of the time. It was as if he had deliberately withdrawn now to allow me some decision which I alone could make, and which was of great importance.

"There is also the matter of food—" Eet finally broke that utter silence.

I still turned the ring around and stared almost unseeingly at the stone. "Do you think this will gain that?" I half sneered.

"No more than you do," he replied. "But neither do I propose to sit here and starve."

Which I thought was the truth, since he seemed well able to provide for himself. And there was something in that realization which held a sour taste for me.

"Take it!" I pulled from the rotting vegetable stuff a long string of fiber, made it into a necklet supporting the ring, and slipped it over Eet's head. He sat up on his haunches when I dropped it around his neck, folding his hand-paws over it for an instant, his eyes closing. I had the feeling he was seeking—though how and where, and for what, I did not know.

"You have chosen well." He fell to four feet and crept to the doorway. "Better than you know—"

With no more than that he was gone, climbing to the top of the rent where plants still stirred in a ragged curtain, pushing through them.

"They are still here," he reported. "Not only under the ship, but along the wall. I think they do not like the sunlight, for they keep to the shadow. Ah—on this side—there is the river! And—another wall—it once fell to make a dam. But now it is broken in two places. Across the water—there lies what the stone seeks!"

He had gone successfully up over the top of the ship. Could I make the same climb? I touched my bruised leg, winced from the pain that followed. I tried to flex it, but it was too stiff. Eet might run easily along that path, but I would have to move slowly. I would have no hope of eluding the watchers, or even of climbing well enough to transverse that slippery surface.

"What lies across the river?"

"Cliffs with holes in them, more tumbled walls," Eet told me. "Now—"

He ceased to communicate. Instead I had from mind to mind, as one might pick up a scent, a sharp emanation of violence.

"Eet!" I tried to get to my feet, bringing down upon my head and shoulders more of the plant life, so that I choked and coughed, and I beat the air, trying to brush aside the foul stuff and get a clean breath again.

"Eet!" Again I sent out that mind call in alarm. There was no answer.

I scrambled to the rent. Had some thrown club knocked him down?

"Eet!" The silence seemed greater than a silence which was only for the ears. For I could hear well enough, wind, water, and other sounds of life outside.

And—something else!

No one who has ever heard the sound of a ship cutting atmosphere, coming in on deter rockets for a landing, can mistake it. The rumbling—the roar. About me the wreck quivered and vibrated in answer to it. A ship under control was about to set down, and not too far away. I slipped back from the rent. The roar was too loud; it sounded as if the ancient ship might be caught in the wash of rocket fire. As the corridor shook about me, I slid down it, striving to break my descent with my hands, around me the foul mess from the rent cascading to blind and choke me. There was a blast and even through the walls I could feel a wave of heat. Whatever had been exposed to that must have been instantly crisped. I wondered about the sniffers. Now would be my chance to escape.

But—who had landed? Some First-in Scout of Survey on a preliminary check of a newly discovered world? Or had there been landings here before for some mysterious reason? At any rate there was a ship down, and from the sound, a small one of a design made for such touchdowns, nothing larger than a Free Trader.

I clawed the debris away and crawled on hands and knees back to the rent. There was a stifling smell of burning. Eet—if he had still been alive on the outer shell when that ship—

"Eet!" My mental call this time must have held the force of a scream. No answer.

A thick steam rose outside, enough to veil most of the landscape. The heat made me cower back for the second time. No one would be going out there until it had had a chance to cool a little. Perhaps some of the rockets' fire had struck into the river, boiling its flow. I shifted impatiently, eager to be out, to see the ship. A very faint chance had come true, as I had never really thought it would. We would not be marooned here for the rest of our lives—*We?* It seemed I was alone now. If Eet had not died in that burst of violence, then certainly he had at the landing of the ship.

The time which passed while the ground cooled and the steam mist cleared was as long to me as those dragging hours when I had been pent in the sanctuary of Tanth. Every impulse pushed me to the rent, to go to claim aid from my own kind. For by one of the most ancient laws of the star lanes any wayfarer marooned as I had been could claim passage on the first ship finding him and be taken off without question.

At last, though the heat was still that of the Arzorian dry lands in midsummer, I pulled myself through the rent and dropped to the charred ground, favoring my bruised leg as best I could. There was a huddled form some distance away, one of the sniffers who had been caught in the backwash of rocket fire. I limped in the opposite direction.

The sound and the heat had made me believe the newcomers had finned down very close to the wreck, but that was not so. However, the rocket wash had cleared that ancient ship of the growth on it. It was not, I saw now, as large as the space derelict, but more the general bulk of a Free Trader. Perhaps it had been left upright on its fins, just as the recently arrived ship was standing a goodly distance away, and the passing of time or some disaster had thrown it over.

I came slowly around to the erose, pitted fins, to look across a fire-bared space at the new ship. It was about the size of the *Vestris*. But no Free Trader's insignia was etched on its side. Nor did it have the blaze of Survey, nor of the Patrol. Yet why would any private vessel land on such a planet as this? There are wealthy Veeps, with a taste for hunting, who crack laws by searching out uncharted worlds where they may indulge their bloodthirsty tastes without falling afoul of the Patrol. If such a hunter had landed here before, that would explain the hostility of the sniffers. But—I drew back into the fin shadow—it would also mean trouble for me. Witnesses to illegal actions are accident prone, and there would be none to ask questions about me.

Only—a Veep's star yacht would have a set of code numbers. There was only one type of ship which would deliberately remain anonymous. I had never seen one, but there were tales in plenty heard in ports. And Vondar's connections had reason to gossip about such matters. The Thieves' Guild maintained ships. Some, under the cover of false papers, made legitimate trading voyages, with only now and then a reason to touch the other side of the law. I suspected the *Vestris* might have been such a ship. But there were other swift cruisers, often fitted with equipment which was experimental, stolen, or bought up before it was generally known.

These were raiders. They did not prey as pirates in space, because that was a very chancy business, to be tried only if a cargo was of such value that one dared a costly gamble. Instead, they looted on planets. Waystar was their legendary base, a satellite or small planet, fortified, hidden, save from those who satisfied its rulers they had no connection with the Patrol or any other law. There had been so many stories, wild tales of Waystar and the shark fleet which operated out of it, that one did not believe in them much. Yet Eet had insisted that I had been unwittingly bound for that place before he had taken steps to separate me from the *Vestris*.

A raiding ship would carry no markings, or else ones which could be changed at will. But a Guild raider here? It was entirely past the bounds of credibility that it was seeking me. My back trail was now so tangled they could

not believe me alive, let alone that chance would land
me here.

Therefore they had some other mission. And the last
thing I must do—until I was sure of that ship—was to
contact its crew or passengers. Though it was closed now,
I could not be sure that I had not already been sighted
on some visa screen. I began to edge back, keeping under
the curving side of the wreck, retreating as eagerly as I
had earlier advanced.

There was a sharp clang and the hatch opened, the
landing ramp protruding like a tongue out over the smoking ground, hunting anchorage on the untouched land.
It angled away from the wreck, so those using it could
not clearly see it or me—I hoped.

I retreated further; I longed to dart back, away now
from the wreckage, which could only draw curious
explorers. There was a brush screen still standing, but I
could not be sure that some of the sniffers were not
lurking there.

The men who came out on the ramp had no protective
suiting, proving that they were aware of the nature of
this world, ready to be about their purpose here. They
wore side arms, and even from this distance, I saw the
short barrels of the lasers, not the long ones of the more
ordinary stunners. So they were prepared to kill.

Though they wore the conventional planetside dress
of any crewmen, coveralls and boots, those had no insignia on breast or collar. Nor was there any choice of color
to suggest a uniform. The first two were human or
humanoid, but behind them came a shorter figure with
four upper limbs which hung at his sides in a way to
suggest an unusual flaccidity. His head, which was round,
lacked hair and appeared to rest directly on his shoulders, with no support of neck. Where a human skull

would show ears, he wore tall feathery appendages which moved constantly back and forth, as Eet's head had moved when he tested for signs of life around him. And of the three I saw, I feared him the most. For as Eet had said, who knows what extra talents an X-Tee might possess. And any among a human crew would be there for no other reason than that he had attributes they found highly useful.

To re-enter the wreck was to be trapped. I must make up my mind to leave the dubious protection of its over-hang and try to reach the brush or the river. And it seemed to me that the river offered the lesser menace.

For as long as I could I watched the three from the ship. They reached the end of the ramp, fanned out. The two humans on either side flanked the X-Tee in the middle. His feathery appendages were no longer whirling about; instead they now pointed their tips straight before him, and I could see more of his face. His features were not as far removed from the human norm as were the sniffers'. He had a short nose, two eyes, and if they were set far to the sides of his head and lacked brows, and if his mouth was wider than seemed symmetrical, he was still not too unlike his crewmates.

Suddenly he halted and in lightning draws two of his upper arms caught at the double set of weapons he wore. The brilliant splash of laser fire pencil-beamed from their tips, blackening the brush. His attack was followed by a scream and a thrashing, which marked the passing of either a sniffer or something of similar bulk. The two humans went into a half crouch, their weapons out and ready. But they had not fired, and it would seem they depended upon the X-Tee for leadership in attack.

I crawled back. Now the ship was between me and those killers. When I came to the river, I saw that blocks had been uprooted from the ruined wall and tumbled by the force of the water. At one time some structure on the other side of the stream had fallen, its masonry joining to the walls on this side to provide a dam. Perhaps that had caused, until the water had broken through again, the flooding of the country.

Now there was a crazy jumble of rocks and stones washed and ringed by the water, forming a broken bridge across that ribbon of river. On the other side was the cliff, some distance away, and as Eet had reported, that was holed with dark openings. Between the water and its face were the remains of buildings.

On this side of the ship the clinging vegetation had not been burned away so thoroughly. Perhaps the river spray gave more moisture, for in some places it grew into long trailing vines.

"Eet?" I tried that call, the life here leading me to hope that he might have survived after all. Or had he fallen to a club? I looked along the rocks, down to the water-washed stones, half expecting to see there a small body lying twisted and broken.

"Eet—?"

The answer I hoped against hope to hear did not come. But what did was an awareness of another kind, a strange groping which could not touch minds as Eet did, but which noted my call. Not that it could trace it back to its source. Only it was alerted.

The X-Tee—could he have "heard" me somehow? My folly struck home as I teetered on the edge of a block, looking down for a possible bridge over the river. To attempt the drop with my dragging leg was more than I dared. I could only be caught out there, helpless, vulnerable to any laser beam.

And so I betrayed myself. For as I hesitated I heard from behind:

"Hold it—right there!"

Basic, spoken with a human intonation. I turned slowly, holding on to a block for support, to face one of the humans from the ship. He was like any other crewman, save that in his hand was a laser pointing directly at me.

I knew then that I had thrown away one small advantage. Had I come out to greet the ship's people in wild joy, as they would expect from one marooned, made up a plausible story, they might not have been suspicious. Of course, it would have been dangerous for me if they wanted to cover up their presence on this world. But I would have gained time. Now my own actions made me suspect. I still had a small trick I could play—I could accentuate my lameness, allow my captors to believe that I was far more handicapped than I really was.

So I waited for the other to approach, making a display of holding to my support as if to loose it for a moment would allow me to collapse. And I hoped my general disreputable appearance would add to my claim of injury. Perhaps I could even build upon those patches of new skin so apparent on my body, using a story of being set adrift in an LB when plague was feared. It would not be the first time such an incident had happened.

My captor did not come too close, though he could see both of my hands in plain sight on the stone and that I had no weapons. And his laser never wavered from its sighting on my chest.

"Who are you?" he demanded in Basic.

In those few moments I had determined on the role which might save me. I cowered away from him and shrieked, in the wildest and least sane voice I could counterfeit.

"No—no! Do not kill me! I am well, I tell you! The fever is gone—I am well—"

He halted and I thought I saw his eyes narrow as he studied my face intently. I trusted those pink patches were very visible.

"Where did you come from?" Was there a subtle alteration in his tone? Could I make him believe that I was a deportee from a plague ship, and that I expected to be burned down on sight for no other reason than that I had been cast adrift?

"A ship—Do not kill me! I tell you I am clean now—the fever is gone! Let me go—I will not come near you—your ship—just let me go!"

"Stand where you are!" His order was sharp. Now he cupped his free hand before his mouth and spoke into a com mike. The words he used were not Basic and I could not understand, save that he must be reporting to a superior. This was a dangerous game I played; a hair's difference could mean life or death.

"You—" He motioned with the laser. "Walk ahead—"

"No—I will go—I will not infect—"

"Walk!" A beam, cut to a finger's breadth in diameter, clipped the stone not far from my left hand. Its heat was searing. I cried out as he expected me to do.

I saw him grin. "Touched you? Want another—closer this time? I said—walk! The Captain's interested in you."

Walk I did, making a clumsy business of pulling myself along as if my bruised leg were hardly more than a dead weight.

"Got hurt?" my captor asked, viewing my very slow progress with impatience.

"There are natives—with clubs—they hunted me—" I mumbled.

"So? They have a liking for meat, and you would be that, as far as they are concerned. Not good—meeting with them." He might have been remembering some earlier experience of his own.

I lurched along as slowly as I could, magnifying my limp. Once more I rounded the end of the wreck and now both the other human and the X-Tee came toward us. The X-Tee had holstered his lasers, but both those feather fronds inclined in my direction.

Whether my communication with Eet had sharpened any esper talent I might have had, though I was sure I was not talented at all, I could not tell. But I was aware of an impact from the alien which was not physical, but mental. Only, if he was trying to batter his way into my mind, he was not successful. There was no smooth meeting as I had known with Eet. And I hoped I could completely bar his probe. It was necessary that I remain what I seemed to be—

"So you flushed him," the other human observed. "What was he trying to do—scramble?"

"Not with that leg. And he may have more wrong with him—take a good look at that face."

So bidden, he did, with a searching stare. And his expression suggested he was not in favor of what he saw. I wondered just how bad my sloughing skin and the shiny new patching looked. It was no longer so noticeable on my hands, or so I thought. But then I was used to seeing it and any fading from those violent purple splotches was an improvement as far as I was concerned.

"Perhaps you had better keep him well away," was the newcomer's verdict. "Tell the Captain about him."

"Captain's waiting—up there. March, you!"

There was someone standing on the ramp. A jerk of the laser sent me on. I stumbled along, hoping I was indeed a miserable object for anyone's eyes to rest upon.

TWELVE

We came to the foot of the ramp and there they bid me stand, ringing me in, their weapons ready. The man awaiting us came several paces farther down to study me in slow appraisal.

He was from one of the old worlds, those first colonized. Generations living under alien conditions had given him differences of physique which were noticeable at more than the first glance. His body, under the coverall with the Captain's shooting star on its standing collar, was thin and lank, his skin dark even beneath the space tan; but his eyes and hair were even more indicative of mutation from the parent stock. The hair, of necessity worn very short to accommodate a helmet, was more blue than gray, thick, and it grew in straight, short spikes. His eyes were a brilliant blue-green, larger than ordinary, and with double eyelids, one almost transparent against the ball, the other, heavier, fitting over it. He visibly lifted both to view me, but I think that the sunlight bothered him, as he quickly dropped the inner ones.

But—I knew him! Not by name, but from the past. Whether the recognition would be mutual, I did not know. I hoped not. This man had visited my father's shop, had been one of those escorted into the inner room, exiting through the private door. He had not worn a Captain's tunic then, nor aught to suggest he was a ship's officer. In fact his hair had then been long enough to brush the outsized, wing-padded shoulders of his foppish tunic—the elegance of an inner-planet dandy.

That he was of the Guild I did not now doubt. But would he know me for Jern's son? And if I were recognized, could such a relationship be useful to me?

I was not to be left long in doubt on either point. He advanced another step and then laughed, raised his hand to his mouth, and made a vee with his two fingers, through which he spat deliberately right and left.

"By the Lips and Limbs of Sorelle Herself! After this day will I burn farn leaves to Her in any shrine I see! That which was lost is found. And see, boys, that it be not lost again. Murdoc Jern—how did you get here? I will believe any tale you spin me after this."

The three guarding me stirred and moved in, making very sure that I was not going to disappear—or even have a chance to attempt escape. I had only my role of late plague victim left. Aside from that, I would use as much of the truth as could be checked if later they set a scanner on me.

I allowed my mouth to hang open a little, and wavered as if I kept my feet only through an exhausting effort.

"Do—do not kill me! The fever—it is gone—I am whole now—"

"Fever?"

"Look at him, Captain," my captor urged. "He is two colors—best take care—"

"You, Jern, hold your head up! Let us see—"

I swayed back and forth. They were still afraid of coming too close. The terror of plague deflated the toughest starman when he faced it.

"I am—am clean—" I repeated. "They put me off in an LB—but now I am well—I swear it."

The Captain palmed his com and spoke into it with a snap in that tongue that was not Basic. We waited in silence until a second man came running lightly out on the ramp. He held before him a small box, from which extended a length of slender cable, ending in a disc not unlike a hand com. I knew it for a portable diagnostic. The ship was apparently very well equipped.

Advancing within touching distance of me, the medico swung his search disc in careful examination, his eyes ever on the indicators of the box.

"Well?" It was plain the Captain found this interruption irritating.

"He is clean, by what we can judge. There is always the possibility though—"

"To what point?" pressed his commander.

"The hundredth perhaps. Who can say definitely?" The medico expressed the caution normal to his calling.

"We shall settle for that." The Captain waved him back. "So," he said to me, "it seems you are right. Your fever or whatever it was is gone and you are no plague risk. But you were on board ship when it struck?"

"On a Free Trader—out of Tanth—" I raised my hands to my head, rubbed them across my forehead as if I were dazed or in pain. "I—it is hard to remember. I was on Tanth—I had to escape. There was trouble. So I paid gems and Ostrend gave me passage. There was another world—the natives were all gone. And after that I was sick. They said it was plague—put me out in the LB. It made landing here—but there were natives—they hunted me—"

"To this place?" The Captain was smiling. "But how fortunate for you. The hunt ended in the one spot you might meet an off-world ship."

"There was a wall—I followed it—and the wood people—they seemed afraid. I got in a wrecked ship, they did not come after me—"

"What fortune favored you, Jern, and us too! We might have met you elsewhere, but time is saved because we meet here. You see, you have been a focus of interest to others. We have long wanted to meet you."

"I—I do not understand—"

"What is the matter with him?" The Captain rounded on the medico. "He is not rated as stupid in our reports."

The medico shrugged. "Who knows what happens to a man when a plague strikes? He is clean of infection as far as I can tell, but I cannot vouch for any changes a strange virus may have caused in mind or body."

"We shall turn him over to you." The Captain had lost his smile. "Suppose you make all the tests you need, and then let us know whether we have an imbecile or a source of reliable information."

"Take him on board?" The medico hesitated.

"Where else? I thought you said he was clean—"

"There is always the chance it is something new."

I felt rather than saw the Captain's indecision. But that did not last long.

"What equipment will you need? Can it be brought out of the ship?" he asked.

"Most of it—yes. Where will you put him?"

"In the workings, where else? Segal, Onund, get what the medico needs. And you, Tusratti, take him over to the west tunnel."

It was as if I had ceased to exist as a person, but had become an object to be moved around at their desire. In my role of dazed plague survivor I was willing to have it so. The X-Tee crewman urged me down to the riverbank, I moving as slowly and with as much of a limp as I could manage. There were others already at work there. Across the rocks and foaming water a section bridge had been anchored into place. It would appear they knew this place very well and had visited it before, making their preparations for setting up a base, if even a temporary one.

At the urging of my guard I wavered across the bridge, and through the ruins beyond. Our goal was one of those holes in the cliff face. But not the one to which the other crewmen were heading. What they carried were mining tools of the kind such as were used to pick riches from dead moons and asteroids.

"In—" commanded the X-Tee. The hole to which he pointed was the farthest to the left. There was debris from recent digging dumped on either side of the opening. But whatever they had been hunting they had not found here. They must be taking the holes in turn and were now working that two away from the one into which I was being ushered.

"I am—am hungry—" I halted as if to get my breath, being careful to steady myself against a rock. "I am hungry—I need food—"

There was no readable expression on the X-Tee's face. The hands of his upper pair of arms rested warningly on the butts of his double supply of lasers. For a long moment he stared at me and then he turned and called to one of the men on his way to the other tunnel.

In answer the other detached a packet from his belt and tossed it in our general direction. He had trusted to the unusual talents of my guard, and it did not fall short. Instead one of the X-Tee's upper limbs snapped out to twice the length I would have believed possible, caught the flying object, and pulled back to hand it to me.

My fingers closed about a tube of E-ration and I did not have to fake the avidity with which I gripped its tip between my teeth, bit through the stopper, and spit it out, before sucking the semiliquid contents. No meal of my imagination could have topped the flavor of what now filled my mouth, or the satisfaction afforded me as it flowed in gulps down into me. The mixture was meant to sustain a man under working conditions; and it would renew my strength even more than usual food.

"On!" My guard thumped me on the shoulder with a stick which one of the extraordinarily agile limbs had picked up from the ground. He was careful, I noted, not to touch me. Apparently X-Tees also shared the fear of plague.

Sucking at the tube, I lurched on. And it seemed that the promised strength of the food was already working in me.

The tunnel was a dark mouth opening to engulf us. But the X-Tee produced a beamer. That this was an artificial way was most apparent. And for some distance inside, the stone showed only the marks of its first working. Then recent scars were displayed in great slashes, both horizontal and vertical, until in places they formed a grid.

I saw the glisten of crystals still embedded in the slashes or lying in broken lumps on the ground. And my interest almost made me betray myself. But I remembered just in time that I was playing stupid. Apparently these were not what the crewmen had been searching for. Though they now caught and reflected the light as if a wealth of gems were spilled, yet they had been discarded. This struck me as odd, since ordinarily no Guild ship would pass up anything remotely suggesting profit.

We came to a hollowed-out space where the tunnel ended. Here the walls had been quarried in great rough arches and niches, as if those who had worked here had been so sure they were about to find what they sought that they had used their tools in a frenzy. The X-Tee motioned to a pile of rock. "Sit!"

I lowered myself stiffly to obey his order, still sucking at the tube of E-ration. He planted the beamer on another pile across the open space and turned it to high-diffuse, to light all but the innermost portions of the hollows in the walls. Then he took his place between me and the tunnel entrance.

During the silence which followed I could hear the drip-drip of water somewhere, though there was no evidence of moisture in the tunnel. And a little later I could both hear and feel through the rock the activities of those working farther along in the cliff.

Was this the place to which the zero stone had been pointing us? The discarded crystals here had no resemblance to that murky stone. But that had been exposed to centuries in space, and to whatever use as a source of energy its discoverers had put it to.

I leaned over to pick up one of the broken prisms. My guard placed a hand on the butt of a laser, but he made no move to stop me. This was a piece of quartz, I thought. But of that I could not be sure. One must never make snap judgments about finds on unknown planets. Vondar would have put any such material through exhaustive tests before he might venture an opinion, and even then I had known him to reserve final classification. He carried with him certain finds he was not sure of, even after years of study, since they possessed qualities which were beyond any code. All dealers accumulated a few such, and one of their principal activities when meeting a fellow gemologist was producing these mystery stones for comparison.

So what I held could be worthless quartz, or something quite different.

There was a sound from the tunnel and the medico entered, pushing before him a box which ran on rollers. Behind him came the two crewmen with other equipment. Then *I* became the object of tests.

I think first they still tried to find in me some seeds of the disease which had left such visible marks on my body. And the medico also applied a renewing ray to my bruised leg, so that I could no longer use lameness as a cover. But I could not, dared not resist—even when they at last locked me into a reader-helm. The very fact that they carried such a thing with them suggested they found its use necessary, illegal as that was.

With its pads locked to my forehead and the nape of my neck I could only answer with the strict truth, or what I thought was the truth. After they had reached that stage of the proceedings they summoned the Captain and it was he who fed me the questions.

"You are one Murdoc Jern, son to Hywel Jern—"

"No."

He was startled by that and looked to the medico, who leaned quickly to read the dial and then nodded to his commander.

"You are not Murdoc Jern?" the Captain began again.

"I am Murdoc Jern."

"Then your father was Hywel Jern—"

"No."

The Captain looked once more to the medico and received a second nod of assurance that the machine was functioning properly.

"Who was your father then?"

"I do not know."

"Were you a member of Hywel Jern's household?"

"Yes."

"Did you consider yourself his son?"

"Yes."

"What do you know of your real parents?"

"Nothing. I was told I was a duty child."

An expression of relief flickered momentarily on the Captain's face.

"But you were in Jern's confidence?"

"He taught me."

"About gems?"

"Yes."

"And he apprenticed you to Ustle?"

"Yes."

"Why?"

"Because, I believe, he wanted a future for me. Since his true son would have the shop upon his death."

I could not stop the flow of words. It was as if I stood slightly apart and listened, as if it was not I who answered. Now I sensed that once again the answer I had given was not the answer the Captain had expected and that he was baffled.

"Did he ever show you a certain ring, one made to fit over the glove of a space suit?"

"Yes."

"Did he tell you where it came from?"

"That it had been brought to him for hock-sale. That it had been found on the body of an alien floating in space."

"What else did he tell you?"

"Nothing except that he believed there was something to be learned about it."

"And he wanted you, during your travels with Ustle, to discover what you could?"

"Yes."

"And what did you discover?"

"Nothing."

The Captain seated himself on a folding stool one of his men had provided. He took from a seal pocket of his tunic a pale-green stick, put it between his teeth, and chewed upon it reflectively, as if studying on some new and vital question. At last he asked:

"Did you ever see the ring in later years?"

"Yes."

"When and where?"

"On Angkor after my father's death."

"What did you do with it?"

"I took it with me."

"You have it now?" He leaned forward, his eyes fully open, both pairs of lids raised.

"No."

"Where is it?"

"I do not know."

Again exasperation, this time strong enough to bring a sharp exclamation from him.

"State the last time you saw it and under what circumstances."

"I gave it to Eet. He took it away."

"*Eet!* And who is Eet?"

"The mutant born of the ship's cat on the *Vestris*."

I think that had he not been so sure of the infallibility of the reader-helm, he would not have taken that for the truth. For it must have been the last answer he expected.

"Was that"—he spoke slowly now—"here on this planet, or on the *Vestris*?"

"Here."

"And when?"

"Just before your ship planeted."

"Where is this Eet now?" Again he leaned forward eagerly.

"Dead, I believe. He was crossing the top of the wreck when you flamed down. He must have been burned off by your deter rockets."

"You—" The Captain turned his head. "Thangsfeld, jump to it! I want every palm's width of that ship's surface searched and all the ground around it! Now!"

One of the crewman left at a run. Once more the Captain turned to me.

"Why did you give the ring to Ect?"

"The ring pulled us toward this place rather than to the wrecked ship. Eet wanted to know why."

"*Eet* wanted to know," he repeated. "What do you mean? You have stated that this creature was a mutant born of a ship's cat—not an intelligent being." Once more he looked to the medico for confirmation of my truthfulness.

"I do not know what Eet is," I replied. "But he is not an animal, save perhaps outwardly."

"Why did he and not you take this ring to the source of attraction?"

"We were besieged by the natives. Eet had a chance of getting out, I did not."

"But why was it so important that the ring get out, via this Eet?"

"I do not know. Eet wanted to take it."

"In what direction?"

"Farther on—over the river."

"So!" He was on his feet in one lithe movement. "We are on the right track after all." Once more he looked down at me. "Do you know what the ring stone is?"

"A source of energy—I think."

"A good enough answer." Still he looked at me, his inner eyelids almost closed, giving his eyes a disquieting opacity.

"What do we do, Captain, with him—?" one of the human crewman asked.

"For the present, nothing. Keep him here. But then, even if he runs loose, I do not think he is going anywhere." He laughed. "After all we owe him some small thanks. More if we find the ring at the wreck."

They unstrapped me. I was very tired and willing to yield to my fatigue. But I remembered they had not asked me the why and how of my leaving the *Vestris*. Had they swallowed my plague story and so would not question me about that? The indications were that they had not been in touch with the Free Trader, at least not since my escape. If these represented those who had bought me free from Tanth for their own purposes, they had not been in direct contact with other members of their team lately.

But this time I did not have Eet to depend upon, and thinking of Eet hurt more than I would have earlier believed possible. I hoped that he had not suffered, that that flash of violence had marked an instantaneous ending for him.

Would they find his body with the ring still tied about his neck? And what did they want it for—to lead them to others of its kind as it had guided me across space to the dead stones in the derelict? That such gems might be a revolutionary source of power was an easy guess. And such power, in the hands of the Guild, was worth far more to them than the ransom of a whole system of planets.

The medico and the other human crewman gathered their apparatus and left. But the X-Tee continued to sit by the door of the tunnel, on the stool left by the Captain. He, too, had pulled a green stick out and was chewing on it, but, while his eyes were half closed in enjoyment, his fronds pointed in my direction.

I slept then, and awoke to a shaking of the rock around me, a roar in my ears. There was another ship coming in. Perhaps the *Vestris*. If so, the Captain might be back with more questions. I lay listening, watching my guard.

He stood looking down the tunnel. However, the fronds still pointed at me, and his upper hands hovered over laser butts.

It was clear from the attitude of the X-Tee that this second ship was not expected. Therefore—who? The Patrol? Or some innocent scout or trader arriving just at the wrong time? That the new arrival was about to walk into a trap, I did not doubt.

The thunder of the planeting died away. Now I could not feel or hear the vibration caused by the workers in the other tunnel.

"What is it?" I dared to ask my guard.

His attentive fronds twitched, but he did not turn his head. Only now the lasers were drawn as if he were prepared to repel an invasion.

We continued to wait. I tried other questions until the wave of a weapon in my direction silenced me. Then there was the tramp of feet in the passage and a voice raised in a hail. My guard restored one laser to its holster, held the other ready.

Three of them came in, human crewmen. They carried a struggling bundle which they dumped without ceremony and with extra roughness on the floor. Once in port I had seen a crewman, drunk on the maddening lorthdrip, subdued by a police tangle gun. And now I looked upon a captive completely enmeshed in the same fashion. Among the coils of gummy rope I caught sight of the black tunic known across space. They had bagged a Patrolman, and securely.

THIRTEEN

He had sense enough to cease struggling as he was dropped, so that his bonds did not tighten. Luckily none had crossed his face or throat. But his captors were so sure of him they walked away, leaving the two of us to the X-Tee. He surveyed the Patrolman, no expression on his face. Then he returned to his stool.

The Patrolman's eyes were open and, I judged, he was busy examining his prison and its occupants. He stared a long time at me. The ordeal of questioning under the probe, though sleep had followed, had left me weak. And not only weak, but caught in a curious lethargy, disinclined to action. I could foresee that at any moment the X-Tee might turn a laser on me. But I was no longer afraid.

After a while one of the human crewmen came in, pitched in my general direction another tube of E-ration. Though I felt hunger stir in me when I saw it, a strong effort of will was required to put out my hand, shift my body to reach it. And I held it in my shaking fingers for some time before I could summon the energy to suck at its contents.

With the flow of food into my mouth, that dreamy, half-awake state broke, and I aroused enough to know that this was no nightmare but grim and threatening reality. The entangled Patrolman lay where they had dropped him, watching me. I had sucked about half the tube before I realized they had left nothing for him. Nor could he feed himself. I started to crawl to where he lay.

"Naw—" It was not good Basic, no more than a guttural bark. A laser appeared in our guard's hand, his intent of using it plain. I halted. He waved me back.

"Staaay—tharrr—"

I stayed. But I did not finish the tube. It would appear that our guard was determined to keep his two charges well apart.

Now I returned the Patrolman's stare. He was immobile in the net casing. Had he landed here alone, as a scout? Or did he have companions who would come seeking him? I would have given a great deal at that moment to be able to communicate with him as I had with Eet.

It could well be that I was a latent esper, and my talent—though limited—had been so aroused by Eet that I could at least make my fellow prisoner aware I was striving to contact him. So I put most of my energy into a beamed call.

What followed was so great a surprise that I betrayed my astonishment and had to dissemble quickly by throwing both hands to my head as if struck by a sudden pain—though how good a cover that could be I did not know. The X-Tee was on his feet, his feather fronds sweeping swiftly back and forth.

I had been answered. Not by the man who lay across the cavern—but by *Eet*! And as quickly as that touch of recognition had come, it was gone—a single flash of light across the dark of a moonless night.

The X-Tee advanced to the center of the working, his fronds still swinging, as if those antennae could pick up our communication. And the Patrolman looked from one of us to the other, inquiry plain on his face.

There was nothing more, and I could guess the reason for Eet's caution. If the X-Tee had been able to sense that touch, then mind speech was to be avoided. But the very fact the mutant was alive was almost as good as if someone had dropped a laser into my reach.

I continued to play a part, huddling together, my hands to my head. The guard halted by me and kicked out, the metal-enforced tip of his boot landing painfully against my shin.

"Whaaat—do—you—?" His guttural mouthing of Basic was hard to understand.

"Pain—in my head—hurts—"

"Mind—talk—you—" He did not make that a question.

I felt then a kind of clumsy, fumbling thought approach which was only a feeble pushing, bearing no relation to Eet's. It was easy to withstand such a probe. The X-Tee must have esper powers to a degree, but perhaps they worked better among his own kind. At any rate he got nothing from me.

Now he began a crisscross search of the cavern, his fronds ever in motion. That they were highly astute sense organs, I did not doubt. But whether they could nose out Eet I did not know.

My confidence arose as I saw that the uneasiness of the X-Tee did not abate, but rather grew. Had he been able to get a quick line on Eet, he would not have continued to prowl but would have gone into action.

Where was Eet? I had no idea from which direction that flash of recognition had come. But that he was alive—! Now I hoped furiously that they would not question me again. But if the guard continued to be suspicious perhaps they would.

He stood close to the Patrolman now, his fronds still seeking. Slowly he turned, then put his head back and looked up at the dim expanse overhead. Eet—was Eet up there somewhere?

Clearly the X-Tee's attention was now riveted and I could only believe that he had a line on the esper tie. But how could he? Eet had been quiet.

The laser swung up, pointed at a spot almost directly above the guard. There were hollows in plenty there, and they might hide anything. A mass of crystals larger than my head was visible. He fired—

A flash of light blinded me. I had reason enough to cry out and cover my eyes now. I heard a gasping which could have come from either the Patrolman or the guard. A thud—and a rattling—

To be blind was horror at that moment. I feared to move, sure that ray was bringing down the rocks over us, to bury us alive. When that did not follow, I tried vainly to see through a blood-red fog.

"Are you dead?" That demand which penetrated my dark was no call from Eet, nor was it the bark of our guard. Basic in a human voice—it could only come from the Patrolman.

"Where are you?" I asked, groping out with one hand.

"Ahead, a little to your right!" he answered swiftly. "You must have been looking up as he fired—"

"What happened?" I did not try to get to my feet, but crawled forward on hands and knees, sweeping now and then a hand before me.

"He beamed straight up. Brought down a hunk of crystal on his head. Look out, he is right before you now—"

But my hands had already encountered the body. I made myself examine it by touch, locate one of the lasers. And all the time I feared I was blind.

I edged around the body and crawled on until one of my hands touched the Patrolman. To burn off his bonds was a job demanding good sight, and I could not do it blind.

"Wait!"

I settled back on my heels, a surge of relief breaking like a high tide in me. "Eet!"

He came out of nowhere as far as I was concerned. I felt the pat of his hand-paws on mine and I released the laser into his hold. I guessed that he was quick and efficient about freeing the Patrolman. For it was only moments later that a human hand fell on my shoulder, drawing me up to my feet. I wavered there, almost as I had when I had played the role of plague wanderer for the Captain. Eet climbed me as if I were a tree and his weight once again ringed my shoulders. I felt the tickle of his whiskers against my cheek.

"Hold still! Let me see your eyes—" That was the Patrolman. I flinched involuntarily from his touch and then obeyed. I could feel him spread the lids, the sting of moisture against the balls.

"Close and hold!" he ordered. "From my aid kit—that ought to help."

"They will have heard—" I put up my hand to touch Eet's wiry fur. "They will come—"

"Not for a while," Eet answered quickly. "It is night and they have posted an outer guard, but there are none in any of the tunnels. We have a good chance of getting free. This guard was the only sensitive among them."

My hand was caught in a firm grip which pulled me on. Eet meanwhile directed my steps around piles of debris. We must have re-entered the tunnel, heading for the outside.

"Who are you?" the Patrolman asked. "A hostage?"

I gave him the version I had edited for the Guild men. "I caught an unknown disease, was spaced from a ship in an LB. It made tape landing here and I was hunted by natives. I took refuge in a wrecked ship. Then these landed. They made me prisoner after their medico pronounced me clean."

"You are lucky they did not just beam you down," he returned. "I wonder why they did not."

I had to supply him with a plausible answer. "They thought I knew about what they hunt here. I am an apprentice gemologist."

"Gems!" He paused and then added, "They are conducting mining operations—that is true."

"Were you tailing them? And where is your ship?" I counterquestioned.

"I am a scout." He gave me the most disheartening answer for one hoping for a quick way out of trouble. "They took me when I came out after landing. But my ship is on time lock—they cannot break into her. If we can reach her—But what—or who—is your friend?"

"I am Eet," Eet answered for himself. "This human and I are in defensive alliance—which was good for you, Patrolman. To get him free I had also to extend aid to you."

"Then you did engineer that fall of rock," I observed.

Eet corrected me. "No, the creature brought it on himself. I only gave him mind direction, confused him to make him think he saw something threatening above. He was esper, but to a limited degree save with his own kind. He lost his head and shot at a shadow which was not there, bringing down the rock."

My hand slipped along Eet's body and he suffered that examination by touch. I did not feel the twined roots about his long neck, or any indication that he still carried the ring. Nor in that company could I ask questions. For the less the Patrolman knew the better. The Patrol ever takes the view that the good of many is superior to the good of the individual.

I sensed that Eet was in complete agreement with me on that point, and that the ring was in a safe place. But I fretted a little—no place save my own custody really satisfied me.

"Try to use your eyes," said the Patrolman.

The sensation of being closed in was gone, and a cool wind laden with outdoor scents blew about us. I lifted my lids and blinked rapidly. That sweep of violent red had faded, and though there were some shadowy blotches, I could see blearily.

Not too far away a rude sentry post had been erected from debris of the mine tunnels and blocks of the ruins. There was a beamer mounted on its uneven wall, and at intervals that swept, not toward the tunnel mouths, but across the jumble of ruins, touching the broken walls which had once dammed the river.

"They fear an attack from the natives," Eet explained.

"Clubs against lasers?" I scoffed.

"Clubs in the night, when one cannot see well—the odds are not as uneven as you think."

"Why do they not just hole up in their ship?" was my second question.

"They have equipment in the tunnels. Once before they tried retreating into the ship at night. The natives smashed things that could not be repaired—they had to go off world for more."

"You seem to know a lot about them!" flashed the Patrolman.

"You," returned Eet in his most insufferable voice, "are one Celph Hory, ten years with the force. You are a native of Loki, one of four sons, two of whom are dead. You were sent here, not on a routine scout, but to search out the source of a well-sustained rumor that the Guild has made a discovery which will give them superiority in space. You have orders to keep under cover (which you did not carry out well, mainly because your ship had been skillfully sabotaged, something you did not discover until you were in orbit here) and to report back, not revealing your presence to the Guild. Is this not true?"

I heard a breath drawn in sharply. "You read minds." Hory made it close to an accusation.

"I merely follow the instinct bred into me, as you follow yours, Hory. Be glad that I do, or you would have been prisoner until Captain Nactitl gave the order for your burning. He was debating the folly of keeping you any longer an hour ago. I would suggest as speedy a withdrawal as possible. These miners have not come upon what they are seeking, but they are close—"

"You found it!" I broke in. By this time I could pick up not only Eet's mental speech but some of his emotions. He was at his smuggest now, suggesting that once again he had bested those physically stronger and bigger.

"So far they look in the wrong place. However, sooner or later that will occur to them. Nactitl is not in the least stupid, and certainly not to be underrated. He has only failed so far because he did not have the right guide."

The right guide! The ring which Eet had taken, which—which must have drawn him to the source. I wanted to ask questions so badly they choked my throat, buzzed in my head. But if he answered them, then Hory, too, would have that information.

"What have they to find here?" broke in the Patrolman, and I knew he would continue to seek an answer. It all depended now on how much he knew of gems. If I guessed wrongly and he had any training in that field, then my secret was threatened. But again Eet took the lead, giving me a briefing in his reply.

"A source of revenue, which also means power." It was very easy to forget at such times he was only a small furred creature. His communication was not that of an equal, but soared only too often into patronizing explanations. "This was a mine of—how many years ago we cannot guess. But I would say the diggings of one of the Forerunner civilizations. Unfortunately for the present-day seekers, they have been picked clean."

"But you said Nactitl was just not looking in the right place—"

"He searches the old diggings. If he looked among the ruins he might find other clues. Unfortunately we cannot linger to investigate on our own. I would suggest that we find your ship," he said to Hory, "and lift as soon as possible. To hide out in this area is unwise. The sniffers are out—"

"Sniffers?"

"The natives; they hunt largely by scent. At any rate the Guild activity here is drawing more and more of them and they have established a ring about the landing field. As yet they are not ready to attack, but they very efficiently serve as a means of confining off-worlder activity to this general vicinity. Even to reach your ship will be something of a problem which will increase materially with every passing moment. But one man alone is not going to change Captain Nactitl's mind and—"

I felt Eet's body stiffen, his head go up and forward. "What is it?"

"We have less time than I had hoped!" His message flashed to us. "They endeavored to reach your late guard by hand com. When he did not answer they ordered a general alert."

We had only those few instants of warning. The beamer mounted on the sentry post went into stepped-up action, sweeping its light wider and farther. But bright as it was in the open, it still could not penetrate the hollow pools of shadow which were to be found among the ruins. And we had luckily dropped into one of those.

"To the right—" Eet took over direction. "Move out at the next sweep."

"To the left." Hory was equally insistent. "My ship—"

"It will not be that easy," Eet snapped. "We must go right to eventually win left. And we shall have to go deeper into the fringe of the ruins, maybe even out into the open—"

"Do we cross the river?" To my mind that would be the point of greatest vulnerability. I did not see how we could pass that under the fire of an alerted camp.

"For so much favor we may thank whatever gods or powers your species recognizes," Eet returned. "Luckily this representative of your law chose to set down on this bank. But it is necessary to flank their post and to avoid any party coming from their ship to reinforce the guard there. Now—right—"

I had been watching the sweep of the beam and it now touched the point farthest from us. So no prompting from Eet was needed to send me scuttling to the next patch of dark I had already marked as a good hiding place. Hory did not leap with me, but my move must have spurred him to action, for he was little behind me in reaching that new lurking place.

Unfortunately the cover seemed designed to lead us farther and farther from our real goal. Yet we could now hear sounds from over the river and see the flash of beamers, which marked a search party setting out from the ship. One of those beamers was set up to illuminate not only their bridge, but a goodly portion of land on our side, an open field of light I saw no way to avoid.

"Not over, but under—at that next hole." Eet's hind claws dug convulsively into my flesh as I gathered my legs under me, readying for the next dash.

He must mean the next patch of deep shadow, but what his "under, not over" meant I was not to learn until I reached it, or rather was engulfed in it. For it was not merely a lurking place behind a pile of stones, but indeed a hole, into which I tumbled.

I flung out my arms, and my fingers scraped rock on three sides. Then Hory landed half on me, sending me teetering toward the fourth. I did not strike any barrier there as I fought for my balance, my feet in their pack coverings skidding on a smooth stone surface. Again I felt about me. Walls not too far away on either side—but open before. And I heard Hory scuffling behind.

"Ahead—" Eet urged.

"How do you know?" I demanded.

"I know." He was confident. "Ahead."

I felt my way along. I was in a passage. Whether it was indeed some runway planned by the builders I did not know. It might have been fashioned by the tumbling of walls. The flooring inclined and I splashed into a pool of water. There was a dank smell which grew thicker as we advanced.

"Where do we travel? Under the river?" I asked.

"No. Though perhaps river water does seep here. Look now to your right."

Ahead was a faint glow which brightened as I slipped and slid on. Through my mind shot a memory of those slime trails within the wreck. Would we find those here also? But at least we could depend upon Eet for a warning—

I came to the site of the glow. There was a square opening in the wall to my right where a block had been removed or had fallen out. And through this improvised window, I looked down into a chamber of some size. Down its center ran a table of the same stone as formed the walls, save that this was not so eroded. And set on it were boxes. They had been metal; now they were pitted and worn, and some had fallen into rusty dust, only their outlines marked on the table. But there was one very near to our window which appeared whole, and in it were stones which gave forth feeble sparks of life. The glow which had drawn my attention did not come from those, but from what lay beside the box. Eet uncurled from my shoulders and passed in a leap through the window to the surface of the table. He raced along it until he came to the ring, thrusting one of his hand-paws through it, using the other to draw it farther up his shoulder like a barbaric armlet.

He made a second leap, back onto the stone ledge of the window, then climbed to my shoulders, stuffing the ring inside my tunic, where it lay, almost too warm for comfort, against my skin.

"What is it?" To my surprise Hory's voice did not come from behind me, but from some distance farther back along the passage. "Where are you? What did you stop for?"

"There is a wall opening here," Eet reported smoothly. "But it is of no service to us. The way ahead, however, is clear."

I was puzzled. I had believed Hory directly on my heels and I had been sure he must have seen what lay in the room. Now it appeared that he had not. But I asked no questions of Eet.

Once more the passage sloped—but now up. It was leading us in the direction we had been aiming for. We took it step by careful step. I listened intently and knew the others must be doing the same.

"There are many loose stones ahead," Eet informed us. "You must move with the greatest care. But it is not too far now before we reach the fringe of the ruins. Beyond that we have yet to avoid the sniffers."

We emerged into heaps of loose rubble. My sight had returned to normal and I saw enough to guess that this material marked the miners' dump. We plotted a path through it with caution. But luckily the higher heaps were between us and the sweeping beam. The activity was now on the cliff side of the river, and at the ruins nearest the tunnel, beamers were turning the night to day.

But our luck held as we crept from the edge of the last rubble pile into the brush. This was tangled and thick, but it made a curtain for us.

"They will expect us to make for the Patrol ship," I pointed out to Eet.

"Naturally. But they will expect that to be bait in a trap for both of you. Probably they have already taken steps there—"

"What!" Hory stopped short. "But they could not interfere with the ship itself—it is on personal time lock."

"Such trifles might not deter a determined Guild expert," Eet replied. "But Nactitl has not been able to foresee my presence or some other minor mishaps. I tell you, keep on. Once we reach the ship we need not worry about escape off world."

Knowing Eet, I trusted that tone of assurance. Hory probably did not, but he followed as if he had no choice—which in truth he did not, unless he proposed to skulk about the terrain or go into suicidal battle with the Guild.

FOURTEEN

"Sniffers!"

Eet's warning halted me. There was enough light and noise behind us to inform the natives that those of the ship's camp were hunting.

"Where?" Perhaps Hory was now willing to depend upon Eet's senses, if not to accept his advice.

"Left—in the tree."

That was not as tall as the forest giants, but it did tower well above us. And its foliage made so impenetrable a cone of dark that no eyes of ours could sight what might hide there.

"He waits to leap as we pass beneath," Eet informed us. "Swing well away; he will leap but fall short."

This time we were not unarmed. Hory had one of the X-Tee's lasers, I another. To spray about without a definite target, however, would be folly. I held the weapon at ready and started around the tree.

It was like a blow in my face, striking deep into my head, then seeming to center in my ears. I staggered under it and heard Hory cry out in equal torment.

Eet twisted on my shoulders, thrust in his claws to keep his position. I forgot all about any menace from the natives; all I wanted was to be rid of the agony in my head.

"—hand—take Hory's hand—hold—"

Eet's mind voice was almost muffled by the pain in my head. His hand-paws had gone to my ears, gripping them, and I could feel his body resting against my head, an addition to my misery.

"Take Hory's hand!" The command was emphasized by a sharp twist of my ears. I tried to lift my hand to pull that tormentor from my shoulders, but found that, instead of obeying me, my flesh and muscle were flung around, and my fingers seemed to close of their own accord on warm skin and bone, in a grip riveted past my breaking. The Patrolman, moaning, tried to break away from me, to no effect.

"Now—on!" Again Eet twisted my ears. Dazed from the pain in my head, I stumbled in the direction he aimed me, towing Hory behind.

There was a shrilling from the tree, and something dark fell, not leaped, from it, to lie writhing on the ground. We dimly heard other sounds, a rustling of movement throughout the brush. Things hiding there were now moving past us toward the cliffs.

Only Eet's sharp hold and constant misuse of my ears kept me going. For, as I moved, it was as if I waded through a swift current determined to bear me back toward the ruins and the Guild ship, which I had to fight with all my strength.

It was dark here, but Eet rode me as a man might mount a beast of burden, guiding me by his hold, steering me here and there. And I could only obey those tugs, always drawing Hory along by a grip I could not release.

For years, or so it seemed, that zigzag march lasted. Then I smelled charred vegetation and we came to where the growth was shriveled by rocket blast, or burned off altogether. Before us, standing on its fins, was the Patrol scout ship.

Only a dark bulk—I could not make out a ramp, or any dark hatch open on its side. And I remembered Hory's talk of a time seal. If he could not lift that at will, we had reached our goal but were still barred from safety.

The pull on me, the pain in my head, still existed, but either its force had lessened, or I was now so accustomed to it that the agony had decreased. Eet still kept his grip on my ears, but when I paused before the ship he did not urge me on.

Instead he turned his attention to Hory, though my brain, too, received his imperative command:

"Hory, the time seal—can you denegate it?"

The Patrolman swayed back and forth, tugging feebly against my grip, trying to turn toward the ruins.

"Hory!" This time Eet's demand for attention was as painful to the receptive mind as the torment from behind.

"What—" Not quite a word, more nearly a moan. With his free hand the Patrolman pawed at his head. The laser was gone; he must have dropped it at the attack.

"The seal—on—the—ship—" Eet's words were heavy in impact, like the ancient solid-type projectiles when they struck into flesh. "Deactivate the seal—now—"

Hory turned his head. I could see him only dimly. With his free hand he fumbled at the front of his tunic. All his movements seemed so uncoordinated that one could not believe he could complete any action. He brought out a hand com.

"Code!" Eet kept at him relentlessly. "What—is—the—code?"

As if he could not even be sure of the position of his mouth, Hory raised his hand in a series of jerks. He mumbled. I could understand none of the sounds clearly. And whether, in spite of his clouded mind, he was responding to Eet's order, I had no idea. His arm dropped heavily, to swing by his side. It seemed he had failed.

Then there was a noise from the ship. The hatch opened and the tongue of a narrow landing ramp licked forth, to touch the seared earth only feet away.

"In!" Eet's order rang almost as shrill as one of the sniffers' screams.

I dragged Hory along. The ramp was very narrow and steep, and I had to negotiate it sideways in order to tow the Patrolman. But step by step we climbed the span to enter the hatch.

It was like walking into a soundproofed chamber and slamming the door behind us. Instantly the tumult in my head ended. I leaned against the wall of the compartment just within the hatch, feeling the drip of my own sweat from my chin. My relief was so great it left me weak and shaking.

By the glow of the light which came on as the hatch closed behind us, I could see that Hory was in no better state. His face was greenish-white under the space tan and slick with sweat. He had bitten his lip and drops of blood still gathered there in bubbles, to feed a thin trickle down his chin.

"They—had—a compeller—on us—" He got out each word as if to form it with his savaged lips was a fearsome task. "They—"

Eet had released his hold on my ears and had dropped down to my shoulders once again.

"Better get off planet." If the compeller had affected the mutant, he did not show it. And now it was far easier to follow his suggestion than to undertake any action on my own.

I think Hory was in much the same state. He lurched away from the wall and drew himself through the inner hatch. As we followed I heard the clang of the rewinding ramp, the automatic sealing of the door behind us. Again I felt a wave of relief.

To get at us now they would have to use a superdestruct. And the Guild ship, as well equipped as it might be, could not carry one of those—it was not large enough.

Hory took the lead, pulling up the core ladder of the ship. Then Eet climbed with a speed which left both of us behind. We passed by two levels to enter the control cabin. The Patrolman reached the pilot's swing chair and began to buckle himself in. He moved as one in a dream, and I do not think he was really aware of my presence, though he must have been of Eet's.

Patrol scouts are not meant to carry more than one man. But in emergencies there might be exceptions, and there was a second blast-off seat in the rear of the cabin. I got into that and was making fast the straps when Hory leaned forward to press the course tape release. Eet sprang from somewhere and lay full length along my body.

There was an awakening of lights on the board, a vibration through the ship. Then came the pressure of blast-off. I had known that of the Free Traders and small freighters, which had seemed so much worse than that of liners. But this was a huge hand squeezing me down into darkness.

When I saw dizzily again, the lights on the board no longer played in flashing patterns but were set and steady. Hory lay in his seat, his head forward on his chest. Eet stirred against me. Then his head arose slowly and his beads of eyes met mine.

"We are out—"

"He set a course tape," I said. "To the nearest Patrol mother ship or base, I suppose."

"If he can reach it," Eet observed. "We may have bought time only."

"What do you mean?"

"Just that Nactitl cannot afford to lose us. The Guild are playing for the largest stakes they have yet found—for many of your human centuries. They will not allow the fate of a single Patrol scout to upset their plans."

"They cannot mount a destruct—not on their ship."

"But they may have other devices, just as useful to them. Also, do you yourself want to be delivered to a Patrol base?"

"What do you mean?" I glanced at Hory. If he was conscious he must be able to "hear" Eet's communications.

"He still sleeps," the mutant reassured me. "But we may not have much time, and I do not know how much an unconscious brain can pick up to retain for the future. This is true—what Nactitl seeks he has not yet found. There are only the stones in the storage vault. But they were not mined on that planet, as Nactitl and the Patrol may continue to believe."

"How do you know that? What about those cliff tunnels?"

"They sought something else there, those old ones. No, the cache under the ruins held their fuel supply. But Nactitl will believe they found them in the mines, and so will others. However, the man who does eventually find the true source of the stones can make his own luck, if he is clever and discreet. Also—those stones looked dead, did they not?"

"Very dead."

"Your ring stone partly activated them. Just as it can give a boost to any conventional fuel in these ships of yours. You have a bargaining point, but you must use it well. There will be those who would kill you for that ring. And you have more to fear than just the Guild." His head swiveled around on that exceedingly mobile neck and he looked meaningfully at the Patrolman.

"To stand against the Patrol would require more resources than I have," I answered. The illegality of it did not bother me. The ring was my heritage, and the fact that some musty law made by men I had never seen or heard of might be produced to wrest it from me only raised my anger. I added, "But I will fight for what I now hold."

"Just so." There was satisfaction in Eet's agreement. "You can seem to yield and yet win."

"Win what? A fortune—with everyone sniping at me to get at the secret and tear me down? I want none of that."

Perhaps Hywel Jern, who could have had wealth and yet had settled prudently for comfort, and might have finished out his life in peace had he not been a curious man, had molded me. Or perhaps the need to be free which had kept Vondar Ustle on the move had rubbed off on his assistant.

"You can buy freedom." Eet's thought followed mine easily. "What have you now with Vondar dead? Nothing. Bargain well, as he taught you, when the time comes. You will know what you want most in that hour."

"What *you* want," I countered.

Now his head turned so that he could eye me. "What I want—just so. But our trails run together. I have told you that before. Apart we are weak, together we are strong, a combination to accomplish much if you have the courage—"

"Eet—what are you?"

"A living being," he replied, "with certain gifts which I have placed at your disposal from time to time, and certainly *not* to your disadvantage." Again he read my thoughts and added, "Of course, I have used you, but also you have used me. You would have been dead long since had we not. And to your species, death of the body is an end—do you not believe it so?"

"Not all of us do."

"That is as it may be," he replied ambiguously. "But at any rate, we are together in this life and it is to our mutual advantage to have this pact continue."

I could not deny his logic, though still the suspicion stayed deep in my mind that Eet had plans of his own and would eventually maneuver me into serving them.

"He is waking." Eet looked at Hory. "Tell him to check his speed."

I was no pilot. But I could see there was a red light flashing on the board. That had about it a suggestion of alarm. Hory made a snorting sound and straightened in his web seat, setting it to swinging. He rubbed his hands across his eyes and then leaned forward to look at the board, his attitude that of one alerted to trouble.

"Eet says—look to the speed—" I said.

His hand shot out to thumb a red button under that red flash. The red spark vanished, a yellow one flashed in its place, held steady for a short space, then became red again. Once more Hory tried the button. But this time there was no change in the light. His fingers played a swift pattern over other buttons and levers, but the signal remained stubbornly red.

"What is the matter?" I asked.

"Traction beam." Hory spit out that explanation as if it were a curse. "They have lifted behind us and slapped a traction on. But a ship of that size, how could they be so equipped?" Still he continued to try his keys. Once the light paled, but only momentarily.

"They can pull us back?"

"They are trying. But they cannot down us—not yet. They can only keep us out of hyper. And they may think they can board—if so they are going to be surprised. But they can keep us tied near that planet."

"Waiting for reinforcements? Why cannot you do the same—call for help?"

"They have a com blanket over us. If they expect reinforcements they were already sure of their coming. I have heard of Guild superships; this must be one of them."

"What do we do then—just wait—?"

"Not if we are wise," Eet cut in. "They do expect aid and it will be of such nature as to take this ship easily.

What you stumbled on here, Hory, is a Guild operation of such magnitude that they are willing to throw many of their undercover reserves in—or did you arrive here with a suspicion that that was so?"

"I suppose you have a suggestion?" Hory asked bitingly. "I can maintain my shield but not break their hold—to do that is to lose my own escape force. They could reel us in before I could fire effectively."

Eet did have an answer. "The ring stone, Murdoc—"

"How?" I had felt the action of the ring on my own body, its drawing power across the wastes of space, and on the planet below. But in what way could it be used on this ship to break a traction beam which held so powerful a vessel in bonds?

"Take it down, to the engine room," Eet ordered.

His knowledge was certainly greater than mine, and I continued to wonder where he had gained it. Reading minds seemed easy enough for him, but how he knew uses for the baffling gem I could not understand. Was it all part of Eet's mysterious past, before he had, as he put it, obtained a body to serve him in the present? Was—could Eet have a link with those who had once used the stones for motive power? How long had Eet been a seed, or stone, or that thing Valcyr had swallowed?

Even as I speculated, I was unbuckling, preparing to leave my seat. I had learned my confidence well; if Eet thought there was a chance the ring might save us, I was willing to try it.

"What will you do?" Hory asked sharply.

Eet answered. "Try to augment your power, Patrolman. We are not sure, we can only try."

It was thoughtful of him to say "we," since, as always, I was merely the one to carry out plans hatched in that narrow head of his.

We descended the ladder to the lowest level and made our way to the reactor room. Eet made the same questing movements of nose and head as he had used to steer us through the forest. Then with a quick stretch of his neck, he pointed his nose at a sealed box.

"There, but you must make it fast. Use a weld torch—"

With the air of one humoring madmen, Hory opened a small compartment on the wall and took out the tool Eet had asked for. I brought out the ring slowly. In spite of Eet's suggestion that we needed its aid, I could not be sure of that. And I had the greatest reluctance to release it to Hory. I had come to trust no one in relation to the stone, which had already left a trail of blood, and blood belonging to those who meant the most to me, across several solar systems.

For a moment I thought Eet was wrong. The stone displayed no signs of life; it was as dead as it had been the first time I saw it. Very much against my will I laid it on top of the box as Eet had ordered.

Then slowly, almost protestingly, it did show life. It did not blaze as it had in space, or even as it had in the underground room, when it had rested near its fellows, bringing them in turn to a glow. That blaze had been blue-white; this was duller, yellow. Hory stared at it, his astonishment so great that he made no attempt to use the welder.

"Affix it—quick!" Eet cried. His whip of tail lashed back and forth on my back as if he would so beat me to the task. I reached for the welder, but Hory roused and touched its tip to the ring metal against the box, joining them firmly.

"Look—" But Eet was not to finish that warning. Hory struck out with a follow through of the weld rod. By the good grace of whatever power might rule space, the lighted end of that improvised weapon did not hit Eet. But the rod swept him from my shoulder and hurled him to the floor with such force that he lay limp and unmoving.

I was so astounded by the attack that I wasted a precious moment in sheer amazement. When I started for Hory, that rod swept up again so that the glowing point menaced my eyes. There was such determination to be read on his face I did not doubt he meant to use it were I to jump him.

So I retreated as he advanced, unable to reach for Eet, for Hory thrust at me when I attempted that. Since the compartment in which we stood was small, my back was swiftly at the wall.

"Why?" I asked. He had me spread there, my hands at shoulder height, palms empty and out, the glowing point of the rod weaving a pattern of threat directly before my eyes.

Hory, the rod in one hand, searched in the front of his tunic. What he produced was a more refined example of the tangler the Guild men had used on him. It flicked out from the tube, not to weave my whole body into a helpless cocoon, but to loop about my wrists, bringing them tightly together.

"Why?" he echoed. "Because I now know who you are. You gave yourself away, or that beast of yours did, when he had you bring out the ring. What happened back there? Could you not agree on the Guild's terms? We have been tracing you for months, Murdoc Jern."

"Why? I am no Guildman—"

"Then you are playing a lone hand, which is enough to label you fool. Or do you reckon your beast high enough to support you? You are rather useless without him, are you not?" Hory kicked out and Eet rolled over. I tried desperately to reach him through mind touch, but met nothing. Once before I had believed him dead; now the evidence of my eyes assured me that was true.

"You accuse me of playing some game." I strove to control my rage; anger can betray a man into foolish error. Perhaps I had not learned the proper submergence of emotions my father had believed necessary to make the superior man, but I had had excellent tutoring and put that to the test now. "What do you mean?"

"You are Murdoc Jern and your father was a notorious Guildman." Hory used the blazing rod as if I were a child and he were an instructor about to indicate some pertinent point on a wall projection from a reading tape. "If you are not a full member of the Guild, you have access to his connections. Your father was killed for information he had, probably about"—with the rod Hory indicated the ring—"that. You were on Angkor when it happened. Then you shipped out, having broken with your family. You were on Tanth when your master Vondar Ustle was killed under circumstances which suggest his death had been arranged. What caused that, Jern? Did he discover what you were carrying and plan to inform the authorities? Whatever happened, matters did not go as you expected, did they? You did not walk out free with your master's private gem stock to back you. But you did get off world—

"The ship you lifted in is suspect as a part-time Guild transport. They dropped you here, didn't they? And later you fell out with your bosses. You ought to have known you could not stand up to the Guild. Or did you believe that with that beast of yours you could do it? We will get the truth out of you with a reader-helm—"

"When and if you get me to a Patrol base!"

"Oh, I think that now there will be no chance of your escaping. You, yourself, obligingly arranged that. But I am forgetting, you are not shipwise, are you? You do not have the 'feel.' We have broken free of the traction and are back on course. Now—" Still facing me with the ready rod, Hory stooped and picked up Eet, a long string of furred body, by the hind legs. "This goes into cold storage. The lab will want to see it. And you shall go into another kind of storage, until you are needed."

He drove me with his heated rod out of the engine compartment, toward the ladder which led to the upper levels. I backed slowly, trying to see any small chance which might work for me. But even though I might be reckless enough to charge him, he need only with pressure of one finger bring that rod to top heat and lay it across my face to discipline me into obedience.

Eet swung, a pitiful pendulum, from Hory's hand. I looked at his body and my hate was no longer hot but cold, clear and deadly in me. And because I did look at Eet at that moment I saw my chance. For Eet came to life, twisting up and around to bury needle-sharp teeth in the hand which held him. And as Hory yelled in pain and surprise I charged.

FIFTEEN

Though I could not use my hands (and I would have used them to some purpose, for my father had had me carefully tutored in those forms of unarmed combat which are useful for a space rover), I did use my head and body as a battering ram, striking Hory hard just below his chest, driving him back against the wall. His breath went out of him in a great gasp. But I could not follow up the small advantage as I wanted; I could only strain to hold him helpless with my weight against his body. And it was a stalemate to which I could see no profitable conclusion.

Eet had played a leading role in the initiation of this fight, but I did not expect any more from him. However, he was not to be counted out, as I discovered. His slim body flew through the air, to land on Hory's bent head, his whip tail lashing my cheek as he passed. He dug in his claws, and caught the Patrolman by the ears as he had me when he steered us away from the cliffs.

Hory screamed and tried to raise his hands to his head, while I wriggled the closer to keep them down and give Eet his chance to win a small victory. Then, regaining some detachment, I backed away, only to charge again, the full force of my shoulder aiming at the base of Hory's throat. Had I been able to deliver that blow as intended, he might have died.

As it was, he made a crowing noise, and when I stood away, he tried to bring his hands up to his throat. But his knees folded under him and he bowed slowly forward. In fact he might have slipped along the ladder and fallen had I not taken his weight, bracing myself, against my thighs.

Eet loosed his hold, leaving bleeding gashes behind, and whipped down Hory's body, using his paws to tear open the Patrolman's tunic and bring forth the tangler. As if he had used one many times before, he turned it on its owner. And in moments Hory was again as neatly packaged as he had been back in the tunnel.

The mutant panted heavily as he drew back on his haunches, holding the tangler between his hand-paws, his attention on the Patrolman. Hory gasped for breath, a dark tinge still in his face. I wondered if my blow had broken some bone, and if I had done worse damage than I had first thought. In spite of the fate he had meant to deal to Eet, and his plans for me, when I had time to think without the heat of rage blinding me, I did not want to kill him. I have killed to defend myself, as I did on Tanth, but never willingly—few men do. And to kill with one's hands is also another matter. Hory was following orders, with, as he believed, law behind him—though

sometimes right and law are not one and the same thing.
I respect the Patrol and have a healthy fear of them. But
that does not mean I tamely submit to a decree which
may not fit with justice. On the frontiers, of necessity,
the law must be more flexible than it is on long-settled
worlds. And it seemed to me, from what Hory had said,
that I had been summarily judged and sentenced without
a chance to defend myself.

"Your hands—" Eet had frisked up the ladder and was
now at my shoulder level.

I held out my bound wrists and his sharp teeth made
short work of clipping through those strands. Freed, I
knelt and settled Hory back against the wall, pressing in
and out on his rib carriage until he was breathing less
painfully and the dark shade had faded from his face.

"You—can—not—Our—course—is locked—" he half
whispered. "Take us—to—base."

His satisfaction at that was plain to read. And perhaps
he was right. If a course tape had been locked in the
autopilot, there was nothing we could do to alter it, and
our freedom would last just as long as it took us to reach
our destination. It would seem that Hory, bound and in
our power as he was, still held the victory.

He smiled, perhaps guessing from some change in my
expression that I knew that. After all, I was no pilot, and
if there was any way of confuting a course tape, I did
not know it. Nor, I was sure, did Eet.

"Bring him—" Eet indicated Hory and the ladder.

"I cannot help you," Hory said. "Once the tape is
locked in—that is that."

"So?" Eet swung his head, keeping his eyes on a level
with Hory's as I boosted the Patrolman to his feet. "We
shall see."

The mutant's confidence did not appear to ruffle Hory. However, he did not fight me as I urged him up the ladder. He could have made it nearly impossible to climb; instead, he seemed to do so willingly enough, allowing me to steady him where he could not use his hands. The lesser gravity in the ship was an aid and I made the most of that.

I think Hory was prepared to savor our dismay when we discovered how right he was and that we could do nothing to halt or change the flight of the ship.

To me the control board meant nothing. But Eet sped across the cabin, leaped to Hory's seat, and from that to the edge of the panel, his head flicking from right to left and back again as if he were searching. Whatever he sought he did not find. Instead he drew back again to the seat, hunching up, his neck pulled in to his body, his eyes staring. His mind was tightly closed, but I knew he was thinking.

Hory laughed. "Your superbeast is baffled, Jern. I told you—make your submission and—"

"Trust the Patrol?" I asked. Perhaps I had come to depend too much on the near-miracles which Eet had achieved. It certainly looked as if Hory was right and we were his prisoners, instead of the situation being reversed.

"Full cooperation will mitigate your sentence," he returned.

"I have not been tried, or sentenced, yet," I parried. "And your charges, or those you stated, are very vague. I inherited the ring from my father. I defended myself from a quite unpleasant death on Tanth, and I paid my own passage off that misformed planet. You yourself saw that I was *not* cooperating with the Guild back there.

So—of just what am I guilty? It seems to me that I have in fact been cooperating with the Patrol, in your person, right along—seeing as how Eet got us away from that tunnel and my ring broke the traction beam—"

Hory still smiled and there was nothing friendly in that stretching of lips. "When you were on Tanth, Jern, did you ever hear the folk-saying they have there—'He who does a demon a service is thereby a demon's servant'? What you have in that ring, if it is what rumor claims it to be, is not for the owning of any one man. We have our orders to destroy it and its owner—if that seems necessary."

"So going beyond the law?"

"There are times when the law must be broken if the race or species is to survive—"

"Now that," Eet's voice rang in our heads, "is a dangerous concept. Either the law exists, or it does not. Murdoc believes that on some occasions the law can be bent, or bypassed for the protection of what seems to be right. And you, Hory, who are pledged to the upholding of the strict letter of the law, now say that it can be broken because of expediency. It would seem that the laws of your species are not held in high respect."

"What do you—" Hory turned on Eet a blast of hate which even I could feel. I moved quickly between him and the furred body now in the pilot's seat.

"What do I, an animal, know about the affairs of humans?" Eet finished for him. "Only what I learn from your thoughts. You do not want to deem me more than 'beast,' do you, Hory? Now I wonder what there is within you that holds you to that point of view, even though you know it is wrong. Or is it all a part of not wishing to admit that you can be wrong in other ways also? You seem to put"—Eet paused to survey the Patrolman closely—"an extraordinary valuation on your own actions."

Hory's face flushed; his lips were tight-set. I wished at that moment I could read his thoughts as well as Eet did. If Eet found them threatening, he did not comment on that, but now struck off on another track.

"If *my* species is to survive, and *I* think that a necessary thing, steps must be taken here and now. You are probably right, Hory, in believing that this ship cannot be turned from its present course. But are you so sure that that cannot be reversed?"

I saw the startled expression on Hory's face. His mind must have been easy for Eet to read.

"Thank you." Satisfaction was plain in Eet's reply. "So that is the way of it!" He leaped again to the edge of the control board and flexed his hand-paws over its surface as one might do preparatory to making some delicate and demanding adjustments on a complicated piece of machinery.

"No!" Hory lunged for him, but he came up against me and did not reach the board. I struck once with the edge of my hand, one of the tricks of personal combat which I had been taught. He went down and out an instant after the blow landed.

I dragged him to the passenger's seat, heaved him up, and buckled him in. Then I turned back to Eet, who was still studying the board, his head darting from side to side, his paws above but not yet touching any of the buttons or levers.

"A pretty problem," he observed. "The result will be complicated by the booster power of the stone. It can be reversed, yes. I read that in his mind when I startled him by such a suggestion. Such a shock will often uncover necessary information. But at our present speed, we shall probably not land near where we took off."

"And what can we gain by returning? Oh," I said, answering my own question, "we cannot alter course until we land again. But I am no pilot. I cannot lift this ship off planet even if we are able to set a second course."

"A fact to consider later, when the time comes to put it to test," was Eet's comment. "But have you any wish to continue this present voyage under the circumstances?"

"What about the Guild ship? It could be on our trail again if we return—"

"Consider the facts—will they be expecting our return? I do not believe that anyone, even someone as shrewd as Captain Nactitl, might foresee that. And if we can set down some distance from their camp, we shall win time. Time is the weapon we need most."

Eet was right, as he always was: I did not want to finish out the voyage on Hory's tape. Even if I were not already under charges, taking over this ship would place me so deeply in the ill graces of the Patrol that I could have small defense.

"Thus and thus and thus—" Having completed his study of the board, Eet made his choices with lightning rapidity. And I was not shipwise enough to know if he had chosen successfully. I watched lights change, fade, others take their places, and hoped fervently that Eet knew what he was doing.

"Now what?" I asked as he scrambled from the edge of the board back into the pilot's seat.

"Since we have only waiting left, I would suggest food—drink—"

He was so right. Now that he mentioned it, the E-ration I had consumed in the tunnel was long behind me and I had nothing but an aching and empty void for a middle. I inspected Hory's lashings. He was still unconscious, but his breathing was regular. Then I went below, accompanied by Eet, who could take the ladder with far more speed than I could. We found a small galley with—to me—a luxurious supply of rations, and had a feast. At that moment it was equal to a Llalation banquet and I savored every mouthful with relish.

Eet shared my food, even if it were not the end product of a hunt. It was when we were both full that I turned again to consider the future.

"I cannot pilot us off world," I said again. "We may be planet-bound on a world which certainly would not be my choice to colonize. If the Guild ship follows us in, they will be able to mark our landing and will be after us. And I do not know enough about this ship to use its weapons. Though I suppose, if it is a matter of his destruction, we could trust Hory enough to man the defenses, whatever they may be."

"Especially, you are thinking, since I can keep reading his mind and will be alert for the moment when he may try to turn those same weapons against us." Eet carefully washed each finger with a dark-red tongue, holding it well out from its fellows to be lapped around. "They will not be expecting us. As for getting off world again, that will come in due time. Do not seek out shadows in the future; you will discover oftentimes that the sun of tomorrow will dispatch them. I would suggest sleep now. That eases the body, rests the brain, and one awakes better prepared to face the inevitable."

He jumped from the swing table and pattered to the door.

"This way—to a bunk—" Pointing with his nose, he indicated a door directly across the level landing. "Do not worry—there is an alarm which will rouse you when we do enter atmosphere once more."

I pushed the door aside. There was a bunk and I threw myself on it, suddenly as tired as I had been hungry. I felt Eet leap to my side and curl up with his head on my shoulder. But his mind was sealed and his eyes closed. There was nothing to do but yield to the demands of my overtired body and follow him into slumber.

I was jerked out of that blissful state by a strident buzzing far too close to my ear. When I looked blearily around I saw Eet sitting up, combing his whiskers between his fingers.

"Re-entry alarm," he informed me.

"Are you sure?" I sat up on the bunk and ran my hands through my hair, but not with the neat results of Eet's personal grooming. It had been far too long since I had had a change of clothing, a bath, a chance to feel really clean. On my hands and body, the pink patches of new skin were fading. It should not be long before my piebald state was past and I would bear none of the stigma of the disease which had taken me from the *Vestris*.

"Back where we started from, yes." Eet did sound sure, though I could not share his complete confidence, and would not until I was able to look outside.

"Might as well strap down right here," he continued.

"But the ship—"

"Is on full automatic. And what could you do if it were not?"

Eet was right, but I would have felt less shaky had Hory been riding in the pilot's seat. It is very true that the autopilots have been refined and refined until they probably are more reliable than humans. But there is always the unusual emergency when a human reflex may save what a machine cannot. And, though the engines of a space ship practically run themselves, no ship ever lifts without pilot, engineer, and those other crewmen whose duties in the past once kept their hands ever hovering over controls.

"You fear your machines, do you not?" As I buckled down on the bunk Eet stretched out beside me. He seemed prepared to carry on a conversation at a time when I was in no mood for light talk.

"Why, I suppose some of us do. I am no techneer. Machines are mysteries as far as I am concerned." Too much of a mystery. I wished I had had some instruction in spacing.

But my thoughts and Eet's answer, if he made one, were blanked out in the discomfort of orbiting before planetfall. And I found that to be twice as great as what I had experienced before. My estimation of Hory arose. If he had constantly to take this sort of thing he was indeed tough. My last stab of fear concerned our actual touchdown. What if the automatic controls did not pick a suitable spot on which to fin in and we were swallowed up in some lake, or tipped over at set-down. Not that there was one thing I could do to prevent either that or any other catastrophe which might arise.

Then I opened my eyes, with the thumping pain of a sun-sized headache behind them, felt the grip of planetside gravity, and knew that we had made it. Since the floor of the cabin appeared to be level, we had had a suitable landing, too.

Eet crawled out from beneath the strap which had gone across my chest and his body. His quick recovery from the strains which always held me in thrall was irritating. I had thought him dead after that violent blow he had taken from the rod. But from the time he had turned to bite the hand which held him, he had shown no sign of nursing even a bruise.

"—see where we are—" He was already going out the cabin door. And in the silent ship I could hear the scraping of his claws as he climbed the ladder. I followed at a far more moderate pace, stopping on the way to pick up a tube of restorative from the rack in the galley. Hory would need that and we would need him—at least until we learned more about where we were and what might be ahead of us.

The Patrolman's eyes were open, fixed on Eet in a stare which suggested he did not in the least want to see the mutant. And Eet was in Hory's lawful place, the pilot's seat. For the first time since I had known him, my companion appeared truly baffled.

As always the control board was rigged with an outside visa-screen. But the button which activated that was now well above Eet's reach, meant to be close to the hand of a human pilot reclining in that swing chair.

Eet had scrambled up as high as he could climb, his neck stretched to an amazing length. But his nose was still not within touching distance of that button. I crossed over to push it.

The screen produced a picture. We seemed to be facing a cliff—and it was too close to have reassured me had I seen it before we landed. Insofar as I could compare it in memory, it was of the same yellow-gray shade as that which had been tunneled by the long-ago miners. But this had no breaks in its surface.

For the first time Hory spoke. "Put on the sweep—that lever there." Bound as he was, he had to indicate with his chin, using it as a pointer. I dutifully pressed that second button.

The cliff face now appeared to travel past us at a slow rate. Then we saw what must lie to the left, open sky with only the tops of greenery showing.

"Depress," ordered Hory almost savagely. "Depress the lever. We want ground level."

There was almost a sensation of falling as our field of vision descended rapidly. The tops of the growth became visible as the crowns of large bushes. There was the usual smoke and fumes left by the deter rockets, a strip of seared ground between the ship and that shriveled wall of green. Nowhere did I see the giant trees which had caught the LB in the forest.

Neither were there any ruins, nor the wreckage of the ancient ship, nor, what I had dreaded the most, the spire of the Guild vessel. As the visa-screen continued to reveal the land about us, it looked very much as if we were in a wilderness. And how far we were from the mining camp was anyone's guess.

"Not too far." Eet climbed up on the webbing to watch the sweep across the countryside. "There are ways of locating a ship, especially on a planet where there is no interference in the way of ordinary electronic broadcasting. He has already thought of that—" The mutant indicated Hory.

I turned to the Patrolman. "What about it? We are back on that planet, I know this vegetation. Can you discover the Guild ship or camp for us?"

"Why should I?" He was not struggling against his bonds, but lying at his ease, as if action was no concern of his. "Why should I put myself into your friends' hands? You have a problem now, have you not, Jern? Take off on the tape set in the autopilot and you will reach my base. Stay here—and sooner or later your friends will come. Then you had better try to make a deal. Perhaps you can use me as a bargaining point."

"You have given me little reason to want to do anything else," I retorted. "But those are not my friends, and I am not about to make any bargain with them." Almost I was tempted to let him believe that his supposition was the truth. But why play murky games when I might well need his cooperation in the future? The ship would take off on a tape, without the need for a human pilot. But whether he had a supply of such tapes on board, whether I could affix and use another, whether I could be sure my choice would not merely take me to another Patrol post, that I must find out. And time to learn might be running out—they might already be tracing us.

I—we—needed Hory, yet we must not make too much of that need lest he play upon it. So I had to convince him that we must cooperate, if only for a short period of truce.

"Do you know what they hunt back there?" I tried a different track.

"It is easy enough to guess. They try to find where those stones were mined."

"Which—" I said slowly, "Eet has discovered, though they have not."

I feared some denial from Eet, but he made no attempt at communication. The mutant was still watching the screen as if the picture on it was the most important thing in the world. I was feeling my way, but it heartened me a little that he had not promptly protested my assertion concerning his knowledge.

"Where is it then—?"

Hory must have known I would not answer that. The screen now showed a wider break in the growth. Beyond the ground our descent had scorched was a slope of yellow sand, of so bright and sharp a color as I had not seen elsewhere on this dusky world. That provided a beach for a lake. The water here was not slime-ringed, murky, and suggestive of evil below its surface; it had not been born of any dying flood. This was as brightly green as the sand was yellow, so vividly colored both they might have been gems set in dingy metal.

"It is the nature of these stones"—I made a lecture of my explanation, supplying nuggets of truth in a vast muffling of words—"that they seek their own kind. One can actually draw you to another. *If* you will yield to the pull of the one you have. Eet took the ring just before the Guild ship landed. We had been following such a pull, and he continued to follow it. He found the source of the attraction—"

Eet gave no sign he heard my words. He was still watching the screen in complete absorption. Suddenly he made one of the few vocal sounds I had ever heard from him. His lips parted to show his teeth, cruelly sharp, and he was hissing. Startled, I looked at the view on the visa-plate.

SIXTEEN

The viewer swept on. What we now saw must be on the other side of the ship. And if the rest of the landscape had been free of any signs that intelligence had ever been there, that was now changed.

An arm of the lake made a narrow inlet. Set in the middle of that was a platform of stone blocks. It was ringed by a low parapet, on which stood stone pillars in the form of heads. Each differed from its fellows so much as to suggest that if they did not resemble imagined gods, they had been fashioned to portray very unlike species. But the oddest thing was not their general appearance, but that from those set at the four corners there curled trails of greenish smoke, almost the shade of the water washing below. It would seem that those heads were hollow and housed fires.

Yet, save for that smoke, there was no sign of any life on the stone surface of the platform. We could see most of it, and unless someone crawled belly-flat below that low parapet, the place was deserted. Eet continued to hiss, his back fur rising in a ridge from nape to root of tail.

I studied those heads, trying to discover in any one of them some small resemblance to something I had seen before on any of the worlds I had visited. And, in the fourth from the nearest smoking one, I thought that I did.

"Deenal!" I must have spoken that word aloud as I recalled the museum on Iona where Vondar had been invited to a private showing of a treasure from remote space. There had been a massive armlet, too large to fit any human arm, and it had borne such a face in high relief. Old, from one of the prehuman space civilizations, named for a legend retold by the Zacathans—that was Deenal. And about it we knew very little indeed.

Yet that was the only one—I counted the heads—out of twelve that I had any clue to. And each undoubtedly represented a different race. Was this a monument to some long-vanished confederation or empire in which many species and races had been united?

We have nonhuman (as we reckon "human") allies and partners, too. There are the reptilian Zacathans, the avian-evolved Trystians, the strange Wyverns, others—a score of them. One or two are deadly strangers with whom our kind has only wary contact. And among those aliens who are seemingly humanoid, there are many divisions and mutations. A man in a lifetime of roving may not even see or hear of them all.

But Eet's reaction to this place was so astounding (his hissing signs of hostility continued), that I asked:

"What is it? That smoke—is there someone there?"

Eet voiced a last hiss. Then he shook his head, almost as if he were coming out of a state of deep preoccupation.

"Storrff—"

It was no sound, nor any word I recognized. Then he corrected himself hurriedly, as if afraid he might have been revealing too much in shock.

"It does not matter. This is an old dead place, of no value—" He could have been reassuring himself more than us.

"The smoke." I brought him back to the important point.

"The sniffers—they take what they do not understand to make of it a new god cult." He appeared sure of that. "They must have fled when we landed."

"Storrff—" Hory voiced that word which Eet had planted in our minds. "Who or what is Storrff?"

But Eet had himself under complete control. "Nothing which has mattered for some thousands of your planet years. This is a place long dead and forgotten."

But not to you, I thought. Since he did not answer that, I knew it was another of those subjects which he refused to discuss. And the mystery of Eet deepened by a fraction more. Whether the Storrff were represented by one of those heads, or whether this place itself was Storrff, he was not going to explain. But I knew that he recognized it or some part of it, and not pleasantly.

Already the screen was sliding past, returning to our first view of the cliff wall. Eet climbed down the webbing.

"The ring—" He was making for the ladder.

"Why?"

But it seemed that was another subject on which he was not going to be too informative. I turned back to

Hory with the restorative. I broke off its cap and held it to his mouth while he sucked deeply at its contents. Must we keep him prisoner? Perhaps for the time being. When he had finished I left him tied in the seat to follow Eet.

The ring was no longer affixed to the top of the box. There was a spot of raw metal where it had been. Eet stood at the wall on the other side of the cabin, his forefeet braced against that surface, staring up at a spot too far above his head for him to reach.

There clung the ring as tightly as if welded. But it was not a cementing of the band which held it so. Instead the stone was tight to the metal. And when I tried to loosen it, I had to exert all my strength to pull it free of the surface. All the while it blazed.

"That platform in the inlet—" I spoke my thought aloud.

"Just so." Eet climbed up me. "And let us now see where and why."

I stopped by the arms rack inside the hatch, the ring, in my palm, jerking my left arm across my body at a painful angle. A laser in my hand would give me more confidence than I had felt earlier.

The ramp cranked out and down and we exited into bright sunlight, my hand pulled away from me. The charred ground was hot under my lightly-covered feet, so that I leaped across it. At the foot of the cliff I turned toward the inlet, allowing the ring to pull me.

"Not a cliff mine." I still wondered about that.

"The stone is not from this world." Eet was positive. "But—there is that out there"—he indicated the platform—"which has more draw than the cache in the ruins. Look at the ring!"

Even in the sunlight its fire blazed. And the heat from it was enough to burn my hand, growing ever more uncomfortable, though I dared not loose my hold on it lest it indeed fly through the air, not to be found again.

I plowed through sand which engulfed my feet above the ankles. It was a thin, powdery stuff into which I sank in a way I did not like. Then I came to the water's edge. In spite of its brilliant color, it was not transparent, but opaque, and I had no idea of its depth. The ring actually jerked me forward and I had to fight against wading in. Nor could I see any way of climbing up to the platform, since it would be well above the head of one in the water and there was no break in its wall.

Had I followed the pull instead of fighting it until I wavered back and forth on the bank, I might have fallen straight into one of the traps of this planet. Only the trap became impatient and reached for me. The emerald surface broke in a great shower of water, and a head which was three-quarters mouth gaped in a hideous display of fangs and avid hunger.

I thumbed the laser as I stumbled back into the thick sand. The beam shot straight into that exposed maw, and the creature turned and twisted frenziedly though it uttered no cry. It was armored in thick scales and, I believed, by chance alone, I had struck its most vulnerable point. Around it the water was beaten into green froth by its struggles and it was still writhing as it sank. Then it arose partly to the surface, drifting from between me and the platform.

Moments later the body began to jerk from side to side and I caught dim glimpses of things which tore at it, devouring the eater in turn. But I was duly warned against trying to cross that strip of inlet, narrow as it was.

"The sniffers—" I remembered Eet's report. "If they use this as a temple, how do they reach it?" Of course they could be immune to the water lurkers, but that I did not accept too readily.

"We have not seen the other side," Eet returned. "We might do well to explore in that direction."

The pull of the ring was a force against which I had continually to fight as I walked along the beach, first paralleling the platform and then away from it. When we reached the end of the water and I could see the other side, Eet was proven right as he had been so many times before.

Lying on the sand was a collection of saplings and poles, tied and woven together with twisted ropes. Properly moved into place, it could span between beach and platform, though it would then be at a sharp slope.

The ring pulled me on, and it seemed to me that its tug was stronger, as if it grew impatient, redoubling its demand on me. I found myself running, or trying to run, through the sand, though it was hard to keep my feet, my left hand, holding the ring so tightly my fingers cramped, straight out, across my body, pointing to the platform.

When I reached the bridge I was caught in a dilemma. To let go of the ring, to holster the laser, both actions might mean disaster. Yet I was not sure I could shift the bridge without using both hands and all my strength. The wood lengths from which it had been made were bleached white and might be lighter than they looked—but—

Carefully, fighting until I was sweating as if I had been in another brawl with Hory, I forced the ring back to my chest, unsealed a slip of the coverall, and clapped the band inside. Within my clothing it pushed out the fabric, but that was tough and would hold.

The laser went into my belt, and I hurried to deal with the bridge. It was unwieldy, but my hopes that it was light were realized. I got it up and swung it around, so that the other end dropped on the top of the wall. And I had no sooner done that than the seal on the breast of my coverall burst open. Not the fabric, but the fastener had yielded to the struggling of the ring.

My grab missed the band. With the stone flashing in triumph, it flew out toward the platform. Now I must follow.

I made that trip on my hands and knees, Eet running as a dark streak ahead. And I felt particularly vulnerable as I climbed. For the span swung alarmingly under my weight and I thought that at any moment it would slide from its hold on the upper wall and hurl me into the water.

There was also the possibility that the sniffers might return. And I had no wish to conduct a running battle up or down this very precarious passage. But at last I was able to put out a hand and rest it on solid and unyielding stone, pull myself to the dubious safety of the wall, and then jump to the platform.

The smoke from the nearest head trailed about me, and I sneezed at its odor. Then I thought, for a second or two, that there was a fifth fire lit in the center of the platform, though this did not smoke. Eet was warily circling that blaze—which was no fire after all, but the stone, in such furious display of energy as I had never seen.

"Keep off!" Eet's warning stopped me. "It is too hot to handle. It is trying to reach what calls it so strongly. And it will either destroy itself now, or reach that which it seeks. But it is beyond our control."

I knelt to see the better. Beyond our control? It had always been that. We had set it to our service in the ship, but how easily it had broken free. And all other times we—or I—had obeyed it and not it me.

Eet was right. The warmth that came from it was now a seething furnace heat. There was a raw radiance which hurt my eyes, a thrust of heat that drove me back and back, until I crouched against the wall beneath one of the smoking heads.

The mutant was probably right in believing that this unendurable burst of energy fought to destroy the stone, burn it to one of those cinders. But if it sought death, it was going in a blaze of glory.

I had to shield not only my eyes but my face against the fury. Eet was not with me. I hoped he was safe on the other side of that inferno.

"Just so," he let me know. "It is still trying to cut through."

I did not try to witness the struggle. The bursting light would have blinded me. Even though I shut my eyes, held my hands tightly across them, and turned my face to the wall, I could feel the effects of the holocaust. Could I bear it much longer? If the heat increased I might be seriously burned, or forced into the lake. Between one fate and the other there was little choice. Then—that lashing heat was gone! The stone had died—

Pushing around, I got to my feet. I did not take my hands from my face and open my eyes until I stood upright. Then I looked away, dreading to face what must lie in front of me.

When I did, I fully expected to see a charred cinder. But what was there was an opening in the platform, a perfect square, as if some door had been burned away. And the light from below was not exactly faded, but was pulsating in a less strident and eye-destroying way.

Eet had already reached the hole. I saw his head shoot out and down as he stretched his neck to its greatest extent to view what lay there. But I went more cautiously, testing each block I stepped upon. That hole bore a likeness to a trap door and I had no wish to be caught in such.

The surface seemed solid enough, and with a couple of hesitant strides I joined my companion to look into the interior. The glowing stone lay on a coffer such as the one we had seen in the derelict ship. But the stones in this were very much alive, more so even than those in the cache of the ruins. And their light, coming through a slit, gave us an excellent view of the vault.

It would seem that the platform was only the outer shell of a room, perhaps a storeroom like that of the ruins. There were many boxes in orderly piles along its walls, and none of them had been affected by time. All were tightly sealed, showing not even hair-thin marks of an opening.

Only after I had studied them for a long moment did their general size and shape make me uneasy. There was something about them—long, narrow, not too deep. What was it—?

"Can you not see?" asked Eet. "These did not give their dead to the fire; they hid them away in boxes, as if they could lock them from the earth and the changes of time!" His contempt was cold.

"But those stones—if this is a tomb, why leave the stones here?"

"Do not many races bury treasures with their dead, that those no longer with them may carry into the Final Dark what they esteemed most in the days of their strength?"

"Primitive peoples, yes," I conceded. But that a race which had achieved space flight would do so—no. And now I noted something else. While many of those boxes did bear too close a resemblance to coffins to dismiss Eet's explanation as fantasy, there were others of different dimensions.

Eet interrupted my thoughts. "Look about you!" His head shot up and turned from side to side, the nose pointing at those rows of heads. "Different species, perhaps different shapes for bodies. This was a composite tomb, made to hold more than one people—"

"Yet all following a single burial ceremony?" I countered. For even among the same species there are different modes of paying honor and bidding farewell to the dead. And to find one vault holding so many burials, seemingly united—

"It might be so," Eet answered. "Let us assume that a composite garrison, even a single ship's company, were marooned here. That there was no chance for their eventual return home. Yet, they would hope that in the future there might come those to seek out their final resting place."

My mind took an imaginative leap. "And the stones were then left as payment for their return to their proper worlds, or for the type of funeral they desired?"

"Just so. Those would do as burial fees."

How long had they waited? Did the worlds which had given them birth still exist? Or did these planets now lie barren under dying suns half the galaxy away? Why had the builders of this place remained here? Had their empire broken apart in some vast and sudden war? Had the relief ships never come? Had the ship fallen at the ruins been their last hope, destroyed before their eyes in some mechanical or natural catastrophe? And the derelict we had found drifting—had that been a relief ship they had awaited? When it did not arrive had they surrendered to the fact of no escape and built this vault to tell their story to the future?

I glanced from wall to wall of that tomb. There was no message left there for our reading. Then I looked once more at the heads on the parapet. These, seen close up, were eroded to some extent, but they had not been as badly aged as the ruins by the cliff. Were they the actual portraits of those resting below, or did they only represent types of races?

Six were definitely nonhuman. Of those, one, I believed, was insectile, at least two vaguely reptilian, one batrachian. The rest were humanoid enough to pass as kin to my own species. Two were as manlike as the space rovers of my own day. There were twelve of them—but what had brought such a mixture to this planet?

I turned to Eet. "This *must* be the source of the stones—and these came to mine them."

"Leaving the galleries picked so clean? That ring did not lead to them. I do not believe that could be true. This may have been a way station for such a shipment. Or it may have had a purpose we cannot conceive of now. But—the fact remains that we do have here a cache of live stones. Enough, as that Patrolman would point out, probably to disrupt the economy of any government. The man or men who take that box and are able to hold it will rule space—for as long as they can keep the stones."

I came back to the vault opening. "The light—it is beginning to die. Perhaps the stones are also—" It was decidedly less light in the crypt.

Eet crossed the platform in a couple of his bounds, leaping now to the parapet. Only for a second did he so face the ship, his whole stance suggesting he was alert to what I could neither see nor hear. Then he was back at the same speed.

"Down!" He dashed against me, his impetus striking me almost waist-high. "Down!"

I did drop, my feet going over the edge of the opening. Then I swung by my hands and landed with a jar on the floor, scraping against the side of the box which held the stones. Though the light they emitted was now no more than a small and flickering fire, it was enough to show me safe footing.

I glanced up just in time to see a spear of light flash across the opening, hardly above the level of the parapet. Laser—but not a hand one! That was from the barrel of a cutter, and it must have been fired from the ship!

Eet climbed a pile of those boxes. He was crouched now well away from the hole, yet near the wall facing the ship, his head laid to the stone blocks as if through them he could still hear something.

I put my hand on the ring. There was warmth in it, and a gleam to the stone, but as far as I could see, it no longer threatened any would-be wearer. And, to my surprise, it did not adhere to the box, but came away easily. For safekeeping I put it into the front of my coverall, making sure the seam was tightly sealed.

Again I looked to Eet. The glow was further reduced, but not entirely gone. I could see him well enough.

"Hory?" I asked.

"Just so. It would seem he had resources we did not know about. Somehow he loosed himself. He has now tried to kill us and failed, so he will search for another and more effective form of attack."

"Go off world—bring in the Patrol?"

"Not yet. We have hurt his pride sorely by what we have done to him. There was more to his being here, I believe, than we—or I—first read in his mind. He may have had an inner shield. Also, he believes if we are left here we shall of necessity join forces with the Guild and perhaps be beyond reach before he can return. No, he wants the ring—and our deaths—before he goes."

"Well, we may not be dead—but how will we get out of here?" To try to climb again to the platform would expose us to Hory's beam. He need only wait; time was now on his side.

"Not altogether," Eet informed me. "If the Guild left men here, and we can safely conclude that they did, they will have monitored our planeting. And they will send to see who landed. Remember, they picked up Hory the first time. Almost too easily. Now I wonder why."

I brushed aside Eet's speculations about the past. "We may be half a continent away from their camp."

"But they must have some form of small aircraft. It would be necessary for their explorations. Yes, they will come—and I do not think we are as far from their base as you suggest. The ruins were once part of a settlement of some size. This tomb would not be located too distant from that."

"Always supposing it is a tomb. So we have to sit here and wait for the Guild to come after Hory. But how will we be any better off then?"

"We shall not, if we do so wait," Eet answered calmly.

"Then how do we get out—just by wishing?" I asked. "If we top that hole, he burns me—though you might be able to make it."

Eet still held his listening position against the wall. "Just so. An interesting problem, is it not?"

"*Interesting!*" I curbed my temper. I could think of several things to call the present situation, all of them more forceful than "interesting."

SEVENTEEN

My hand kept returning to the ring beneath my coverall. It had led us on a wild chase, probably to our deaths—where we would lie in company. I glanced around the vault. The light was low, and shadows crept toward us from the rows of ominous boxes. Behind those was only the heavy masonry of the walls. Even if we were able to cut through on the opposite side from the ship so that Hory might not sight our going, we would still have the water to cross.

The ring. It had saved me and Eet before, though perhaps that was only incidental to its seeking for its kind. Could it do anything to get us out of here? Hory wanted it—wanted it badly—

I glanced at Eet, who was now a barely discernible blot against the wall.

"Could you reach Hory's mind from this distance?"

"If there was a reason—I think so. His has—at least on the surface—a relatively simple pattern—like yours."

"How much influence could you bring to bear on him under contact?"

"Very little. Such a tie needs cooperation to be successful. The Patrolman does not trust me, nor would he open his mind to me now. It would be necessary to break down active resistance. I could not hold him in any thrall."

"But—you could me?" I did not know just what I fished for. I was one feeling his way through the dark by touch alone. If I chose rightly it meant life; if I failed—well—we might not be worse off than at present.

"If you surrendered your full will. But that is not in you. There is a stubborn core in your species which would resist any take-over. Whether you wished to cooperate or not, I would have a struggle on my hands."

"But Hory does not know that. All he knows is that you communicate mentally. He knows, though he will not admit it, that you are not an animal. Suppose he were led to believe that you have been controlling me all along, that I am only hands and feet to serve you. Suppose I acted that part now, got out there saying you were dead, I was free and wanted nothing more than to get back with him—bringing the ring?"

"And just how are you going to make that clear to him?" Eet inquired. He left the wall, flowed over the boxes to hunch before me, his eyes level with mine. "If you emerge on the platform he will burn you instantly."

"Can you die spectacularly in a way he can see?" I countered.

There was amusement rather than any direct answer. "Clutching my throat and flopping about?" he asked after a moment. "But with a laser you cannot perform so. I would be scorched fur and a dead body instantly. However, always supposing we *could* convince Hory I had made my exit permanently—what then?"

"I would emerge, dazed, cowed, ready to be taken prisoner—"

"While I would later come to your rescue? Do you remember that we played somewhat similar roles before? No, I do not believe Hory is so gullible. Do not underestimate him. He may be more than he seems."

"What do you mean?"

"I believe he has a mind shield—that I have read only surface thoughts—perhaps what he was programmed to reveal. Did not you yourself once say 'Do not underrate your opponents'? However, your suggestion has some points worth considering. Suppose you were the one to meet his laser beam?"

"But—he hates you. Would he treat with you?"

"Just so—a question. However, there is an implanted feeling in your race that size and superior muscularity count much. Hory hates me as a freak, a thing which belies his superiority. Therefore, he *must* deal with me—for his own emotional satisfaction—not by a flash of fire, but rather by delivering me to his superiors in triumph. So far we have bested him, and that rankles. I wish we knew more." Eet hesitated. "He is a puzzle. And he is also intelligent enough to know that time is his enemy. Do you think he has not already figured out a Guild detachment may be on its way here?

"But they could not shake him out of his ship. Only—he needs the ring as a booster to take off. He wants the ring, and he would like me—you are merely incidental."

"Thank you!" But Eet's dissection of the problem was not irritating—it was true. "So I die—"

"As conspicuously as possible. I will then endeavor to take over the noble mind of Hory, promising him the sun, any vagrant moon, and, of course, the stars, all via the help of the ring. I think he will use a stun beam on me—"

"But—"

"Oh, I do not think that weapon will be as effective as he thinks it is. I shall be transported to the ship, doubtless installed in a cage, and Hory will see his way clear to departing."

"Leaving me here? How—"

Again amusement from Eet. "I said I could not control Hory without his assistance. But there is one time when that assistance, unconsciously, may be mine for a short period. When he thinks I am totally in his power, he will then, by our hope, relax his guard. I do not need to advise you that period will be short. I am his shocked and docile prisoner, you are dead. He has full control—"

"And if the stunner really works on you?"

"Do you want to await death here?" Eet countered. "What one can say this or that sore stroke will not fall on his shoulders, aimed by the strong arm of fortune? Do you wish to sit here waiting for the Guild, or perhaps for Hory to switch on whatever heavy armament his ship affords and burn us to the bare rocks, setting even those to bubbling around our roasted ears? What I have learned of your minds suggests I have a good chance for what I propose to do. Esper powers are not used much and to mechanical devices such as cages there are always keys."

Perhaps my partnership with Eet had made me particularly susceptible to his self-confidence, or perhaps I merely wanted to believe that his plan could work because I could not turn up a better. But I made tacit agreement when I asked:

"And how do I die by laser beam without being crisped in the process? That is a weapon one does not dodge, or survive. And Hory will not be aiming over my head, or any place except where it will do him the most good and me the least!"

It was now twilight in the vault and I could see Eet, but not too clearly. If he had a plausible answer I was willing to agree that in this partnership he was the senior.

"I can give you five, perhaps ten heartbeats—" he answered slowly.

"To do what? Act as if I were going to jump in the lake? And how—"

"I can expend a little power over Hory, confusing his sight. He will aim at what he thinks is his target. But that will not be you."

"Are you sure?" My skin crawled. Death by fire is something no one of my kind faces with equanimity.

"I am sure."

"What if he comes to view the remains?"

"I can again confuse his sight—for a short period." After a long moment's pause he spoke more briskly: "Now—we make sure of a future bargaining point—"

"Bargaining point?" My imagination was still occupied with several unpleasant possible future happenings.

"The cache of stones here. I do not think that without the ring they will be visible."

"The ring." I took it out. "You will take the ring and leave the stones here as bait to draw him back?"

Eet appeared to consider that. "If he had more time perhaps. But I think not now. Give me the ring.

These—we do not want them in sight, if and when he comes to pick me up."

It was my muscle which dragged the box from below the opening and concealed it back behind one of the rows of coffins.

"Now!" Eet sat on a box. "He will not fire until you are out in the open, making a dash for the parapet. The laser may beam close enough so that you will feel its heat. The rest is up to you."

My good sense belabored me as I climbed up, reached out to grasp the edges of the opening. If—if—and if again—

Eet popped out, running, heading for the parapet. I had only an instant and then I fell, a searing, biting pain along my side—a pain so intense that I was aware of nothing else for a second. I could smell my clothes smoldering. Then Eet was back with me, pulling at my coverall as if to urge me up and on, though in reality putting out those lickings of fire.

His mind was closed to me, and I knew he was on the defensive, waiting for a second attack from our common enemy. Suddenly he stiffened, fell over, and lay still, though his eyes were open and I could see the fluttering of his breathing along his side. Hory had used a stunner even as Eet had foreseen, but how effectively? And I could not query Eet as to that.

Around one of his forelegs was the ring. Perhaps his pawing at my smoldering clothing might have been translated by the watcher into a hunt for that. Now we lay still, I belly down, my head turned toward Eet, he flattened out, his legs stiff. Where was Hory?

It seemed to me that we lay there for hours. Since we must be under observation from the ship, there was no chance to move. I had gone down at the touch of that searing beam, not in a planned fall, and my right leg, half doubled under my body, began to cramp. I would be in no shape to carry on battle should Hory decide I was not safely dead. In fact he would be a fool not to crisp us now as we lay.

Except that Eet was sure the Patrolman wanted him. And he had contrived to collapse so close to me that now a sweeping beam aimed from the ship could not remove one of us without killing the other into the bargain.

I could not raise my head to watch the shore line or the span, both hidden by the parapet. Winged things came out of nowhere to buzz about us, crawl across my flesh. And I had to lie and take their attention with no show of life. In that period it was driven home to me again that a man's hardest ordeal is waiting.

Then I heard a crackling. Someone, or something, was climbing the span from the shore; the frail structure creaking and crackling under the weight. A many-legged thing crawled across my cheek and I shrank from its touch, so that it seemed my very skin must shrivel.

My field of vision was so limited! I was not even facing the direction where booted feet would be visible as they crossed the parapet. I heard the metallic click of the sole plates of space footgear on the stone.

Now—would Hory finish the job by simply turning a hand laser on me? Or would the illusion Eet promised hold long enough to deceive him? Perhaps Eet was truly stunned, unable to provide such cover.

Those few moments were the longest of my life. I think had I come out of them with the touch of old age upon me I would not have been surprised.

The boots came into my restricted line of vision. The crawling thing on my face now rested across my nose. A hand reached down, and I saw the sleeve of a uniform. Fingers closed on Eet, swung him aloft out of my sight. I waited for a burning flash.

But (and for an instant I could not believe it) the boots turned, were gone. I was not yet safe; he could pause before he climbed the parapet and fire at me again.

I heard the scrape of his boot plates die away and listened once more to the creak of the span. He had only to pull that down or burn it to make me a prisoner.

How long before I dared move? The need to do that became a growing agony in me. I lay and endured as best I could. What came at last was enough to fill me with despair—the clatter of a ship's ramp being rolled in. Hory was back in his fortress and he had activated the sealing of the ship. Preparing to take off?

I waited no longer, struggling against the stiffness and pain in my body, rolling into the shadow of the parapet. Then I pulled along to reach the span. It was still in place; Hory had not stopped to destroy it. Perhaps he intended to return and investigate what lay here after he had made sure of Eet and the ring.

Half sliding, at a speed which left splinters in my hands, for I lay almost flat on that fragile link with land and allowed its slope to carry me to the beach, I reached the sand. Once ashore, I sprinted for the underbrush, expecting at any instant to be enveloped by fire.

The very uncertainty of what might be happening, or Hory's next move, was as hard to take as if I were under physical attack. I must rely entirely on Eet. And whether at this moment he was a helpless captive I did not know. But I could not expect more than the worst.

There was one fairly safe place if I could reach it— directly under the fins of the ship. Always supposing

Hory did not choose that particular moment to press the off button and crisp my cowering body by rocket blast. Throwing all caution to the winds, I dashed straight for the ship and somehow reached that hiding place. My side was ablaze with pain. The laser had not really caught me—I would have been dead if it had—but it had passed close enough to burn away the fabric and leave a red brand on my ribs.

So far I had managed to keep alive. But now what? The ship was sealed, Eet imprisoned in it, and Hory the master of the situation. Would he lift off world? Or could his curiosity be so aroused by the vault that he would make another visit to it? The ring! What if he used the ring even as we had done and followed its guide? But would he be so incautious—

"Murdoc!"

Eet's summons was as demanding as a shout from an aroused sentry.

"Here!"

"He is now under my control—for how long—" Eet's thread of communication broke. I waited, tense. Dare I beam to him where I was and how helplessly outside the sealed ship? If his control had slipped, then perhaps Hory would be able to pick that up too. I knew too little about his own powers.

Then I saw the loops set in the fin, surely meant to be hand—and footholds, leading up to the body of the ship. But would they bring me to any hatch? They might be for the convenience of workmen only. That they might—a thin chance—be indeed a way in, made me move.

My seared side hurt so badly as I wracked it by my struggles that only will power kept me going. I reached the top of the fin. My ladder did not end there as I feared it would. The holds were now smaller, less easy to negotiate, but beyond them was the outline of a hatch.

I took a chance—"Eet!" I am sure my summons was as strident as the one he had roused me with, because I knew this to be my last chance. "A hatch—lower—can you activate the opening?"

I knew that I was asking the impossible. But still I made my way toward it, clung to the side of the ship as sweat poured down my face and arms, threatening my hold on those slippery loops.

But the crack around the sealing was more pronounced. It was giving. I loosed one hand and beat upon it with all my strength. Whether that small expenditure of effort did hasten the process, or whether the controls suddenly loosened, I had no way of knowing, but the whole plate fell away.

What I crawled into was a much larger space than the upper hatch into which the ramp led. And it was occupied, almost to the full extent of the area, by a one-man flitter—a scout intended for exploration use.

I had found not only a door in but a possible escape out. Before I crawled over and around the machine to the inner hatch, I got out of the flitter one of its store of emergency tools, a bar for testing the composition of ground, and wedged it with all the strength I could to hold the hatch open. Now, even if Hory tried to take off, the ship would not rise. That hatch would have to be closed and he must do it by hand. The protection alarms of the ship would see to that.

The inner hatch had no latch, and it gave easily. I was out in a corridor. I had a laser, and I had also taken an aid kit from the flitter. Now I leaned back against the wall to open that. I brought out a tube of plasta-heal and plastered its contents liberally over my ribs. That almost instantly-hardening crust banished pain and began the healing, giving me renewed strength and mobility.

Then, feeling far more able to tackle what might await me above, I slipped along to the ladder. Had I had more than a passenger's knowledge of the ship I might have found a more secretive way from level to level, but I did not. So I had to go openly, up to the control cabin, where I was sure I would find both Eet and Hory.

I did not attempt to touch minds with Eet again. If my last appeal to him had alerted the Patrolman, then Hory would guess I was in the ship and would be readying traps for me.

One small advantage I had. My feet had nearly worn through those coverings which had been the linings of the space boots. The material was tough but it had become very thin. The lack of boots now gave me silence as I took the core ladder one hesitant step at a time, listening ever for either a betraying noise from above, or the sound of engines.

I had advanced to the level which held the galley. As yet I had heard nothing, nor had I had any message from Eet. The silence which covered my advance now seemed ominous to me. Perfect confidence on Hory's part could keep him waiting for me. And since I would emerge from a well in the floor there, he would have me at his mercy when I reached my goal.

Now I had only those last few steps. I flattened myself against the ladder, tried to make of my body one giant ear, listening, listening.

"I know you are down there—" Hory's voice. But it sounded thin, strained, almost desperate, as if its owner was in such a vice of tension as to be on the raw edge of breaking. What could have reduced him to such a state?

"I know you are there! I am waiting—"

To burn my head off, I deduced. And then Eet broke in, but he was not addressing me.

"It is no use, you cannot kill him."

"You—you—" Hory's voice arose in an eerie shriek. "I'll burn you!"

I heard the crackle of a laser beam and cringed against the ladder. Then I found myself climbing without my mind ordering my hands and feet into action. There was ozone in the air and I saw, shooting across the mouth of the well, flashes of light.

Eet once more: "Your fear is self-defeating, as I have shown you." He seemed very calm. "Why not be sensible? You are not unintelligent. Do you not see that a temporary alliance is going to be the only solution? Look up at that screen—look!"

I heard an inarticulate exclamation from Hory. And then Eet spoke to me.

"Up!"

I took the last two steps with a rush, remained half crouched, my laser ready. But I did not need that. Hory stood, his back to me, a laser in his hand, but that hand had fallen to his side. He was staring at the visa-screen and I saw over his shoulder what held him oblivious.

Across the inlet, facing the platform of the vault, a square of gleaming metal pushed out of the brush, advancing onto the sand at a crawl. I do not know what type of machinery it hid, but there was a small port open at its top. And I thought that whatever lurked behind it was certainly a deadly promise.

How well protected this ship might be I could not tell, but there are some weapons which it might not be able to withstand. A quick lift could be our only hope. But—the bar I had left in the hatch—an anchor keeping us grounded.

"Eet—" I paid no attention to Hory. "I have to unstopper a hatch—so we can lift—"

I half threw myself into the well, skidding down the ladder in a progress which was a series of falls I delayed from level to level by grabs at the rails. Then I slammed along the corridor at the bottom, wedged past the flitter once more. I had done my work of locking the hatch open almost too well. Though I jerked at the bar, I finally had to use the butt of the laser to pound it loose. At last it fell with a clang. I pulled at the far-too-slowly moving door, brought it shut, dogged it down as fast as I could.

Panting, I started back up the ladder. Would Hory's solution be the same? If so, I would have to reach a shock cushion before we lifted. Also—what was going on in the control cabin?

My ascent was not as speedy as the descent had been, but I wasted no time in making it. And I half expected to be greeted by a laser blast, or at least threatened into submission.

But Hory stood with both hands on controls, not those of the pilot, but another set to one side. A beam flashed out from the ship. The visa-screen allowed us to follow its track as it struck across the platform. But it was mounted on a higher course now, to hit directly on that wall of metal moving slowly out of the brush.

There was no resulting glow of the sort that would have followed such an impact on any surface I knew. It was almost as if the shield simply absorbed the ray Hory hurled at it.

I glanced from the screen to look for Eet. There was a burned-out, melted-down mass of wiring to one side of the passenger webbing. But if that had caged the mutant, it had not done so for long. Now he clung to the pilot's seat, swinging back and forth, as intent upon the screen as Hory.

A second or two later, and the ship rocked as if a giant fist had beat upon it. Not from the direction of that advancing shield, but from behind. We had been intent upon one enemy and lowered our guard to another. There was no time to assess the nature of that second, only to feel what attack it launched. I kept my feet by grabbing at the back of the seat. Hory crashed against the bank of buttons he tended, caromed off to the floor. Lights flickered and ran wild across both boards.

Eet sprang from his hold to the edge of the board. We were slightly aslant, enough to make it noticeable that we had been rocked from a straight three-fin stand. Another such blow would send us over, to lie as helpless as a sea dweller stranded ashore.

"Cushions!" Eet's warning rang in my head. "Blast off—!"

I caught at Hory, pulled him over against the pilot's chair so that we both lay half across the webbing. The quiver of the ship's awaking was about us. I saw Eet's paws playing across the board, his long body seemingly plastered to that. Then we did indeed blast off—into a nothingness of mind.

EIGHTEEN

There was the sickly taste of blood in my mouth, a lack of clarity in my mind—

"Murdoc!"

I tried to raise my head. Under me, for I lay on a smooth surface, a vibration reached into my body, bringing into life every ache and pain I had. I rolled, brought up against a wall, clawed above me for support, and at last got to my feet.

Fighting against dizziness, I stared slowly about. Eet still clung to the edge of the control board. And drawing himself aloft, even as I had done, was Hory, blood trickling from a gash along his jaw, his movements discordant and fumbling.

I turned to Eet. "We upped ship?"

"After a fashion." Seemingly he was not so affected by the force of the take-off.

"Back on the sealed course again—" I could remember better now.

Hory shook his head as if trying to clear it from some bewildering fog. He looked at me, but in an unfocused way, as if he did not really see me. Or, if he did, my presence had no meaning for him. He put out a hand to catch at the pilot's seat, pulled himself laboriously into that, and relaxed in its embrace.

"We are on course." His voice was drained and weak. "Back where we were. Next set down will be at the Patrol base—or do you want to reverse again?"

He did not turn his head to look at me as he spoke. If the active combativeness had gone out of him, there was still a core of determination to be read in his tone as his voice grew stronger and steadied.

"The Guild are in control down there." I did not know what I wanted, save to keep from sudden and painful death, a fate which had dogged me far too long. Perhaps some men savor such spice in their lives, but it was not to my taste. I was so tired I wanted nothing but peace. And a way out—with neither the Guild nor the Patrol snapping at my heels. The only obstacle to that was that neither organization was one to relinquish easily what it desired. In that moment I damned the day I had first laid eyes on the zero stone. Yet when I looked to Eet and saw he wore the ring about his forelimb, something about it drew and held my eyes. And I do not think I could have hurled it from me had it lain within my grasp. I was as tied to it now as if I were bound by a tangle cord.

"To no purpose—" That was Eet. For a moment I did not understand him, so far had my thoughts ranged. "Look—"

His paws moved and on the visa-screen appeared a picture.

"This registered as we took off," he explained. "It remained."

I saw the platform of the heads approaching sharply, as if we had crossed above it. And I remembered the ship had been slightly aslant.

"The tail flames of the rockets"—Eet used his instructor's voice—"must have swept across it."

He did not enlarge on that but I understood. The flames—could they have resealed, or cleaned out the crypt? If sealed, then the cache of the best stones was once more hidden. And we were the only ones who knew of their existence! A bargaining point? The stones we had seen in the room of the ruins had been close to exhaustion, those in the vault fresh. They were probably the cream of those owned by the ones who had established the tomb. If the Guild depended upon those from the ruins, they could still be defeated by whoever had the others.

I knew that Eet was reading my mind. But he remained silent, so that Hory could not share my realization of that small superiority. The mutant continued to watch the visa-screen until it went blank.

"They are not going to find what they want," he said to Hory.

The Patrolman lay in the webbing as one exhausted. The blood on his cheek was clotting. His eyes were half closed.

"You have not won either," he said, his words slurred.

"We never wanted to win anything," I responded, "except our own freedom."

Then I felt a sudden strange sensation, a sharpening of contact—Eet's thoughts? NO! For the first time I touched, not Eet, in such communication, but another human brain directly.

I tried to break away. It had been hard at first to accept that Eet could so invade my mind at will. But somehow I had been able to stand it because he was alien. This was far different. I was being pushed against my will into a raging torrent which whirled me on and on. And even to this day I can find no proper words to express what happened. I learned what—who—Hory really was—as no man should ever know one of his fellows. It is too harsh a stripping, that. And he must have learned the same of me. I knew that he meant to bring me to his form of justice, that he looked upon me with scorn because of my association with Eet. I could see—and see—and see—and that enforced sharing went on forever and ever. I saw Hory not only as he was now, but as he had been back and back down a trail of years—all of which had formed him into the man he now was—just as he must also see me—

I fought vainly against the power which made me see so, for I feared I would be utterly lost in that other mind, that Hory was becoming me, and I Hory. And we would be so firmly welded together in the end that there would be no Hory and Jern, but some unnatural whirling mass fighting itself—trapped so—

Then I was released and flew out of the mind stream as if some whirlpool had thrust me off and out. I lay retching on the floor, aware again that I had a body, an identity of my own. I heard noises from the pilot's chair which suggested my sickness was shared, even as we had shared other things—too many of them.

Somehow I got to my hands and knees and crawled to the wall again, once more pulled myself up by holding to the equipment there. I faced around slowly to stare at Hory, while he looked back at me, dully, with a kind of shrinking.

Beyond him, on the floor, lay a small flaccid body—Eet!

Keeping hold on the wall, for without that support I was now helpless to move, I edged along until I passed Hory to stand above the mutant. Then I let go, fell to the floor rather than knelt, to gather up Eet's body and hold it tight against me. That same emotion which had moved me when Hory had tried to kill Eet in the engine room flooded through me once more. It strengthened me, shaking me completely out of my daze.

Eet had done that—had made us free of one another's minds. And he had done it for a purpose. I cradled Eet's too-limp body, smoothing his wiry fur, trying to discover some indication he still lived.

"You know," I said to Hory, "why—"

"I know—" His words came with long pauses between them. "Is—he—dead?"

I stroked and smoothed, tried to feel some light breathing, the pound of a heartbeat, but to no purpose. Even so, I could not allow myself to believe the worst.

However, I did not try to reach Eet's mind. Now I shrank painfully from such contact. I had wounds which must heal, the strangest wounds any of my species may ever have borne.

"The—aid—kit—" Hory's right hand rose, shaking badly. Yet he managed to point to a compartment in the far wall. "A stimulant—"

Perhaps. But how well medication intended for our breed would serve Eet I did not know. I worked up to my feet again, holding the mutant tightly to me, and began that long journey around the cabin. One-handed, I fumbled with the latch, snapped open the cubby. There was a box—in it a capsule. And that was slippery between my fingers, so I had to use care to bring it forth. One-handed, I could not crush it.

Holding it and Eet, I retraced my steps, bracing myself erect by one shoulder against the wall, back to Hory. I held out the capsule. He took it from me with trembling fingers while I steadied Eet's body. Hory broke the capsule under that pointed nose, released the fumes of the volatile gas. His hands fell back into his lap, as if even that small exertion had completely exhausted him.

Eet sneezed, gasped. His eyes opened and his head moved feebly as it turned so he could see who held him. He did not try to leave my hands.

Once more I gathered him close to me, so that the head, raised a little as if to welcome such contact, now rested on my shoulder close to my chin.

"He is alive," Hory whispered. "But he—did—that—"

"Yes."

"Because we must know—and knowing—" The Patrolman hesitated until I prompted:

"And knowing—what? You are wedded to your purposes. But you must know now that mine were not as you believed."

"Yes. But—I have my duty."

He gazed at me, but again as if he did not see me for what I was, but rather beyond, into some future.

"We are not meant—" He continued after a pause, "to know our own kind in that way. I do not want to see you now, it makes me—sick—" His mouth worked as if he were about to be physically ill.

My stomach churned in sympathy. He was right. To look at him and remember—Man is not vile—most men—nor depraved, nor monstrous. But neither is he meant to violate another as we had done. Having Eet as a conductor between our minds was one thing; to be directly joined—never again!

"It was meant that we might understand. Words can be screens—we needed free minds," I said. Were he to retreat now into a denial, an attempt to be as we were before, he would negate all Eet had done to save us. That I dared not allow.

"Yes. You—are—not as we thought." He appeared to make that concession against his will. "But—I have my orders—"

"We can bargain." I repeated Eet's earlier suggestion. "I have something to offer—a cache, untouched, of the stones. Did you read that also?" That was my one fear. That when my thoughts had been laid bare to him, he had uncovered all I needed, for the sake of the future, to hide.

"Not that." He turned his head away. Looking at me bothered him. "But the Guild—"

"Does not know of this one. Nor shall they find it." I could not be sure of that, I could only hope. However, I thought I had a right to argue.

"What do you want in return?"

I made my first offer as I did because there is no reason why one should not begin at the highest point, as every trader knows. "Freedom—to begin with. After that—well, I am a masterless man with Vondar Ustle gone—in a way he died for this. I want a ship—"

"Ship?" Hory repeated the word as if it were new to him. "You—a ship—?"

"Because I am no pilot?" I chose thus to interpret his surprise. "True, but pilots can be hired. I want payment—our freedom and credits enough to buy a ship. In return—the position of the cache. It seems to me the price is low—"

"I am not authorized to make any such bargains—"

"No?" And then I repeated two words, drawing them out of the time when we had been one.

He turned his head laboriously to look at me again, his face very cold and set.

"True—you know that also. So—" He added nothing, but closed his eyes.

I felt a soft bump against my chin as Eet moved his head, almost as if he nodded approval. Eet had been suspicious of Hory. He had reported a shield—had he suspected what might lie below that? Known that this was no simple scout but a Double Star Commander, sent on a special mission? Or had only suspicion been his before he hurled us mind to mind?

A Double Star, one of those whose word could be accepted at once in an agreement. If Hory did now so agree, we were safe.

"We get all the stones," he said. "That ring also."

My fingers had found the ring on Eet's limb; now they closed about it tightly. Not that! But Eet's head once more bumped my chin. He dared not use mind reach intelligible to Hory, but he was trying in this way to communicate. Without the ring—I could not—

I saw Hory's eyes glitter in rising triumph, and knew that he believed he had found my weak point and would thus regain control of the situation and us. In that moment I had the strength for our last battle of wills.

"The ring also—after an agreement is taped."

Hory hitched himself up, reached to the control board. He used his forefinger to release a print seal, bring out a treaty com. There was no mistaking its white and gold casing. And its very presence here told me of his importance among his command.

Now he held it to his lips. But he wet those with the tip of his tongue and hesitated a long moment before he began to dictate:

"In the name of the Council, the Four Confederacies, the Twelve Systems, the Inner and Outer Planets," he recited formally, as he must have done many times before, it came so easily to him, "this agreement shall hold by planet law and star law." He added figures which held no meaning for me but must have been an identification code. Once more he switched to words:

"Murdoc Jern, status, assistant gem buyer, late apprentice to Vondar Ustle, deceased, is hereby declared free of all charges made against him—"

"Erroneously," I prompted as he paused for breath.

"Erroneously," he agreed, not looking at me, but at the com in his hand. "In addition, free of all charges is one Eet, an alien mutant, now in association with Jern."

So now it was officially recognized that Eet was no animal but an intelligent entity coming under the protection of laws made for the defense of such.

"In return, Murdoc Jern agrees to release to the custody of the Patrol certain information, classified"—once more he rattled off a series of code numbers—"which is his. Accepted, sealed, coded by—" and he unemotionally gave that name which was not Hory, and certainly not on a roster of scouts.

"You have forgotten," I broke in sharply. "The bargain is also for compensation—"

For a moment I thought he would refuse even now. His eyes caught mine and I read in them a cold enmity which I knew would exist on his side for all time. He had been humbled here as he thought I had not, or rather he felt a humbling, though I had not in any way triumphed over him. For our embroilment had been mutual and if he felt invaded, was I any the less violated? Now I added:

"Was it any worse for you than for me?"

"Yes!" He made of that an oath. "I am who I am."

I supposed he meant his Double Star, his training, the fact that in the service he was above and beyond some regulations. But if he was a man who had climbed to that post, and the Patrol was as incorruptible as it claimed to be, then also he must be a man of some breadth of mind. I hoped that was true.

Yes, he had said, but now his eyes changed. There was still hatred for me in them, but perhaps he was a bigger man than he had been only moments earlier.

"No—perhaps it was not—" He was just.

"And there was to be compensation." I pressed my point. "After all, whether you accept it or not, we have been battle comrades—"

"To save yourselves!" was his quick retort.

"No more than yourself."

"Very well." Once more he raised the treaty com. "Murdoc Jern is to receive compensation in connection with his information, this to be set by a star court, not to fall below ten thousand credits, nor rise above fifteen."

Ten thousand credits—enough for a small ship of the older type. Again Eet's head moved. My comrade found that acceptable.

"Agreed to by Murdoc Jern." He held out the com and I bent my head to speak into it.

"I, Murdoc Jern, accept and agree—"

"The alien, Eet—" For the first time during this ceremony Hory was at a loss. How could a creature without vocal communication agree on an oral recording?

Eet moved. He swung his head toward the com and from his lips issued a weird sound, part the mew of a cat, yet holding some of the Basic "yes."

"So be it recorded." Hory's tone had the solemnity of a thumb seal pressed by some planet ruler before his court.

"Now"—he reached for another taper, taken from the same recess as the treaty com—"to your part."

I held it before my lips. "I, Murdoc Jern, do hereby surrender"—might as well get the worst done first—"into the hands of a duly registered member of the Patrol a ring set with an unknown stone, the gem having unusual and as yet unexplored possibilities. In addition I do hereby state that there are two caches of similar stones on a planet unknown to me by name. These can be found as follows—" And I launched into descriptions of the cache in the ruins and that of the vault.

The knowledge that he had been so close to both and had not realized it must have been bitter to Hory. But he did not reveal his feelings. Now that his true identity was known he was a different man, one lacking the more emotional reactions of Hory the scout. When I had described both caches and their locations to the best of my ability, I handed the tape mike back. He took it from me as if he feared to touch my fingers, as if I were unclean.

"There is a passenger cabin to the left of the galley," he said remotely, not ordering me to it, but making his desire plain. And I wanted his company no more than he wanted mine.

I descended the ladder wearily, Eet riding in his old place on my shoulders. But before we had gone the mutant had shaken the ring loose, to leave it lying on the edge of the control board. I did not want to look at it again. Perhaps Hory locked it away with the tapes—I did not want to know.

The passenger cabin was small and bare. I lay down on the bunk. But though my body ached for rest I could not quiet my mind. I had given up the ring, the small knowledge I had of the caches. In return I had our freedom and enough to buy a ship—

Buy a ship? Why—why had I asked for that? I was no pilot, I had no reason to want a ship of my own. But ten thousand credits could be used—

"To buy a ship!" Eet answered.

"But I do not want—or need—and cannot use a ship!"

"You will—all three." His reply was assured. "Do you think I went close to ending my being to earn us anything else? We shall have a ship—"

I was too tired to argue. "To what purpose?"

"That shall be discussed at the proper time."

"But—who is to pilot it?"

"Do not dwell so much on the skills you have not; consider rather those you have. There is something else—look within the inner pocket where you carry what is left of your gems."

It had been so long since I had thought of that poor store, a most meager base for the future, that I could not guess what he meant. I fingered that inner pouch and the stones in it moved under my touch. I loosed the seal to turn out the sorry collection. Among them was—I snatched at it and between thumb and forefinger I held a zero stone in its lifeless phase.

"But—!"

Eet read my thought. "You have broken no oath. You surrendered exactly what you promised—the ring and the location of the caches. If another has seen to a better bargain for you—accept it without question."

Hory—above—could he tune in on our exchange? Would he now know what I had?

Eet was plainly alert to the same danger. "He sleeps. He was close to the end of his strength though he did not reveal that to you. But do not mention this again. Not until we are free."

I dropped the stone among the others—all the bits from my wanderings. To the uninitiated it would certainly seem worth no more than, perhaps not as much as, the rest. Eet's cleverness needed no comment.

Then I, too, surrendered to sleep. And sleep I did, off and on for much of the rest of the voyage. But at times Eet and I talked together. Not of the stones, but rather of other worlds, and I reviewed my gem knowledge. I had none of Vondar's prestige, but I knew his methods of trade. And were I to have a ship, there was no reason why I could not continue on my own. Eet encouraged me in such speculations, leading me on to discuss my chances. I was glad to turn my thoughts from the past, and perhaps it gave me some pleasure to play the informant and instructor. For this was one field in which Eet lagged behind.

But there came a time when I was interrupted by a sharp order over the ship's com. We were nearing the base port, it was necessary to strap down for landing. And Hory continued, saying that I would find my cabin a temporary prison until he could make the proper arrangements. I would have protested, but Eet's shake of the head counseled discretion.

The mutant had a listening attitude after we set down. And I heard the clang of boot plates on the ladder, passing my cabin. Eet became communicative when their echoes died away.

"He is out of the ship. And he will carry out his part of the bargain. He takes with him the ring, to put it in safekeeping—as I had hoped. Now it will not betray you should you pass near it with the other stone."

"Why did it not do that in the cabin?"

"It did. But at that time you were too occupied otherwise to notice. Get free of these Patrolmen as fast as you can. Then we shall be about our own business—"

"That being?"

Eet was amused. "Gem hunting—what else? I told you that world was not the source of the stones. The Guild and the Patrol will believe so for some time. They will search, they will mine. But they shall not find what they seek. We have only sniffed out the first few steps on a long cold trail. But we have what will serve us as a guide."

"You mean—we are to keep on hunting the zero stones? But how? Space is very wide—there are many worlds—"

"Which makes our quest only the more worth the trying. I tell you—we are meant to do this thing."

"Eet—who—what are you? Did you—were you of the people who owned the stones?"

"I am Eet," he replied with his old arrogance. "That is all that means aught in this life. But if it troubles you—no, I was not of those who used the stones."

"But you know much of them—"

He interrupted me. "The Patrolman is returning; he brings others. They are angry, but they will hold by

Hory's bargain. However, walk softly. They would be only too pleased to have some reason to pull you down."

I faced the door as it opened. Hory stood there, with him another, wearing a uniform with signs of high rank. Both men watched me with cold and wary eyes, their antagonism like a blow. Eet was very right, they would like nothing better than to get me by some infraction. I must walk as warily as in a quaking swamp.

"You will come with us. The bargain will be kept." The officer with Hory spoke as if it hurt him. "But for your own protection you will be in maximum security while you are here."

There was a spark in Hory's eyes. "We can keep you safe. The arm of the Guild is long, it can reach far, but *not* into a Patrol base."

So he made clear his thoughts. I had had two enemies. I might have now dealt successfully with one, but there was still the second. My hand wanted to cup over the stones in my inner pocket. Would the zero stone only lead me further and further into danger? I remembered my father and Vondar—and the legendary might of the Guild.

However, who may seize upon time and hold it fast, not allowing the moments to slip by him? I had said I was not a gambler. But Fortune appeared determined to make me one. With Eet warm and heavy about my shoulders, and the future, misty and threatened as it was, before me, I left the cabin to walk into a new slice of life.

Perhaps I went better armed and armored than I had once been; the sum of a man's knowledge may change from day to day, and experience is both sword and buckler. As long as Eet and I walked the same road, free under the stars, then could the present be savored, and let the future take care for itself—After all, what man can influence that knowingly?

I found it enough to have this hour, this day, this small moment, as a victory over odds which I now marveled at our facing. Perhaps I was true son to Hywel Jern in spirit if not body. And still I could cup hand at my will across a zero stone. The door of the cabin was open. So was that of life, and I had not yet found its limit.

UNCHARTED STARS

For Patrick Terry
because he has been kind enough
to approve my work

ONE

It was like any other caravansary at a space port, not providing quarters for a Veep or some off-planet functionary, but not for a belt as sparsely packed with credits as mine was at that moment either. My fingers twitched and I got a cold chill in my middle every time my thoughts strayed to how flat that belt was at present. But there is such a thing as face, or prestige, whatever name you want to give it, and that I must have now or fail completely. And my aching feet, my depressed spirits told me that I was already at the point where one surrendered hope and waited for the inevitable blow to fall. That blow could only fell me in one direction. I would lose what I had played the biggest gamble of my life to win—a ship now sitting on its tail fins in a field I could have sighted from this hotel had I been a Veep and able to afford one of the crown tower rooms with actual windows.

One may be able to buy a ship, but thereafter it sits eating up more and more credits in ground fees, field service—more costs than my innocence would have believed possible a planet month earlier. And one cannot lift off world until he has a qualified pilot at the controls, the which I was not, and the which I had not been able to locate.

It had all sounded so easy in the beginning. My thinking had certainly been clouded when I had plunged into this. No—been plunged! Now I centered my gaze on the door which was the entrance to what I could temporarily call "home," and I had very unkind thoughts, approaching the dire, about the partner waiting me behind it.

The past year had certainly not been one to soothe my nerves, or lead me to believe that providence smiled sweetly at me. It had begun as usual. I, Murdoc Jern, had been going about my business in the way any roving gem buyer's apprentice would. Not that our lives, mine and my master Vondar Ustle's, had been without exciting incident. But on Tanth, in the spin of a diabolical "sacred" arrow, everything had broken apart as if a laser ray had been used to sever me not only from Vondar but from any peace of mind or body.

When the sacrifice arrow of the green-robed priests had swung to a stop between Vondar and me, we had not feared; off-worlders were not meat to satisfy their demonic master. Only we had been jumped by the tavern crowd, probably only too glad to see a choice which had not included one of them. Vondar had died from a knife thrust and I had been hunted down the byways of that dark city, to claim sanctuary in the hold of another of their grisly godlings. From there I had, I thought, paid my way for escape on a Free Trader.

But I had only taken a wide stride from a stinking morass into a bush fire—since my rise into space had started me on a series of adventures so wild that, had another recited them to me, I would have thought them the product of fash-smoke breathing, or something he had heard from a story tape.

Suffice it that I was set adrift in space itself, along with a companion whose entrance into my time and space was as weird as his looks. He was born rightly enough, in the proper manner, out of a ship's cat. Only his father was a black stone, or at least several men trained to observe the unusual would state that. Eet and I had been drawn by the zero stone—the zero stone! One might well term that the seed of all disorder!

I had seen it first in my father's hands—dull, lifeless, set in a great ring meant to be worn over the bulk of a space glove. It had been found on the body of an alien on an unknown asteroid. And how long dead its suited owner was might be anyone's guess—up to and including a million years on the average planet. That it had a secret, my father knew, and its fascination held him. In fact, he died to keep it as a threatening heritage for me.

It was the zero stone on my own gloved hand which had drawn me, and Eet, through empty space to a drifting derelict which might or might not have been the very ship its dead owner had once known. And from that a lifeboat had taken us to a world of forest and ruins, where, to keep our secret and our lives, we had fought both the Thieves' Guild (which my father must have defied, though he had once been a respected member of its upper circles) and the Patrol.

Eet had found one cache of the zero stones. By chance we both stumbled on another. And that one was weird enough to make a man remember it for the rest of his days, for it had been carefully laid up in a temporary tomb shared by the bodies of more than one species of alien, as if intended to pay their passage home to distant and unknown planets of origin. And we knew part of their secret. Zero stones had the power to boost any energy they contacted, and they would also home on their fellows, activating such in turn. But that the planet we had landed upon by chance was the source of the stones, Eet denied.

We used the caches for bargaining, not with the Guild, but with the Patrol, and we came out of the deal with credits for a ship of our own, plus—very sourly given—clean records and our freedom to go as we willed.

Our ship was Eet's suggestion. Eet, a creature I could crush in my two hands (sometimes I thought that solution was an excellent one for me), had an invisible presence which towered higher than any Veep I had ever met. In part, his feline mother had shaped him, though I sometimes speculated as to whether his physical appearance did not continue to change subtly. He was furred, though his tail carried only a ridge of that covering down it. But his feet were bare-skinned and his forepaws were small hands which he could use to purposes which proved them more akin to my palms and fingers than a feline's paws. His ears were small and set close to his head, his body elongated and sinuous.

But it was his mind, not the body he informed me had been "made" for him, which counted. Not only was he telepathic, but the knowledge which abode in his memory, and which he gave me in bits and pieces, must have rivaled the lore of the famed Zacathan libraries, which are crammed with centuries of learning.

Who—or what—Eet was he would never say. But that I would ever be free of him again I greatly doubted. I could resent his calm dictatorship, which steered me on occasion, but there was a fascination (I sometimes speculated as to whether this was deliberately used to entangle me, but if it was a trap it had been very skillfully constructed) which kept me his partner. He had told me many times our companionship was needful, that I provided one part, he the other, to make a greater whole. And I had to admit that it was through him we had come out of our brush with Patrol and Guild as well as we had—with a zero stone still in our possession.

For it was Eet's intention, which I could share at more optimistic times, to search out the source of the stones. Some small things I had noted on the unknown planet of the caches made me sure that Eet knew more about the unknown civilization or confederation which had first used the stones than he had told me. And he was right in that the man who had the secret of their source could name his own price—always providing he could manage to market that secret without winding up knifed, burned, or disintegrated in some messy fashion before he could sell it properly.

We had found a ship in a break-down yard maintained by a Salarik who knew bargaining as even my late master (whom I had heretofore thought unbeatable) did not. I will admit at once that without Eet I would not have lasted ten planet minutes against such skill and would have issued forth owning the most battered junk the alien had sitting lopsidedly on rusting fins. But the Salariki are feline-ancestered, and perhaps Eet's cat mother gave him special insight into the other's mind. The result was we emerged with a useful ship.

It was old, it had been through changes of registry many times, but it was, Eet insisted, sound. And it was small enough for the planet hopping we had in mind. Also, it was, when Eet finished bargaining, within the price we could pay, which in the end included its being serviced for space and moved to the port ready for takeoff.

But there it had sat through far too many days, lacking a pilot. Eet might have qualified had he inhabited a body humanoid enough to master the controls. I had never yet come to the end of any branch of knowledge in my companion, who might evade a direct answer to be sure, but whose supreme confidence always led me to believe that he *did* have the correct one.

It was now a simple problem: We had a ship but no pilot. We were piling up rental on the field and we could not lift. And we were very close to the end of that small sum we had left after we paid for the ship. Such gems as remained in my belt were not enough to do more than pay for a couple more days' reckoning at the caravansary, if I could find a buyer. And that was another worry to tug at my mind.

As Vondar's assistant and apprentice, I had met many of the major gem buyers on scores of planets. But it was to Ustle that they opened their doors and gave confidence. When I dealt on my own I might find the prospect bleak, unless I drifted into what was so often the downfall of the ambitious, the fringes of the black market which dealt in stolen gems or those with dubious pasts. And there I would come face to face with the Guild, a prospect which was enough to warn me off even more than a desire to keep my record clean.

I had not found a pilot. Resolutely now I pushed my worries back into the immediate channel. Deal with one thing at a time, and that, the one facing you. We had to have a pilot to lift, and we *had* to lift soon, very soon, or lose the ship before making a single venture into space with her.

None of the reputable hiring agencies had available a man who would be willing—at our wages—to ship out on what would seem a desperate venture, the more so when I could not offer any voyage bond. This left the rejects, men black-listed by major lines, written off agency books for some mistake or crime. And to find such a one I must go down into the Off-port, that part of the city where even the Patrol and local police went on sufferance and in couples, where the Guild ruled. To call attention to myself there was asking for a disagreeable future—kidnapping, mind scanning, all the other illegal ways of gaining my knowledge. The Guild had a long and accurate memory.

There was a third course. I could throw up everything—turn on my heel and walk away from the door I was about to activate by thumb pressure on personal seal, take a position in one of the gem shops (if I could find one), forget Eet's wild dream. Even throw the stone in my belt into the nearest disposal to remove the last temptation. In fact, become as ordinary and lawabiding a citizen as I could.

I was greatly tempted. But I was enough of a Jern not to yield. Instead I set thumb to the door and at the same time beamed a thought before me in greeting. As far as I knew, the seals in any caravansary, once set to individual thumbprints, could not be fooled. But there can always be a first time, and the Guild is notorious for buying up or otherwise acquiring new methods of achieving results which even the Patrol does not suspect have been discovered. If we had been traced here, then there just might be a reception committee waiting beyond. So I tried mind-touch with Eet for reassurance.

What I got kept me standing where I was, thumb to doorplate, bewildered, then suspicious. Eet was there. I received enough to be sure of that. We had been mind-coupled long enough for even tenuous linkage to be clear to my poorer human senses. But now Eet was withdrawn, concentrating elsewhere. My fumbling attempts to communicate failed.

Only it was not preoccupation with danger, no warn-off. I pressed my thumb down and watched the door roll back into the wall, intent on what lay beyond.

The room was small, not the cubby of a freeze-class traveler, but certainly not the space of a Veep suite. The various fixtures were wall-folded. And now the room was unusually empty, for apparently Eet had sent every chair, as well as the table, desk, and bed, back into the walls, leaving the carpeted floor bare, a single bracket light going.

A circle of dazzling radiance was cast by that (I noted at once that it had been set on the highest frequency and a small portion of my mind began calculating how many minutes of that overpower would be added to our bill). Then I saw what was set squarely under it and I was really startled.

As was true of all port caravansaries, this one catered to tourists as well as business travelers. In the lobby was a shop—charging astronomical prices—where one could buy a souvenir or at least a present for one's future host or some member of the family. Most of it was, as always, a parade of eye-catching local handicrafts to prove one had been on Theba, with odds and ends of exotic imports from other planets to attract the attention of the less sophisticated traveler.

There were always in such shops replicas of the native fauna, in miniature for the most part. Some were carved as art, others wrought in furs or fabrics to create a very close likeness of the original, often life-size for smaller beasts, birds, or what-is-its.

What sat now in the full beam of the lamp was a stuffed pookha. It was native to Theba. I had lingered by a pet shop (intrigued in spite of my worries) only that morning to watch three live pookhas. And I could well understand their appeal. They were, even in the stuffed state, luxury items of the first class.

This one was not much larger than Eet when he drew his long thin body together in a hunched position, but it was of a far different shape, being chubby and plump and with the instant appeal to my species that all its kind possess. Its plushy fur was a light green-gray with a faint mottling which gave it the appearance of the watered brocade woven on Astrudia. Its forepaws were bluntly rounded pads, unclawed, though it was well provided with teeth, which in live pookhas were used for crushing their food—tich leaves. The head was round with no visible ears, but between the points where ears might normally be, from one side of that skull-ball to the other, there stood erect a broad mane of whisker growth fanning out in fine display. The eyes were very large and green, of a shade several tints darker than its fur. It was life-size and very handsome—also very, very expensive. And how it had come here I did not have the slightest idea. I would have moved forward to examine it more closely but a sharp crack of thought from Eet froze me where I stood. It was not a concrete message but a warning not to interfere.

Interfere in what? I looked from the stuffed pookha to my roommate. Though I had been through much with Eet and had thought I had learned not to be surprised at any action of my alien companion, he now succeeded very well in startling me.

He was, as I had seen, hunched on the floor just beyond the circle of intense light cast by the lamp. And he was staring as intently at the toy as if he had been watching the advance of some enemy.

Only Eet was no longer entirely Eet. His slim, almost reptilian body was not only hunched into a contracted position but actually appeared to have become plumper and shorter, aping most grotesquely the outward contours of the pookha. In addition, his dark fur had lightened, held a greenish sheen.

Totally bewildered, yet fascinated by what was occurring before my unbelieving eyes, I watched him turn into a pookha, altering his limbs, head shape, color, and all the rest. Then he shuffled into the light and squatted by the toy to face me. His thought rang loudly in my head.

"Well?"

"You are that one." I pointed a finger, but I could not be sure. To the last raised whisker of crest, the last tuft of soft greenish fur, Eet was twin to the toy he had copied.

"Close your eyes!" His order came so quickly I obeyed without question.

A little irritated, I immediately opened them again, to confront once more two pookhas. I guessed his intent, that I should again choose between them. But to my closest survey there was no difference between the toy and Eet, who had settled without any visible signs of life into the same posture. I put out my hand at last and lifted the nearest, to discover I had the model. And I felt Eet's satisfaction and amusement.

"Why?" I demanded.

"I am unique." Was there a trace of complacency in that remark? "So I would be recognized, remarked upon. It is necessary that I assume another guise."

"But how did you do this?"

He sat back on his haunches. I had gone down on my knees to see him the closer, once more setting the toy beside him and looking from one to the other for some small difference, though I could see none.

"It is a matter of mind." He seemed impatient. "How little you know. Your species is shut into a shell of your own contriving, and I see little signs of your struggling to break out of it." This did not answer my question very well. I still refused to accept the fact that Eet, in spite of all he had been able to do in the past, could *think* himself into a pookha.

He caught my train of thought easily enough. "Think myself into a hallucination of a pookha," he corrected in that superior manner I found irking.

"Hallucination!" Now *that* I could believe. I had never seen it done with such skill and exactitude, but there were aliens who dealt in such illusions with great effect and I had heard enough factual tales of such to believe that it could be done, and that one receptive to such influences and patterns could be made to see as they willed. Was it because I had so long companied Eet and at times been under his domination that I was so deceived now? Or would the illusion he had spun hold for others also?

"For whom and as long as I wish," he snapped in reply to my unasked question. "Tactile illusion as well—feel!" He thrust forth a furred forelimb, which I touched. Under my fingers it was little different from the toy, except that it had life and was not just fur laid over stuffing.

"Yes." I sat back on my heels, convinced. Eet was right, as so often he was—often enough to irritate a less logical being such as I. In his own form Eet was strange enough to be noticed, even in a space port, where there is always a coming and going of aliens and unusual pets. He could furnish a clue to our stay here. I had never underrated the Guild or their spy system.

But if they had a reading on Eet, then how much more so they must have me imprinted on their search tapes! I had been their quarry long before I met Eet, ever since after my father's murder, when someone must have guessed that I had taken from his plundered office the zero stone their man had not found. They had set up the trap which had caught Vondar Ustle but not me. And they had laid another trap on the Free Trader, one which Eet had foiled, although I did not know of it until later. On the planet of ruins they had actually held me prisoner until Eet again freed me. So they had had innumerable chances of taping me for their hounds—a fact which was frightening to consider.

"You will think yourself a cover." Eet's calm order cut across my uneasiness.

"I cannot! Remember, I am of a limited species—" I struck back with the baffled anger that realization of my plight aroused in me.

"You have only the limits you yourself set," Eet returned unruffled. "Perceive—"

He waddled on his stumpy pookha legs to the opposite side of the room, and as suddenly flowed back into Eet again, stretching his normal body up against the wall at such a lengthening as I would not have believed even his supple muscles and flesh capable of. With one of his paw-hands he managed to touch a button and the wall provided us with a mirror surface. In that I saw myself.

I am not outstanding in any way. My hair is darkish brown, which is true of billions of males of Terran stock. I have a face which is wide across the eyes, narrowing somewhat to the chin, undistinguished for either good looks or downright ugliness. My eyes are green-brown, and my brows, black, as are my lashes. As a merchant who travels space a great deal, I had had my beard permanently eradicated when it first showed. A beard in a space helmet is unpleasant. And for the same reason, I wear my hair cropped short. I am of medium height as my race goes, and I have all the right number of limbs and organs for my own species. I could be anyone— except that the identification patterns the Guild might hold on me could go deeper and be far more searching than a glance at a passing stranger.

Eet flowed back across the room with his usual liquid movement, made one of his effortless springs to my shoulder, and settled down in position behind my neck, his head resting on top of mine, his hand-paws flat on either side of my skull just below my ears.

"Now!" he commanded. "Think of another face—anyone's—"

When so ordered I found that I could not—at first. I looked into the mirror and my reflection was all that was there. I could feel Eet's impatience and that made it even more difficult for me to concentrate. Then that impatience faded and I guessed that he was willing it under control.

"Think of another." He was less demanding, more coaxing. "Close your eyes if you must—"

I did, trying to summon up some sort of picture in my mind—a face which was not my own. Why I settled for Faskel I could not say, but somehow my foster brother's unliked countenance swam out of memory and I concentrated upon it.

It was not clear but I persevered, setting up the long narrow outline—the nose as I had last seen it, jutting out over a straggle of lip-grown hair. Faskel Jern had been my father's true son, while I was but one by adoption. Yet it had always seemed that I was Hywel Jern's son in spirit and Faskel the stranger. I put the purplish scar on Faskel's forehead near his hairline, added the petulant twist of lips which had been his usual expression when facing me in later years, and held to the whole mental picture with determination.

"Look!"

Obediently I opened my eyes to the mirror. And for several startled seconds I looked at someone. He was certainly not me—nor was he Faskel as I remembered him, but an odd, almost distorted combination of us both. It was a sight I did not in the least relish. My head was still gripped in the vise maintained by Eet's hold and I could not turn away. But as I watched, the misty Faskel faded and I was myself again.

"You see—it can be done," was Eet's comment as he released me and flowed down my body to the floor.

"You did it."

"Only in part. There has been, with my help, a break-through. Your species use only a small fraction of your brain. You are content to do so. This wastage should shame you forever. Practice will aid you. And with a new face you will not have to fear going where you can find a pilot."

"If we ever can." I push-buttoned a chair out of the wall and sat down with a sigh. My worries were a heavy burden. "We shall have to take a black-listed man if we get any."

"Ssssss—" No sound, only an impression of one in my mind. Eet had flashed to the door of the room, was crouched against it, his whole attitude one of strained listening, as if all his body, not just his ear, served him for that purpose.

I could hear nothing, of course. These rooms were completely screened and soundproofed. And I could use a hall-and-wall detect if I wished to prove it so. Space-port caravansaries were the few places where one could be truly certain of not being overlooked, overheard, or otherwise checked upon.

But their guards were not proofed against such talents as Eet's, and I guessed from his attitude not only that he was suspicious of what might be arriving outside but that it was to be feared. Then he turned and I caught his thought. I moved to snap over a small luggage compartment and he folded himself into hiding there in an instant. But his thoughts were not hidden.

"Patrol snoop on his way—coming here," he warned, and it was alert enough to prepare me.

TWO

As yet, the visitor's light had not flashed above the door. I moved, perhaps not with Eet's speed, but fast enough, to snap the room's furnishings out and in place so that the compartment would look normal even to the searching study of a trained Patrolman. The Patrol, jealous of its authority after long centuries of supremacy as the greatest law-enforcement body in the galaxy, had neither forgotten nor forgiven the fact that Eet and I had been able to prove them wrong in their too-quick declaration of my outlawry (I had indeed been framed by the Guild). That we had dared, actually dared, to strike a bargain and keep them to it, galled them bitterly. We had rescued their man, saved his skin and his ship for him in the very teeth of the Thieves' Guild. But he had fought bitterly against the idea that we did have the power to bargain and that he had to yield on what were practically our terms. Even now the method of that bargaining made me queasy, for Eet had joined us mind to mind with ruthless dispatch. And such an invasion, mutual as it was, left a kind of unhealed wound.

I have heard it stated that the universe is understood by each species according to the sensory equipment of the creature involved, or rather, the meaning it attaches to the reports of those exploring and testing senses. Therefore, while *our* universe, as we see it, may be akin to that of an animal, a bird, an alien, it still differs. There are barriers set mercifully in place (and I say mercifully after tasting what can happen when such a barrier goes down) to limit one's conception of the universe to what he is prepared to accept. Shared minds between human and human is not one of the sensations we are fitted to endure. The Patrolman and I had learned enough—too much—of each other to know that a bargain could be made and kept. But I think I would face a laser unarmed before I would undergo that again.

Legally the Patrol had nothing against us, except suspicions perhaps and their own dislike for what we had dared. And I think that they were in a measure pleased that if they had to swear truce, the Guild still held us as a target. And it might well be that once we had lifted from the Patrol base we had been regarded as expendable bait for some future trap in which to catch a Veep of the Guild—a thought which heated me more than a little every time it crossed my mind.

I gave a last hurried glance around the room as the warn light flashed on, and then went to thumb the peephole. What confronted my eye was a wrist, around which was locked, past all counterfeiting, the black and silver of a Patrol badge. I opened the door.

"Yes?" I allowed my real exasperation to creep into my voice as I fronted him.

He was not in uniform, wearing rather the ornate, form-fitting tunic of an inner-world tourist. On him, as the Patrol must keep fit, it looked better than it did on most of the flabby, paunchy specimens I had seen in these halls. But that was not saying much, for its extreme of fashion was too gaudy and fantastic to suit my eyes.

"Gentle Homo Jern—" He did not make a question of my name, and his eyes were more intent on the room behind me than on meeting mine.

"The same. You wish?"

"To speak with you—privately." He moved forward and involuntarily I gave a step before I realized that he had no right to enter. It was the prestige of the badge he wore which won him that first slight advantage and he made the most of it. He was in, with the door rolled into place behind him, before I was prepared to resist.

"We are private. Speak." I did not gesture him to a chair, nor make a single hospitable move.

"You are having difficulty in finding a pilot." He looked at me about half the time now, the rest of his attention still given to the room.

"I am." There was no use in denying a truth which was apparent.

Perhaps he did not believe in wasting time either, for he came directly to the point.

"We can deal—"

That really surprised me. Eet and I had left the Patrol base with the impression that the powers there were gleefully throwing us forth to what they believed certain disaster with the Guild. The only explanation which came to me at the moment was that they had speedily discovered that the information we had given them concerning the zero stones had consisted of the whereabouts of caches only and they suspected the true source was still our secret. In fact, we knew no more than we had told them.

"What deal?" I parried and dared not mind-touch Eet at that moment, much as I wanted his reception to this suggestion. No one knows what secret equipment the Patrol has access to. And it might well be that, knowing Eet was telepathic, they had some ingenious method of monitoring our exchange.

"Sooner or later," he said deliberately, almost as if he savored it, "the Guild is going to close in upon you—"

But I was ready, having thought that out long ago. "So I am bait, and you want me for some trap of yours."

He was not in the least disconcerted. "One way of putting it."

"And the right way. What do you want to do, plant one of your men in our ship?"

"As protection for you and, of course, to alert us."

"Very altruistic. But the answer is no." The Patrol's highhanded method of using pawns made me aware that there was something to being their opponent.

"You cannot find a pilot."

"I am beginning to wonder"—and at that moment I was—"how much my present difficulty may be due to the influence of your organization."

He neither affirmed nor denied it. But I believe I was right. Just as a pilot might be black-listed, so had our ship been, before we had even had a chance for a first voyage. No one who wanted to preserve his legal license would sign our log now. So I must turn to the murky outlaw depths if I was to have any luck at all. I would see the ship rust away on its landing fins before I would raise with a Patrol nominee at her controls.

"The Guild can provide you with a man as easily, if you try to hire an off-rolls man, and you will not know it," he remarked, as if he were very sure that I would eventually be forced to accept his offer.

That, too, was true. But not if I took Eet with me on any search. Even if the prospective pilot had been brainwashed and blanked to hide his true affiliation, my companion would be able to read that fact. But that, I hoped, my visitor and those who had sent him did not know. That Eet was telepathic we could not hide—but Eet himself—

"I will make my own mistakes," I allowed myself to snap.

"And die from them," he replied indifferently. He took one last glance at the room and suddenly smiled. "Toys now—I wonder why." With a swoop as quick and sure as that of a harpy hawk he was down and up again, holding the pookha by its whisker mane. "Quite an expensive toy, too, Jern. And you must be running low in funds, unless you have tapped a river running with credits. Now why, I wonder, would you want a stuffed pookha."

I grimaced in return. "Always provide my visitors with a minor mystery. You figure it out. In fact, take it with you—just to make sure it is not a smuggling cover. It might just be, you know. I am a gem buyer—what better way to get some stones off world than in a play pookha's innards?"

Whether he thought my explanation was as lame as it seemed to me I do not know. But he tossed the toy onto the nearest chair and then, on his way to the door, spoke over his shoulder. "Dial 1–0, Jern, when you have stopped battering your head against a stone wall. And we shall have a man for you, one guaranteed not to sign you over to the Guild."

"No—just to the Patrol," I countered. "When I am ready to be bait, I shall tell you."

He made no formal farewell, just went. I closed the door sharply behind him and was across the room to let Eet out as quickly as I could. My alien companion sat back on his haunches, absent-mindedly smoothing the fur on his stomach.

"They think that they have us." I tried to jolt him—though he must already have picked up everything pertinent from our visitor's mind, unless the latter had worn a shield.

"Which he did," Eet replied to my suspicion. "But not wholly adequate, only what your breed prepares against the mechanical means of detecting thought waves. They are not," he continued complacently, "able to operate against my type of talent. But yes, they believe that they have us sitting on the palm of a hand"—he stretched out his own—"and need only curl their fingers, so—" His clawed digits bent to form a fist. "Such ignorance! However, it will be well, I believe, to move swiftly now that we know the worst."

"Do we?" I asked morosely as I hustled out my flight bag and began to pack. That it was not intelligent to stay where we were with Patrol snoops about, I could well understand. But where we would go next—

"To the Diving Lokworm," Eet replied as if the answer was plain and he was amused that I had not guessed it for myself.

For a moment I was totally adrift. The name he mentioned meant nothing, though it suggested one of those dives which filled the murky shadows of the wrong side of the port, the last place in the world where any sane man would venture with the Guild already sniffing for him.

But at present I was more intent on getting out of this building without being spotted by a Patrol tail. I rolled up my last clean undertunic and counted out three credit disks. In a transit lodging, one's daily charges are conspicuous each morning on a small wall plate. And no one can beat the instant force field which locks the room if one does not erase these charges when the scanner below says he is departing. The room might be insured for privacy in other ways, but there are precautions the owners are legally allowed to install.

I dropped the credits into the slot under the charge plate and that winked out. Thus reassured I could get out, I must now figure how. When I turned, it was to see that Eet was again a pookha. For a moment I hesitated, not quite sure which of the furry creatures was my companion until he moved out to be picked up.

With Eet in the crook of one arm and my bag in my other hand, I went out into the corridor after a quick look told me it was empty. When I turned toward the down grav shaft Eet spoke:

"Left and back!"

I obeyed. His directions took me where I did not know the territory, bringing me to another grav shaft, that which served the robos who took care of the rooms. There might be scanners here, even though I had paid my bill. This was an exit intended only for machines and one of them rumbled along toward us now.

It was a room-service feeder, a box on wheels, its top studded with call buttons for a choice of meal. I had to squeeze back against the wall to let it by, since this back corridor had never been meant for the human and alien patrons of the caravansary.

"On it!" Eet ordered.

I had no idea what he intended, but I had been brought out of tight corners enough in the past to know that he generally did have some saving plan in mind. So I swung Eet, my bag, and myself to the table top of the feeder, trying to take care that I did not trigger any of the buttons.

My weight apparently was nothing to the machine. It did not pause in its steady roll down the remainder of the corridor. But I was tense and stiff, striving to preserve my balance on this box where there was nothing to grip for safety.

When it moved without pause off the floor and onto the empty air of the grav shaft I could have cried out. But the grav supported its weight and it descended as evenly under me as if it had been a lift platform bringing luggage and passengers out of a liner at the port. A sweeper joined us at the next level, but apparently the machines were equipped with avoid rays, as they did not bump, but kept from scraping against each other. Above and below us, in the dusk of the shaft, I could see other robo-servers descending, as if this was the time when they were through their morning work.

We came down floor by floor, I counting them as we passed, a little more relieved with each one we left behind, knowing that we were that much nearer our goal. But when we reached ground level we faced only blank surface, and my support continued to descend.

The end was some distance below the surface, at least equal, I believed, to three floors above. And the feeder, with us still aboard, rolled out in pitch dark, where the sounds of clanging movement kept me frozen. Nor did Eet suggest any answer to this.

I did gain enough courage to bring out a hand beamer and flash it about us, only to gain disturbing glimpses of machines scuttling hither and thither across a wide expanse of floor. Nor were there any signs of human tenders.

I was now afraid to dismount from my carrier, not knowing whether the avoid rays of the various busy robos would also keep them from running me down. To this hour I had always taken the service department of a caravansary for granted and such an establishment as this I had never imagined.

That the feeder seemed to know just where it was going was apparent, for it rolled purposefully on until we reached a wall with slits in it. The machine locked to one of these and I guessed that the refuse and disposable dishes were being deposited in some sort of refuse system. Not only the feeder was clamped there. Beyond was a sweeper, also dumping its cargo.

A flash of my beamer showed that the wall did not reach the roof, so there might be a passage along its top to take us out of the paths of the roving machines—though such a way might well lead to a dead end.

I stood up cautiously on the feeder, and Eet took the beamer between his stubby pookha paws. The bag was easy to toss to the top of the wall, my furry companion less so, since his new body did not lend itself well to such feats. However, once aloft, he squatted, holding the beamer in his mouth, his teeth gripping more easily than his paws.

With that as my guide I leaped and caught the top of the wall, though I was afraid for a moment my fingers would slip from its slick surface. Then I made an effort which seemed enough to tear my muscles, and drew my whole body up on an unpleasantly narrow surface.

Not only was it narrow but it throbbed and vibrated under me, and I mentally pictured some form of combustion reducing the debris dumped in, or else a conveyer belt running on into a reducer of such refuse.

Above me, near enough to keep me hunched on my hams, was the roof of the place. A careful use of the beamer showed me that the wall on which I crouched ran into a dark opening in another wall met at right angles, as if it were a path leading into a cave.

For want of a better solution I began to edge along, dragging my bag, my destination that hole. Luckily Eet did not need my assistance but balanced on his wide pookha feet behind me.

When I reached that opening I found it large enough to give me standing room in a small cubby. The beam lighted a series of ladder steps bolted to the wall, as though this was an inspection site visited at intervals by a human maintenance man. Blessing my luck, I was ready to try that ladder, for the clanging din of the rushing machines, the whir of their passing rung in my ears, making me dizzy. The sooner I was out of their domain the better.

Eet's paws were not made for climbing, and I wondered if he would loose the disguise for the attempt. I had no desire to carry him; in fact I did not see how I could.

But if he could release the disguise he was not choosing to do so. Thus, in the end, I had to sling the bag on my back by its carrying strap and loosen my tunic to form a sling, with Eet crawling part-way down inside my collar at my shoulders. Both burdens interfered cruelly with my balance as I began to climb. And I had had to put away the beamer, not being conveniently endowed with a third hand.

For the moment all I wanted was to get out of the dark country of the robo-servers, even though I was climbing into the unknown. Perhaps I had come to depend too much on Eet's warnings against approaching dangers. But he had not communicated with me since we had taken transport on the feeder.

"Eet, what is ahead?" I sent that demand urgently as I became aware of just what might lie ahead of us.

"Nothing—yet." But his mind-send was faint, as a voiced whisper might be, or as if most of his mind was occupied with some other pressing problem.

I found, a second or two later, the end of the ladder, as my hand, rising to grope for a new hold, struck painfully instead against a hard surface. I spread my fingers to read what was there. What I traced by touch was a circular depression which must mark a trap door. Having made sure of that, I applied pressure, first gently and then with more force. When there was no reassuring yield I began to be alarmed. If the bolt hole of this door was locked, we would have no recourse but to return to the level of the robos, and I did not want to think of that.

But my final desperate shove must have triggered whatever stiff mechanism held the door and it gave, letting in a weak light. I had wit and control enough left to wait for a very long moment for any warning from Eet.

When he sent nothing I scrambled out into a place where the walls were studded with gauges, levers, and the like, perhaps the nerve center that controlled the robos. Since there was no one there and a very ordinary door in the nearest wall, I breathed a sigh of heart-felt relief and set about making myself more presentable, plucking Eet out of my unsealed tunic and fastening that smoothly. As far as I could tell, examining my clothes with care, I bore no 'traces of my late venture through the bowels of the caravansary and I should be able to take to the streets without notice. Always providing that the door opposite me would eventually lead me to freedom.

What it did give on was a very small grav lift. I set the indicator for street level and was wafted up to a short corridor with doors at either end. One gave upon a walled court with an entrance for luggage conveyers. And I hop-skipped with what speed I could along one of those, to drop into an alley where a flitter from the port unloaded heavier transport boxes.

"Now!" Eet had been riding on my shoulder, his pookha body less well adapted to that form of transport than his true form. I felt his paws clamp on either side of my head as he had earlier done when showing me how one's face could be altered. "Wait!"

I did not know his purpose, since he did not demand I "think" a face. And though that waiting period spun out, making me uneasy, he did not alter his position. I was sure he was using his own thought power to provide me with a disguise.

"Best—I—can—do—" The paws fell away from my head and I reached up to catch him as he tumbled from his place. He was shaking as if from extreme fatigue and his eyes were closed, while he breathed in short gasps. Once before I had seen him so drained—even rendered unconscious—when he had forced me to share minds with the Patrolman.

Carrying Eet as I might a child, and shouldering my flight bag, I went down the alley. A back look at the building had given me directions. If I had a tail who had not been confused by our exit, he had no place to hide here.

The side way fed into a packed commercial street where the bulk of the freight from the port must pass. There were six heavy-duty transport belts down its middle, flanked on either side by two light-duty, and there remained room for a single man-way, narrow indeed, which scraped along the sides of the buildings it passed. There was enough travel on it to keep me from being unduly conspicuous, mainly people employed at the port to handle the shipments. I dropped my bag between my feet and stood, letting the way carry me along, not adding speed by walking.

Eet had spoken of the Diving Lokworm, which was still a mystery to me, and I had no intention of visiting the Off-port before nightfall. Daytime visitors, save for tourists herded along on a carefully supervised route, were very noticeable there. Thus I would have to hole up somewhere. Another hotel was the best answer. With what I thought a gift of inspiration I chose one directly across from the Seven Planets, from where I had just made my unusual exit.

This was several steps down from the Seven Planets in class, which suited my reduced means. And I was especially pleased that instead of a human desk clerk, who would have added to the prestige, there was a robo—though I knew that my person was now recorded in the files from its scanners. Whether the confusing tactics on my behalf via Eet's efforts would hold here I did not know.

I accepted the thumb lock plate with its incised number, took the grav to the cheapest second-floor corridor, found my room, inserted the lock, and once inside, relaxed. They could force that door now only with super lasers.

Depositing Eet on the bed, I went to the wall mirror to see what he had done to me. What I did sight was not a new face, but a blurring, and I felt a disinclination to look long at my reflection. To watch with any concentration was upsetting, as if I found my present appearance so distasteful that I could not bear to study it.

I sat down on the chair near the mirror. And as I continued to force myself to look at that reflection I was aware that the odd feeling of disorientation was fading, that in the glass my own features were becoming clearer, sharper, visible and ordinary as they had always been.

That Eet could work such a transformation again when the time came to leave here, I doubted. Such a strain might be too much, especially when it was imperative that his esper talents be fully alert. So I might well walk out straight into the sight of those hunting me. But—could I reproduce Eet's effect by my own powers? My trial with Faskel's features had certainly not been any success. And I had had to call upon Eet's help to achieve even that.

But suppose I did not try for so radical a disguise? Eet had supplied me this time, not with a new face, but with merely an overcast of some weird kind which had made me difficult to look at. Suppose one did not try to change a whole face, but only a portion of it? My mind fastened upon that idea, played with it. Eet did not comment, as I thought he might. I looked to the bed. By all outward appearances he was asleep.

If one did not subtract from a face but added to it—in such a startling fashion that the addition claimed the attention, thus overshadowing features. There had been a time in the immediate past when my skin was piebald, due to Eet's counterfeiting of a plague stigma. I could remember only too well those loathsome purple patches. No return to those! I had no wish to be considered again a plague victim. However, a scar—

My mind wandered to the days when my father had kept the hock-lock shop at the space port on my home planet. Many spacers had sought out his inner room to sell finds into whose origin it was best not to inquire too closely. And more than one of those had been scarred or marked unpleasantly.

A scar—yes. Now where—and what? A healed knife gash, a laser burn, an odd seam set by some unknown wounding? I decided on a laser burn which I had seen and which should fit in well with the Off-port. With it as clear in my mind as I could picture it, I stared into the mirror, striving to pucker and discolor the skin along the left side of my jaw and cheek.

THREE

It was an exercise against all the logic of my species. Had I not seen it succeed with Eet, seen my partial change under his aid, I would not have believed it possible. Whether I *could* do it without Eet's help was another question, but one I was eager to prove. My dependence upon the mutant, who tended to dominate our relationship, irked me at times.

There is a saying: If you close doors on all errors, truth also remains outside. Thus I began my struggle with errors aplenty, hoping that a small fraction of the truth would come to my aid. I had not, since I had known Eet, been lax in trying to develop any esper talents I might have. Primarily because, I was sure, it was not in my breed to admit that a creature who looked so much an animal could out-think, out-act a man—though in the galaxy the term "man" is, of course, relative, having to do with a certain level of intelligence rather than a humanoid form. In the beginning, this fact was also difficult for my breed, with their many inborn prejudices, to realize. We learned the hard way until the lesson stuck.

I closed the channels of my mind as best I could, tamping down a mental lid on my worries about our lack of a pilot, a shrinking number of credits, and the fact that I might right now be the quarry in a hunt I could sense but not see or hear. The scar—that must be the most important, the *only* thing in my mind. I concentrated on my reflection in the mirror, on what I wanted to see there.

Perhaps Eet was right, as he most always was—we of Terran stock do not use the full powers which might be ours. Since I had been Eet's charge, as it were, I must have stretched, pulled, without even being aware of that fact, in a manner totally unknown to my species heretofore. Now something happened which startled me. It was as if, in that part of me which fought to achieve Eet's ability, a ghostly finger set tip to a lever and pressed it firmly. I could almost feel the answering vibration through my body—and following on that, a flood of certainty that this I could do, a heady confidence which yet another part of me observed in alarm and fear.

But the face in the mirror—Yes! I had that disfiguring seam, not raw and new, which would have been a giveaway to the observant, but puckered and dark, as though it had not been tended quickly enough by plasta restoration, or else such a repair job had been badly botched—as might be true for a crewman down on his luck, or some survivor of a planetary war raid.

So real! Tentatively I raised my hand, not quite daring to touch that rough, ridged skin. Eet's illusion had been—was—tactile as well as visual. Would mine hold as well? I touched. No, I was not Eet's equal as yet, if I could ever be. My fingers traced no scar, as they seemed to do when I looked into the mirror. But visually the scar was there and that was the best protection I could have.

"A beginning, a promising beginning—"

My head jerked as I was startled out of absorption. Eet was sitting up on the bed, his unblinking pookha eyes watching me in return. Then I feared the break in my concentration and looked back to the mirror. But contrary to my fears, the scar was still there. Not only that, but I had chosen rightly—it drew attention, the face behind it blotted out by that line of seamed and darkened skin—as good as a mask.

"How long will it last?" If I ventured out of this room, went delving into the Off-port as I must, I would not be able to find another hole in a hurry into which I could settle safely for the period of intense concentration I would need to renew my disfigurement.

Eet's round head tilted a little to one side, giving the appearance of critical observation of my thought work.

"It is not a large illusion. You were wise to start small," he commented. "With my aid, I think it will hold for tonight. Which is all we need. Though I shall have to change myself—"

"You? Why?"

"Need you parade your incomprehension of danger?" The whisker mane had already winked out of being. "Take a pookha into the Off-port?"

He was right as ever. Pookhas alive were worth more than their weight in credits. To carry one into the Off-port would be to welcome a stun ray, if lucky, a laser burn if not, with Eet popped into a bag and off to some black-market dealer. I was angry with myself for having made such a display of nonthinking, though it was due to the need for concentration on maintaining the scar.

"You must hold it, yes, but not with your whole mind," Eet said. "You have very much to learn."

I held. Under my eyes Eet changed. The pookha dissolved, vanished as though it were an outer husk of plasta meeting the cold of space and so shattering into bits too tiny for the human eye to see. Now he was Eet again, but as unusual to the observer as the pookha had been.

"Just so," he agreed. "But I shall not be observed. I need not change. It will simply be a matter of not allowing the eye to light on me."

"As you did with my face, coming here?"

"Yes. And the dark will aid. We'll head straight for the Diving Lokworm—"

"Why?"

One of my own species might have given an exaggerated sigh of annoyance. The mental sensation which emanated from my companion was not audible but it had the same meaning.

"The Diving Lokworm is a possible meeting place for the type of pilot we must find. And you need not waste time asking me how I know that. It is the truth."

How much Eet could pick out of nearby minds I did not know; I thought that I did not want to know. But his certainty now convinced me that he had some concrete lead. And I could not argue when I had nothing of my own to offer in return.

He made one of his sudden leaps to my shoulder and there arranged himself in his favorite riding position, curled about my neck as if he were an inanimate roll of fur. I gave a last look into the mirror, to reassure myself that my creation was as solid-seeming as ever, and knew a spark of triumph when I saw that it was, even though I might later have to depend upon Eet to maintain it.

So prepared, we went out and took the main crawl walk toward the port, ready to drop off at the first turn which led to the murk of the Off-port. It was dusk, the clouds spreading like smoke across a dark-green sky in which the first of Theba's moons pricked as a single jewel of light.

But the Off-port was awake as we entered it by the side way. Garish signs, not in any one language (though Basic was the main tongue here), formed the symbols, legible to spacemen of many species and races, which advertised the particular wares or strange delights offered within. Many of them were a medley of colors meant to attract nonhuman races, and so, hurtful to our organs of vision. Thus one was better advised not to look above street level. There was also such a blare of noise as was enough to deafen the passerby, and scents to make one long for the protection of a space suit which could be set to shut out the clamor and provide breathable, filtered air.

To come into this maze was to believe one had been decanted on another world, not only dangerous but inhospitable. How I was to find Eet's Diving Lokworm in this pool of confusion was a problem I saw no way of solving. And to wander, deafened and half asphyxiated, through the streets and lanes was to ask for disaster. I had no belted weapon and I was carrying a flight bag, so perhaps ten or more pairs of eyes had already marked me down as possible prey for a portside rolling.

"Right here—" Eet's thought made as clean a cut as a force blade might make through the muddle of my mind.

Right I turned, out of the stridence of the main street, into a small, very small, lessening of the clamor, with a fraction less light, and perhaps one or two breaths now and then of real air. And Eet seemed to know where we were going, if I did not.

We turned right a second time and then left. The spacemen's rests now about were such holes of crime that I feared to poke a nose into any of them. We were fast approaching the last refuge of the desperate, and the stinking hideups of those who preyed upon them, driven from the fatter profits of the main streets.

The Diving Lokworm had, not its name, but a representation of that unwholesome creature set in glow lines about its door. The designer had chosen to arrange it so that one apparently entered through the open mouth—which was perhaps an apt prophecy of what might really await the unwary within. The stench of the outside was here magnified materially by the fumes of several kinds of drink and drug smoke. Two I recognized as lethal indeed to those who settled down to make their consumption the main business of what little life remained to them.

But it was not dark. The outer Lokworm had here its companions, who writhed about the walls in far too life-like fashion. And though parts of those gleaming runnels of light had darkened through want of replacement, the whole gave enough radiance so one could actually see the customers' faces after a fashion, if not what might be served in the cups, beakers, tubes, and the like placed before them.

Unlike the drinking and eating places in the more civilized (if that was the proper term) part of the port, the Diving Lokworm had no table dials to finger to produce nourishment, no robo-servers whipping about. The trays were carried by humans or aliens, none of whom had a face to be observed long without acute distaste. Some of them were noticeably female, others—well it could be a guess. And frankly, had I been drinking the local poison, it would have stopped a second order to have the first slopped down before me by a lizardoid with two pairs of arms. Unless the drink had been more important than what I saw when I looked about me.

The lizardoid was serving three booths along the wall, and doing it most efficiently; four hands were useful. There was a very drunk party of Regillians in the first. In the second something gray, large, and warty squatted. But in the third slumped a Terran, his head supported on one hand, with the elbow of that arm planted firmly on the table top. He had on the remains of a space officer's uniform which had not been cleaned for a long time. One insignia still clung by a few loose threads to his tunic collar, but there was no house or ship badge on the breast, only a dark splotch there to show he had sometime lost that mark of respectability.

To take a man out of this stew was indeed combing the depths. On the other hand, all we really needed to clear the port was a pilot on board. I did not doubt that Eet and I together could get us out by setting automatic for the first jump. And to accept a black-listed man—always supposing he was not a plant—was our only chance now.

"He is a pilot and a fash-smoker." Eet supplied information, some of which I did not care to hear.

Fash-smoke does not addict, but it does bring about a temporary personality change which is dangerous. And a man who indulges in it is certainly not a pilot to be relied upon. If this derelict was sniffing it now, he was to be my last choice instead of my first. The only bright thought was that fash-smoke is expensive, and one who set light to the brazier to inhale it was not likely to patronize the Diving Lokworm.

"Not now," Eet answered. "He is, I believe, drinking veever—"

The cheapest beverage one could buy and enough to make a man as sick as a sudden ripple of color in the tube worm on the wall made this lounger appear. The fact that the light was a sickly green might have had something to do with his queasy expression. But he roused to pull the beaker before him into place and bend his head to catch the suck tube between his lips. And he went on drinking as we came to the side of the booth.

Perhaps he would not have been my first choice. But the stained insignia on his collar was that of a pilot, and he was the only one I had sighted here. Also, he was the only humanoid with a face I would halfway trust, and Eet appeared to have singled him out.

He did not look up as I slipped into the bench across from him, but the lizard waiter slithered up and I pointed to the drinker, then raised a finger, ordering a return for my unknown boothmate. The latter glanced at me without dropping the tube from his lip hold. His brows drew together in a scowl and then he spat out his sipper and said in a slurred mumble:

"Blast! Whatever you're offering—I'm not buying."

"You are a pilot," I countered. The lizardoid had made double time to whatever sewer the drinks had been piped from and slammed down another beaker. I flipped a tenth-point credit and one of his second pair of hands clawed it out of the air so fast I never really saw it disappear.

"You're late in your reckoning." He pushed aside his first and now empty beaker, drew the second to him. "I *was* a pilot."

"System or deep-space ticket?" I asked.

He paused, the sipper only a fraction away from his lips. "Deep space. Do you want to see it all plain and proper?" There was a sneer in his growl. "And what's it to you, anyway?"

There is this about fash-smoking—while it makes a man temporarily belligerent during indulgence, it also alters the flow of emotion so that between bouts, where rage might normally flare, one gets only a flash of weak irritation.

"A lot maybe. Want a job?"

He laughed then, seemingly in real amusement. "Again you're too late. I'm planet-rooted now."

"You offered to show your plate. That hasn't been confiscated?" I persisted.

"No. But that's just because no one cares enough to squawk. I haven't lifted for two planet years, and that's the truth. Quite a spiller tonight, aren't I? Maybe they've cooked some babble stuff into this goop." He stared down into his beaker with dim interest, as if he expected to see something floating on its turgid surface.

Then he mouthed the sipper, but with one hand he pulled at the frayed front seam of his tunic and brought out, in a shaking hand, a badly-worn case, which he dropped on the table top, not pushing it toward me, but rather as if he were indifferent to any interest of mine in its contents. I reached for it just as another ripple of light in the wall pattern gave me sight of the plate within that covering.

It had been issued to one Kano Ryzk, certified pilot for galactic service. The date of issuance was some ten years back, and his age was noted as problematical, since he had been space-born. But what did startle me was the small symbol deeply incised below his name—a symbol which certified him as a Free Trader.

From their beginnings as men who were willing to take risks outside the regular lines, which were the monopolies of the big combines, the Free Traders, loners and explorers by temperament, had become, through several centuries of space travel, more and more a race apart. They tended to look upon their ships as their home worlds, knowing no planet for any length of time, ranging out where only First-in Scouts and such explorers dared to go. In the first years they had lived on the short rations of those who snatch at the remnants of the feast the combines grew fat upon.

Not able to bid at the planet auctions when newly discovered worlds were put up for sale to those wanting their trade, they had to explore, take small gains at high risks, and hope for some trick of fate which would render a big profit. And such happened just often enough to keep them in space.

But seeing their ships as the only worlds to which they owed allegiance, they were a clannish lot, marrying among themselves when they wed at all. They had space-hung ports now, asteroids they had converted, on which they established quasi family life. But they did not contact the planet-born save for business. And to find one such as Ryzk adrift in a port—since the Free Traders cared for their own—was so unusual as to be astounding.

"It is true." He did not raise his eyes from the beaker. He must have encountered the same surprise so many times before that he was weary of it. "I didn't roll some star-stepper to get that plate."

That, too, must be true, since such plates were always carried close to a man's body. If any other besides the rightful owner had kept that plate, the information on it would be totally unreadable by now, since it had a self-erase attuned to personal chemistry.

There was no use in asking what brought a Free Trader shipless into the Diving Lokworm. To inquire might turn him so hostile I would not be able to bargain. But the very fact he was a Free Trader was a point in his favor. A broken combine man would be less likely to take to the kind of spacing we planned.

"I have a ship"—I put it bluntly now—"and I need a pilot."

"Try the Register," he mumbled and held out his hand. I closed the case and laid it on his palm. How much was the exact truth going to serve me?

"I want a man off the lists."

That did make him look at me. His pupils were large and very dark. He might not be on fash-smoke, but he was certainly under some type of mind-dampening cloud.

"You aren't," he said after a moment, "a runner."

"No," I replied. Smuggling was a paying game. However, the Guild had it sewed up so well that only someone with addled brains would try it.

"Then what are you?" His scowl was back.

"Someone who needs a pilot—" I was beginning when Eet's thought pricked me.

"We have stayed here too long. Be ready to guide him."

There was silence. I had not finished my sentence. Ryzk stared at me, but his eyes seemed unfocused, as if he did not really see me at all. Then he grunted and pushed aside the still unfinished second beaker.

"Sleepy," he muttered. "Out of here—"

"Yes," I agreed. "Come to my place." I was on his left, helping him to balance on unsteady feet, my hand slipped under his elbow to guide him. Luckily he was still enough in command of his body to walk. I could not have pulled him along, since, though he was several inches shorter than I, his planet days had given him bulk of body which was largely ill-carried lard.

The lizard stepped out as if to bar our way and I felt Eet stir. Whether he planted some warning, as he seemed to have planted the desire to go in Ryzk, I do not know. But the waiter turned abruptly to the next booth, leaving us a free path to the door. And we made it out of the stink of the place without any opposition. Once in the backways of the Off-port, I tried to put on speed, but found that Ryzk, though he did keep on his feet and moving, could not be hurried. And pulling at him seemed to disturb the thought Eet had put in his mind, so I did not dare to put pressure on him. I was haunted by the feeling that we were being followed, or at least watched. Though whether our cover had been detected or we had just been marked down for prey generally by one of the lurking harpies, I did not try to deduce. Either was dangerous.

The floodlights of the port cut out the night, reducing all three moons now progressing at a stately pace over our heads to pallid ghosts of their usual brilliance. To pass the gates and cut across the apron to our ship's berth was the crucial problem. If, as I thought, the Patrol and perhaps the Guild were keeping me under surveillance, there would be a watch on the ship, even if we had lost them in the town. And my scar, if I still wore it, would not stand up in the persona scanner at the final check point. Escape might depend on speed, and Ryzk did not have that.

I lingered no longer at the first check point than it took to snap down my own identity plate and Ryzk's. Somehow he had fumbled it out of hiding as we approached, some part of his bemused brain answering Eet's direction. Then I saw a chance to gain more speed. There was a luggage conveyer parked to one side, a luxury item I with my one flight bag had never seen reason to waste half a credit on. But there was need for it now.

Somehow I pushed and pulled Ryzk to it. There was a fine for using it as a passenger vehicle, but such minor points of law did not trouble me at that moment. I got him flat on it, pulled a layer of weather covering over his more obvious outlines, and planted my flight bag squarely on top to suggest that it did carry cargo. Then I punched the berth number for our ship, fed in my credit, and let it go. If Ryzk did not try to disembark en route I could be sure he would eventually arrive at the ramp of our ship.

Meanwhile Eet and I had to reach the same point by the least conspicuous and quickest route. I glanced around for some suggestions as to how to accomplish that. A tourist-class inter-system rocket ship was loading, with a mass of passengers waiting below its ramp and more stragglers headed for it. Many of the travelers were being escorted by family parties or boisterous collections of friends. I joined the tail of one such, matching my pace to keep at the end of the procession. Those I walked with were united in commiserating with a couple of men wearing Guard uniforms and apparently about to lift to an extremely disliked post on Memfors, the next planet out in this system, and one which had the reputation of being far from a pleasure spot.

Since most of the crowd were male, and looked like rather hard cases, I did not feel too conspicuous. And it was the best cover I saw. However, I still had to break away when we reached the rocket slot and cross to my own ship. It was during those last few paces I would be clearly seen.

I edged around the fringes of the waiting crowd, putting as many of those between me and the dark as I could, trying to be alert to any attention I might attract. But as far as I could see, I might once more be enveloped in Eet's vision-defying blur.

I wanted to run, or to scuttle along under some protective shell like a pictick crab. But both of those safety devices were denied me. Now I dared not .even look around as though I feared any pursuit, for wariness alone could betray me.

Ahead I saw the luggage conveyer crawling purposefully on a course which had been more of a straight line than my own. My bag had not shifted from the top, which meant, I trusted, that Ryzk had not moved. It reached the foot of the ramp well before me and stood waiting for the lifting of its burden to release it.

"Watcher—to the right—Patrol—"

Eet came alive with that warning. I did not glance in the direction he indicated.

"Is he moving in?"

"No. He took a video shot of the carrier. He has no orders to prevent take-off—just make sure you do go."

"So they can know the bait is ready and they need only set their trap. Very neat," I commented. But there was no drawing back now, and I did not fear the Patrol at this moment half as much as the Guild. After all, I had some importance to the Patrol—bait has until the moment for sacrificing it comes. Once we were off planet I had the feeling it was not going to be so easy for them to use me as they so arrogantly planned. I still had what they did not suspect I carried—the zero stone.

So I gave no sign that I knew I was under observation as I hauled Ryzk off the luggage carrier, guided him up the ramp, snapped that in, and sealed ship. I stowed my prize, such as he was, in one of the two lower-level cabins, strapped him down, taking his pilot's plate with me, and climbed with Eet to the control cabin.

There I fed Ryzk's plate into the viewer to satisfy the field law and prepared for take-off, Eet guiding me in the setting of the automatics. But I had no trip tape to feed in, which meant that once in space Ryzk would have to play his part or we would find another port only by the slim margin of chance.

FOUR

Since we lacked a trip tape, we could not go into hyper until Ryzk found us jump co-ordinates. So our initial thrust off world merely set us voyaging within the system itself, an added danger. While a ship in hyper cannot be traced, one system-traveling can readily be picked up. Thus, when I recovered from grav shock, I unstrapped myself and sought out my pilot, Eet making better time, as usual, down the inner stair of the ship.

Our transport, the *Wendwind*, was not as small as a scout, though not as large as a Free Trader of the D class. She might once have been the private yacht of some Veep. If so, all luxury fittings had long since been torn out, though there were painted-over scars to suggest that my guess was correct. Later she had been on system runs as a general carrier. And her final fate had been confiscation by the Patrol for smuggling, after which she had been bought by the Salarik dealer as a speculation.

She had four cabins besides the regular crew quarters. But three of these had been knocked together for a storage hold. And one feature within attracted me, a persona-pressure sealed strongbox, something a dealer in gems could put to use.

At one time the *Wendwind* must have mounted strictly illegal G-lasers, judging by the sealed ports and markings on decks and walls. But now she had no such protection.

Ryzk had been left in the last remaining passenger cabin. As I came in he was struggling against the grav straps, looking about him wildly.

"What—where—"

"You are in space, on a ship as pilot." I gave it to him without long explanation. "We are still in system, ready to go into hyper as soon as you can set course—"

He blinked rapidly, and oddly enough, the slack lines of his face appeared to firm, so that under the blurring of planetside indulgence you could see something of the man he had been. He stretched out his hand and laid it palm flat against the wall, as if he needed the reassurance of touch to help him believe that what I said was true.

"What ship?" His voice had lost the slur, just as his face had changed.

"Mine."

"And who are you?" His eyes narrowed as he stared up at me.

"Murdoc Jern. I am a gem buyer."

Eet made one of his sudden leaps from deck to the end of the bunk, where he squatted on his haunches, his hand-paws resting on what would have been his knees had he possessed a humanoid body.

Ryzk looked from me to Eet and then back again. "All right, all right! I'll wake up sooner or later."

"Not"—I picked up the thought Eet aimed at Ryzk—"until you set us a course—"

The pilot started, then rubbed his hands across his forehead as if he could so rub away what he had heard, not through his ears, but in his mind.

"A course to where?" he asked, as one humoring some image born out of fash-smoke or veever drink.

"To quadrant 7-10-500." At least I had had plenty of time to lay plans such as these during the past weeks when I feared we would never be space-borne. The sooner we began to earn our way the better. And I had Vondar's experience to suggest a good beginning.

"I haven't set a course in—in—" His voice trailed off. Once more he put his hand to the ship's wall. "This is—this is a ship! I'm not dreaming it!"

"It is a ship. Can you get us into hyper now?" I allowed some of my impatience to show.

He pulled himself out of his bunk, moving unsteadily at first. But perhaps the feel of a ship about him was a tonic, for by the time he reached the core ladder to the control cabin he had picked up speed, and he swung up that with ease. Nor did he wait to be shown the pilot's seat, but crossed to sit there, giving quick, practiced looks to the control board.

"Quadrant 7-10-500—" It was not a question but a repetition, as if it were a key to unlock old knowledge. "Fathfar sector—"

Perhaps I had done far better than I had hoped when I had picked up a planeted Free Trader. A pilot for one of the usual lines would not have known the fringes of the travel lanes which must be my hunting trails now.

Ryzk was pushing buttons, first a little slowly, then picking up speed and sureness, until a series of equations flashed on the small map screen to his left. He studied those, made a correction or two with more buttons, and then spoke the usual warning—"Hyper."

Having seen that he did seem to know what he was doing, I had already retired to the second swing chair in the cabin, Eet curled up tightly against me, ready for that sickening twist which would signal our snap into the hyper space of galactic travel. Though I had been through it before, it had been mostly on passenger flights, where there had been an issue of soothe gas into the cabin to ease one through the wrench.

The ship went silent with a silence that was oppressive as we passed into a dimension which was not ours. Ryzk pushed a little away from the board, flexing his fingers. He looked to me and those firmer underlines of his face were even more in evidence.

"You—I remember you—in the Diving Lokworm." Then his brows drew together in a frown. "You—your face is different."

I had almost forgotten the scar; it must be gone now.

"You on the run?" Ryzk shot at me.

Perhaps he was entitled to more of the truth, since he shared a ship which might prove a target were we unlucky.

"Perhaps—"

But I had no intention of spouting about the past, the secret in my gem belt, and the real reason why we might go questing off into unexplored space, seeking out uncharted stars. However, "perhaps" was certainly not an explanation which would serve me either. I would have to elaborate on it.

"I am bucking the Guild." That gave him the worst, and straight. At least he could not jump ship until we planeted again.

He stared at me. "Like trying to jump the whole nebula, eh? Optimistic, aren't you?" But if he found my admission daunting, it did not appear in any expression or hesitation in his reply. "So we get to the Fathfar sector, and when we set down—on which world by the way?—we may get a warm welcome, crisped right through by lasers!"

"We set down on Lorgal. Do you know it?"

"Lorgal? You picked that heap of sand, rock, and roasting sun for a hide-out? Why? I can give you a nice listing of more attractive places—" It was plain he did know our port. Almost I could suspect he was a plant, except that I had voiced to no one at all my selection for my first essay as a buyer. Lorgal was as grim as his few terse words had said—with hellish windstorms and a few other assorted planetside disasters into the bargain. But its natives could be persuaded to part with zorans. And I knew a place where a selection of zorans, graded as I was competent to do, could give us half a year's supply of credits for cruising expenses.

"I am not hunting a hide-hole. I am after zorans. As I told you, I buy gems."

He shrugged as if he did not believe me but was willing to go along with my story, since it did not matter to him one way or another. But I triggered out the log tape and pushed its recorder to him, setting before him the accompanying pad for his thumbprint to seal the bargain.

Ryzk examined the tape. "A year's contract? And what if I don't sign, if I reserve the right to leave ship at the first port of call? After all, I don't remember any agreement between us before I woke up in this spinner of yours."

"And how long would it take you to find another ship off Lorgal?"

"And how do you know I'll set you down there in the first place? Lorgal is about the worst choice in the Fathfar sector. I can punch out any course I please—"

"Can you?" inquired Eet.

For the second time Ryzk registered startlement. He stared now at the mutant and his gaze was anything but pleasant.

"Telepath!" He spat that out like a curse.

"And more—" I hastened to agree. "Eet has a way of getting things we want done, done."

"You say that you have the Guild after you and you want me to sign on for a year. Your first pick of a landing is a hellhole. And now this—this—"

"Partner of mine," I supplied when he seemed at a loss for the proper term.

"This partner suggests he can make me do as he wishes."

"You had better believe it."

"What do I get out of it? Ship's wages—?"

This was a fair enough protest. I was willing to concede more.

"Take Trade share—"

He stiffened. I saw his hand twitch, his fingers balled into a fist which might have been aimed at me had he not some control over his temper. But I read then his dislike for my knowledge of that fragment of his past. That I had used a Free Trader's term, offering him a Trader deal, was not to his liking at all. But he nodded.

Then he pressed his thumb on the sign pad and recited his license number and name into the recorder, formally accepting duty as pilot for one planet year, to be computed on the scale of the planet from which we had just lifted, which was a matter of four hundred days.

There was little or nothing to do while the ship was in hyper, a matter of concern on the early exploring and trading ships. For idle men caused trouble. It was usually customary for members of a ship's crew to develop hobbies or crafts to keep their minds alert, their hands busy. But if Ryzk had had such in the past, he did not produce them now.

He did, however, make systematic use of the exercise cabin, as I did also, keeping muscles needed planetside from growing flabby in the reduced gravity of space flight. And as time passed he thinned and fined down until he was a far more presentable man than the one we had steered out of the Off-port drinking den.

My own preoccupation was with the mass of records I had managed, with the reluctant assistance of the Patrol, to regain from several storage points used by Vondar Ustle. With some I was familiar, but other tapes, especially those in code, were harder. Vondar had been a rover as well as a gem merchant. He could have made a fortune had he settled down as a designer and retailer on any inner-system planet. But his nature had been attuned to wandering and he had had the restlessness of a First-in Scout.

His designing was an art beyond me, and of his knowledge of stones I had perhaps a tenth—if I was not grossly overestimating what I had been able to assimilate during the years of our master-apprentice relationship. But the tapes, which I could claim under the law as a legally appointed apprentice, were my inheritance and all I had to build a future upon. All that was reasonably certain, that is. For the quest for the source of the zero stone was a gamble on which we could not embark without a backing of credits.

I watched the viewer as I ran the tapes through, concentrating on that which I had not already absorbed in actual tutelage under Vondar. And my own state of ignorance at times depressed me dismally, leaving me to wonder if Eet had somehow moved me into this action as one moves a star against a comet in that most widely spread galactic game of chance, named for its pieces—Stars and Comets.

But I was also sure that if he had, I would never be really sure of that fact, and it was far better for my peace of mind not to delve into such speculation. To keep at my task was the prime need now and I was setting up, with many revisions, deletions, and additions, a possible itinerary for us to follow.

Lorgal had been my first choice, because of the simplicity of its primitive type of exchange barter. In my first solo deal I needed that simplicity. Though I had cut as close as I could in outfitting the *Wendwind*, I had had to spend some of our very meager store of credits on trade goods. These now occupied less than a third of the improvised storeroom. But the major part of the wares had been selected for dealing on Lorgal.

As wandering people, traveling from one water hole to the next across a land which was for the most part volcanic rock (with some still-active cones breathing smoke by day, giving forth a red glow at night), sand, wind to a punishing degree, and pallid vegetation growing in the bottom of sharp-cut gullies, the Lorgalians wanted mainly food for their too often empty bellies, and water, which for far too many days seemed to have vanished from, or rather into, their earth's crust.

I had visited there once with Vondar, and he had achieved instantaneous results with a small solar converter. Into this could be fed the scabrous leaves of the vegetation, the end product emerging as small blocks about a finger in length containing a highly nutritious food which would keep a man going for perhaps five of their dust—and wind-filled days, one of their plodding beasts for three. The machine had been simple, if bulky, and had had no parts so complicated that a nontechnically-inclined people could put it out of running order. The only trouble was that it was so large that it had to be slung between two of their beasts for transport— though that had not deterred the chieftain from welcoming it as he might have a supernatural gift from one of his demon gods.

I had found, in my more recent prowlings through supply warehouses where the residue of scout and exploration ships was turned in for resale, a similar machine which was but half the size of that we had offered before. And while I could raise the price of only two of these, I had hopes that they would more than pay for our voyage.

I knew zorans, and I also knew the market for them. They were one of those special gems whose origin was organic rather than mineral. Lorgal must once have had an extremely wet climate which supported a highly varied vegetable growth. This had vanished, perhaps quite suddenly in a series of volcanic outbreaks. Some gas or other had killed certain of those plants, and their substance was then engulfed in earth fissures which closed to apply great pressure. That, combined with the gas the plants had absorbed, wrought the changes to produce zorans.

In their natural state they were often found still in the form of a mat of crushed leaves or a barked limb, sometimes even with a crystallized insect (if you were very lucky indeed) embedded in them. But once polished and cut, they were a deep purple-blue-green through which ran streaked lines of silver or glittering gold. Or else they were a crystalline yellow (probably depending upon some variation in the plant, or in the gas which had slain it) with flecks of glittering bronze.

The chunks or veins of the stuff were regularly mined by the nomads, who, until the arrival of the first off-world traders, used it mainly to tip their spears. It could be sharpened to a needle point which, upon entering flesh, would break off, to fester and eventually kill, even though the initial wound had not been a deep one.

And during the first cutting a zoran had to be handled with gloves, since any break in the outer layer made it poisonous. Once that had been buffed away, the gems could be shaped easily, even more so by the application of heat than by a cutting tool. Then, plunged into deep freeze, they hardened completely and would not yield again to any treatment. Their cutting was thus a complicated process, but their final beauty made them prized, and even in the rough they brought excellent prices.

So it would be zorans, and from Lorgal we could lift next to Rakipur, where zorans could be sold uncut to the priests of Mankspher and the pearls of lonnex crabs bought. From there perhaps to Rohan for caberon sapphires or—But there was no use planning too far ahead. I had learned long ago that all trading was a gamble and that to concentrate on the immediate future was the best way.

Eet wandered in and out while I studied my tapes. Sometimes he sat on the table to follow with a show of interest some particular one, at other times curling up to sleep. At length Ryzk, probably for lack of something to do, also found his way to where I studied, and his casual interest gave way to genuine attention.

"Rohan," he commented when I ran through Vondar's tape on that world. "Thax Thorman had trading rights on Rohan back in 3949. He made a good thing out of it. Not sapphires, though. He was after mossilk. That was before the thrinx plague wiped out the spinners. They never did find out what started the thrinx, though Thorman has his suspicions."

"Those being?" I asked when he did not continue.

"Well, those were the days when the combines tried to make it hard for the Free Men." He gave their own name to the Free Traders. "And there were a lot of tricks pulled. Thorman bid for Rohan in a syndicate of five Free ships, and he was able to overtop the Bendix Combine for it. The Combine had the auction fixed to go their way and then a Survey referee showed up and their bribed auctioneer couldn't set the computer. So their low bid was knocked out and Thorman got his. It was a chance for him. Bendix had a good idea of what was there, and he was just speculating because he knew they were set on it.

"So—he and the other ships had about four planet years of really skimming the good stuff. Then the thrinx finished that. Wiped out three of the other captains. They had been fool enough to give credit for two years running. But Thorman never trusted Bendix and he kind of expected something might blow up. No way, of course, of proving the B people had a hand in it. Nowadays, since the Free Men have had their own confederation, combines can't pull such tricks. I've seen a couple of those sapphires. Tough to find, aren't they?"

"They wouldn't be if anyone could locate the source. What is discovered are the pieces washed down the north rivers in the spring—loose in the gravel. Been plenty of prospectors who tried to get over the Knife Ridge to hunt the blue earth holes which must be there. Most of them were never heard from again. That's taboo country in there."

"Easier to buy 'em than to hunt them, eh?"

"Sometimes. Other times it is just the opposite. We have our dangers, too." I was somewhat irked by what I thought I detected underlying his comment.

But he was already changing the subject. "We come out of hyper on the yellow signal. Where do you want to set down on Lorgal, western or eastern continent?"

"Eastern. As near the Black River line as you can make it. There is no real port, as perhaps you know."

"Been a lot of time spinning by since I was there. Things could be changed, even a port there. Black River region." He looked over my shoulder at the wall of the cabin as if a map had been video-cast there. "We'll fin down in the Big Pot, unless that has boiled over into rough land again."

The Big Pot was noted on Lorgal, a giant crater with a burned-out heart which was relatively smooth and which had been used as an improvised space port. Though we had not landed there on my one visit to Lorgal, I knew enough from what I had heard then to recognize that Ryzk had chosen the best landing the eastern continent could offer.

Though the Big Pot was off the main nomad route along the series of water holes the Black River had shrunk to, we had a one-man flitter in our tail hold. And that could scout out the nearest camp site, saving a trek over the horribly broken land, which could not be traveled on foot by any off-worlder.

I looked to the recorded time dial. It was solidly blue, which meant that the yellow signal was not too far off. Ryzk arose and stretched.

"After we come out of hyper, it will take us four color spans to get into orbit at Lorgal, then maybe one more to set down, if we are lucky. How long do we stay planet-side?"

"I cannot say. Depends upon finding a tribe and setting up a talk fire. Five days, ten, a couple of weeks—"

He grimaced. "On Lorgal that is too long. But you're the owner, it's your ration supply. Only hope you can cut it shorter."

He went out to climb to the control cabin. I packed away the tapes and the viewer. I certainly shared his hope—though I knew that once I entered upon the actual trading, I would find in it the zest which it always held for me. Yet Lorgal was not a world on which one wanted to linger. And now it was for me only a means to an end, the end still lying too far ahead to visualize.

I was not long behind Ryzk in seeking the control cabin and the second seat there. While I could not second his duties, I wanted to watch the visa-screen as we came in. This was my first real venture, and success or failure here meant very much. Perhaps Eet was as uncertain as I, for though he curled up in his familiar position against my chest and shoulder, his mind was closed to me.

We snapped out of hyper and it was plain that Ryzk deserved so far the trust I had had to place in him, for the yellow orb was certainly Lorgal. He did not put the ship on automatic, but played with fingers on the controls, setting our course, orbiting us about that golden sphere.

As we cut into atmosphere, the contours of the planet cleared. There were the huge scars of old seas, now shrunken into deep pockets in the centers of what had once been their beds, their waters bitterly salt. The continents arose on what were now plateaus, left well above the dried surface of the almost-vanished seas. In a short time we could distinguish the broken chains of volcanic mountains, the river valley with lava, country in between.

And then the pockmark of the Big Pot could be seen. But as we rode our deter rockets into that promise of a halfway fair landing, I caught a startling glimpse of something else.

We sat down, waiting that one tense moment to see if it had indeed been a fair three-fin landing. Then, as there came no warning tilt of the cabin, Ryzk triggered the visa-screen, starting its circular sweep of our immediate surroundings. It was only a second before I was able to see that we were indeed not alone in the Big Pot.

There was another ship standing some distance away. It was plainly a trader-for-hire. Which meant dire competition, because Lorgal had only one marketable offworld product—zorans. And the yield in any year from one tribe was not enough to satisfy two gem merchants, not if one had to have a large profit to continue to exist. I could only wonder which one of Vondar's old rivals was now sitting by a talk fire and what he had to offer. The only slim chance which remained to me was the fact that he might not have one of the reduced-in-size converters, and that I could so outbid him.

"Company," Ryzk commented. "Trouble for you?" With that question he disassociated himself from any failure of mine. He was strictly a wage man and would get his pay, from the value of the ship if need be, if I went under.

"We shall see," was the best answer I could make as I unstrapped to go and see to the flitter and make a try at finding a nomad camp.

FIVE

My advantage lay in that I had been to Lorgal before, though then the trade responsibility had lain with Vondar, and I had only been an observer. Our success or failure now depended upon how well I remembered what I had observed. The nomads were humanoid, but not of Terran stock, so dealing with them required X-Tee techniques. Even Terrans, or Terran colonist descendants, could not themselves agree over semantics, customs, or moral standards from planet to planet, and dealing with utterly alien mores added just that much more confusion.

The small converter I selected as my best exhibit could be crowded into the flitter's tail storage section. I strapped on the voca-translator and made sure that a water supply and E-rations were to hand. Eet was already curled up inside waiting for me.

"Good luck." Ryzk stood ready to thumb open the hatch. "Be sure to keep contact beam—"

"That is one thing I will not forget!" I promised. Though we had little in common, save that we shared the same ship and some of the duties of keeping it activated, we were two of the same species on an alien world, a situation which tended to make a strong, if temporary, bond between us now.

Ryzk would monitor me all the time the flitter was away from the ship. And I knew that should disaster strike either of us the other would do what he could to aid. It was a ship law, a planet law—one never put onto actual record tape but one which had existed since the first of our breed shot into space.

My memory of my first visit to Lorgal gave me one possible site for a nomad meeting, a deep pool in the river bed which had been excavated time and time again by the wandering tribes until they were always sure of some moisture at its bottom. I set off in that direction, taking my marking from two volcanic cones.

The churned ground passing under the flitter was a nightmare of broken ridges, knife-sharp pinnacles, and pitted holes. I do not believe that even the nomads could have crossed it—not that they ever wandered far from the faint promise of water along the ancient courses of the river.

While most of the rock about the Big Pot had been of a yellow-red-brown shade, here it was gray, showing a shiny, glassy black in patches. We had planeted about midmorning and now the sun caught those gleaming surfaces to make them fountains of glare. There were more and more of these as the flitter dipped over the Black River, where even the sands were of that somber color.

Here the water pits broke the general dark with their side mounds of reddish under-surface sand, which had been laboriously dug out in the past by the few native animals or the nomads. And on the inner sides of those mounds, ringing what small deposits of moisture there might be, grew the stunted plants which were the nomads only attempts at agriculture.

They saved every seed, carrying them where they went, as another race on a more hospitable world might treasure precious stones or metal, planting them one by one in the newly-dug sides of any hole before they left. When they circled back weeks or months later, they found, if they were fortunate, a meager harvest waiting.

Judging by the height of the scrubby brush around the first two pits I dipped to inspect, the Lorgalians had not yet reached them—which meant I must fly farther east to pick up their camp.

I had seen no sign of life about that other ship as I had taken off. Nor had my course taken me close to it. However, I had noted that its flitter hatch was open and guessed that the trader was already out in the field. Time might already have defeated me.

Then the Black River curved and I saw the splotch of tents dotted about. There was movement there, and as I throttled down the flitter to lowest speed and came in for a set-down I knew I was indeed late. For the cloaked and cowled figures of the tribesmen were moving with rhythmic pacing about the circumference of their camp site, each swinging an arm to crack a long-lashed whip at the nothingness beyond, a nothingness which they believed filled with devils who must be driven away by such precautions before any ceremony or serious business could be transacted.

There was another flitter parked here. It had no distinguishing company markings, so I was not about to buck a combine man. Of course I hardly expected to find one here. The pickings, as far as they were concerned, were too small. No, whoever was ready to deal with the camp was a free lance like myself.

I set down a length from the other transport. Now I could hear the high-pitched, almost squealing chant voiced by the devil-routers. With Eet on my shoulders I plunged into dry, stinging air, and the glare of a sun against which my goggles were only part protection. That air rasped against the skin as if it were filled with invisible but very tangible particles of grit. Feeling it, one did not wonder at the long robes, the cowls, the half-masks the natives wore for protection.

As I approached the ring of devil-lashers, two of the whips curled out to crack the air on either side, but I did not flinch, knowing that much of nomad custom. Had I shown any surprise or recoil, I would have labeled myself a demon in disguise and a shower of zoran-pointed spears would have followed that exposure of my true nature.

The tribesmen I passed showed no interest in me; they were concentrating on their duty of protection. I cut between two of the closed tents to a clear space where I could see the assembly the whippers were guarding.

There was a huddle of nomads, all males, of course, and so enwrapped in their robes that only the eye slits suggested that they were not just bales of grimy lakis-wool cloth. The lakises themselves, ungainly beasts with bloated bodies to store the food and water for days when there was need, perched on long, thin legs with great wide, flat feet made for desert travel. These were now folded under them, for they lay to serve as windbreaks behind their masters. Their thick necks rested across each other's bodies if they could find a neighbor to so serve them, and their disproportionately small heads had the eyes closed, as if they were all firmly asleep.

Facing this assembly was the suited and helmeted figure of one of my own race. He stood, some packages about his feet, making the Four Gestures of Greeting, which meant, considering his ease, that he had either visited such a camp before, or else had made a careful study of record tapes.

The chieftain, like everyone else in that muffled crowd, could certainly not be recognized by features, but only by his badge of office, the bloated abdomen which was the result of much prideful padding. That layer upon layer of swaddling was not simply a shield against assassination (chieftainship among the Lorgalians was based upon weapon skill, not birthright); to be fat was a sign of wealth and good fortune here. And he who produced a truly noticeable belly was a man of prestige and standing.

I could not even be sure that this was the tribe with whom Vondar had traded. Only luck might help me in that. But surely, even if it was not, they would have heard of the wonder machine he had introduced and would be the more eager to acquire one of their own.

When I had entered the gathering I had come up behind the trader. And the nomads did not stir as they sighted me. Perhaps they thought me one of the stranger's followers. I do not think he was aware of me until I stepped level with him and began my own gestures of greeting, thus signifying that he was *not* speaking for me, but that I was on my own.

He turned his head and I saw one I knew—Ivor Akki! He had been no match for Vondar Ustle; few were. But he was certainly more than I would have chosen to contend against at the beginning of my independent career. He stared at me intently for a moment and then grinned. And that grin said that in me he saw no threat. We had fronted each other for several hours once at a Salarik bargaining, but there I had been only an onlooker, and he had been easily defeated by Vondar.

He did not pause in his ritual gestures after that one glance to assess his opposition and dismiss it. And I became as unseeing of him. We waved empty hands, pointed north, south, east, and west, to the blazing sun, the cracked, sandy earth under us, outlined symbols of three demons, and that of the lakis, a nomad, and a tent, signifying that by local custom we were devout, honest men, and had come for trade.

By right Akki had the first chance, since he was first on the scene. And I had to wait while he pulled forward several boxes, snapped them open. There was the usual small stuff, mostly plastic—some garish jewelry, some goblets which were fabulous treasure to the eye but all plastic to the touch, and a couple of sun torches. These were all make-gifts—offered to the chief. And seeing their nature I was a little relieved.

For such an array meant this was not a return visit but a first try by Akki. If he was here on spec and had not heard of Vondar's success with the food converter, I could beat him yet. And I had had this much luck, a small flag fluttering by the chieftain's tent told me—this *was* the tribe Vondar had treated with. And I needed only tell them that I had a more easily transported machine to sweep all the zorans they had to offer out of their bags.

But if I felt triumph for a few seconds it was speedily swept away as Akki opened his last box, setting out a very familiar object and one I had not expected to see.

It was a converter, but still more reduced in size and more portable than those I had chanced upon in the warehouse, undoubtedly a later and yet further improved model. I could only hope that he had just the one and that I might halve or quarter his return by offering two.

He proceeded to demonstrate the converter before that silent, never-moving company. Then he waited.

A hairy hand with long dirty nails flipped out from under the bundle of the chieftain's robes, making a sign. And one of his followers hunched forward to unfold a strip of lakis hide on which were many loops. Each loop held a chunk of zoran and only strict control kept me standing, seemingly indifferent, where I was. Four of those unworked stones were of the crystalline type and each held an insect. It was a better display than I had ever heard of. Vondar had once taken two such stones and the realization of their value off world had seemed fabulous to me. Four—with those I would not have to worry about a year's running of the ship. I would not even have to trade at all. We could be off after the zero stone after a single sale.

Only Akki was the one to whom they were offered, and I knew very well that none of them was ever going to come to me.

He deliberated, of course—that was custom again. Then he made his choice, sweeping up the insect pieces, as well as three of the blue-green-purple stones of size large enough to cut well. What was left after his choices had been fingered seemed refuse.

Then he raised his head to grin at me again as he slipped his hoard into a travel case, clapped his hand twice on the converter, and touched the rest of the goods he had spread out, releasing them all formally.

"Tough luck," he said in Basic. "But you've been having that all along, haven't you, Jern? To expect to fill Ustle's boots—" He shook his head.

"Good fortune," I said, when I would rather have voiced disappointment and frustration. "Good fortune, smooth lifting, with a sale at the end." I gave him a trader's formal farewell.

But he made no move to leave. Instead he added the insulting wave of hand signifying among the Lorgalians a master's introduction of a follower. And that, too, I had to accept for the present, since any dispute between us must be conducted outside the camp. A flare of temper would be swift indication that a devil had entered and all trading would be under ban, lest that unchancy spirit enter into some piece of the trade goods. I was almost tempted to do just that, in order to see Akki's offerings ritually pounded into splinters, the zorans treated the same way. But though such temptation was hot in me for an instant, I withstood it. He had won by the rules, and I would be the smaller were I to defeat him so, to say nothing of destroying all thought of future trade with Lorgal not only for the two of us, but for all other off-worlders.

I could take a chance and try to find another tribe somewhere out in the stark wilderness of the continent. But to withdraw from this camp now without dealing would be a delicate matter and one I did not know quite how to handle. I might offend some local custom past mending. No, like it or not, I would have to take Akki's leavings.

They were waiting and perhaps growing impatient. My hands spun into the sign language, aided by the throaty rasping my translator made as it spoke words in their own sparse tongue.

"This"—I indicated the converter—"I have also—but larger—in the belly of my sky lakis."

Now that I had made that offer there was no turning back. In order to retain the good will of the nomads I would have to trade, or lose face. And inwardly I was aware of my own inaptitude in the whole encounter. I had made my mistake in ever entering the camp after I had seen Akki's flitter already here. The intelligent move would have been then to prospect for another clan. But I had rushed, believing my wares to be unduplicated, and so lost.

Again that hairy hand waved and two of the bundled warriors arose to tail me to the flitter, cracking their whips above us as we crossed the line kept by the lashing guards. I pulled the heavy case from where I had so hopefully wedged it. And with their aid, one protecting us from the devils, the other helping me to carry it, I brought it back to the camp.

We set it before the chieftain. Either by accident or design, it landed next to Akki's, and the difference in bulk was marked. I went through the process of proving it was indeed a food converter and then awaited the chieftain's decision.

He gestured and one of my assistants booted a lakis to its feet, the creature bubbling and complaining bitterly with guttural grunts. It came up with a splayfooted shuffle which, awkward as it looked, would take it at an unvarying pace day after day across this tormented land.

A kick on one foreknee brought it kneeling again and the two converters were set beside it. Then proceeded a demonstration to prove the inferiority of my offering.

Akki's machine might be put in a luggage sling on one side of the beast, a load of other equipment on the other—while if it bore the one I had brought, it could carry nothing else.

The chieftain wriggled his fingers and a second roll of lakis hide was produced. I tensed. I had thought I would be offered Akki's leavings, but it would seem I was too pessimistic. My elation lasted, however, only until the roll was opened.

What lay within its loops were zorans right enough. But nothing to compare with those shown to Akki. Nor was I even allowed to choose from his rejects. I had to take what was offered—or else return to the ship empty-handed, with a profitless set-down to my credit, or rather discredit. So I made the best of a very bad bargain and chose. There were, naturally, no insect pieces, and only two of the more attractive yellow ones. The blues had faults and I had to examine each for flaws, taking what I could, though in the end I was certain I had hardly made expenses.

I still had the second converter, and I might just be able to contact another tribe. With that small hope, I concluded the bargain and picked up what still seemed trash compared with Akki's magnificent haul.

He was grinning again as I wrapped the pieces of my choice into a packet and stood to make the farewell gestures. All this time Eet had been as inert as if he were indeed a fur piece about my shoulders. And it was not until I had to walk away from the camp, badly defeated, that I wondered why he had not taken some part in the affair. Or had I come to lean so heavily on him that I was not able to take care of myself? As that thought hit me I was startled and alarmed. Once I had leaned upon my father, feeling secure in his wisdom and experience. Then there had been Vondar, whose knowledge had so far exceeded my own that I had been content to accept his arrangement of both our lives. Soon after disaster had broken that tie, Eet had taken over. And it would seem that I was only half a man, needing the guidance of a stronger will and mind.

I could accept that, become Eet's puppet. Or I could be willing to make my own mistakes, learn by them, hold Eet to a partnership rather than a master-servant relationship. It was up to me, and perhaps Eet wanted me to make such a choice, having deliberately left me to my own bungling today as a test, or even an object lesson as to how helpless I was when I tried to deal on my own.

"Good fortune, smooth lifting—" That was Akki mockingly echoing my farewell of minutes earlier. "Crab pearls next, Jern? Want to wager I will take the best there, too?"

He laughed, not waiting for my answer. It was as if he knew that any defiance on my part would be in the nature of a hollow boast. Instead, he tramped off to his flitter, letting me settle into mine.

I did not take off at once to follow him back to his ship. If he also expected to hunt another camp, I did not want him to follow my path—though he might put a scanner on me.

Triggering the com, I called Ryzk. "Coming in." I would not add to that. The channels of all flitter coms were the same and Akki could pick up anything I now said.

Nor did I try to contact Eet, stubbornly resolved I would leave him in mental retirement as I tried to solve my own problems.

Those problems were not going to become any lighter, I saw as I took off. There was an odd greenish-yellow cast to the sky. And the surface of the ground, wherever there was a deposit of sand, threw up whirling shapes of grit. Seconds later the very sky about us seemed to explode, and the flitter was caught in a gust which even her power could not fight.

For a space we were caught in that whirlwind and I knew fear. The flitter was never meant for high altitudes, and skimming the surface beneath the worst of the wind carried with it the danger of being smashed against some escarpment. But I had little choice. And I fought grimly to hold the craft steady.

We were driven south and west, out over the dead sea bottom. And I knew bleakly that even if I did get back to the *Wendwind* my chances of finding another tribe were finished. Such a storm as this drove them to shelter and I could spend fruitless weeks hunting them. But I was able bit by bit to fight back to the Big Pot. And when I finally entered the hatch I was so weak I slumped forward over the controls and was not really aware of anything more until Ryzk forced a mug of caff into my hands and I knew I was in the mess cabin.

"This pest hole has gone crazy!" He was drumming with his fingers on the edge of the table. "According to our instruments we are sitting over a blowhole now. We up ship, or we are blown out!"

I did not quite realize what he meant and it was not until we had spaced that he explained tersely; the readings of planet stability under the Big Pot had suddenly flared into the danger zone, and he had feared I would not get back before he would be forced to lift. That I had squeezed in by what he considered a very narrow margin he thought luck of a fabulous kind.

But that danger was not real to me, since I had not been aware of it until afterward. The realization of my trade failure was worse. I must lay better plans or lose out as badly as I would have, had we never raised from Theba.

Akki had mentioned crab pearls—which might or might not mean that his itinerary had been planned along the same course as mine. I laid out the poor results of my zoran dealing and considered them fretfully. Akki might have done two things: he might have boastfully warned me off the planet where he was going to trade (his ship had lifted, Ryzk informed me, at once upon his return), or he might just have said that out of malice to make me change my own plans.

I wondered. Eet could tell me. But straightaway I rebelled. I was not going to depend on Eet!

Where was my next-best market? I tried to recall Vondar's listings. There was—Sororis! And it was not from Ustle's notes that memory came, but from my father. Sororis had been an "exit" planet for years, that is, a very far out station in which outlaws could, if they were at the end of their resources and very desperate indeed, find refuge. It had no regular service of either passenger or trade ships, though tramps of very dubious registry would put in there now and then. The refuse of the galaxy's criminal element conjoined around the half-forgotten port and maintained themselves as best they could, or died. They were too useless for even the Guild to recruit.

However, and this was the important fact, there was a native race on Sororis, settled in the north where the off-worlders found the land too inhospitable. And they were supposed to have some formidable weapons of their own to protect themselves against raiders from the port.

The main thing was that they had a well-defined religion and god-gifts were an important part of it. To present their god with an outstanding gift was the only real means of winning status among them. Such presentations gave the donor the freedom of their city for a certain number of days.

My father had been given to telling stories, always supposedly about men he knew during his years as a Guild appraiser. I believed, however, that some concerned his own exploits as a youth. He had told of an adventure on Sororis in detail, and now I could draw upon that for a way to retrieve the Lorgal fiasco.

To the inhabitants of Sororis these chunks of zoran would be rare and strange, since they would not have seen them before. Suppose I presented the largest at the temple, then offered the rest to men who wished to make similar gifts and thus enhance their standing among their fellows? What Sororisan products might be taken in exchange I did not know. But the hero of my father's story had come away with a greenstone unheard of elsewhere. For there was this about the Sororisans—they traded fairly.

It was so wild a chance that no one but a desperate man would think of it. But the combination of my defeat by Akki and the need for asserting my independence of Eet made me consider it. And after I had finished the caff I went to the computer in the control cabin and punched the code for Sororis, wagering with myself that if I received no answer I would accept that as meaning there was no chance of carrying through such a wild gamble.

Ryzk watched me speculatively as I waited for the computer's answer. And when, in spite of my half-hopes, a series of numbers did appear on the small screen, he read them aloud:

"Sector 5, VI—Norroute 11–Where in the name of Asta-Ivista is that? Or what?"

I was committed now. "That is where we are going." I wondered if he had heard of it. "Sororis."

SIX

"Where are your beam lasers and protect screens?" Ryzk asked in the voice, I decided, one used for addressing someone whose mental balance was in doubt. He even glanced at the control board, as if expecting to see such armaments represented there. And so convincing was his question that I found myself echoing that glance—which might not have been so fruitless had the ship still carried what scars proclaimed she once had.

"If you don't have those," he continued, his logic an irritation, "you might just as well blow her tubes and end us all right here without wasting the energy to take us to Sororis—if you do know what awaits any ship crazy enough to planet there. It's a rock prison and those dumped on it will storm any ship for a way to lift off again. To set down at whatever port they do have is simply inviting take-over."

"We are not going in—that is, the ship is not." At least I had planned that far ahead, drawing on my father's very detailed account of how his "friend" had made that single visit to the planet's surface. "There is the LB. It can be fitted with a return mechanism if only one is to use it."

Ryzk looked at me. For a very long moment he did not answer, and when he did, it was obliquely.

"Even a parking orbit there would be risky. They may have a converted flitter able to try a ship raid. And who is going down and why?"

"I am—to Sornuff—" I gave the native city the best pronunciation I could, though its real twist of consonants and vowels was beyond the powers of the human tongue and larynx to produce. The Sororisans were humanoid, but they were not of Terran colony stock, not even mutated colony stock.

"The temple treasures!" His instant realization of what I had in mind told me that his Free Trader's knowledge of the planet's people was more than just surface.

"It has been done," I told him, though I was aware that I was depending perhaps too much on my father's story.

"An orbit park for Sornuff," Ryzk continued, almost as if thinking aloud, "could be polar, and so leave us well away from the entrance route for anything setting down at the real port. As for the LB, yes, there can be lift-off modifications. Only"—he shrugged—"that's a job you don't often tackle in space."

"You can do it?" I demanded. I would admit frankly that I was no mech-tech and such adjustments were beyond either my knowledge or my skill. If Ryzk could not provide the knowledge, then we would have to risk some other and far more dangerous way to gain Sornuff.

"I'll take a look—" He was almost grudging.

But that was all I wanted for now. Free Traders by the very nature of their lives were adept in more fields than the usual spacer. While the fleet men were almost rigorously compartmented as to their skills, the men of the irregular ships had to be able to take over some other's duties when need arose.

The LB must have been periodically overhauled or it would not have had the certification seal on its lock. But it still dated to the original fitting of the ship, and so must have been intended to carry at least five passengers. Thus we were favored in so much room. And Ryzk, dismantling the control board with the ease of one well used to such problems, grunted that it was in better shape for conversion than he had supposed.

It suddenly occurred to me that, as on Lorgal, Eet had made no suggestions or comments. And that started a small nagging worry in my mind, gave me a twinge of foreboding. Had Eet read in my mind my decision for independence? If so, had he some measure of foreknowledge? For never yet had I been able to discover the limit of his esper powers. Whenever I thought I knew, he produced something new, as he had on Theba. So, possessing foreknowledge, was he now preparing to allow me to run into difficulty from which he alone could extricate us, thus proving for once and for all that our association was less a partnership than one of master and servant, with Eet very much in the master's seat? He had closed his mind, offering no comments or suggestions. Nor did he now ever accompany us to the lock where Ryzk and I—I as the unhandy assistant—worked to give us possible entry to a hostile world where I had a thin chance of winning a gamble. I began to suspect he was playing a devious game, which made me more stubborn-set than ever to prove I could plan and carry through a coup which did not depend upon his powers.

On the other hand, I was willing enough to use what I had learned from Eet, even though it now irked me to admit I owed it to him. The hallucinatory disguise was so apt a tool that I systematically worked at the exercise of mind and will which produced the temporary changes. I found that by regular effort I could hold a minor alteration such as the scar I had worked so hard to produce as long as I pleased. But complete change, a totally new face for instance, came less easily. And I must labor doggedly even to produce the slurring of line which would pass me through a crowd unnoticed for a short space. It was Eet's added force which had held that before, and I despaired of ever having enough power to do it myself.

Practice, Eet had said, was the base of any advance I could make, and practice I had time for, in the privacy of my own cabin, with a mirror set up on a shelf to be my guide in success or failure.

At the back of my mind was always the hope that so disguised I might slip through Guild watch at any civilized port. Sororis might be free of their men, but if I won out with a precious cargo, I would have to reach one of the inner planets and there sell my spoil. Stones of unknown value were only offered at auction before the big merchants. Peddled elsewhere, they were suspect and could be confiscated after any informer (who got a percentage of the final sale) turned in a tip. It did not matter if they had been honestly enough acquired on some heretofore unmarked world; auction tax had not been paid on them and that made them contraband.

So I spent our voyage time both acting as an extra pair of inept hands for Ryzk and staring into a mirror trying to reflect there a face which was not that I had seen all my life.

We came out of hyper in the Sororis system with promptitude, which again testified to Ryzk's ability, leading me to wonder what had grounded him in the scum of the Off-port. There were three planets, two, dead worlds, balls of cracked rock with no atmosphere, close enough to the sun to fuse any ship finning down on them like a pot to fry its crew.

On the other hand, Sororis was a frozen world, or largely so, with only a belt of livable land, by the standards of my species, about its middle. It was covered by glaciers north and south of that, save where there were narrow fingers of open land running into that ice cover. In one of these Sornuff was supposed to exist, well away from the outcast settlement about the port.

Ryzk, whom I left at the controls, set up his hold orbit to the north while I packed into the LB what I judged I would need for my visit to the ice-bound city. Coordinates would be fed to the director, and that, too, was Ryzk's concern. On such automatic devices would depend my safe arrival not too far from Sornuff and my eventual return to the ship, the latter being even less sure than the former.

If Ryzk's fears were realized and a high-altitude-conditioned flitter from the port raised with a pilot skillful or reckless enough to attempt a take-over of the *Wendwind*, it might be that the ship would be forced out of orbit in some evasive maneuvering during my absence. If so, I had a warning which would keep me planetside until the ship was back on a course the LB was programmed to intercept.

I checked all my gear with double care, as if I had not already checked it at least a dozen times while we were in hyper. I had a small pack containing special rations, if the local food was not to be assimilated, a translator, a mike call Ryzk would pick up if he were safely in orbit, and, of course, the stones from Lorgal. There was no weapon, not even a stunner. I could not have smuggled one on board at Theba. I could only depend upon my knowledge of personal defense until I was able to outfit myself with whatever local weapons were available.

Ryzk's voice rasped over the cabin com to say that all was clear, and I picked up the pack. Eet was stretched on the bunk, apparently asleep as he had been every time I had come in recently. Was he sulking, or simply indifferent to my actions now? That small germ of worry his unexpected reaction to my bid for independence had planted in me was fast growing into a full-sized doubt of myself—one I dared not allow if I were to face the tests of my resourcefulness below.

Yet I hesitated just to walk out and leave him. Our growing rift hurt in an obscure way, and I had to hold stubbornly to my purpose to keep from surrender. Now I weakened to the degree that I aimed a thought at him.

"I am going—" That was weakly obvious and I was ashamed I had done it.

Eet opened his eyes calmly. "Good fortune." He stretched out his head as if savoring a comfort he was not in the least desirous of leaving. "Use your hind eyes as well as the fore." He closed his own and snapped our linkage.

"Hind eyes as well as fore" made little sense, but I chewed angrily upon it as I went to the LB, setting the door seals behind me. As I lay down in the hammock I gave the eject signal to Ryzk, and nearly blacked out when the force of my partition from the ship hit.

Since I was set on automatics, using in part the LB's built-in function to seek the nearest planet when disaster struck the ship, I had nothing to do but lie and try to plan for all eventualities. There was an oddly naked feel to traveling without Eet, we had been in company for so long. And I found that my rebellion did not quite blank out that sense of loss.

Still, there was an exultation born of my reckless throwing over of all prudent warnings, trying a wholly new and dangerous venture on my own. This, too, part of me warned against. But I was not to have very long to think about anything. For the cushioning for landing came on and I knew I had made the jump to planetside and was about to be faced by situations which would demand every bit of my attention.

The LB had set down, I discovered, in the narrow end of one of those claw-shaped valleys which cut into the ice. Perhaps the glacial covering of Sororis was now receding and these were the first signs of thaw. There was water running swiftly and steadily from the very point of the earth claw, forming a good-sized stream by the time it passed the LB. But the air was so chill that its freezing breath was a blow against the few exposed portions of my face. I snapped down the visor of my helmet as I set the LB hatch on persona lock and, taking up my pack, crunched the ice-packed sand under my space boots.

If Ryzk's reckoning had been successful I had only to go down this valley to where it joined a hand-shaped wedge from which other narrow valleys stretched away to the north and I would be in sighting distance of the walls of Sornuff. When I reached that point I must depend upon my father's tale for guidance. And now I realized he had gone into exhaustive detail in describing the country, almost as if he were trying to impress it upon my memory for some reason—though at the time it had not seemed so. But then I had listened eagerly to all his stories, while my foster brother and sister had apparently been bored and restless.

Between me and the city wall was a shrine of the ice spirit Zeeta. While she was not the principal deity of the Sororisans, she had a sizable following, and she had acted for the hero of my father's story as an intermediary with the priests of the major temple in the city. I say "she" for there was a living woman—or priestess—in that icy fane who was deemed to be the earth-bound part of the ice spirit, and was treated as a supernatural being, even differing in body from her followers.

I came to the join of "claw" and "hand" and saw indeed the walls of the city—and not too far away, the shrine of Zeeta.

My landing had been made just a little after dawn, and only now were thin beams of the hardly warm sun reaching to raise glints from the menace of the tall ice wall at my back. There was no sign of any life about the shrine and I wondered, with apprehension, if Zeeta had been, during the years since that other visitor was here, withdrawn, forsaken by those who had petitioned her here.

My worries as to that were quickly over as I came closer to the building of stone, glazed over with glistening ice. It was in the form of a cone, the tip of which had been sliced off, and it was perhaps the size of the *Wend-wind*. Outside, a series of tables which were merely slabs of hewn ice as thick as my arm mounted on sturdy pillars of the same frozen substance encircled the whole truncated tower. On each of these were embedded the offerings of Zeeta's worshippers, some of them now so encased in layers of ice that they were only dark shadows, others lying on the surface with but a very thin coat of moisture solidifying over them.

Food, furs, some stalks of vegetable stuff black-blasted by frost lay there. It would seem that Zeeta never took from these supplies, only left them to become part of the growing ice blocks on which they rested.

I walked between two of these chill tables to approach the single break in the rounded wall of the shrine, a door open to the wind and cold. But I was heartened to see further proof of my father's story, a gong suspended by that portal. And I boldly raised my fist to strike it with the back of my gloved hand as lightly as I could—though the booming note which answered my tap seemed to me to reach and echo through the glacier behind.

My translator was fastened to my throat and I had rehearsed what I would say—though the story had not supplied me with any ceremonial greeting and I would have to improvise.

The echoes of the gong continued past the time I thought they would die. And when no one came to answer, I hesitated, uncertain. The fairly fresh offerings spelled occupancy of the shrine, but perhaps that was not so, and Zeeta, or her chosen counterpart, was not in residence.

I had almost made up my mind to go on when there was a flicker of movement within the dark oblong of the door. That movement became a shape which faced me.

It was as muffled as a Lorgalian. But they had appeared to have humanoid bodies covered by ordinary robes. This was as if a creature completely and tightly wound in strips or bandages which reduced it to the likeness of a larva balanced there to confront me.

The coverings, if they were strips of fabric, were crystalled with patterns of ice which had the glory of individual snowflakes and were diamond-bright when the rising sun touched them. But the body beneath was only dimly visible, having at least two lower limbs (were there any arms they were bound fast to the trunk and completely hidden), a torso, and above, a round ball for a head. On the fore of that the crystal encrustations took the form of two great faceted eyes—at least they were ovals and set where eyes would be had the thing been truly humanoid. There were no other discernible features.

I made what I hoped would be accepted as a gesture of reverence or respect, bowing my head and holding up my hands empty and palm out. And though the thing had no visible ears, I put my plea into speech which emerged from my translator as a rising and falling series of trills, weirdly akin in some strange fashion to the gong note.

"Hail to Zeeta of the clear ice, the ice which holds forever! I seek the favor of Zeeta of the ice lands."

There was a trilling in return, though I could see that the head had no mouth to utter it.

"You are not of the blood, the bones, the flesh of those who seek Zeeta. Why do you trouble me, strange one?"

"I seek Zeeta as one who comes not empty-handed, as one who knows the honor of the Ice Maiden—" I put out my right hand now, laying on the edge of the nearest table the gift I had prepared with some thought—a thin

chain of silver on which were threaded rounded lumps
of rock crystal. On one of the inner worlds it had no
value, but worth is relative to the surroundings and here
it flashed bravely in the sunlight as if it were a string of
the crystals such as adorned Zeeta's wrappings.

"You are not of the blood, the kind of my people,"
came her trilling in reply. She made no move to inspect
my offering, nor even, as far as I could deduce, to turn
her eyes to view it. "But your gift is well given. What ask
you of Zeeta? Swift passage across ice and snow? Good
thoughts to light your dreams?"

"I ask the word of Zeeta spoken into the ear of mighty
Torg, that I may have a daughter's fair will in
approaching the father."

"Torg also does not deal with men of your race,
stranger. He is the Guardian and Maker of Good for
those who are not of your kind."

"But if one brings gifts, is it not meet that the gift-
giver be able to approach the Maker of Good to pay
him homage?"

"It is our custom, but you are a stranger. Torg may
not find it well to swallow what is not of his own people."

"Let Zeeta but give the foreword to those who serve
Torg and then let him be the judge of my motives and
needs."

"A small thing, and reasonable," was her comment.
"So shall it be done."

She did turn her head then so those blazing crystal
eyes were looking to the gong. And though she raised
nothing to strike its surface, it suddenly trembled and
the sound which boomed from it was enough to summon
an army to attack.

"It is done, stranger."

Before I could give her any thanks she was gone, as suddenly as if her whole crystal-encrusted body had been a flame and some rise of wind had extinguished it. But though she vanished from my sight, I still lifted my hand in salute and spoke my thanks, lest I be thought lacking in gratitude.

As before, the gong note continued to rumble through the air about me, seemingly not wholly sound but a kind of vibration. So heralded, I began to walk to the city.

The way was not quite so far as it seemed and I came to the gates before I was too tired of trudging over the ice-hardened ground. There were people there and they, too, were strangely enough clad to rivet the attention.

Fur garments are known to many worlds where the temperature is such that the inhabitants must add to their natural covering to survive. Such as these, though, I had not seen. Judging by their appearance, animals as large as a man standing at his full height had been slain to obtain skins of shaggy, golden fur. These had not been cut and remade into conventional garb but had retained their original shape, so that the men of Sornuff displayed humanoid faces looking out of hoods designed from the animal heads and still in one piece with the rest of the hide; the paws, still firm on the limbs, they used as cover for hands and feet. Save for the showing of their faces they might well be beasts lumbering about on their hind legs.

Their faces were many shades darker than the golden fur framing them, and their eyes narrow and slitted, as if after generations of holding them so in protection against the glare of sun on snow and ice this had become a normal characteristic.

They appeared to keep no guard at their gate, but three of them, who must have been summoned by the

gong, gestured to me with short crystal rods. Whether
these were weapons or badges of office I did not know,
but I obediently went with them, down the central street.
Sornuff had been built in circular form, and its center
hub was another cone temple, much larger than Zeeta's shrine.

The door into it was relatively narrow and oddly fashioned to resemble an open mouth, though above it were
no other carvings to indicate the rest of a face. This was
Torg's place and the test of my plan now lay before me.

I could sense no change in warmth in the large circular
room into which we came. If there was any form of
heating in Sornuff it was not used in Torg's temple. But
the chill did not in any way seem to bother my guides
or the waiting priests. Behind them was the representation of Torg, again a widely open mouth, in the wall
facing the door.

"I bring a gift for Torg," I began boldly.

"You are not of the people of Torg." It was not quite
a protest, but it carried a faint shadow of warning and it
came from one of the priests. Over his fur he wore a
collar of red metal from which hung several flat plaques,
each set with a different color stone and so massively
engraved in an intertwined pattern that it could not be
followed.

"Yet I bring a gift for the pleasures of Torg, such as
perhaps not even his children of the blood have seen."
I brought out the best of the zorans, a blue-green,
roughly oval stone which nearly filled the hollow of my
hand when I had unrolled its wrappings and held it forth
to the priest.

He bent his head as if he sniffed the stone, and then
he shot out a pale tongue, touching its tip to the hard

surface. Having to pass it through some strange test, he plucked it out of my hold and turned to face the great mouth in the wall. The zoran he gripped between the thumb and forefinger of each hand, holding it in the air at eye level.

"Behold the food of Torg, and it is good food, a welcome gift," he intoned. I heard a stir and mutter from behind me as if I had been followed into the temple by others.

"It is a welcome gift!" the other priests echoed.

Then he snapped his fingers, or appeared to do so, in an odd way. The zoran spun out and away, falling through the exact center of the waiting mouth, to vanish from sight. The ceremony over, the priest turned once more to face me.

"Stranger you are, but for one sun, one night, two suns, two nights, three suns, three nights, you have the freedom of the city of Torg and may go about such business as is yours within the gates which are under the Guardianship of Torg."

"Thanks be to Torg," I answered and bowed my head. But when I in turn faced around I found that my gift giving had indeed had an audience. There were a dozen at least of the furred people staring intently at me. And though they opened a passage, giving me a free way to the street without, one on the fringe stepped forward and laid a paw-gloved hand on my arm.

"Stranger Who Has Given to Torg." He made a title of address out of that statement. "There is one who would speak with you."

"One is welcome," I replied. "But I am indeed a stranger within your gates and have no house roof under which to speak."

"There is a house roof and it is this way." He trilled that hurriedly, glancing over his shoulder as if he feared interruption. And as it did seem that several others now coming forth from the temple were minded to join us, he kept his grasp on my arm and drew me a step or two away.

Since time was a factor in any trading I would do here, I was willing enough to go with him.

SEVEN

He guided me down one of the side streets to a house which was a miniature copy of shrine and temple, save that the cone tip, though it had been cut away, was mounted with a single lump of stone carved with one of the intricate designs, one which it somehow bothered the eyes to study too closely.

There was no door, not even a curtain, closing the portal, but inside we faced a screen, and had to go between it and the wall for a space to enter the room beyond. Along its walls poles jutted forth to support curtains of fur which divided the outer rim of the single chamber into small nooks of privacy. Most of these were fully drawn. I could hear movement behind them but saw no one. My guide drew me to one, jerked aside the curtain, and motioned me before him into that tent.

From the wall protruded a ledge on which were more furs, as if it might serve as a bed. He waved me to a seat there, then sat, himself, at the other end, leaving a goodly expanse between us as was apparently demanded by courtesy. He came directly to the point.

"To Torg you gave a great gift, stranger."

"That is true," I said when he paused as though expecting some answer. And then I dared my trader's advance. "It is from beyond the skies."

"You come from the place of strangers?"

I thought I could detect suspicion in his voice. And I had no wish to be associated with the derelicts of the off-world settlement.

"No. I had heard of Torg from my father, many sun times ago, and it was told to me beyond the stars. My father had respect for Torg and I came with a gift as my father said must be done."

He plucked absent-mindedly at some wisps of the long fur making a ruff below his chin.

"It is said that there was another stranger who came bringing Torg a gift from the stars. And he was a generous man."

"To Torg?" I prompted when he hesitated for the second time.

"To Torg—and others." He seemed to find it difficult to put into words what he wanted very much to say. "All men want to please Torg with fine gifts. But for some men such fortune never comes."

"You are, perhaps, one of those men?" I dared again to speak plainly, though by such speech I might defeat my own ends. To my mind he wanted encouragement to state the core of the matter and I knew no other way to supply it.

"Perhaps—" he hedged. "The tale of other days is that the stranger who came carried with him not one from-beyond-the-stars wonders but several, and gave these freely to those who asked."

"Now the tale which I heard from my father was not quite akin to that," I replied. "For by my father's words the stranger gave wonders from beyond, yes. But he accepted certain things in return."

The Sororisan blinked. "Oh, aye, there was that. But what he took was token payment only, things which were not worth Torg's noting and of no meaning. Which made him one of generous spirit."

I nodded slowly. "That is surely true. And these things which were of no meaning—of what nature were they?"

"Like unto these." He slipped off the ledge to kneel on the floor, pressing at the front panel of the ledge base immediately below where he had been sitting. That swung open and he brought out a hide bag from which he shook four pieces of rough rock. I forced myself to sit quietly, making no comment. But, though I had never seen greenstone, I had seen recorder tri-dees enough to know that these were uncut, unpolished gems of that nature. I longed to handle them, to make sure they were unflawed and worth a trade.

"And what are those?" I asked as if I had very little interest in the display.

"Rocks which come from the foot of the great ice wall when it grows the less because the water runs from it. I have them only because—because I, too, had a tale from my father, that once there came a stranger who would give a great treasure for these."

"And no one else in Sornuff has such?"

"Perhaps—but they are of no worth. Why should a man bring them into his house for safekeeping? They have made laughter at me many times when I was a youngling because I believed in old tales and took these."

"May I see these rocks from the old story?"

"Of a surety!" He grabbed up the two largest, pushed them eagerly, with almost bruising force, into my hands. "Look! Did your tale speak also of such?"

The larger piece had a center flaw, but it could be split, I believed, to gain one medium-sized good stone and maybe two small ones. However, the second was a very good one which would need only a little cutting. And he had two other pieces, both good-sized. With such at auction I had my profit, and a bigger, more certain one than I had planned in my complicated series of tradings beginning with the zorans.

Perhaps I could do even better somewhere else in Sornuff. I remembered those other men who had moved to contact me outside the temple before my present host had hurried me off. On the other hand, if I made this sure trade I would be quicker off world. And somehow I had had an eerie sensation ever since I had left the LB that this was a planet it was better to visit as briefly as possible. There were no indications that the outlaws of the port came this far north, but I could not be sure that they did not. And should I be discovered and the LB found—No, a quick trade and a speedy retreat was as much as I dared now.

I took out my pouch and displayed the two small and inferior zorans I had brought.

"Torg might well look with favor on him who offered these."

The Sororisan lunged forward, his fur-backed hands reaching with the fingers crooked as if to snatch that treasure from me. But that I did not fear. Since I had fed Torg well this morning, I could not be touched for three days or the wrath of Torg would speedily strike down anyone trying such a blasphemous act.

"To gift Torg," the Sororisan said breathlessly. "He who did so—all fortune would be his!"

"We have shared an old tale, you and I, and have believed in it when others made laughter concerning that belief. Is this not so?"

"Stranger, it is so!"

"Then let us prove their laughter naught and bring truth to the tale. Take you these and give me your stones from the cold wall, and it shall be even as the tale said it was in the days of our fathers!"

"Yes—and yes!" He thrust at me the bag with the stones he had not yet given me, seized upon the zorans I had laid down.

"And as was true in the old tale," I added, my uneasiness flooding in now that I had achieved my purpose, "I go again into beyond-the-sky."

He hardly looked up from the stones lying on the fur.

"Yes, let it be so."

When he made no move to see me forth from his house, I stowed the bag of greenstones into the front of my weather suit and went on my own. I could not breathe freely again until I was back in the ship, and the sooner I gained that safety the better.

There was a crowd of Sororisans in the street outside, but oddly enough none of them approached me. Instead they looked to the house from which I had come, almost as if it had been told them what trade had been transacted there. Nor did any of them bar my way or try to prevent my leaving. Since I did not know how far the protection of Torg extended, I kept a wary eye to right and left as I walked (not ran as I wished) to the outer gate.

Across the fields which had been so vacant at my coming a party was advancing. Part of them wore the fur suits of the natives. But among them were two who had on a queer mixture of shabby, patched, off-world weather clothing. And I could only think they must have connection with the port. Yet I could not retreat now; I was sure I had already been sighted. My only hope was to get back to the LB with speed and raise off world.

The suited men halted as they sighted me. They were too far away for me to distinguish features within their helmets, and I was sure they could not see mine. They would only mark my off-world clothing. But that was new, in good condition, which would hint to them that I was not of the port company.

I expected them to break from their traveling companions, to cut me off, and I only hoped they were unarmed. I had been schooled by my father's orders in unarmed combat which combined the lore of more than one planet where man made a science of defending himself using only the weapons with which nature had endowed him. And I thought that if the whole party did not come at me at once I had a thin chance.

But if such an attack was in the mind of the off-worlders, they were not given a chance to put it to the test. For the furred natives closed about them and hustled them on toward the gate of the city. I thought that they might even be prisoners. Judging by the tales I had heard of the port, an inhabitant there might well give reason for retaliation by the natives.

My fast walk had become a trot by the time I passed the shrine of Zeeta and I made the best speed I could back to the LB, panting as I broke the seal and scrambled in. I snapped switches, empowering the boat to rise and latch on to the homing beam to the *Wendwind*, and threw myself into a hammock for a take-off so ungentle that I blacked out as if a great hand had squeezed half the life out of me.

When I came groggily to my senses again, memory returned and I knew triumph. I had proved my belief in the old story right. Under the breast of my suit was what would make us independent of worry—at least for a while—once we could get it to auction.

I rendezvoused with the ship, thus proving my last worry wrong, and stripped off the weather suit and helmet, to climb to the control cabin. But before I could burst out with my news of success, I saw that Ryzk was frowning.

"They spy-beamed us—"

"What!" From a normal port such a happening might not have been too irregular. After all, a strange ship which did not set down openly but cruised in a tight orbit well away from any entrance lane would have invited a spy beam as a matter of regulation. But by all accounts Sororis had no such equipment. Its port was not defended, needed no defense.

"The port?" I demanded, still unable to believe that.

"On the contrary." For the first time in what seemed to me days, Eet made answer. "It came from the direction of the port, yes, but it was from a ship."

This startled me even more. To my knowledge only a Patroller would mount a spy beam, and that would be a Patroller of the second class, not a roving scout. The Guild, too, of course, had the reputation of having such equipment. But then again, a Guild ship carrying such would be the property of a Veep. And what would any Veep be doing on Sororis? It was a place of exile for the dregs of the criminal world.

"How long?"

"Not long enough to learn anything," Eet returned. "I saw to that. But the very fact that they did not learn will make them question. We had better get into hyper—"

"What course?" Ryzk asked.

"Lylestane."

Not only did the auction there give me a chance to sell the greenstones as quickly as possible, but Lylestane was one of the inner planets, long settled, even overcivilized, if you wish. Of course the Guild would have some connections there; they had with every world on which there was a profit to be made. But it was a well-policed world, one where law had the upper hand. And no Guild ship would dare to follow us boldly into Lylestane skies. So long as we were clear of any taint of illegality, we were, according to our past bargain with the Patrol, free to go as we would.

Ryzk punched a course with flying fingers, and then signaled a hyper entrance, as if he feared that at any moment we might feel the drag of a traction beam holding us fast. His concern was so apparent it banished most of my elation.

But that returned as I brought out the greenstones, examined them for flaws, weighed, measured, set down my minimum bids. Had I had more training, I might have attempted cutting the two smaller. But it was better to take less than to spoil the stones, and I distrusted my skill. I had cut gems, but only inferior stones, suitable for practice.

The largest piece would cut into three, and the next make one flawless one. The other two might provide four stones. Not of the first class. But, because greenstone was so rare, even second—and third-quality stones would find eager bidders.

I had been to auctions on Baltis and Amon with Vondar, though I had never visited the more famous one of Lylestane. Only two planet years ago one of Vondar's friends, whom I knew, had accepted the position of appraiser there, and I did not doubt that he would remember me and be prepared to steer me through the local legalities to offer my stones. He might even suggest a private buyer or two to be warned that such were up for sale. I dreamed my dreams and spun my fantasies, turning the stones around in my fingers and thinking I had redeemed my stupidity on Lorgal.

But when we had set down on Lylestane, being relegated to a far corner of the teeming port, I suddenly realized that coming to such as a spectator, with Vondar responsible for sales and myself merely acting as a combination recording clerk and bodyguard, was far different from this. Alone—For the first time I was almost willing to ask Eet's advice again. Only the need to reassure myself that I could if I wished deal for and by my lone kept me from that plea. But as I put on the best of my limited wardrobe—inner-planet men are apt to dress by station and judge a man by the covering on his back—the mutant sought me out.

"I go with you—" Eet sat on my bunk. But when I turned to face him I saw him become indistinct, hazy, and when the outlines of his person again sharpened I did not see Eet, but rather a pookha. On this world such a pet would indeed be a status symbol.

Nor was I ready to say no. I needed that extra feeling of confidence Eet would supply by just riding on my shoulder. I went out, to meet Ryzk in the corridor.

"Going planetside?" I asked.

He shook his head. "Not here. The Off-port is too rich for anyone less than a combine mate. This air's too thick for me. I'll stay ramp-up. How long will you be?"

"I shall see Kafu, set up the auction entry, if he will do it, then come straight back."

"I'll seal ship. Give me the tone call." I wondered a little at his answer. To seal ship meant expectation of trouble. Yet of all the worlds we might have visited we had the least to fear from violence here.

There were hire flitters in the lanes down-field and I climbed into the nearest, dropping in one of my now very few credit pieces and so engaging it for the rest of the day. At Kafu's name it took off, flying one of the low lanes toward the heart of the city.

Lylestane was so long a settled world that for the most part its four continents were great cities. But for some reason the inhabitants had no liking for building very high into the air. None of the structures stood more than a dozen stories high—though underground each went down level by level deep under the surface.

The robo-flitter set down without a jar on a rooftop and then flipped out an occupied sign and trundled off to a waiting zone. I crossed, to repeat Kafu's name into the disk beside the grav shaft, and received a voiced direction in return:

"Fourth level, second crossing, sixth door."

The grav float was well occupied, mostly by men in the foppish inner-planet dress, wherein even those of lower rank went with laced, puffed, tagged tunics. To my frontier-trained eyes they seemed more ridiculous than in fashion. And my own plain tunic and cropped hair attracted sideways eyeing until I began to wish I had applied some of the hallucinatory arts at least to cloud my appearance.

Fourth level down beneath the ground gave Kafu's standing as one of reasonably high rank. Not that of a Veep, who would have a windowed room or series of rooms above surface, but not down to the two—and three-mile depth of an underling.

I found the second crossing and stopped at the sixth door. There was an announce com screwed in its surface, a pick-up visa-plate above it—a one-way visa-plate which would allow the inhabitant to see me but not reveal himself in return.

I fingered the com to on, saw the visa-plate come to life.

"Murdoc Jern," I said, "assistant to Vondar Ustle."

The wait before any answer came was so long I began to wonder if perhaps Kafu was out. Then there did come a muffled response from the com.

"Leave to enter." The barrier rolled back to let me into a room in vivid contrast to the stone-walled Sorori-san house where I had done my last trading.

Though men went in gaudy and colorful wear, this room was in subdued and muted tones. My space boots trod springy summead moss, a living carpet of pale yellow. And along the walls it had raised longer stalks with dangling green berries which had been carefully twined and massed together to form patterns.

There were easirests, the kind which yielded to one's weight and size upon bodily contact, all covered in earth-brown. And the light diffused from the ceiling was that of the gentle sun of spring. Directly ahead of me as I came in, one of the easirests had been set by the wall where the berry stalks had been trained to frame an open space. One might have been looking out of a window, viewing miles upon miles of landscape. And this was not static but flowed after holding for a time into yet another view, and with such changes in vegetation one could well believe that the views were meant to show not just one planet but many.

In the easirest by this "window" sat Kafu. He was a Thothian by birth, below what was considered to be the norm in height for Terran stock. His very brown skin was pulled so tightly over his fragile bones that it would seem he was the victim of starvation, hardly still alive. But from the deep sockets of his prominent skull, his eyes watched me alertly.

Instead of the fripperies of Lylestane he wore the robe of his home world, somewhat primly, and it covered him from throat, a stiffened collar standing up in a frame behind his skull, to ankles, with wide sleeves coming down over his hands to the knucklebones.

Across the easirest a table level had been swung, and set out on that were flashing stones which he was not so much examining as arranging in patterns. They might be counters in some exotic game.

But he swept these together as if he intended to clear the board for business, and they disappeared into a sleeve pocket. He touched his fingers to forehead in the salute of his people.

"I see you, Murdoc Jern."

"And I, you, Kafu." The Thothians accepted no address of honor, making a virtue of an apparent humbleness which was really a very great sense of their own superiority.

"It has been many years—"

"Five." Just as I had been suddenly restless on Sororis, so this room, half alive with its carefully tended growth, affected me with a desire to be done with my business and out of it.

Eet shifted weight on my shoulder and I saw, I thought, a flicker of interest in Kafu's eyes.

"You have a new companion, Murdoc Jern."

"A pookha," I returned, tamping down impatience.

"So? Very interesting. But you are thinking now that you did not come to discuss alien life forms or the passage of years. What have you to say to me?"

I was truly startled then. Kafu had thrown aside custom in coming so quickly to the point. Nor had he offered me a seat or refreshment, or gone through any of the forms always used. I did not know whether I faced veiled hostility, or something else. But that I was not received with any desire to please I did know.

And I decided that such an approach might be met by me with its equal in curtness.

"I have gems for auction."

Kafu's hands came up in a gesture which served his race for that repudiation mine signified by a shake of the head.

"You have nothing to sell, Murdoc Jern."

"No? What of these?" I did not advance to spill the greenstones onto his lap table as I might have done had his attitude been welcoming, but held the best on the palm of my hand in the full light of the room. And I saw that that light had special properties—no false, doctored, or flawed stone could reveal aught but its imperfections in that glow. That my greenstones would pass this first test I did not doubt.

"You have nothing to sell, Murdoc Jern. Here or with any of the legally established auctions or merchants."

"Why?" His calmness carried conviction. It was not in such a man as Kafu to use a lie to influence a sale. If he said no sale, that was true and I was going to find every legitimate market closed to me. But the magnitude of such a blow had not yet sunk in, and as yet I only wanted an answer.

"You have been listed as unreliable by the authorities," he told me then.

"The lister?" I clung desperately to that one way of possible clearance. Had my detractor a name, I could legally demand a public hearing, always supposing I could raise the fees to cover it.

"From off world. The name is Vondar Ustle."

"But—he is dead! He was my master and he is dead!"

"Just so," Kafu agreed. "It was done in his name, under his estate seal."

This meant I had no way of fighting it. At least not now, and maybe never, unless I raised the astronomical fees of those legal experts who would be able to fight through perhaps more than one planet's courts.

Listed, I had no hope of dealing with any reputable merchant. And Kafu said I had been listed in the name of a dead man. By whom, and for what purpose? The Patrol, still wishing to use me in some game for the source of the zero stones? Or the Guild? The zero stone—I had not really thought of it for days; I had been too intent on trying my trade again. But perhaps it was like a poison seeping in to disrupt my whole life.

"It is a pity. They look like fine stones—" Kafu continued.

I slapped the gems back in their bag, stowing it inside my tunic. Then I bowed with what outward impassiveness I could summon.

"I beg the Gentle Homo's pardon for troubling him with this matter."

Kafu made another small gesture. "You have some powerful enemy, Murdoc Jern. It would be best for you to walk very softly and look into the shadows."

"If I go walking at all," I muttered and bowed again, somehow getting myself out of that room where all my triumph had been crushed into nothingness.

This was bottom. I would lose the ship now, since I could not pay field fees and it would be attached by the port authorities. I had a small fortune in gems I could not legally sell.

Legally—

"This may be what they wish." Eet followed my thoughts.

"Yes, but when there is only one road left, that is the one you walk," I told him grimly.

EIGHT

On some worlds I might have moved into the shadowy places with greater ease than I could on Lylestane. I did not know any contacts here. Yet it seemed to me when I had a moment to think that there had been something in Kafu's talk with me—perhaps a small hint—

What had he said? "You have nothing to sell with any of the legally established merchants or auctions—" Had he or had he not stressed that word "legally"? And was he so trying to bait me into an illegal act which would bring him an informer's cut of what I now carried? With a lesser man than Kafu my suspicions might be true. But I believed that the Thothian would not lend his name and reputation to any such murky game. Vondar had considered Kafu one of those he could trust and I knew there had been an old and deep friendship between my

late master and the little brown man. Did some small
feeling of friendliness born of that lap over to me, so
that he had been subtly trying to give me a lead? Or was
I now fishing so desperately for anything which might
save me that I was letting my imagination rule my common sense?

"Not so—" For the second time Eet interrupted my
train of thought. "You are right in supposing he had
friendly feelings for you. But there was such in that room
that he could not express them—"

"A spy snoop?"

"A pick-up of some sort," Eet returned. "I am not as
well attuned to such when they are born of machines
rather than the mind. But while this Kafu spoke for more
than your ears alone, his thoughts followed different
paths, and they were thoughts of regret that he must do
this thing. What does the name Tacktile mean to you?"

"Tacktile?" I repeated, speculating now as to why Kafu
had been under observation and who had set the spy
snoop. My only solution was that the Patrol was not done
with me and were bringing pressure to bear so that I
would agree to the scheme their man had outlined when
he offered me a pilot of their choosing.

"Yes—yes!" Eet was impatient now. "But the past does
not matter at this moment—it is the future. Who is
Tacktile?"

"I do not know. Why?"

"The name was foremost in this Kafu's mind when he
hinted of an illegal sale. And there was a dim picture
there also of a building with a sharply pointed roof. But
of that I could see little and it was gone in an instant.
Kafu has rudimentary esper powers and he felt the mind-
touch. Luckily he believed it some refinement of the spy
snoop and did not suspect us."

Us? Was Eet trying to flatter me?

"He had a crude shield," the mutant continued. "Enough of a one to muddle reception when I did not have time to work on him. But this Tacktile, I believe, would be of benefit to you now."

"If he is an IGB—a buyer of illegal gems—he might just be the bait in someone's trap."

"No, I think not. For Kafu saw in him a solution for you but no way to make that clear. And he is on this planet."

"Which is helpful," I returned bitterly, "since I lack the years it could take to run him down on name alone. This is one of the most densely populated worlds in the inner systems."

"True. But if a man such as Kafu saw this Tacktile as your aid, then he would be known to other gem dealers also, would he not? And I would suggest—"

But this time I was ahead of him. "I make the rounds, not accepting Kafu's word that I am listed. While you try to mind-pick those I meet."

It might just work, though I must depend upon Eet's gifts and not my own this time. However, there was also the thin chance that some one of the minor merchants might take a chance at an undercounter sale when they saw the quality of the stones I had to offer. And I decided to begin with these smaller men.

Evening was close when I had finished that round of disappointing refusals. Disappointing, that is, on the surface. For though some of those I had visited looked with greed on what I had to offer, all of them repeated the formula that I was listed and there was no deal. Only Eet had done his picking of minds, and as I sat in the ship's cabin again, very tired, I was not quite so discouraged as I might have been, for we knew now who Tacktile was and that he was right here in the Off-port.

As my father had done, so did Tacktile here—he operated a hock-lock for spacers wherein those who had tasted too deeply of the pleasures of the Off-port parted with small portable treasures in return for enough either to hit the gaming tables unsuccessfully again or to eat until they shipped out.

Being a hock-lock, he undoubtedly had dealings with the Guild, no matter how well policed his establishment might be. But, and this was both strange and significant, he was an alien from Warlock, a male Wyvern, which was queer. Having for some reason fled that matriarchy and reached Lylestane, he kept his own planet's citizenship and had some contact with it still which the Patrol did not challenge. Thus his holding was almost a quasi consulate for the world of his birth. His relationship with the female rulers of Warlock no one understood, but he was able to handle some off-world matters for them and was given a semidiplomatic status here which allowed him the privilege of breaking minor laws.

Tacktile was not his right name, but a human approximation of the sounds of his clacking speech—for audible speech was used by the males of Warlock while the females were telepathic.

"Well"—Ryzk faced me—"what luck?"

There was no reason to keep the worst from him. And I did not think he would jump ship here in a port where he had already decided he could not even afford to visit the spacer's resorts.

"Bad. I am listed. No merchant will buy."

"So? Do we move out now or in the morning?" He leaned back against the wall of the cabin. "I don't have anything to be attached. And I can always try the labor exchange." His tone was dry and what lay behind it was the dull despair of any planet-bound spacer.

"We do nothing—until I make one more visit—tonight." Time, as it had been since the start of our venture, was our enemy. We must raise our port fees in a twenty-four hour period or we would have the ship base-locked and confiscated.

"But not," I continued, "as Murdoc Jern." For I had this one small thread of hope left. If I were listed and suspect, then this ship and its crew of two—for Eet might well be overlooked as a factor in our company—would be watched and known. I would have to go in disguise. And already I was working out how that might be done.

"Dark first, then the port passenger section—" I thought out loud. Ryzk shook his head.

"You'll never make it. Even a Guild runner could be picked up here. That entrance is the focus of every scanner in the place. They screen out all the undesirables when they are funneled through at landing."

"I shall chance it." But I did not tell him how. My attempts at Eet's art were still my secret. And all the advantages of any secret lie in the fact that it is not shared.

We ate and Ryzk went back to his own cabin—I think to consider gloomily what appeared to be a black future. That he had any faith in me was now improbable. And I could not be sure he was not right.

But I set up the mirror in my cabin and sat before it. Nothing as simple as a scar now. I must somehow put on another face. I had already altered my clothing, taking off my good tunic and donning instead the worn coveralls of an undercrew man on a tramp freighter.

Now I concentrated on my reflection. What I had set up as a model was a small tri-dee picture. I could not hope to make my copy perfect, but if I could only create a partial illusion—

It required every bit of my energy, and I was shaking with sheer fatigue when I could see the new face. I had the slightly greenish skin of a Zorastian, plus the large eyes, the show of fanged side teeth under tight-stretched, very thin, and near colorless lips. If I could hold this, no watcher could identify me as Murdoc Jern.

"Not perfect." I was shaken out of my survey of my new self by Eet's comment. "The usual beginner's reach for the outre. But in this case, possible, yes, entirely possible, since this is an inner planet with a big mingling of ship types."

Eet—I had turned to look—was no longer a pookha. Nor was he Eet. Instead there lay on my bunk a serpent shape with a narrow, arrow-shaped head. The kind of a life form it was I could not put name to.

There was no question that Eet was going to accompany me. I could not depend now on my limited human senses alone, and what rested on my visit to Tacktile was more important than my pride.

The reptile wound about my arm, coiled there as a massive and repulsive bracelet, its head a little upraised to view. And we were ready to go, but not openly down the ramp.

Instead I descended through the core of the ship to a hatch above the fins, and in the dark felt for the notches set on one of those supports for the convenience of repair techs. So that we hit ground in the ship's shadow.

I had Ryzk's ident disk, but hoped I would not have to show it. And luckily there was a liberty party from one

of the big intersolar ships straggling across the field. As
I had done when disembarking from our first port, I
tailed this and we tramped in a group through the gate.
Any reading on me would be reported as my own and I
had the liberty of the port. But the scanners, being robos,
would not report that my identity did not match my
present outward appearance. Or so I hoped as I continued to tag along behind the spacers, who steered straight
for the Off-port.

This was not as garish and strident as that in which I
had found Ryzk—at least on the main street. I had a
very short distance to go, since the sharply peaked roof
of Tacktile's shop could be seen plainly from the gate.
He appeared to depend upon the strange shape of his
roof rather than a sign for advertisement.

That roof was so sharply slanted that it formed a very
narrow angle at the top and the eaves well overhung
the sides. There was an entrance door so tall it seemed
narrower than it was, but no windows. The door gave
easily under my touch.

Hock-locks were no mystery to me. Two counters on
either side made a narrow aisle before me. Behind each
were shelves along the wall, crowded with hock items,
protected by a thin haze of force field. It would seem
Tacktile conducted a thriving business, for there were
four clerks in attendance, two on either side. One was
of Terran blood, and there was a Trystian, his feathered
head apparently in molt, as the fronds had a ragged
appearance. The gray-skinned, warty-hided clerk nearest
me I did not recognize, but beyond him was another
whose very presence there was a jarring note.

In the galaxy there is an elder race, of great dignity
and learning—the Zacathans, of lizard descent. These

are historians, archaeologists, teachers, scholars, and never had I seen one in a mercantile following before. But there was no mistaking the race of the alien, who stood in a negligent pose against the wall, fitting the strip of reader tape in his clawed hands into a recorder.

The gray creature blinked sleepily at me, the Trystian seemed remote in some personal misery, and the Terran grinned ingratiatingly and leaned forward.

"Greetings, Gentle Homo. Your pleasure is our delight." He mouthed the customary welcome of his business. "Credits promptly to hand, no hard bargaining—we please at once!"

I wanted to deal directly with Tacktile and that was going to be a matter of some difficulty—unless the Wyvern had Guild affiliations. If that were so, I could use the knowledge of the correct codes gained from my father to make contact. But I was going to have to walk a very narrow line between discovery and complete disaster. If Tacktile was honest, or wanted to protect a standing with the Patrol, the mere showing of what I carried would lead to denunciation. If he was Guild, the source of my gems would be of interest. Either way I was ripe for betrayal and must make my deal quickly. Yet I knew well the value of what I held and was going to lose no more of the profit than I was forced to.

I gave the Terran what I hoped was a meaningful stare and out of the past I recalled what I hoped would work—unless the code had been changed.

"By the six arms and four stomachs of Saput," I mumbled, "it is pleasing I need now."

The clerk did not show any interest. He was either well schooled or wary.

"You invoke Saput, friend. Are you then late from Jangour?"

"Not so late that I am forgetful enough to wish to return. Her tears make a man remember—too much." I had now given three of the Guild code phrases which in the old days had signified an unusual haul, for the attention of the master of the shop only. They had been well drilled into me when I had stood behind just such a counter in my father's establishment.

"Yes, Saput is none too kind to off-worlders. You will find better treatment here, friend." He had placed one hand palm-down on the counter. With the other he pushed out a dish of candied bic plums, as if I must be wooed as a buyer in one of the Veep shops uptown.

I picked up the top plum, laying the smallest of the greenstones in its place. A quick flicker of eyes told him what I had done. He withdrew the dish, putting it under the counter, where I knew a small visa-com would pick up the sight for Tacktile.

"You have, friend?" he continued smoothly. I laid down one of the lesser zorans from my unhappy Lorgal trade.

"It is flawed." He gave it a quick professional examination. "But as it is the first zoran we have taken in in some time, well, we shall do our best for you. Hock or sale?"

"Sale."

"Ah, we can hock but not buy. For sale you must deal with the master. And sometimes he is not in the mood. You would do better at hock, friend. Three credits—"

I shook my head as might a stupid crewman set for a higher price. "Four credits—outright sale."

"Very well, I shall ask the master. If he says no, it will not even be hock, friend, and you will have lost all." He allowed his finger to hover over the call button set in the counter as if awaiting some change in my mind. I shook my head, and with a commiserating shrug he pressed the button.

Why the elaborate byplay I did not know. Except for me there was no one else in the shop, and surely the other clerks were equally well versed in the code. The only answer must be that they feared some type of snoop ray, at least in the public portion of the shop.

A brief spark of light flashed by the button and the clerk motioned me toward the back of the shop. "Don't say you weren't warned, friend. Your stone is not enough to interest the master, and you shall lose all the way."

"I will see." I passed the other clerks, neither of whom looked at me. As I came to the end of the aisle, a section of wall swung in and I was in Tacktile's office.

It did not surprise me to see the dish of sticky plums on his desk, the greenstone already laid out conspicuously in a pool of light. He raised his gargoyle head, his deep-set eyes searching me, and I was glad that he lacked that other sense given Wyvern females and could not read my thoughts.

"You have more of these?" He came directly to the point.

"Yes, and better."

"They are listed stones, with a criminal history?"

"No, received in fair trade."

He rapped his blunted talons on the desk top, almost uneasily. "What is the deal?"

"Four thousand credits, on acceptance of value."

"You are one bereft of wits, stranger. These on the open market—"

"At auction they would bring five times that amount." He did not offer me a seat, but I took the stool on the other side of the desk.

"If you want your twenty thousand, let them go at auction," he returned. "If they are indeed clean stones, there is no reason not to."

"There is a reason." I moved two fingers in a sign.

"So that is the way of it." He paused. "Four thousand—well, they can go off world. You want cash?"

I gave an inward sigh of relief. My biggest gamble had paid off—he had accepted me as a Guild runner. Now I shook my head. "Deposit at the port."

"Well, very well." Eet's words were in my mind: "He is too afraid not to be honest with us."

Tacktile pulled a recorder to him. "What name?"

"Eet," I told him. "Port credit, four thousand, to one Eet. To be delivered on a voice order repeating," and I gave him code numerals.

I had come to Lylestane with high hopes. I was getting away with a modest return of port fees and supplies, and the danger of making a contact which could alert my enemies.

Now I produced the greenstones, and the Wyvern rapidly separated them. I could tell by his examination that he had some knowledge of gems. Then he nodded and gave the final signal to the recorder.

I retraced my path through the shop and now none of the clerks noticed me. The word had been passed I was to be invisible. When I reached the outside Eet spoke.

"It might be well to drink to your good fortune at the Purple Star." And so out of the ordinary was that suggestion that I was startled into breaking stride. It would be far wiser and better to get back to the ship, to prepare for take-off and rise off world before we got into any more difficulty. Yet Eet's suggestions were, as I well knew from the past, never to be disregarded.

"Why?" I asked and kept on my way, the port lights directly ahead.

"That Zacathan has been planted in Tacktile's," Eet returned as smoothly as if he were reading it all from a tape. "He is hunting for information. Tacktile has it. The Wyvern is to meet someone at the Purple Star within the hour and it is of vast importance."

"Not to us," I denied. The last thing to do was to become involved in some murky deal, especially one with the Guild—

"Not Guild!" Eet cut into my train of thought. "Tacktile is not of the Guild, though he deals with them. This is something else again. Piracy—or Jack raiding—"

"Not for us!"

"You are listed. If the Patrol has done this, you can perhaps buy your way out with pertinent information."

"As we did before? I do not think we can play that game twice. It would have to be information worth a lot—"

"Tacktile was excited, tempted. He visualized a fortune," Eet continued. "Take me into the Purple Star and I can discover what excites him. If you are listed, what kind of future voyages can you expect? Let us buy our freedom. We are still far from seeking the zero stones."

The source of the zero stones had receded from my mind to a half-remembered dream, smothered by the ever-present need to provide us with a living. All my instincts told me that Eet proposed running us headlong into a meteor storm, but the gamble might go two ways. Supposing he could mind-read a meeting between the Wyvern and some mysterious second party—the affair must be important if the Zacathans had seen fit to plant an agent in the shop. And having a drink in a spacers' bar would add to my disguise as an alien crewman who had made a successful deal at the hock-lock.

"Back four buildings," Eet dictated. And when I turned I saw the purple five-pointed light.

It was one of the better-class drinking places, and the door attendant eyed me questioningly as I entered with all the boldness I could muster. I thought he was going to bar me, but if that was so he changed his mind and stepped aside.

"Take the booth to the right under the mask of Iuta," Eet ordered. There was another beyond that but the curtain had been dropped to give its occupants privacy. I settled in and punched the robo-server on the table for the least expensive drink in the house—it was all I could afford and I did not intend to drink it anyway. The lights were dim and the occupants very mixed, but more were of Terran descent than alien. I had no sight of Tacktile. Eet moved on my arm so that his arrow head now pointed to the wall between me and the curtained booth.

"Tacktile has arrived," he announced. "Through a sliding wall panel. And his contact is already there. They are scribo-writing."

I could hear the murmur of voices and guessed that those behind me were discussing some ordinary matter while their fingers were busy with the scribos, which could communicate impervious to any snoop ray. But if their thoughts were intent upon their real business, that dodge would not hide their secrets from Eet.

"It is a Jack operation," my companion reported. "But Tacktile is turning it down. He is too wary—rightly so—the victims are Zacathans."

"Some archaeological find, then—"

"True. One of great value apparently. And this is not the first one to be so jacked. Tacktile says the risk is too great, but the other one says it has been set up with much care. There is no Patrol ship within light-years, it will be easy. The Wyvern is holding fast, telling the other to try elsewhere. He is going now."

I raised my glass but did not sip the brew it contained. "Where and when is the raid?"

"Co-ordinates for the where—he thought of them while talking. No when."

"No concrete proof then for the Patrol," I said sourly, and spilled most of my glass's contents on the floor.

"No," Eet agreed with me. "But we do have the co-ordinates and a warning to the intended victims—"

"Too risky. They might already have been raided and then what? We are caught suspiciously near a Jack raid."

"They are Zacathans," Eet reminded me. "The truth cannot be hid from them, not with one telepath contacting another."

"But you do not know when—it might be now!"

"I do not believe so. They have failed with Tacktile. They must now hunt another buyer, or they may feel they can eventually persuade him. You took a gamble on Sororis. Perhaps this is another for you, with a bigger reward at the end. Get Zacathan backing and your listing will be forgotten."

I got up and went out on the noisy street, the port my goal. In spite of my intentions it would seem that Eet could mold my future, for reason and logic were on his side. Listed, I no longer had a trade. But suppose I did manage to warn some Zacathan expedition of a Jack raid. Not only would it mean that I would gain some very powerful patrons, but the Zacathans dealt only in antiquities, and the very great treasure the stranger had used to tempt Tacktile might well be zero stones!

"Just so." There was smug satisfaction in Eet's thought. "And now I would advise a speedy rise from this far-from-hospitable planet."

I jogged back to the ship, wondering how Ryzk would accept this latest development. To go up against a Jack raid was no one's idea of an easy life. More often it was quick death. Only, with Zacathans involved, the odds were the least small fraction inclined to our side.

NINE

Below us the ball of the planet was a sphere of Sirenean amber, not the honey-amber or the butter-amber of Terra, but ocher very lightly tinged with green. The green areas grew, assumed the markings of seas. There were no very large land masses but rather sprays of islands and archipelagoes, with only two providing possible landing sites.

Ryzk was excited. He had protested the co-ordinates we had brought back from the Purple Star, saying they were in a sector completely off any known map. Now I think all his Free Trader instincts awoke when he realized that we had homed in on an uncharted world.

We orbited with caution, but there was no trace of any city, no sign that this was anything but an empty world. However, we decided at last that the same tactics used at Sororis would be best here—that Eet and I should leave the ship in orbit and make an exploratory trip in the converted LB. And since it seemed logical that the two largest land masses were the most probable sites for any archaeological dig, I made a choice of the northern.

Dawn was the time we descended. Ryzk, having experimented with the LB, had added some refinements to his original adaptations, making it possible to switch from automatics to hand controls. He had run through the drill patiently with me until he thought I could master the craft. Though I did not have the training of a spacer pilot, I had used flitters since I was a child and the techniques of the LB were not too far from that skill.

Eet, once more in his own form, curled up on the second hammock, allowing me to navigate unhindered as we went in. As the landscape became more distinct on the view-plate I saw that its ocher color was due to trees, or rather giant, lacy growths, waving fronds with delicate trunks hardly thicker than my two fists together. They were perhaps twenty or thirty feet tall and swayed and tossed as if they were constantly swept by wind. In color they shaded from a bright rust-brown to a pale green-yellow with brighter tints of reddish tan between. And they seemed to grow uniformly across the ground, with no sign of any clearing where the LB might set down. I had no desire to crash into the growth, which might be far tougher than it looked, and I went on hand controls to cruise above it, searching vainly for some break. So untouched was that willowy expanse that I had about decided my choice of island had been wrong and that we must head south to investigate the other.

Now the fronds gave way from tall to shorter. Then there was a stretch of red sand in which the sunlight awoke points of sharp glitter. This was washed by the green waves of the sea, and such green I had only seen in the flawless surface of a fine Terran emerald.

At this point the beach was wide and in the middle of it was my first signpost, a broad blot of glassified sand blasted by deter rockets, a ship's landing place. I guided the LB past that a little along the fringe of the growth, bringing it down under the overhang of vegetation with a care of which I was rightfully proud. Unless that mark had been left by a scout, I should be able to find traces of the archaeological camp not too far away, or so I hoped.

The atmosphere was breathable without a helmet. But I took with me something Ryzk had put together. We might not be allowed lasers or stunners, but the former Free Trader had patiently created a weapon of his own, a spring gun which shot needle darts. And those darts were tipped with my contribution, made from zorans too flawed to use, cut with a jeweler's tool, and deadly.

I have used a laser and a stunner, but this, at close range, was to my mind an even deadlier weapon, and only the thought that I might have to front a Jack crew prepared me to carry it. Those in space learned long ago that the first instinct of our species, to attack that which is strange as being also dangerous, could not be allowed to influence us. And in consequence, mind blocks were set on the first explorers. Such precautions continued until those who were explorers and colonizers became inhibited against instant hostility. But there were times when we still needed arms, mainly against our own species.

The stunner with its temporary effect on the opponent was the approved weapon. The laser was strictly a war choice and outlawed for most travelers. But as a former

Patrol suspect, I could not have my permit to carry either renewed for a year. I was a "pardoned" man, pardoned for an offense I never committed—something they conveniently forgot. And I had no wish to demand a permit and give them some form of control over me again.

Now that I dropped out of the LB, Eet riding on my shoulder, I was very glad Ryzk had found such an arm. Not that this seemed a hostile world. The sun was bright and warm but not burning hot. And the breeze which kept the fronds ever in play was gentle, carrying with it a scent which would have made a Salarik swoon in delight. From ground level I could see that the trunks of those fronds had smaller branches and those bent under the weight of brilliant scarlet flowers rimmed with gold and bronze. Insects buzzed thickly about these.

The soil was a mixture of red sand and a darker brown earth where the beach gave way to forested land. But I kept to the edge between sand and wood, angling along until I was opposite that patch of glass formed by the heat of the rockets at some ship's fin-down.

There I discovered what had not been visible from above, covered by the trees and vegetation—a path back into the interior of the forest. I am no scout, but elementary caution suggested that I not walk that road openly. However, I soon found that forcing a passage along parallel to the route was difficult. The clusters of flowers beat against my head and shoulders, loosing an overpowering scent, which, pleasant as it was, became a cloying, choking fog when close to the nose. That and a shower of floury, rust-yellow pollen which made the skin itch where it settled finally forced me into the path.

Though fronds had been cut down to open that way, yet the press of the thick growth had spread out overhead to again roof in the channel, providing a dusky, cooling shade. On some of the trees the clusters of flowers were gone and pods hung there, pulling the trunks well out of line with their weight.

The path ran straight, and in the ground underfoot were the marks of robo-carriers. But if the camp had been so well established, why had I not been able to sight it from the air as the LB had passed overhead? Certainly they must have cut down enough fronds to make a clearing for their bubble tents.

Suddenly the trail dipped, leaving rising banks on either side. They had not had to cut a path here, for the earth had been scraped away by their carriers to show a pavement, while the fronds growing on the bank spread to cover the cut completely.

I knelt to examine the pavement, sure that it had been set of a purpose a long time ago, that it was no fortuitous rock shelf. Thus the banks on either hand might well be walls long covered by earth.

The passage continued to deepen and narrow, growing darker and more chill as it went. I slowed my advance to a creep, trying to listen, though the constant sighing of the wind through the fronds might cover any sound.

"Eet?" Finally, out of a need for more than my own five senses, I appealed to my companion.

"Nothing—" His head was raised, swaying slowly from side to side. "This is an old place, very old. There have been men here—" Then he stopped short and I could feel his small body tense against mine.

"What is it?"

"Death smell—there is death ahead."

I had my weapon ready. "Danger for us?"

"No, not now. But death here—"

The cut had now led underground, the earth lips closing the slit above, and what lay ahead was totally dark. I
had a belt beamer, but to use it might bring on us the
very attention which would be danger.

"Is there anyone here?" I demanded of Eet as I halted,
unwilling to enter that pocket of utter black.

"Gone," Eet told me. "But not long ago.
And—no—there is a trace of life, very faint. I think
someone still lives—a little—"

Eet's answer was obscure, and I did not know whether
we dared go on.

"No danger to us," he flashed. "I read pain—no
thoughts of anger or of waiting our coming—"

I dared then to trigger the beamer, which flashed on
stone walls. The blocks had been so set together that
only the faintest of lines marked their joining, with no
trace of mortar at all, only a sheen on their surface, as if
their natural roughness had been either polished away
or given a slick coating. They were a dull red in hue, a
shade unpleasantly reminiscent of blood.

As we advanced, the space widened, the walls almost
abruptly expanding on either side to give one the feeling
of being on the verge of some vast underground chamber. But my beamer had picked up something else, a
tangle of wrecked gear which had been thrown about,
burned by lasers. It was as if a battle had been fought
in this space.

And there were bodies—

The too-sweet scent of the flowers was gone, lost in
the stomach-twisting stench of seared flesh and
blood—until I wanted to reel out of that hole into the
clean open.

Then I heard it, not so much a moan as a kind of
hissing plaint, with that in it which I could not refuse to

answer. I detoured around the worst of the shambles to a place near the wall where something had crawled, leaving a ghastly trail of splotches on the floor that glistened evilly in the beam ray.

It was a Zacathan and he had not been burned down in a surprise attack as had the others I had caught glimpses of amid the chaos of the camp. No, this was such treatment as only the most sadistic and barbaric tribe of some backward planet might have dealt a battle slave.

That he still lived was indicative of the strong bodies of his species. That he would continue to live I greatly doubted. But I would do all I could for him.

I summoned up determination enough to search through the welter of the camp until I found their medical supplies. Even these had been smashed about. In fact, the whole mess suggested either a wild hunt for something hidden or else destruction for the mere sake of wanton pillage.

One who roves space must learn a little of first aid and what I knew I applied now to the wounded Zacathan, though I had no idea of how one treated alien ills. But I did my best and left him in what small comfort I could before I went to look about the chamber. To take him back to the LB I needed some form of transportation, and the camp trail had the marks of robo-carriers. I had not seen any such machines among the wreckage, which might mean they were somewhere in the dark.

I found one at last, its nose smashed against the wall at the far end of that space as if it had been allowed to run on its own until the stone barrier halted it. But beside it was something else, a dark opening where stones had been taken out of the wall, piled carefully to one side.

Curiosity was strong and I pushed in through that slit and flashed the beamer. There was no mistaking the purpose of the crypt. It had been a tomb. Against the wall facing me was a projecting stone outline, still walled up. Instead of being set horizontally as might be expected of a tomb, it was vertical, so that what lay buried there must stand erect.

There were shelves, but all of them were now bare. And I could imagine that what had stood there once had been taken to the camp and was now Jack loot. I had been too late. Perhaps he who had dealt with Tacktile had not known that the raid was already a fact, or had chosen to suppress that knowledge.

I returned to the carrier. In spite of the force with which it had rammed the wall it was still operative, and I put it in low gear, so that it crawled, with a squeal of protesting metal, back to the Zacathan. Since he was both taller and heavier than I, it was an effort to load his inert body on the top of the machine. But fortunately he did not regain consciousness and I thought one of the balms Eet had suggested I employ had acted as an anesthetic.

There was no use searching the wreckage. It was very plain that the raiders had found what they came for. But the wanton smashing was something I did not understand—unless Jacks were a different breed of thief from the calmly efficient Guild.

"Can you run the carrier?" I asked Eet. It obeyed a simple set of buttons, usable, I believed, by his hand-paws. And if he could run it I would be free to act as guard. Though I thought the Jacks had taken off, there was no sense in not being on the alert.

"Easy enough." He leaped to squat behind the controls, starting the machine, though it still complained noisily.

We reached the LB without picking up any sign that the raiders had lingered here or that there were any other survivors of the archaeological party. Getting the Zacathan into the hammock of the craft was an exhausting job. But I did it at last and flipped the automatic return which would take us to the *Wendwind.*

With Ryzk's help I carried the wounded survivor to one of the lower cabins. The pilot surveyed my improvised treatment closely and at last nodded.

"Best we can do for him. These boys are tough. They walk away from crashes that would pulp one of us. What happened down there?"

I described what I had found—the opened tomb, the wreckage of the camp.

"They must have made a real find. Now there's something worth more than all your gem hunting, even if you made a major strike! Forerunner stuff—must have been," Ryzk said eagerly.

The Zacathans are the historians of the galaxy. Being exceptionally long-lived by our accounting of planet years, they have a bent for the keeping of records, the searching out of the source of legends and the archaeological support for such legends. They knew of several star-wide empires which had risen and fallen again before they themselves had come into space. But there were others about whom even the Zacathans knew very little, for the dust of time had buried deep all but the faintest hints.

When we Terrans first came into the star lanes we were young compared to many worlds. We found ruins, degenerate races close to extinction, traces over and over again of those who had preceded us, risen to heights we had not yet dreamed of seeking, then crashed suddenly or withered slowly away. The Forerunners, the first explorers had called them. But there were many Forerunners, not just of one empire or species, and those Forerunners had Forerunners until the very thought of such lost ages could make a man's head whirl.

But Forerunner artifacts were indeed finds to make a man wealthy beyond everyday reckoning. My father had shown me a few pieces, bracelets of dark metal meant to fit arms which were not of human shape, odds and ends. He had treasured these, speculated about them, until all such interest had centered upon the zero stone. Zero stone—I had seen the ruins with the caches of these stones. Had there been any in this tomb which the Zacathans had explored? Or was this merely another branch of limitless history, having no connection with the Forerunner who had used the stones as sources of fantastic energy?

"The Jacks have it all now anyway," I observed. We had rescued a Zacathan who might well die before we could get him to any outpost of galactic civilization, that was all.

"We did not miss them by too much," Ryzk said. "A ship just took off from the south island—caught it on radar as it cut atmosphere."

So they might have set down there and used a flitter to carry out the raid—which meant they had either scouted the camp carefully or had a straight tip about it. Then what Ryzk had said reached my inner alarms.

"You picked them up—could they have picked us up in return?"

"If they were looking. Maybe they thought we were a supply ship and that's why they cut out so fast. In any case, they will not be coming back if they have what they wanted."

No, they would be too anxious to get their loot into safe hiding. Zacathans, armed with telepathic powers, did not make good enemies, and I thought that the Jacks who had pulled this raid must be very sure of a safe hiding place at some point far from any port or they would not have attempted it at all.

"Makes you think of Waystar," commented Ryzk. "Sort of job those pirates would pull."

A year earlier I would have thought Ryzk subscribing to a legend, one of the tall tales of space. But my own experience, when Eet had informed me that the Free Traders who had taken me off Tanth, apparently to save my life after Vondar's murder, had intended to deliver me at Waystar, had given credibility to the story. At least the crew of that Free Trader had believed in the port to which I had been secretly consigned.

But Ryzk's casual mention of it suddenly awoke my suspicions. I had had that near-fatal brush with one Free Trader crew who had operated on the shady fringe of the Guild. Could I now have taken on board a pilot who was also too knowing of the hidden criminal base? And was Ryzk—had he been planted?

It was Eet who saved me from speculation and suspicion which might have been crippling then.

"No. He is not what you fear. He knows of Waystar through report only."

"He"—I indicated the unconscious Zacathan—"might just as well write off his find then."

My try at re-establishing our credit had failed, unless the Zacathan lived long enough for us to get him to some port. Then perhaps the gratitude of his House might work in my favor. Perhaps a cold-blooded measuring of assistance to a fellow intelligent being. Only I was so ridden by my ever-present burden of worry that it was very much a part of my thinking—though I would not have deserted any living thing found in that plundered camp.

I appealed to Ryzk for the co-ordinates to the nearest port. But, though he searched through the computer for any clue as to where we were, he finally could only suggest return to Lylestane. We were off any chart he knew of and to try an unreckoned jump through hyper was a chance no one took, except a First-in Scout as part of his usual duty.

But we did not decide the matter, for as we were arguing it out Eet broke into our dispute to say that our passenger had regained consciousness.

"Leave it up to him," I said. "The Zacathans must have co-ordinates from some world to reach here. And if he can remember those, we can return him to his home base. Best all around—"

However, I was not at all sure that the alien, as badly wounded as he was, could guide us. Yet a return to Lylestane was for me a retracing of a way which might well lead to more and more trouble. If he died and we turned up with only his body on board, who would believe our story of the Jacked camp? It could be said that we had been responsible for the raid. My thinking was becoming more and more torturous the deeper I went into the muddle. It seemed that nothing had really gone right for me since I had taken the zero stone from its hiding place in my father's room, that each move I made, always hoping for the best, simply pushed me deeper into trouble.

Eet flashed down the ladder at a greater speed than we could make. And we found him settled by the head of the bed we had improvised for the wounded alien. The latter had his bandaged head turned a little, was watching the mutant with his one good eye. That they were conversing telepathically was clear. But their mental wave length was not mine, and when I tried to listen in, the sensation was like that of hearing a muttering of voices at the far side of a room, a low sound which did not split into meaning.

As I came from behind Eet the Zacathan looked up, his eye meeting mine.

"Zilwrich thanks you, Murdoc Jern." His thoughts had a sonorous dignity. "The little one tells me that you have the mind-touch. How is it that you came before the last flutters of my life were done?"

I answered him aloud so Ryzk could also understand, telling in as few words as possible about our overhearing of the Jack plot, and why and how we had come to the amber world.

"It is well for me that you did so, but ill for my comrades that it was not sooner." He, too, spoke Basic now. "You are right that it was a raid for the treasures we found within a tomb. It is a very rich find and a remainder of a civilization not heretofore charted. So it is worth far more than just the value of the pieces—it is worth knowledge!" And he provided that last word with such emphasis as I might accord a flawless gem. "They will sell the treasure to those collectors who value things enough to hide them for just their own delight. And the knowledge will be lost!"

"You know where they take it?" Eet asked.

"To Waystar. So it would seem that that is not a legend after all. They have one there who will buy it from them, as has been done twice lately with such loot. We have tried to find who has betrayed our work to these stit beetles, but as yet we have no knowledge. Where do you take me now?" He changed the subject with an abrupt demand.

"We have no co-ordinates from here except those for return to Lylestane. We can take you there."

"Not so!" His denial was sharp. "To do that would be to lose important time. I am hurt in body, that is true, but the body mends when the will is bent to its aid. I must not lose this trail—"

"They blasted into hyper. We cannot track them." Ryzk shook his head. "And the site of Waystar is the best-guarded secret in the galaxy."

"A mind may be blocked where there is fear of losing such a secret. But a blocked mind is also locked against needful use," returned Zilwrich. "There was one among those eaters of dung who came at the last to look about, see that nothing of value was left. His mind held what we must know—the path to Waystar."

"Oh, no!" I read enough of the thought behind his words to deny what he suggested at once. "Maybe the Fleet could blast their way in there. We cannot."

"We need not blast," corrected Zilwrich. "And the time spent on the way will be used to make our plans."

I stood up. "Give us the co-ordinates of your base world. We will set you down there and you can contact the Patrol. This is an operation for them."

"It is anything but a Patrol operation," he countered. "They would make it a Fleet matter, blast to bits any opposition. And how much would then be left of the treasure? One man, two, three, four"—he could not move his head far but somehow it was as if he had pointed to each of us in turn—"can go with more skill than an army. I shall give you only those co-ordinates."

I had opened my mouth for a firm refusal when Eet's command rang in my head. "Agree! There is an excellent reason."

And, in spite of myself, in spite of knowing that no excellent reason for such stupidity could exist, I found myself agreeing.

TEN

It was so wild a scheme that I suspected the Zacathan
of exerting some mental influence to achieve his
ends—though such an act was totally foreign to all I had
ever heard of his species. And since we were committed
to this folly, we would have to make plans within the
framework of it. We dared not go blindly into the
unknown.

To my astonishment, Ryzk appeared to accept our destination with equanimity, as if our dash into a dragon's
mouth was the most natural thing in the world. But I
held a session in which we pooled what we knew of
Waystar. Since most was only legend and space tales, it
would be of little value, a statement I made gloomily.

But Zilwrich differed. "We Zacathans are sifters of
legends, and we have discovered many times that there

411

are rich kernels of truth hidden at their cores. The tale of Waystar has existed for generations of your time, Murdoc Jern, and for two generations of ours—"

"That—that means it antedates our coming into space!" Ryzk interrupted. "But—"

"Why not?" asked the Zacathan. "There have always been those outside the law. Do you think your species alone invented raiding, crime, piracy? Do not congratulate or shame yourselves that this is so. Star empires in plenty have risen and fallen, and always they had those who set their own wills and desires, lusts and envies, against the common good. It is perfectly possible that Waystar has long been a hide-out for such, and was rediscovered by some of your kind fleeing the law, who thereafter put it to the same use. Do you know those coordinates?" he asked Ryzk.

The pilot shook his head. "They are off any trade lane. In a 'dead' sector."

"And what better place—in a sector where only dead worlds spin about burned-out suns? A place which is avoided, since there is no life to attract it, no trade, no worlds on which living things can move without cumbersome protection which makes life a burden."

"One of those worlds could be Waystar?" I hazarded.

"No. The legend is too plain. Waystar is space-borne. Perhaps it was even once a space station, set up eons ago when the dead worlds lived and bore men who reached for the stars. If so, it has been in existence longer than our records, for those worlds have always been dead to us."

He had given us a conception of time so vast we could not measure it. Ryzk frowned.

"No station could go on functioning, even on atomics—"

"Do not be too sure even of that," Zilwrich told him. "Some of the Forerunners had machines beyond our comprehension. You have certainly heard of the Caverns of Arzor and of that Sargasso planet of Limbo where a device intended for war and left running continued to pull ships to crash on its surface for thousands of years. It is not beyond all reckoning that a space station devised by such aliens would continue to function. But also it could have been converted, by desperate men. And those criminals would thus have a possession of great value, if they could continue to hold it—something worth selling—"

"Safety!" I cut in. Though Waystar was not entirely Guild, yet surely the Guild had some ties there.

"Just so," agreed Eet. "Safety. And if they believe they have utter safety there, we may be sure of two things. One, that they do have some defenses which would hold perhaps even against Fleet action, for they cannot think that the situation of their hole would never be discovered. Second, that having been so long in the state of safety, they might relax strict vigilance."

But before Eet had finished, Ryzk shook his head. "We had better believe the former. If anyone not of their kind had gotten in and out again, we would know it. A story like that would sweep the lanes. They have defenses which really work."

I called on imagination. Persona detectors, perhaps locked, not to any one personality, but rather to a state of mind, so that any invader could pass only if he were a criminal or there on business. The Guild was rumored to buy or otherwise acquire inventions which the general public did not know existed. Then they either suppressed them or exploited them with care. No, such a persona detector might be possible.

"But such could be 'jammed,'" was Eet's answer.

Ryzk, who could follow Eet's mental broadcast but not mine (which was good for us both, as I well knew), looked puzzled. I explained. And then he asked Eet:

"How could you jam it? You can't tamper with a persona beam."

"No one ever tried telepathically," returned the mutant. "If disguise can deceive the eye, and careful manipulation of sound waves, the ear, a change in mental channels can do the same for a persona detector of the type Murdoc envisioned."

"That is so," Zilwrich agreed. I must accept the verdict of the two of our company who best knew what was possible with a sixth sense so few of my own species had.

Ryzk leaned back in his seat. "Since we two do not have the right mental equipment, that lets us out. And you, and you"—he nodded to Eet and Zilwrich—"are not able to try it alone."

"Unfortunately your statement is correct," said the alien. "Limited as I now am by my body, I would be a greater hindrance than help—in person—to any such penetration. And if we wait until I am healed"—he could not move enough to shrug—"then we are already lost. For they will have disposed of what they have taken. We were under Patrol watch back there—"

I stiffened. So we had been lucky indeed in our quick descent and exit from the island world. Had we come during a Patrol visit—

"When the expedition's broadcast signal failed they must have been alerted. And since the personnel of our expedition are all listed, they will be aware of my absence. But also they have evidence of the raid. The

Jacks must have foreseen this, since they have been acting on a reliable source of information. And so they will
be quick to dispose of their loot."

I thought I saw one fallacy in his reasoning. "But if
they have taken the loot to Waystar, and they need not
fear pursuit there, then they may believe they have
plenty of time to wait for a high bid on it and not be so
quick to sell."

"They will sell it, probably to some resident buyer. No
Jack ship will have the patience to sit on a good haul."
Surprisingly Ryzk took up the argument. "They may even
have a backer. Some Veep who wants the stuff for a
private deal."

"Quite true," said Zilwrich. "But we must get there
before the collection is dispersed, or even, Zludda forbid,
broken up for the metal and gems! There was that among
it—yes, I will tell you so you may know the prime importance of what we seek. There was among the pieces a
star map!"

And even I who was sunk in foreboding at that
moment knew a thrill at that. A star map—a chart which
would give those who could decode it a chance to trace
some ancient route, even the boundaries of one of the
fabled empires. Such a find had never been made before.
It was utterly priceless and yet its worth might not be
understood by those who had stolen it.

Not be recognized for what it was—my thoughts clung
to that. From it sprang a wilder idea. My father had had
fame throughout the Guild for appraising finds, especially antiquities. He had had no ambition to climb to
Veep status with always the fear of death from some
equally ambitious rival grinning behind his shoulder. He
had indeed bought out and presumedly retired when his

immediate employer in the system had been eliminated. But he was so widely known that he had become an authority, borrowed at times from his Veep to assist in appraising elsewhere. And he had been noted for dealing with Forerunner treasure.

Who would be the appraiser on Waystar? He would have to be competent, trusted, undoubtedly with Guild affiliations. But supposing that a man of vast reputation turned up at Waystar fleeing the Patrol, which was a very common occupational hazard. He might make his way quietly at first, but then that very reputation would spread to the Veep who had the treasure and he might be asked for an independent report. All a series of ifs, ands, buts, but still holding together with a faint logic. The only trouble was that the man who could do this was dead.

I was so intent upon my thoughts that I was only dimly aware that Ryzk had begun to say something and had been silenced by a gesture from Eet. They were all staring at me, the two who were able to follow my thoughts seemingly bemused. My father was dead, and that appeared to put a very definite end to what might have been accomplished had he been alive. It was a useless speculation to follow, yet I continued to think about the advantage my father would have had. Suppose an appraiser in good standing with the Guild when he retired, one with special knowledge of Forerunner artifacts, were to show up at Waystar, settle down without any overt approach to the Veep who had the treasure. It would very logically follow that he would be asked to inspect the loot and then—But at that point my speculation stopped short. I could not foresee action leading to the retaking of the treasure—that could only be planned after the setup on Waystar had been reconnoitered.

Must be planned! I was completely moon-dazed to build on something impossible. Hywel Jern was dead for near to three planet years now. And his death, which had undoubtedly been ordered by the Guild, would be common knowledge. His reputation, in spite of his years of retirement, was too widespread for it to be otherwise. He was *dead*!

"Reports have been wrong before." That suggestion slid easily into my thoughts before I knew Eet had fed it.

"Not in the case of executions carried out by the Guild," I retorted, aroused from my preoccupation with a plan which might have been useful had I only stood in my father's boots.

My father's boots—had that been a sly manipulation of Eet's? No, I was sensitive enough now to his insinuations to be sure that it had been born inside my own mind. When I was a child I had looked forward to being a copy of Hywel Jern. He had filled my life nearly to the exclusion of all else. I did not know until years later that my lukewarm feeling for his wife, son, and daughter must have come from the fact that I was a "duty" child, one of those babies sent from another planet for adoption by a colony family in order to vary what might become too inborn a strain. I had felt myself Jern's son, and I continued to feel that even when my foster mother disclosed the true facts after Jern's death, jealously pointing out that my "brother" Faskel was the rightful heir to Jern's shop and estate.

Hywel Jern had done as well by me as he could. I had been apprenticed to a gem buyer, a man of infinite resources and experience, and I had been given the zero stone, as well as all I could absorb of my father's teachings. He had considered me, I was fully convinced, the son of his spirit, if not of his body.

There might be some record somewhere of my true parentage; I had never cared to pursue the matter. But I thought that the same strain of aloof curiosity and restlessness which had marked Hywel Jern must also have been born into me. Given other circumstances I might well have followed him into the Guild.

So—I had wanted to be like Hywel Jern. Would it be possible for me to *be* Jern for a period of time? The risk such an imposture would entail would be enormous. But with Eet and his esper powers—"

"I wondered," the mutant thought dryly, "when you would begin to see clearly."

"What's this all about?" Ryzk demanded with some heat. "You"—he looked almost accusingly at me—"you have some plan to get into Waystar?"

But I was answering Eet, though I did so aloud, as if to deny the very help which might be the key to the whole plan. "It is too wild. Jern is dead, they would be sure of that!"

"Who is Jern and what has his death got to do with it?" Ryzk wanted to know.

"Hywel Jern was the top appraiser for one sector Veep of the Guild, and my father." I stated the facts bleakly. "They murdered him—"

"On contract?" asked Ryzk. "If he's dead, how is he of any use to us now? Sure, I can see how an appraiser with Guild rank might get into Waystar. But—" He paused and scowled. "You got some idea of pretending to be your father? But they would know—if there was a contract on him, they'd know."

Only now I was not quite so sure of that. My father had been in retirement. True enough, he had been visited from time to time by Guild men. I had had my proof of that when I had recognized as one of those visitors the captain of the Guild ship who had ordered my questioning on the unknown world of the zero-stone caches. Jern must have been killed by Guild orders for the possession of the zero stone, which his slayers did not find. But supposing they had left a body in which they thought life extinct and my father had revived? There had been a funeral service carried out by his family. But that, too, was an old cover for a man's escape from vengeance. And on the sparsely settled frontier planet he had chosen for his home, they could not have investigated too much for fear of detection.

So, we had Hywel Jern resurrected, smuggled off world perhaps—There were many radical medical techniques—plastic surgery which could alter a man. No, that was wrong. It must be an unmistakable Hywel Jern to enter Waystar. I tried again to dismiss the plan busy fitting itself together piece by piece in my mind—utter folly, logic told me it was. But I could not. I must look like Hywel Jern. And my appearance would be baffling, for who would believe that someone would assume the appearance of a dead man, and one who had been killed by Guild orders? Such a circumstance might give me even quicker access to the Veeps on Waystar. If past rumor spoke true, there was a rivalry between the Veeps of Waystar and the center core of the Guild. The former might well receive a fugitive, one they could use, even if he were now Guild-proscribed. After all, once at their station, he would be largely a prisoner they could control utterly.

Thus—Hywel Jern, running from the Patrol. After all, I *had* been a quarry of both sides for a while because I had the zero stone. The zero stone. My thoughts circled

back to that. I had not put to any use the one I carried
next to my body—not experimented to step up the *Wen-dwind's* power as Eet and I had discovered it could do.
I had not even looked at it in weeks, merely felt in my
belt at intervals to know I still carried it.

To dare even hint that I carried such would make me
an instant target for the Guild, break the uneasy truce,
if that still held, between the Patrol (who might suspect
but could not be sure) and me. No, that I could not use
to enter the pirate station. Back to Hywel Jern. He had
never been on Waystar. Of that I was reasonably certain.
So he would not have to display familiarity with any part
of it. And with Eet to pick out of minds what I *should*
know—

But could I be Hywel Jern for the length of time it
would—might well—take for the locating of the loot? I
had held my scar-faced disguise for only hours, the alien
countenance I had devised for the Lylestane venture
even less. And I would have to be Hywel Jern perhaps
for days, keeping up that facade at all times lest I be
snooped or surprised.

"It cannot be done, not by me," I told Eet, since I
knew that he, of the three facing me, was the one waiting
for my decision, preparing arguments to counter it.

"You could not hold it either," I continued, "not for
so long."

"There you speak the truth," he agreed.

"Then it is impossible."

"I have discovered"—Eet assumed that pontifical air
which I found most irksome, which acted on me as a
spur even when I was determined not to be ridden by
him in any direction—"that few things, very few things,
are impossible when one has all the facts and examines

them carefully. You did well with the scar—for one of your limited ability—your native ability. You did even better with your alien space man. There is no reason why you cannot—"

"I cannot hold it—not for the necessary length of time!" I shot back at him, determined to find, for once and all, an answer which would satisfy my own thoughts as well as the subtle compulsion I sensed coming from both telepaths.

"That, too, can be considered," Eet returned evasively. "But now, rest is needed for our friend."

And I awoke to the fact that the Zacathan had indeed slumped on his bed. His eye was near closed and he appeared to be completely exhausted. Together with Ryzk I worked to make him as comfortable as possible and then I went to my own cabin.

I threw myself on my bunk. But I found that I could not shut off my thoughts, bent as they were, in spite of my desires, on the solving of what seemed to be the first of the insurmountable problems. So I lay staring up at the ceiling of the cabin, trying to break my problem down logically. Hywel Jern might get into Waystar. Possibly I could use Eet's form of disguise to become Hywel Jern. But the exertion of holding that would be a drain which could exhaust both of us and might not leave my mind clear enough to be as alert as I must be to cope with the dangers awaiting us in the heart of the enemies' territory.

If there was only some way to increase my power to hold the illusion without draining myself and Eet. For Eet must have freedom for the mind reading which would be the additional protection we had to have. Increase the power—just as we were able to increase the power of the Patrol scout with the zero stone. The zero stone!

My fingers sought that very small bulge in my belt. I sat up and swung my feet to the cabin floor. For the first time in weeks I unsealed that pocket and brought out the colorless, unattractive lump which was the zero stone in its unawakened phase.

Zero stone—energy, extra energy for machines, for stepping up their power. But when I strove to create the illusions, I used energy of another kind. Still it was energy. But my race had for so long been used to the idea of energy only in connection with machines that this was a new thought. I closed both my hands over the gem, so that its rough edges pressed tightly, painfully, into my flesh.

The zero stone plus a machine already alive with energy meant a heightened flow, an output which had been almost too much for the engine in the scout ship to handle. Zero stones had apparently powered the drifting derelict we had found in space, Eet and I. And it had been their energy broadcast that had activated the stone I then carried, causing it to draw us to the derelict in the first place. Just as on the unnamed planet a similar broadcast had guided us to the long-forsaken ruins where the stones' owners had left their caches.

Energy—But the idea which was in my mind was no wilder than others that had visited me lately. There was a very simple trial. Not on myself, not yet. I was wary of experimentation I might not be able to control. I looked about me hurriedly, seeing Eet curled, apparently asleep, on the foot of my bunk. For a moment I hesitated—Eet? There was humor in that, and something else—the desire to see Eet for once startled out of his usual competent control over the situation.

I stared at Eet. I held the zero stone, and I thought—

The cold gem between my hands began to warm, grew hotter. And the lines of Eet's body began to dim. I dared not allow one small spark of triumph to break my concentration. The stone was afire almost past the point where I could continue to hold it. And Eet—Eet was gone! What lay on the foot of my bunk now was what his mother had been, a ship's cat.

I had to drop the stone. The pain was too intense for me to continue to hold it. Eet came to his feet in one of those quick feline movements, stretched his neck to right and left, to look along his body, and then faced me, his cat's ears flattened to his skull, his mouth open in an angry hiss.

"You see!" I was exultant.

But there was no answer to my mind-touch—nothing at all. It was not that I met the barrier which Eet used to cut off communication when he desired to retire into his own thoughts. Rather it seemed that Eet was not!

I sank down on the pull seat to stare back at the angry cat now crouched snarling, as if to spring for my throat. Could it be true that I had done more than create an illusion? It was as if Eet *was* now a cat and not himself at all! I had indeed stepped up energy and to what disastrous point? Frantically I took the stone tightly into my seared hands, grasped it between my painful palms, and set about undoing what I had done.

No cat, I thought furiously, but Eet—Eet in his mutation from the enraged bundle of fur now facing me with anger enough, had it been larger, to tear out my life. Eet, my thoughts commanded as I fought panic and tried only to concentrate on what I *must* do—get Eet back again.

Again the stone warmed, burned, but I held it in spite of the torment to my flesh. The furry contours of the cat dimmed, changed. Eet crouched there now, his rage even somehow heightened by the change into his rightful body. But was it truly Eet?

"Fool!" That single word, hurled at me as a laser beam might be aimed, made me relax. This was Eet.

He leaped to the table between us, stalked back and forth, lashing his ridged tail; in his fury, very feline.

"Child playing with fire," he hissed.

I began to laugh then. There had been little to amuse one in the weeks immediately behind us, but the relief of having pulled off this impossibility successfully, plus the pleasure of having at last surprised and bested Eet in his own field, made me continue to laugh helplessly, until I leaned weakly back against the wall of the cabin, unwitting of the pain in my hands.

Eet stopped his angry pacing, sat down in a feline posture (it seemed to me his cat ancestry was more notable than before) with his tail curled about him so that its tip rested on his paws. He had closed his mind tightly, but I was neither alarmed nor abashed by his attitude. I was very sure that Eet's startled reaction to transformation was only momentary and that his alert intelligence would speedily be bent to consider the possibilities of what we had learned.

I stowed the stone carefully in my belt and treated my burned hands with a soothing paste. The mutant continued to sit statue-still and I made no further attempts at mind-touch, waiting for him to make the first move.

That I had made a momentous discovery exhilarated me. At that moment nothing seemed outside my grasp. It was not only machine energy which the zero stone furthered; it could also be mental. As a cat, Eet had been silenced and, I was sure, unable by himself to break the image I had thought on him, even for his own defense. This must mean that any illusion created with the aid of the stone would have no time limit, remaining so until one thought it away.

"Entirely right." Eet came out of his sulk—or perhaps it was a deep study. His rage also seemed to have vanished. "But you were indeed playing with a fire which might have consumed us both!" And I knew that he did not mean the burns on my hands. Even so, I was not going to say that I was sorry the experiment had worked. We needed it. Hywel Jern could indeed go to Waystar and it would require no expenditure of energy to keep the illusion intact as long as he carried the zero stone.

"To take that in," remarked Eet, "is a great hazard." And his reluctance puzzled me.

"You suspect"—I thought I guessed what bothered him—"they might have one, able to pick up emanations from ours?"

"We do not know what the Guild had as their original guide to the stones. And Waystar would be an excellent stronghold for the keeping of such. But I agree that we cannot be choosers. We must take such a chance."

ELEVEN

"It must be here." Ryzk had brought us out of hyper in a very old system where the sun was an almost-dead red dwarf, the planets orbiting around it black and burned-out cinders. He indicated a small asteroid. "There is a defense shield up there. And I don't see how you are going to break through that. They must have an entrance code and anything not answering that and getting within range—" He snapped his fingers in a significant gesture of instantaneous extinction.

Zilwrich studied what showed on the small relay visa-screen we had set up in his cabin. He leaned against the back rest we had improvised, his inert head frill crum-pled about his neck. But though he appeared very weak, his eye was bright, and I think that the interest in the unusual which motivated his race made him forget his wounds now.

"If I only had my equipment!" He spoke Basic with the hissing intonation of his species. "Somehow I do not believe that is a true asteroid."

"It may be a Forerunner space station. But knowing that is not going to get us in undetected," rasped Ryzk.

"We cannot all go in," I said. "We play the same game over. Eet and I shall take in the LB."

"Blasting through screens?" scoffed Ryzk. "I tell you, our detect picked up emanations as strong as any on a defensive Patrol outpost. You'd be lasered out of existence quicker than one could pinch out an angk bug!"

"Suppose one dogged in a ship which did have the pass code," I suggested. "The LB is small enough not to enlarge the warn beep of such a one—"

"And when are you going to pick up a ship to dog in?" Ryzk wanted to know. "We might hang here for days—"

"I think not," Eet cut in. "If this is truly Waystar, then there will be traffic, enough to cut down days of waiting. You are the pilot. Tell us if this could be done—could the LB ride in behind another ship in that way?"

It secretly surprised me that there were some things Eet did not know. Ryzk scowled, his usual prelude to concentrated thought.

"I could rig a distort combined with a weak traction beam. Cut off the power when that connected with another ship. You'd have this in your favor—those defenses may only be set for big stuff. They'd expect the Fleet to burn them out, not a one-man operation. Or they might detect and let you through. Then you'd find a welcome-guard waiting, which would probably be worse than being lasered out at first contact."

He seemed determined to paint the future as black as possible. I had only what I had learned of the zero stone to support me against the very unpleasant possibilities ahead. Yet the confidence my experiment had bred in me wavered only in the slightest degree.

In the end, Ryzk turned his Free Trader's ingenuity to more work on the LB, giving it what defenses he could devise. We could not fight, but we were now provided with distorters which would permit us to approach the blot our ship's radar told us was Waystar, and then wait for the slim chance of making a run into the enemies' most securely guarded fortress.

Meanwhile, the *Wendwind* set down on the moon of the nearest dead planet, a ball of creviced rock so bleak and black that it should afford a good hiding place. And the co-ordinates of that temporary landing site were fed into the computer of the LB to home us if and when we left the pirate station—though Ryzk was certain we would never be back and said so frankly, demanding at last that I make a ship recording releasing him from contract and responsibility after an agreed-upon length of time. This I did, Zilwrich acting as witness.

All this did not tend to make me set about the next part of our venture with a great belief in success. I kept feeling the lump of the zero stone as a kind of talisman against all that could go wrong, too long a list of possible disasters to count.

Eet made a firm statement as we prepared our disguise.

"I choose my own form!" he said in a manner I dared not question.

We were in my cabin, for I had no wish to share the secret of the zero stone with either Ryzk or the

Zacathan—though what they might think of our disguises I could not tell.

But Eet's demand was fair enough. I took the dull, apparently lifeless gem and laid it on the table between us. My own change was already thought out. But in case I needed a reminder on some details, I had something else, a vividly clear tri-dee of my father. He had never willingly allowed such to be taken, but this had belonged to my foster mother and had been the one thing I had taken, besides the zero stone, from my home when his death closed its doors to me. Why I had done so I could not have said—unless there was buried deep inside me a fragment of true esper talent, that of precognition. I had not looked at the tri-dee since the day I had lifted from that planet. Now, studying it carefully, I was very glad I had it. The face I remembered had, as usual, been hazed by time, and I found memory differed from this more exact record.

Warned by the fury of heat in the stone when I had used it on Eet, I touched it now with some care, my attention centering on the tri-dee, concentrating on the face appearing therein. I was only dimly aware that Eet crouched on the table, a clawed hand-paw joining mine in touching the jewel.

I could not be sure of the change in my outward appearance. I felt no different. But after an interval I glanced at the mirror ready for the necessary check, and indeed saw a strange face there. It was my father, yes, but in a subtle way younger than I remembered him last. But then I was using as my guide a picture taken planet years before I knew him, when he had first wed my foster mother.

There could certainly be no mistaking his sharp, almost harsh features by anyone who had ever known him. And I hoped that Eet could help me carry out the rest of the deception by mind reading and supplying me with the memories necessary to make me a passable counterfeit of a man known in Guild circles.

Eet—what had been his choice of disguise? I fully expected something such as the pookha or the reptilian form he had taken on Lylestane. But this I did not foresee. For it was no animal sitting cross-legged on the table, but a humanoid perhaps as large as a human child of five or six years.

The skin was not smooth, but covered with a short plushy fur, much like that of the pookha. On the top of the head this grew longer, into a pointed crest. Only the palms of the hands were bare of the fur, which in color was an inky black, and the skin bared there was red, as were the eyes, large and bulging a little from their sockets, the red broken only by vertical pupils. The nose had a narrow ridge of fur up and down it, giving a greater prominence to that feature. But the mouth showed only very narrow slits of lips and those as black as the fur about them.

To my knowledge I had neither seen nor heard described such a creature, and why Eet had chosen to assume this form first intrigued and then bothered me. Space-rovers were addicted to pets and one met with many oddities accompanying their masters. But this was no pet, unusual as it looked. It had the aura of an intelligent life form, one which could be termed "man."

"Just so." Eet gave his old form of agreement. "But I think you will discover that this pirate hold will have varied life forms aboard. And also this body has possibilities which may be an aid in future difficulties."

"What are you?" curiosity made me ask.

"You have no name for me," Eet returned. "This is a life form which I believe long gone from space."

He ran his red-palmed hands over his furred sides, absent-mindedly scratching his slightly protrudent middle. "You, yourselves, admit you are late-comers to the stars. Let it suffice that this is an adequate body for my present need."

I hoped Eet was right, as there was no use in arguing with him. Now I saw something else. That hand not occupied with methodical hide-scratching hovered near the zero stone—though if Eet was preparing to snatch that treasure I did not see where, in his present unclothed state, he would stow it. However, my fingers closed promptly on the gem and sealed it back in my belt. Eet was apparently not concerned, for his straying hand dropped back on his knee.

We bade good-by to Ryzk and the Zacathan. And I did not miss that Zilwrich watched Eet with an attention which might have been rooted in puzzlement but which grew into a subdued excitement, as if he recognized in that black-furred body something he knew.

Ryzk stared at us. "How long can you keep that on?" It was plain that he thought our appearances the result of some plasta change. But how he could have believed we carried such elaborate equipment with us I did not know.

"As long as necessary," I assured him and we went to board the greatly altered LB.

As we took off, forcibly ejected from the parent ship by the original escape method, we aimed in the general direction of the pirate station. But Ryzk's modifications allowed us to hover in space, waiting a guide. And it was Eet in his new form who took over the controls.

How long we would have to patrol was the question. Waiting in any form is far more wearisome than any action. We spent the slowly dragging time in silence. I was trying to recall every small scrap of what my father had said about his days with the Guild. And what lay in Eet's mind I would not have tried to guess. In fact, I was far too occupied with the thought that my father had been remarkably reticent about his Guild activities and that there might be as many pitfalls ahead as those pocking the dead moon, with only hair-thick bridges spanning them.

But our silence was broken at last by a clatter from the control board and I knew our radar had picked up a moving object. The tiny visa-screen gave us a ship heading purposefully for the station. Eet glanced over his shoulder and I thought he was looking at me for orders. The mutant was not accustomed, once a matter had been decided, to wait for permission or agreement. I found myself nodding my head, and his fingers made the necessary adjustments to bring us behind that other ship, a little under its bulk where we might apply that weak traction beam without being sighted, or so we hoped.

The size of the newcomer was in our favor. I had expected something such as a scout ship, or certainly not larger than the smallest Free Trader. But this was a bulk-cargo vessel, of the smallest class, to be sure, but still of a size to be considered only a wallowing second-rate transfer ship.

Our traction beam centered and held, drawing us under the belly of the bigger vessel, which overhung us, if anyone had been out in space to see, as a covering shadow. We waited tensely for some sign that those in the other ship might be alarmed. But as long moments slipped by we breathed more freely, reassured by so much, though it was very little.

However, on the visa-screen what we picked up now was not the ship, but what lay ahead. For additional safety Eet had snapped on the distort beam and through that we could see just a little of the amazing port we neared.

Whatever formed its original core—an asteroid, a moon, an ancient space station—could not be distinguished now. What remained was a mass of ships, derelicts declared so by their broken sides, their general decrepit appearances. They were massed, jammed tightly together into an irregular ovoid except in one place directly before us, where there was a dark gap, into which the ship controlling our path was now headed.

"Looted ships—" I hazarded, ready to believe now in every wild story of Waystar. Pirates had dragged in victim ships to help form their hiding place—though why any such labor was necessary I could not guess. Then I saw—and felt—the faint vibration of a defense screen. The LB shuddered but it did not break linkage with the ship. Then we were through without any attack.

As the wall of those crumpled and broken ships funneled about us, I foresaw a new danger, that we might be scraped or caught by the wreckage, for that space down which we were being towed narrowed the farther we advanced.

Also, though the ships had seemed tightly massed at first sight, this proved not to be so upon closer inspection. There were evidences that they had been intended as an enveloping cover for whatever core lay at the heart. There were girders and patches of skin welded together, anchoring one wreck to another. But it was a loose unity

and there were spaces in between, some large enough
to hold the LB.

Seeing those, and calculating that we might come to
grief ahead were the passage to narrow to the point
where only the cargo ship might wedge through, I
decided one gamble was better than another.

"Wedge in here"—I made this more a suggestion than
an order—"then suit up and go through?"

"Perhaps that is best," Eet answered. However, I suddenly remembered that though I might suit up, there
was no protective covering on board which would take
Eet's smaller body.

"The disaster bag," Eet reminded me as his hands
moved to loose our tie with the bulk of ship overhead.

Of course, the baglike covering intended to serve a
seriously injured escapee using the LB, one whose hurt
body could not be suited up if the emergency landing
had been made on a planet with a hostile atmosphere
and it was necessary to leave the boat. I unstrapped, and
opened the cupboard where the suit lay at full length.
The disaster bag was in tight folds beside its booted feet.
Passage in that would leave Eet helpless, wholly depen-
dent on me, but there was hope it would not be for long.

He was busy at the controls, turning the nose of the
LB to the left, pointing it into one of those hollows in
the mass of wreckage. The impetus left us by the pull of
the ship sufficed to give us forward movement, and two
girders welded just above the hole we had chosen held
the pieces of wreckage forming its walls steady. There
was a bump as we scraped in, and another, moments
later, as the nose of the LB rammed against some obstacle. We could only hope that the crevice had swallowed
us entirely and that our tail was not sticking betrayingly
into the ship passage.

I suited up as fast as I could, wanting to make sure of that fact—though what we could do to remedy matters if that had happened I did not have the slightest idea. Then I hauled out the disaster bag and Eet climbed in so that I could make the various sealings tight and inflate its air supply. Since it was made for a man he had ample room, in fact moved about in it in the manner of one swimming in a very limited pool, for there was no gravity in this place and we were in free fall.

Activating the exit port, I crawled out with great care, fearing more than I wanted to admit some raw edge which could pierce the protecting fabric of the suit or Eet's bag. But there was space enough to wriggle down the length of the LB, mostly by feel, for I dared not flash a beamer here.

Fortune had served us so far. The tail of the LB was well within the hole. And I had to hitch and pull, the weight of Eet dragging me back, by grasping one piece of wreckage and then the next for several lengths until I was in the main passage.

There was a weak light here, though I could not see its source, enough to take me from one handhold to the next, boring into the unknown. I made that journey with what speed I could, always haunted by the fear that another ship might be coming in or going out and I would be caught and ground against the wreckage.

The band of murdered ships ended suddenly in a clear space, a space which held other ships—three I could see. One was the cargo ship which had brought us in, another was one of those needle-nosed, deadly raiders I had seen used by the Guild, and the third was plainly a yacht. They were in orbit around what was the core of this whole amazing world in space. And it was a station, oval in shape like the protecting mass of wreckage, with landing stages at either end. Its covering was opaque, but with a crystalline look to the outer surface, which was pitted and pocked and had obviously been mended time and time again with substances that did not match the original material.

The cargo ship had opened a hatch and swung out a robo-carrier, heavily laden. I held on to my last anchorage and watched the robo spurt into a landing on a stage. The top half carrying the cargo dropped off and moved into an open hatch of the station while the robo took off for another load. There was no suited overseer to be seen, just robos. And I thought I saw a chance to make use of them to reach the station, just as we had used the robos to leave the caravansary.

Only I was not to have an opportunity to try. Out of nowhere came a beam, the force of which plastered me as tightly to the wreckage at my back as if my suit had indeed been welded in eternal bondage.

There was no breaking that hold. And my captors were very tardy about coming to collect me, finally spurting from the hatch of the yacht on a mini air sled. They lashed me into a tangle cord and used it as a drag to pull me behind them, not back to the ship from which they had issued, but to the landing stage where the robo had set down. Then, dismounting from their narrow craft, they tugged us both through a lock and into the interior of the station, where a weak gravity brought my boots and Eet's relaxed body to the floor.

Those who had taken me prisoner were humanoid, perhaps even of Terran breed, for they had that look. They snapped up their helmets and one did the same for me, letting in breathable air, though it had that peculiar faint odor of reprocessed oxygen. Leaving the tangle about my arms, they loosed me enough to walk, pointing with a laser to enforce my going. One of them took the bag from me and towed Eet, turning now and then to study the mutant narrowly.

So it was as prisoners that we came to the legendary Waystar, and it was an amazing place. The center was open, a diffused light filling it, a greenish light which gave an unpleasant sheen to most of the faces passing. By some unknown means there was a light gravity giving a true up and down to the corridors and balconies opening on that center. I caught sight of what could be labs, passed other doors tightly shut. There was population enough to equal that of a village on an ordinary planet—though, as I guessed, those who used the station as home base were often in space and the permanent dwellers were limited in number.

It was one of the latter I was taken before. He was an Orbsleon, his barrel bulk immersed in a bowl chair with the pink fluid he needed for constant nourishment washing about his wrinkled shoulders, his boneless upper tentacles floating just beneath its surface. His head was very broad in the lower part, dwindling toward a top in which two eyes were set far apart, well to the sides. His far-off ancestor of the squid clan was still recognizable in this descendant. But that alien body housed a very shrewd and keen intelligence. A Veep in Waystar would be a Veep indeed, no matter what form of body held him.

A tentacle tip flashed from the bowl chair to trigger keys on a Basic talker, for the Orbsleon was a tactile communicator.

"You are who?"

"Hywel Jern." I gave him an answer as terse as his question.

Whether that name meant anything to him I had no way of knowing. And I received no aid from Eet. For the first time I doubted that the mutant could carry some of the burden of my impersonation. It might well be that the alien thought process would prove, in some cases, beyond his reading. Then I would be in danger. Was this such a time?

"You came—how?" The tentacle tip played out that question.

"On a one-man ship. I crashed on a moon—took an LB—" I had my story ready. I could only hope it sounded plausible.

"How through?" There was of course no readable expression on the alien's face.

"I saw a cargo ship coming in, hung under it. The LB played out halfway through the passage. Had to suit up and come along—"

"Why come?"

"I am a hunted man. I was Veep Estampha's value expert, I thought to buy out, live in peace. But the Patrol were after me. They sent a man on contract when they could not take me legally. He left me for dead. I have been on the run ever since." So thin a tale it might hold only if I were recognized as Hywel Jern. Now that I was well into this I realized more and more my utter folly.

Suddenly Eet spoke to me. "They have sent for one who knew Jern. Also they did not register 'dead' when you gave your name."

"What do here?" my questioner went on.

"I am an appraiser. There is perhaps need for one here. Also—this is the one place the Patrol is not likely to take me." I kept as bold a front as I could.

A man came in at the slow and rather stately pace the low gravity required. To my knowledge I had not seen him before. He was one of the mutants of Terran stock having the colorless white hair and goggle-protected eyes of a Faltharian. Those goggles made his expression hard to read. But Eet was ready.

"He did not know your father well, but had seen him several times in Veep Estampha's quarters. Once he brought him a Forerunner piece, a plaque of iridium set with bes rock. Your father quoted him a price of three hundred credits but he did not want to sell."

"I know you," I said swiftly as Eet's mind read that for me. "You had a piece of Forerunner loot—iridium with bes setting—"

"That is the truth." He spoke Basic with a faint lisp. "I sold it to you."

"Not so! I offered three hundred, you thought you could do better. Did you?"

He did not answer me. Rather his goggled head swung toward the Orbsleon. "He looks like Hywel Jern, he knows what Jern would know."

"Something—you do not like?" queried the tentacles on the keys.

"He is younger—"

I managed what I hoped would register as a superior smile. "A man on the run may not have time or credits enough for a plasta face change, but he can take rejub tablets."

The Faltharian did not reply at once. I wished I could see the whole of his face without those masking goggles. Then, almost reluctantly, he did answer.

"It could be so."

During all those moments the Orbsleon's gaze had held on me. I did not see his small eyes blink; perhaps they did not. Then he played the keys of the talker again.

"You appraiser, maybe use. Stay."

With that, not sure whether I was a prisoner or perhaps now an employee, I was marched out of the room and led to a cubby on a lower level, where Eet and I, having been searched for weapons and had the suit and bag taken from us, were left alone. I tried the door and was not surprised to find it sealed. We were prisoners, but to what degree I could not be sure.

TWELVE

What I needed most at that moment was sleep. Life in space is always lived to an artificial timetable which has little relationship to sun or moon, night or day, in the measured time of planets. In hyper, when there is little to do for the smooth running of the ship, one simply sleeps when tired, eats when hungry, so that regular measurement of time does not apply. I did not know really how long it had been since I had had a meal or slept. But now sleep and hunger warred in me.

The room in which we had been so summarily stowed was a very small one, having little in the way of furnishings. And what there was resembled that planned for the economy of space, such as is found in a ship. There was a pull-down bunk, snapped up into a fold in the wall when not in use, a fresher, into which I would have to pack myself, when needful, with some care, and a food slot. On the off chance that it might be running, I whirled the single dial above it (there seemed to be no choice of menu). And somewhat to my surprise, the warn lights in the panel snapped on and the front flipped open to display a covered ration dish and a sealed container of liquid.

It would appear that the inhabitants of Waystar were on tight rations, or else they believed that uninvited guests were entitled only to the bare minimum of sustenance. For what I uncovered were truly space rations, nutritious and sustaining, to be sure, but practically tasteless—intended to keep a man alive, not in any way to please his taste buds.

Eet and I shared that bounty, as well as the somewhat sickening vita drink in the container. I did have a fleeting suspicion that perhaps some foreign substance had been introduced into either, one of those drugs which will either make a man tell all he knows or eradicate his will, so that for a time thereafter he becomes merely the tool of whoever exerts mastery over him. But that suspicion did not keep me from eating.

As I dumped the empty containers down the disposal unit I knew that just as I had had to eat, so I must now sleep. But it seemed that Eet did not agree, or not as far as he himself was concerned.

"The stone!" He made a command of those two words.

I did not have to ask what stone. My hand was already at the small pocket in my belt.

"Why?"

"Do you expect me to go exploring in the body of a phwat?"

Go exploring? How? I had already tried the cabin door and found it sealed. Nor did I doubt that they had guards outside, perhaps in the very walls about us—scan rays—

"Not here." Eet appeared very sure of that. "As to how—through there." He indicated a narrow duct near the ceiling, an opening which, if the grill over it were removed, might offer a very small exit.

I sat on the bunk and glanced from the hairy man-thing Eet now was to that opening. When we had first tried this kind of change I had believed it all illusion, though tactile as well as visual. But now, had Eet really altered in bulk so that what I saw before me was actually many times the size of my alien companion? If so—how had that been done? And (in me a sharp fear stabbed) if one did not have the stone, would changes remain permanent?

"The stone!" Eet demanded. He did not answer any of my thoughts. It was as if he were suddenly pressed for time and must be off on some important errand from which I detained him.

I knew I was not going to get any answers from Eet until he was ready to give them. But his ability to read minds was perhaps our best key to this venture and if he now saw the necessity for crawling through ventilation ducts, then I must aid him.

I kept my hand cupped about the stone. Though Eet had said there were no snoop rays on us, yet I would not uncover that treasure in Waystar. I stared at Eet where he hunkered on the floor and forced myself to see with the mind's eye, not a furred humanoid, but rather a mutant feline, until just that crouched at my feet.

It was easy to screw out the mesh covering of the duct. And then Eet, using me as a ladder, was up into it with speed. Nor did he leave me with any assurance as to when he would return, or where his journey would lead, though perhaps he did not know himself.

I wanted to keep awake, hoping that Eet might report via mind-touch, but my body needed sleep and I finally collapsed on the bunk into such slumber as might indeed have come from being drugged.

From that I awoke reluctantly, opening eyes which seemed glued shut. The first thing I saw was Eet, back in his hairy disguise, rolled in a ball. I sat up dazedly, trying to win out over the stupor of fatigue.

Eet was back, not only in this cell but in his other body. How had he managed the latter? Fear sharpened my senses and sent my hand to my belt again, but I felt with relief the shape of the stone in the pocket.

Even as I watched bleerily, he unwound, sat up blinking, and stretched his arms, as if aroused from a sleep as deep as mine had been.

"Visitors coming." He might give the outward seeming of one only half awake, but his thought was clear.

I shambled to the fresher. Best not let any arrival know I had warning. I used the equipment therein and emerged feeling far more alert. Even as I looked to the food server, the door opened and one of the Orbsleon's followers looked in.

"Veep wants you."

"I have not eaten." I thought it well to show some independence at the suggestion that I was now the Orbsleon's creature.

"All right. Eat now." If he made that concession (and the very fact that he did was a matter of both surprise and returning confidence for me) he was not going to enlarge upon it. For he stood in the doorway watching me dial the unappetizing food and share it with Eet.

"You—" The guard stared at the mutant. "What do you do?"

"No good talking to him," I improvised hurriedly. "You would need a sonic. He is—was—my pilot. Only fourth part intelligence, but good as a tech."

"So. What is he anyway?" Whether he spoke out of idle curiosity or was following an order to learn more, I did not know. But I had made a reasonable start on providing Eet with a background and I enlarged upon it a little with the name he had given himself.

"He is a phwat, from Formalh—" I added to my inventions. With so many planets supporting intelligent or quasi-intelligent life in the galaxy, no one could be expected to know even a thousandth of them.

"He stays here—" As I prepared to leave, the guard stepped in front of Eet.

I shook my head. "He is empathic-oriented. Without me he will will himself to death." Now I referred to something I had always thought a legend—that two species could be so emotionally intertied. But since I had believed, until last year, that the place in which I now stood was also a legend, there might be truth in other strange tales. At least the guard seemed inclined to accept what I said as a fact; he allowed Eet to shamble along behind me.

We did not return to the room in which the Orbsleon had interviewed me, but rather to one which might be a small edition of the hock-locks I well knew. There was a long table, with various specto-devices clamped on it. In fact, it was a lab which many an appraiser on a planet might have envied. And on the walls were outlines of "safe" cupboards, each one with the locking thumb hole conspicuous in the center, where only the thumb of one authorized to open it would register to release its contents.

"Snooper ray on us," Eet informed me. But I had already guessed that, knowing why I had been brought here. They were going to prove my claim of being an appraiser, which meant tricky business. I would have to call on all I had learned from the man I seemed to be, all that I had picked up since I had left his tutelage, in order to survive such a test.

The things to be valued were spread on the table, under a protective ull web. I went straight to it, for in that moment my lifetime preoccupation took command.

There were four pieces in all, gemmed and set in metal—their glitter sparking life clear across the room. The first was a necklace—koro stones, those prized gems from out of the Sargolian seas which the Salariki doubly value because of their ability to give forth perfume when warmed by the body heat of the wearer.

I held it up to the light, weighed each of the jewels in my hand, sniffed at each stone. Then I let it slide carelessly from my grasp to the bare surface of the table.

"Synthetic. Probably the work of Ramper of Norstead—or of one of his apprentices—about fifty planet years old. They used marquee scent on it—five, maybe six steepings." I gave my verdict and turned to the next piece, knowing I did not have to impress the guard, or the two other men in the room, but rather those who held the snooper ray on me.

The second piece was set in a very simple mounting. And its dark rich fire held me for a moment or two. Then I put it in the cup below the infrascope and took two readings.

"This purports to be a Terran ruby of the first class. It is unflawed, true enough. But it has been subjected to two forms of treatment. One I can identify, the other is new to me. This has resulted in a color shift. I think it was originally a much lighter shade. It will pass, save for quality lab testing. But any expert gemologist would be uneasy about it."

The third on that table was an arm band of metal which was reddish but carried a golden overcast that shifted across the surface when the ornament was handled. The maker had taken advantage of that overcast in working out the pattern on it, which was of flowers and vine, so that the gold appeared to line some of the leaves at all times. There was no mistaking it and my mind jumped back to the day my father had shown me such work, but then as a small pendant he had sold to a museum.

"This is Forerunner, and it is authentic. The only piece I have previously seen was taken from a Rostandian tomb. That was decided by the archaeologists to be very much older than the tomb even. Perhaps it had been found by the Rostandian buried there. Its origin is unknown as yet."

In contrast to the three other offerings the fourth was dull, leaden-gray, ugly metal set with an ill-formed cluster of badly-cut stones. It was only the center stone, one of perhaps four carats, which seemed to have any real life, and that, too, had been unimaginatively treated.

"Kamperel work. The centerpiece is a sol sapphire and would pay recutting. The rest"—I shrugged—"not worth working with. A tourist bauble. If this"—I turned to the two men, who had not spoken—"is the best you have to show me, then indeed, rumor has greatly overrated the take of Waystar."

One of them came around the table to restow the four pieces under the web. I was wondering if I were now to be returned to my cell when the monotonous click of the Veep's voice sounded from some concealed com.

"As you think, this was test. You will see other things. The sol—can you recut?"

Inwardly I sighed with relief. My father had not had that training, I need not be forced to claim it.

"I am an appraiser, not a cutter. It will take skill to make the most out of that stone after it has been mishandled the way it has. I would suggest that it be offered as is"—I thought furiously—"to such a firm as Phatka and Njila." Again I pulled names from my memory, but this time from Vondar's warning about borderline dealers whose inventories of stones were kept in two or three different accountings, those they could sell openly, those to be sold privately. That they had Guild affiliations was suspected but unproved. But my ability to name them would be more proof that I had dealt on the borderline of the law.

There was a period of silence. The man who had rewrapped the treasures in the web now sealed them into one of the wall cubbies. No one commented, nor did the com speak again. I shifted from one foot to the other, wondering what would happen now.

"Bring here—" the com finally clicked.

So I was taken back to the room where the Orbsleon Veep wallowed in his fluid-filled seat. Swung out over the surface of that was a lap table and on it lay a single small piece of metal.

It had no gem and it was an odd size. But the shape I had seen before and knew very well indeed. A ring—meant to fit, not a bare finger, but over the bulky glove of a space suit. Only this had no zero stone, dull and lifeless, in its empty prongs. That it was, or had been,

twin to the ring which had caused my father's death, I
was sure. Yet the most important part was missing. I
knew instantly that this was another test, not of my
knowledge as an appraiser, but of how much I might
know on another subject. My story must hold enough
truth to convince them.

"There is a snooper ray on." Eet had picked up my
thought.

"What this?" The Veep wasted no time in coming to
the test.

"May I examine it?" I asked.

"Take, look, then say," I was ordered.

I picked up the ring. Without its stone it was even
more like a piece of battered junk. How much dared I
say? They must know a great deal about my father's
"death"—So I would give them all my father had known.

"I have seen one of these before—but that had a
stone." I began with the truth. "A dim stone. It had been
subjected to some process which rendered it lifeless, of
no value at all. The ring was found on the space glove
of a dead alien—probably a Forerunner—and brought
to me for hock-lock."

"No value," clicked the voice of the Veep. "Yet you
bought."

"It was alien, Forerunner. Each bit we learn about
such things is knowledge, which makes some men richer.
A hint here, a hint there, and one can be led to a find.
This in itself has no value, but its age and why it was
worn over a space glove—that makes it worth payment."

"Why worn on glove?"

"I do not know. How much do we know of the Forerunners? They were not even all of one civilization, species, or time. The Zacathans list at least four different

star empires before they themselves developed a civilization, and claim there are more. Cities can crumble, suns burn out, sometimes artifacts remain—given proper circumstances. Space itself preserves, as you know well. All we can learn of those Forerunners comes in bits and pieces, which makes any bit of value."

"He asks," Eet told me, "but the questions are now from another."

"Who?"

"One more important than this half-fish." For the first time Eet used a derogatory expression, allowed an aura of contempt to pervade his mind-touch. "That is all I know. The other wears a protective antiesper, antisnoop device."

"This was a ring," I repeated aloud and laid the plundered circlet back on the lap table. "It held a stone now gone, and it resembles the one I held for a time which had been found on a Forerunner."

"You held—now where?"

"Ask that," I returned sharply, "of those who left me for dead when they plundered my shop." False now, but would any snooper detect that? I waited, almost expecting some loud contradiction of my lie. If any had been made perhaps those in the room were not aware of it yet. And if my last statement was accepted as truth, perhaps there might be awkward questions asked inside the ranks of the Guild, the which would do me no harm at all.

"Enough," the voicer clicked. "You go—sales place—watch."

My escort moved for the door. He did not snap to attention as a Patrolman, but he wore a tangler at his belt and I did not dispute his right to see me to where the Veep ordered my attendance.

We passed along one of the balcony corridors which rimmed the open center. It was necessary to shuffle, not lifting the feet much, keeping a handhold on the wall rail, or the low gravity became a hazard. When our way led down on a curled rod with handholds instead of stair-steps, we managed almost as if we were in a grav lift, coming to the third level below that where the Veep had his quarters.

This possessed some of the bustle of a market place. There was a coming and going of many races and species, Terrans, Terran-mutants, humanoids, and nonhuman-oid aliens.

Most of them wore ship uniforms, though unmarked by any official badges. And all of them wore stunners, though I saw no lasers. And I thought perhaps there might be some rule against more lethal weapons here.

The booth into which I was ushered lacked the elabo-rate detection equipment of the lab. Another Orbsleon (plainly of inferior caste, since he still had the crab legs long ago removed from the Veeps) squatted in a bowl with just enough liquid washing in it to keep him on the edge of comfort. It was plain he was in charge and must have expected me. He clicked nothing on his talker, but gestured with one tentacle to a stool back against the wall, where I obediently sat down, Eet hunkering at my feet. There were two others there, and seeing them, I realized, with a shudder I hoped I successfully sup-pressed, just how far outside the bounds of law I was.

There has always been slavery within the galaxy, some-times planet-orientated, sometimes spread through a solar system, or systems. But there are some kinds of slavery which make men's stomachs turn more readily than the war-captive, farm-labor type most widely known. And these—these—*things*—were the result of selective breeding in a slavery the Patrol had worked for years to eliminate from any star lane.

The Orbsleon's servants were humanoid—to a point. But there had been both surgical and genetic modifications, so that they were not truly "men" as the Lankorox scale defines men in an alien-Terran-mutant society. They were rather living machines, each programmed for a special type of service, knowing nothing else. One sat now with his hands resting limply on the table, his whole puffy body slack, as if even the energy which brought him pseudo life had drained away. The other worked with precise and delicate speed at a piece of jewelry, a gem-studded collar such as is worn at a feast of state by a Warlockian Wyvern. He pried each gem from its setting, sorting them with unerring skill, and at the same time graded them, placing the gems in a row of small boxes before him. The many-lensed orbs in his misshapen, too large, too round head were not turned upon what he did but rather stared straight ahead out of the booth, though they were not focused on anything beyond.

"He is a detect—" Eet told me. "He sees all, reports without defining what he sees. The other is a relay."

"Esper!" I was suddenly afraid, afraid that that loosely sprawling hulk of flesh before us might tune in on Eet, know that we two together were far more than we seemed.

"No, he is on a lower band," Eet returned. "Only if his master wishes—"

He lapsed into silence and I knew he, too, knew the danger.

Why I had been sent here I did not know. Time passed. I watched those go to and from outside. The detect slave continued his work until the collar was entirely denuded of its jewels and then the metal went into a larger box. Now the busy fingers brought out a filigree tiara. Selections were made from the boxes of gems, and with almost the same speed with which they had been pried forth from their first settings they were put into the tiara. Though all the jewels were not used, I could see that the result of the work would be a piece which would easily bring a thousand certified credits in any inner planet shop. But all the time he worked, the slave never looked at what he wrought.

What were to be my duties, if any, I was not told. And while the activities of the detect slave interested me for awhile, it was not enough to hold my attention too long. I found the inactivity wearing and I was restless. But surely anyone in my situation would want employment after awhile and no one would be suspicious if I showed my boredom.

I was shifting on what became an increasingly hard stool the longer I sat on it when a man stepped inside the booth. He wore the tunic of a space captain without any company insignia and he appeared to be familiar with the establishment, as he bypassed the table where the slaves sat and came directly to the Orbsleon.

He had been pressing his left hand against his middle—reminding me of my own frequent check on my gem belt. Now he unsealed his tunic and fumbled under its edge. The alien pushed forward a swing table much like the one his Veep had used to display the ring.

The spacer produced a wad of ull web, picked it apart to show a very familiar spot of color—a zoran. The Orbsleon's tentacle curled about the stone and without warning threw it to me. Only instinct gave me the reflex to catch the flying stone out of the air.

"What!" With a sharp exclamation the captain swung around to eye me, his hand on the butt of his stunner. I was turning the stone around, examining it.

"First grade," I announced. Which it was—about the best I had seen for some time. Also it was not a raw stone but had been carefully cut and mounted in a delicate claw setting, hooked to hang as a pendant.

"Thank you." There was sarcasm in the captain's voice. "And who may you be?" He lost now some of his aggressive suspicion.

"Hywel Jern, appraiser," I answered. "You wish to sell?"

"I wouldn't come here just for you to tell me it's first grade," he retorted. "Since when has Vonu added an appraiser?"

"Since this day." I held the stone between me and the light to look at it again. "A fleck of clouding," I commented.

"Where?" He was across the booth in two strides, snatched the jewel out of my hand. "Any clouding came from your breathing on it. This is a top stone." He swung around to the Orbsleon. "Four trade—"

"Zorans are not four trade," the talker clicked. "Not even top grade."

The captain frowned, half turned, as if to march out of the booth. "Three then."

"One—"

"No! Tadorc will give me more. Three!"

"Go Tadorc. Two only."

"Two and a half—"

I had no idea what they bid, since they did not use the conventional credits. Perhaps Waystar had its own scale of value.

The Orbsleon seemed to have reached a firm decision. "Two only. Go Tadorc—"

"All right, two." The captain dropped the zoran on the lap table and the alien's other tentacle stretched to a board of small buttons. When that mobile tip punched out a series on it there was no vocal reply. But he used the talker again.

"Two trade—at four wharf—take supplies as needed."

"Two!" The captain made an explosive oath of that word as he left with a force which might have been a stamp in a place of higher gravity.

The alien again threw the zoran, this time to be caught by the detect, who tucked it away in one of his boxes. And it was then that my earlier guide-guard came to the front of the booth.

"You"—he gestured to me—"come along."

Glad for the moment to be released from the boredom of the booth, I went.

THIRTEEN

"Top Veep," Eet's warning came, to match my own guess as to where we were being taken. We again climbed through the levels to the higher ways of the station, this time passing the one where the Orbsleon had his quarters. Now the time-roughened walls about us showed dim traces of what had once been ornamentation. Perhaps for whatever creatures had built this station this had been officer territory.

I was motioned through a roll door, my guards remaining outside. They made a half-hearted attempt to stop Eet, but he suddenly developed an agility he had not shown before and pushed past them. I thought it odd they did not follow. Then, a moment later, I discovered why the inhabitant of these particular quarters did not need their attendance, for with another step I struck rather painfully against a force wall.

Also, inside this room the light gravity to which I had partially adjusted not only had become full for my race, but had an added pull, so it was an effort to take a step.

Beyond that invisible barrier the room was furnished as might be one in a luxury caravansary on some inner planet. Yet the furniture did not harmonize but was jammed together, showing even differences in scale size, as if some pieces had been made for bodies smaller or larger than my own. The one thing these had in common was their richness, which in some cases was gaudy and blatantly flamboyant.

Stretched in an easirest was the Veep. He was of Terran descent, but with certain subtle differences, modifications of feature, which suggested mutation. Probably he came from a race which had been among the early colonists. His hair had been cut so that it stood above his partially shaven skull in a stiffened roach, making him resemble one of the mercenaries of old times, and I wondered how he got a space helmet over that crest, if he ever did. His skin was brown, not just space-tanned, and there were two scars, too regular to be anything but inflicted on purpose for a patterning, running from corner of eye to chin on either side of his mouth.

Like the gaudy room, his clothing was a colorful mixture of planetary styles from several worlds. His long legs, stretched out in the rest, which fitted itself to give him greatest comfort, were encased in tight-fitting breech-legging-boots of a pliable, white-furred hide, the fur patterned with a watered rippling. Above his waist he wore the brilliant black-and-silver combination of a Patrol admiral's dress tunic complete with begemmed stars and ribbons of decorations. But the sleeves of that had been cut out, leaving his arms bare to the shoulders. Below his elbows he wore on both arms very wide bracelets or armlets of iridium, one mounted with what could only be Terran rubies of the first water, the other with sol sapphires and lokerals running in alternate rows, the vivid greens and blues in harmonious contrast. Both armlets were barbaric in taste.

In addition, his stiffened top ridge of hair was encircled by a band of mesh metal, green-gold—from which hung, flat against his forehead, a pendant bearing a single koro—about ten carats and very fine. The whole effect was that of what he must be, a pirate chief on display.

Whether he wore that mixture of splendor and bad taste by choice or for the effect such a bold showing of wealth might have on his underlings, I did not know. The Guild men in the upper echelons were usually inclined to be conservative in dress rather than ostentatious. But perhaps as master, or one of the masters, of Waystar, he was not Guild.

He watched me reflectively. Meeting his dark eyes, I had the impression that his clothing was a mask of sorts, meant to bedazzle and mislead those with whom he dealt. He was holding a small plate of white translucent jade in one hand, from time to time raising it to his mouth to touch tongue tip in a small licking movement to the gob of blue paste it held.

"They tell me"—he spoke Basic with no definable accent—"that you know Forerunner material."

"To some extent, Gentle Homo. I have seen, have been able to examine perhaps ten different art forms."

"Over there—" He pointed, not with his empty hand, but with his chin, to my left. "Take a look at what lies there and tell me—is it truly Forerunner?"

A round-topped table of Salodian marble supported what he wanted appraised. There was a long string of interwoven metal threads dotted here and there with tiny brilliant rose-pink gems; it could have been intended as either a necklace or a belt. Next to it was a crown or tiara, save that no human could have worn it in comfort, for it was oval instead of round. There was a bowl or basin, etched with lines and studded here and there with gems, as if they had been scattered by chance or whim rather than in any obvious pattern. And last of all, there was a weapon, still in a sheath or holster—its hilt or butt of several different metals, each of a different color but inlaid and mingled with the others in a way I knew we had no means of duplicating.

But what was more, I knew we had found what we had entered this kolsa's den to seek. This was the larger part of the treasure the Zacathans had found in the tomb; I had been too well briefed by Zilwrich to mistake it. There were four or five other pieces, but the best and most important lay here.

It was the bowl which drew my attention, though I knew if the Veep had not already caught the significance of those seemingly random lines and gems he must not be given a hint, by any action of mine, that it was a star map.

I walked toward the table, coming up against the barrier again before I reached it—a circumstance which gave me a chance to assert myself as I was sure Hywel Jern would have done.

"You cannot expect an appraisal, Gentle Homo, if I cannot inspect closely."

He tapped a stud on the chair arm and I could advance, but I noted that he tapped it again, twice, when

I reached the table, and I did not doubt I was now sealed in.

I picked up the woven cord and ran it through my fingers. In the past I had seen many Forerunner artifacts, some in my father's collection, some through the aid of Vondar Ustle. Many others I had studied via tri-dee representation. But this stolen treasure was the richest it had ever been my good fortune to inspect. That the pieces were Forerunner would of course have been apparent even if I had not known their recent past history. But as everyone knew, there were several Forerunner civilizations and this workmanship was new to me. Perhaps the Zacathan expedition had stumbled upon the remains of yet another of those forgotten stellar empires.

"It is Forerunner. But, I believe, a new type," I told the Veep, who still licked at his confection and watched me with an unwavering stare. "As such it is worth much more than its intrinsic value. In fact, I cannot set a price on it. You could offer it to the Vydyke Commission, but you might even go beyond what they could afford—"

"The gems, the metal, if broken up?"

At that moment his question was enough to spark revulsion and then anger in me. To talk of destroying these for the worth of their metal and gems alone was a kind of blasphemy which sickened anyone who knew what they were.

But he had asked me a direct question and I dared not display my reaction. I picked up each piece in turn, longing to linger in my examination of the bowl map, yet not daring to, lest I arouse his suspicion.

"None of the jewels is large," I reported. "Their cutting is not of the modern fashion, which reduces their value, for you would lose even more by attempting to recut. The metal—no. It is the workmanship and history which makes them treasure."

"As I thought." The Veep gave a last lick to his plate and put it aside empty. "Yet a market for such is difficult to find."

"There are collectors, Gentle Homo, who are perhaps not as freehanded as the Vydyke, but who would raise much on all their available resources to have a single piece of what lies here. They would know it for a black deal and so keep what they obtained hidden. Such men are known to the Guild."

He did not answer me at once, but continued to stare, as if he were reading my mind more than concentrating on my words. But I was familiar enough with mind-touch to know he was not trying that. I judged rather that he was considering carefully what I had just said.

But I was now aware of something else which first alarmed and then excited me. There was warmth at my middle, spreading from the pocket which held the zero stone. And that could only mean, since I was not putting it to service, that somewhere near was another of those mysterious gems. I looked to the most obvious setting, that of the crown, but I saw no telltale glow there. Then Eet's thought reached me.

"The bowl!"

I put out my hand, as if to reinspect that piece. And I saw that on the surface nearest me, luckily turned away from the Veep, there was a bright spark of light. One of those seemingly random jewels I had thought were meant to mark stars had come to life!

Picking up the bowl, I turned it idly around, holding my palm to cover the zero stone, and felt both at my middle and from the bowl the heat of life.

"Which do you think of greatest importance?" the Veep asked.

I put down the bowl, the live gem again turned away from him, looking over the whole array as if to make up my mind.

"This perhaps." I touched the strange weapon.

"Why?"

Again I sensed a test, but this time I had failed.

"He knows!" Eet's warning came even as the Veep's hand moved toward the buttons on the chair arm.

I threw the weapon I held. And by some superlative fortune I did not have any right to expect, it crashed against his forehead just beneath that dangling koro stone, as if the force field no longer protected him, or else I was inside it. He did not even cry out, but his eyes closed and he slumped deeper into the hold of the easirest. I whirled to face the door, sure he had alerted his guards. The force field might protect me, but it would also hold me prisoner.

I saw the door open, the guards there. One of them cried out and fired a laser beam. The force field held, deflected that ray enough to send a wave of flame back, and the man farthest into the room staggered, dropped his weapon, and fell against the one behind him.

"There is a way." Eet was by the easirest. He reached up and grabbed at the strange weapon now lying in the Veep's lap. I swept up the other treasures, holding them between my body and arm as I followed Eet to the wall, where he fingered a stud and so opened a hidden door. As that fell into place behind us, he mind-touched again.

"That will not hold them for long, and there are alarms and safeguards all through this wall way. I snouted them out when I explored. They need only throw those into action and we are trapped."

I leaned against the wall, unsealing my tunic and making its front into a bag to hold what I had snatched up. It was so awkward a bundle that I had difficulty in closing the tough fabric over it.

"Did your exploring see a way out?" I asked now. Our escape from that room had been largely a matter of unthinking reflex action. Now I was not sure we had not trapped ourselves.

"These are old repair ways. There are suits in a locker. They still have to patch and repatch the outside. It depends now upon how fast we can reach the suit locker."

The gravity here was practically nonexistent, and we made our way through the dark, which was near absolute, by swimming through the air. Luckily there were handholds at intervals along the outer wall, proving that this method of progression had been used here before. But my mind worried at what lay ahead. Supposing fortune did favor us enough to let us reach the suits, get into them, and out on the outer shell of the station. We still had a long strip of space to cross to the ring of wreckage, and then to find our LB. This time the odds were clearly too high against us. I believed that the whole of Waystar would be alerted to track us down, they to hunt over familiar ground, we lost in their territory.

"Wait—" Eet's warning brought me up with a bump against him. "Trap ahead."

"What do we do—?"

"You do nothing, except not distract me!" he snapped.

I half expected him to make some move forward, for I thought his intention was to disarm what waited us. But he did not. Though no mind-touch was aimed at me, I felt what could only be waves of mental energy striking some distance ahead—and the zero stone in my belt grew uncomfortably warm against my body.

"Well enough," Eet reported. "The energy is now burned out. We have a clear path for a space."

We encountered two more of what Eet declared to be pitfalls, but which I never saw, before we came out of a sliding panel in the wall into a blister compartment on the outer skin of the hull. There we found the suits, just as Eet had foretold. Since I could not stuff myself plus the loot I carried into the one nearest my size, I had to pass the bowl and the tiara on to Eet, who was in the smallest, still much too large for him.

But how we would reach the outer shell of wreckage and the LB, I had not the least idea. The suits were both equipped, it was true, with blast beams, intended to give any worker who was jolted off into open space a chance of returning to the surface of the station. But if we used those, their power might not be enough to take us all the way to the wreckage, and in addition, we would be in plain sight of any watcher or radar screen. However, we did have the treasure and—

"That mistake I made—does the Veep know the importance of the bowl?" I demanded now.

"Part of it. He knows it is a map."

"Which they would not destroy willingly." I hoped that was true.

"You argue from hope, not knowledge," the mutant returned. "But it is all the hope we may have."

I signaled exit from the bubble, and crawled out, the magnetic plates on my boots anchoring me to the surface of the station. Once before Eet and I had so gone into space and I was touched now with the terrible fear which had gripped me then when I had lost my footing on the skin of the Free Trader ship and my contact with security, and floated into empty space.

But here there was a limit to emptiness. The cargo ship which we had followed into this port was gone, but the needle-nosed raider and the yacht were still in orbit, and above, all around, was the mass of wreckage—though I could sight no landmarks there and wondered how we were ever going to discover the narrow inlet in the jagged, tangled mass which hid the LB.

I could see no reason to wait. Either we would coast across to the wreckage or our power would fail. But to wait here any longer was to risk being captured before we had even tried. However, we did take the precaution of linking together by one of the hooked lines meant to anchor a worker to the surface of the station. So united, we took off between the two ships hanging ominously above.

"I cannot reach the controls of my jet—" Eet delivered what might be a final blow, dooming us to capture. Would the power in my own shoulder-borne rocket be enough to take us both over?

I triggered the controls, felt the push thrust which sent me and the suit containing Eet away from the station. My aim was the nearest rim of wreckage. I might be able to work my way along that in search of the passage if I could get to it. But every moment I expected to be caught by tangle beams, somehow sure that the Veep would not risk an annihilating weapon which would destroy his treasure.

The spurt of thrust behind me continued, in spite of the drag Eet caused as he spun slowly about at the end of the line, and there did not come any pursuit or pressure beam. I did not feel any triumph, only a foreboding which wore on my nerves. It is always worse to wait for an attack. I was certain that we had been sighted and that any moment we would be caught in a net.

The thrust failed while we were still well away from the wreckage. And though I got one more small burst by frantic fingering of the controls, it did little more than set me spinning across a small portion of that gap. Eet had been carried ahead of me by some chance of my own efforts, and now I saw his suit roll from side to side, as if, within it, he fought to reach his controls and so activate his own power.

What he did I could not tell, but suddenly there was a lunge forward of his spinning suit, and he towed me with him. The power of his progress intensified, for he no longer rolled. Now he was as straight as a dart flung at some target, and he dragged me easily behind as he headed for the wreckage. Still I could not guess why we had not been followed.

The splintered and dangerous mass of that wall of derelict ships grew more distinct. I trusted Eet could control his power, so that we would not be hurled straight into it. The merest scrape of some projection could tear suits and kill us in an instant.

Eet was rolling again, fighting against the full force of the power. Though I could do little to control my own passage, I rolled, too, hoping to meet feet first a piece of ship's side which would afford a reasonably smooth landing among the debris.

We whirled on at a faster pace than my own pack had sent us. And I guessed suddenly that Eet was making use of the zero stone on the map to trigger the energy of his rocket.

"Off!" I thought that as an order. "We'll be cut to ribbons if you do not."

Whether he could not control the force now, I did not know, but my feet slammed with bone-shaking impact against the smooth bit I had aimed for. I reached out, trying to grip Eet's suit. He had managed to turn, to coast alongside of the debris, just far enough away not to be entangled in it, yet. The magnetic plates in my boots kept me anchored, but not for long. Though I stopped Eet's advance with a sharp jerk, I was immediately thereafter torn loose by the power which dragged him on.

We nudged along beside the wreckage, twisting and turning as best we could to avoid any contact. Even if we might not be picked up by sight scanners against the camouflaging irregularities of that mass of metal, any heat identification ray could pick us up. And I did not doubt in the least that such equipment was in use at Waystar.

Was it that they dared not attack for fear of losing the treasure? Had they sent ahead of us some command to activate the outer defenses, to keep us bottled up until they could collect us at their leisure? Perhaps when loss of air had rendered us perfectly harmless?

"I think they want you alive." Eet's answer came in response to my last dark speculation. "They guess that you know the value of the map. They want to know why. And perhaps they know that Hywel Jern did not really rise from the dead. I may read minds, but in that nest back there I could not sort out all thoughts."

I was not interested in the motives of the enemy. I was absorbed now in escape, if that was at all possible. Given time, we might work our way completely around the wall of debris to find the entrance. But such time our air supply would not offer.

"Ahead—the ship with the broken hatch," Eet said suddenly. "That I have seen before!"

I could make out the broken hatch. It took the shape of a half-opened mouth. And in me, too, memory stirred. I had set gloved hand to the edge of that very same hatch just before the pressure beam had made us captive. We could not be far now from the entrance, though I could hardly believe in such fortune.

Eet put on an extra burst of speed, drawing out a space from the wreckage, and certainly this energy could not all come from the suit rocket. The spurt was enough to bring us inside the ship passage. And we worked our way back from one handgrip to another, or rather I did so, pulling Eet's suit along. Only the fact that we were both relatively weightless made it possible. And even then, I was weak, shaking with fatigue, not certain I could make the full journey.

Every handhold I won to and from was a struggle. I did not direct my attention to the whole passage yet ahead, but limited it to the next hold only, and then to the next. I even lost my fear of what might lie behind, my concentration was so great on just swinging to the next hold—

We gained, I was not quite sure how, the crevice in which we had left the LB and crawled to its hatch. But once I slammed that door shut behind us I lost my last ounce of energy, and slid down, unable to move, watching Eet, in the clumsy suit, lift one arm with visible effort to reach the inner controls, fail, and then with grim patience try again.

Eventually he succeeded. Air hissed in around me, and the inner hatch opened. The suit holding Eet squirmed and wriggled, and then the mutant emerged, kicked the suit away in an almost vindictive gesture, and scrambled over to me to fumble with the sealings which held me in the protective covering.

The ship air revived me to the extent that I was able to shed that shell and crawl on into the cabin. Eet had preceded me, and now squatted in the pilot's web, fingering the buttons to ease us out and away.

I dragged myself to the hammock, lay weakly back in it. I did not believe at that moment that we had the least chance of breaking through the outer defenses of Waystar. We and our ship must meet some force field which would hold us, intact, as our captors wanted. But some reckless desire to go down fighting made me take the zero stone out in my shaking hands. I broke the disguise it had given me, or hoped I did. Having no mirror I could not be sure.

Now—there was something I could do which would at least confuse them if they slapped a spy ray on us.

"Such comes now," Eet reported and then closed his mind tightly, intent only on getting us out of the tunnel.

How much time did I have? The stone burned my hands but I held on. I had no mirror to mark the course of my transformation, but I willed it with all the energy and resource I had left. Then I lay back weakly, unable even to put away the precious source of my pain.

I looked blearily down what I could see of my prone body. There were, surely I could not be mistaken, the furred breeches, and above them the brilliance of a space admiral's tunic. I turned my head a fraction from side to side. My arms were bare, below the elbow wearing the gemmed armlets. I was, I hoped, by the power of the zero stone, a complete copy of the Veep. If they now snooped us with a seeing ray, the change might give us a small advantage, a few moments of confusion among our enemies.

Eet did not turn to look at me but his thought rang in my head.

"Very well done. And—here comes their snoop ray!"

Not having his senses, I must take his word for that. I levered myself up in the hammock with what energy I could summon, which was only enough to keep me braced with some small semblance of alertness. Eet suddenly slapped a furred fist on the board and the answering leap of the LB pinned me against the hammock. My head spun, I was sick—then I was swept into darkness.

FOURTEEN

When I roused groggily I lay staring at the rounded expanse above me, not able at once to remember where I was, or perhaps even *who* I was. With what seemed painful and halting slowness, memory of the immediate past returned. At least we were still in existence; we had not been snuffed out by some defense weapon of the pirate stronghold. But were we free? Or held captive by a force beam? I tried to lever myself up and the LB hammock swayed.

But I had had a look at my own body and I was not now wearing the semblance of the Veep—though a furry dwarf still hunched at the controls of the small craft. My hand went to the bulge in my belt. The sooner I was sure I was myself again, the better. I had a strange feeling that I could not think or plan until I was Murdoc Jern outwardly as well as inwardly, as if the outer disguise could change me from myself into a weak copy of the man my father had been. Eet had been a cat, but I had willed that on him without his desire. This I had taken upon myself by my own wish, meant to be outer, not complete. What did make sense any more?

"You are yourself," came Eet's thought.

But there was something else. My hand rested upon a pocket wherein all those days, months, I had carried the zero stone. And there was no reassuring hard lump to be felt. It was flat—empty!

"The stone!" I cried that aloud. I drew myself up, though my body was weak and drained of energy. "The stone—"

Then Eet turned to me. His alien face was a mask as far as I was concerned. I could read no expression there.

"The stone is safe," he thought-flashed.

"But where—?"

"It is safe," he repeated. "And you are Murdoc Jern outwardly again. We are through their defenses. The snooper ray caught you in the Veep's seeming and was deceived long enough for the stone to boost us out of range."

"So that is the way you used it. I will take it now." I held myself upright, though I must still clutch at the hammock to keep that position. Eet had used the zero stone even as we had once used it to boost the power of a Patrol scout ship and so escape capture. I was angry with myself for having overlooked that one weapon in our armament. "I will take it now," I repeated when Eet made no move to show me where it was. Though I had worked on the LB under Ryzk's direction I could not be sure where Eet had put it for the greatest effect in adding to our present drive.

"It is safe," he told me for the third time. Now the evasiveness of that reply made an impression on me.

"It is mine—"

"Ours." He was firm. "Or, rather, it was yours by sufferance."

Now I was thinking clearly again. "The—the time I turned you into a cat. . . . You are afraid of that—"

"Once warned, I cannot be caught so again. But the stone is danger if used in an irresponsible fashion."

"And you"—I controlled my rising anger with all the strength I had learned—"are going to see that it is not!"

"Just so. The stone is safe. And what is more to the purpose—look here." He pointed with one of his fingers to something which, for the want of other safekeeping, lay in the second hammock.

I loosed one hand to pull that webbing a little toward me. There lay the bowl with the map incised on its outer surface. A moment later I held it close to my eyes.

With the bowl turned over, the bottom was a half sphere on which the small jewels which must be stars winked in the light. And I saw, now that I had the time and chance to view it searchingly, that those varied. My own species rate stars on our charts by color—red, blue, white, yellow, dwarfs and giants. And here it would seem that the unknown maker of this chart had done the same. Save in one place alone, where next to a yellow gem which might denote a sun was a zero stone!

Quickly I spun the bowl around, studying the loose pattern. Yes, there were other planets indicated about those colored suns, but they were done in tiny, almost invisible dots. Only the one was a gem.

"Why, think you?" Eet's question reached me.

"Because it was the source!" I could hardly believe that we might hold the answer to our quest. I think my unbelief was born in the subconscious thought that it would be one of those quests, such as fill the ancient ballads and sagas, wherein the end is never quite in the grasp of mortals.

But it is one thing to hold a star map and another to find on it some already known point. I was no astro-navigator and unless some point of reference marked on this metal matched our known charts, we could spend a lifetime looking, unable even to locate the territory it pictured.

"We know where it was found," Eet suggested.

"Yes, but it may be another case of a relic of an earlier civilization treasured by its finder long after and buried with one who never even knew the life form that fashioned it, let alone the planets it lists."

"The Zacathan may furnish our key, together with Ryzk, who does know these star lanes. The stars this shows may be largely uncharted now. But still, those two together might give us one point from which we can work."

"You will tell them?" That surprised me somewhat, for Eet had never before suggested hinting to anyone that the caches we had disclosed to the Patrol were not the sum total of the stones now in existence. In fact, our quest had been his plan from its inception.

"What is needful. That this is the clue to another trea-sure. The Zacathan will be drawn by his love of knowl-edge, Ryzk because it will be a chance for gain."

"But Zilwrich is to be returned with the treasure to the nearest port. Of course—" I began to see that per-haps Eet was not so reckless as he seemed in suggesting that we plunge into the unknown with a map which might be older than my species itself as our only guide. "Of course, we did not say when we would return him."

There was in the back of my mind the thought that the Zacathan might even willingly agree to our plan to go exploring along the bowl route, the thirst for knowledge being as keen as it was among his kind.

But though I held that star map in my hand, my attention returned to the more important point for now.

"The stone, Eet."

"It is safe." He did not enlarge upon that.

There was, of course, this other stone, which, compared to the one we had used, was a mere pin point of substance, now so dull as to be overlooked by anyone not aware of its unusual properties. Did the amount of energy booster depend upon the size of the stone? I remembered how Eet had produced that burst of power which had brought us along the barrier of the wreckage. Had all that come from this dull bit which I could well cover with only a fraction of the tip of my little finger? It must be that we had learned only a small portion of what the stones could do.

I was most eager to get back to the ship, away from Waystar. And as the LB was on course, I began to wonder at the length of our trip. Surely we had not been this far from where we had set down on the dead moon.

"The homer—" I moved to see that dial. Its indicator showed set to bring us back on automatics to the *Wendwind*. Suddenly I doubted its efficiency. Most of the alterations in the controls of the LB had been rigged by Ryzk, were meant to be only temporary, and had been made with difficulty—though it was true that a Free Trader had training in repairs and extempore rigging which the average spacer never learned.

Suppose the linkage with the parent ship was faulty? We could be lost in space. Yet it was true we were holding to a course.

"Certainly," Eet broke into my ominous chain of thought. "But not, I believe, to the moon. And if they go into hyper—"

"You mean—they have taken off? Not waiting for us?" Perhaps that fear, too, had ever lain in the depths of my mind. Our visit to Waystar had been so rash an undertaking that Ryzk and the Zacathan could well have written us off almost as soon as we left for the pirate station. Or Zilwrich might have begun to fail and the pilot, realizing the Zacathan was too far spent to object, and wanting to get him to some aid—There were many reasons I could count for myself for the *Wendwind* to have taken off. But we were still on course for something—a course which would hold only until the ship went into hyper for a system jump. If that happened, our guide line would snap and we would be adrift—with only a return to Waystar or a landing on one of the dead worlds for our future.

"If they left for out-system they would hyper—"

"If they do not know the system they must reach its outermost planet before they do," Eet reminded me.

"The stone—if we use that to step up energy to join them—"

"Such a journey must be made with great care. To maneuver the LB and the ship together during flight—" But it was apparent that Eet was thinking for himself as well as for my enlightenment. He studied the control board and now he shook his head. "It is a matter of great risk. These are not true controls, only improvised, and so might not serve us at a moment of pressing need."

"A choice between two evils," I pointed out. "We stay here and die, or we take the chance of meeting with the ship. As long as we remain on course we are linked with her. Why doesn't"—I was suddenly struck by a new thought—"Ryzk know we are following? The fact that we are should have registered—"

"The indicator in the ship may have failed. Or perhaps he does not choose to wait."

If the pilot did not want to wait—he had the *Wendwind*, he had the Zacathan, and he had an excellent excuse for our disappearance. He might return to the nearest port with the rescued archaeologist, the co-ordinates of Waystar to deliver to the Patrol, a ship he could claim for back wages. All in all, the master stars lay in his hand in this game and we had no comets to cut across the playing board to bring him down—except the zero stone.

"Into the hammock," Eet warned now. "I shall cut in the stone power. And hope that the ship does not hyper before we can catch up."

I lay down again. But Eet remained by the controls. Could the alien body he had wished upon himself stand the strain of not using such protection as the LB afforded? If Eet blacked out, I could not take his place, and we could well strike the *Wendwind* with projectile speed.

In the past I had been through the strain of take-offs in ships built for speed. But the LB was not such. I could only remember that the original purpose of the craft was to flee a stricken ship, and that it must thus be fit to take the strain of a leap away from danger. To sustain such energy, however, was another matter. Now I lay in the hammock and endured, though I did not quite black out. It seemed as if the very material of the walls about us protested against the force. And the bowl, which I still held, had a fiery spot of light on its surface where the infinitely smaller stone answered the burst of power from the larger, which Eet had concealed.

I endured and I watched through a haze the furred body of Eet, his arms flung out, his fingers crooked to hold in position at the controls. Then I heard the loud rasp of painful breathing which was not mine alone. And every second I expected a break in the link tying us to the ship, the signal that the *Wendwind* has gone into hyper, vanished out of the space we knew.

Either my sight was affected by the strain or else Eet was so pinned by our speed that he could not function well, but I saw mistily his one hand creep at a painfully slow rate to thumb a single lever. Then we were free of that punishing pressure. I clawed my way out of the hammock, swung across to elbow Eet aside, and took his place, facing the small battery of winking lights and warnings I did understand and which Ryzk had patiently drilled me to respond to.

We had reached match distance of the *Wendwind* and must now join her. Automatics had been set up to deal with much of this, but there were certain alarms I must be ready to answer if they were triggered. And if Ryzk had ignored our following signal, he could not, short of winking instantly into hyper, avoid our present homing.

I sweated out those endless seconds at the board, my fingers poised and ready to make any correction, watching the dials whose reading could mean life or death not only to us but to the ship we fought to join. Then we were at our goal. The visa-screen winked on to show the gap of the bay for the LB and we bumped into it. The screen went dark again as the leaves of the bay closed about us. I was weak with relief. But Eet arose from where he had crouched, hanging to one end of the other hammock.

"There is trouble—"

He did not complete that thought. I cannot tell how—there are no words known to my species to describe what happened then—for we were not bedded down, prepared for the transition as was needful. We were not even warned. Seconds only had brought us in before the ship went into hyper.

There was the taste of blood in my mouth. I drooled it forth to flow stickily down my chin. When I opened my eyes I was in the dark, a dark which brought the terror of blindness with it. My whole body was one great ache which, when I tried to move, became sheer agony. But somehow I got my hand to my head, wiped it without knowing across the stickiness of blood. I could not *see*!

"Eet!" I think I screamed that. The sound echoed in my ears, adding to the pain in my head.

There was no answer. The dark continued. I tried to feel about me and my hand struck against solid substance as memory stirred. I was in the LB, we had returned to the ship just an instant before it had gone into hyper.

How badly I was hurt I did not know. As the LBs had originally been fashioned to take care of injured survivors of some space catastrophe, I needed only get back to the hammock and the craft would be activated into treating me.

I felt about me, seeking the touch of webbing. But though my one arm obeyed me, I could not move the other at all. And I touched nothing but wall. I tried to inch my body along, sliding my fingers against that wall, seeking some break, some change in its surface. The quarters of the LB were so confined that surely I could soon find one of the hammocks. I flung my arm up and out, rotating it through the thick darkness. It encountered nothing.

But I was in the LB and it was too small for me not to have found the hammock by now. The thought of the hammock, that it was ready to soothe my pain, to apply restoratives and healing, so filled me that I forced myself to greater efforts to find it. But my agonizing movements, so slow and limited, told me that there was no hammock. And whatever space in which I now lay was not in the LB. My hand fell to the floor and touched a small, inert body. Eet! Not as I had seen him last, my exploring fingers reported. But Eet, the mutant, as he had been from birth.

I drew my fingers down his furred side and thought I detected a very faint fluttering there, as if his heart still beat. Then I tried to discover by touch alone whether he bore any noticeable wounds. The darkness—I would not allow myself to accept the thought that I was blind—took on a heavy, smothering quality. I was gasping as if the lack of light was also a lack of air. Then I feared that it was, and that we had been sealed in somewhere to suffocate.

Eet did not answer my thoughts, which I tried to make coherent. I felt on, beyond him, and sometime later gave up the hope we were in the LB. Instead we lay in a confined space with a door which would not yield to the small force I could exert against it. We must be on board the *Wendwind*—and I believed we were now imprisoned in one of those stripped lower cabins which had been altered for cargo transport. This could only mean that Ryzk had taken command. What he might have told the Zacathan I did not know. Our actions had been strange enough to give credence to some story that we operated outside the law, and Ryzk could testify truly that we had brought him on board without his knowledge. The

Zacathans were esper—telepaths. Ryzk could tell the exact truth and Zilwrich would have to believe him. We could well be on our way now to being delivered to the Patrol as kidnapers and shady dealers with the pirates of Waystar. Yes, as I painfully marshaled the facts as another would see them I realized that Ryzk could make an excellent case, and Zilwrich would back him up.

That we brought back part of the treasure meant nothing. We could have done that and still planned to keep it, and the Zacathan, for ransom. Such deals were far from unknown.

If Ryzk had been black-listed, bringing us in might return him to the rolls. And if we underwent, or I underwent, deep interrogation—the whole affair of the zero stone would be known. It would be clear that we were guilty of what the Patrol might deem double-dealing. Ryzk had only to play a completely honest man at the nearest port and we would have lost our big gamble.

It seemed so hopeless when I thought it all out that I could see no possible counter on our part. Had we one of the zero stones we might—so much had I come to accept the unusual powers of those strange gems—have a fighting chance. Eet—if he were not dead—or dying—might just—

I felt my way back to that small body, gathered it carefully up so that Eet's head rested against me, and put my good arm protectingly around it. I thought now that I no longer felt that small stirring of a heartbeat. There was no answer to my mind-call. So there was good reason to believe that Eet was dead. And in that moment I forgot all my annoyance at his interference in my life, the way he had taken over the ordering of my days. Perhaps I was one who needed such dependence upon a stronger will. There had been my father, then Vondar Ustle, then Eet—

Only I would not accept that this was the end. If Eet was dead, then Ryzk would pay for that death. I had thought of the aid of the stone, and the aid of Eet, and both of them were gone. What remained was myself, and I was not ready to say I was finished.

I had always believed that I was no esper. Certainly no such talent was apparent in me before I met Eet. He had touched my mind for communication and I had learned that use from him. He had at one uncomfortable time given me mental contact with another human in order to prove our innocence to a Patrol officer. Then he had taught me to use the hallucinatory change and I had been the one to discover that the zero stone could bring about an almost total change.

But Eet—he was either dead or very close to it. I had neither Eet nor the stone. I was hurt, how badly I could not tell, and I was a prisoner. There was only one small—very small—spark of hope left—the Zacathan.

He was normally esper, as was Eet. Could I possibly reach him now? Make some appeal?

I stared into a dark which I hoped would not be my portion all the rest of my life, but in my mind I pictured the face of Zilwrich as I had seen it last. And I strove to hold that face in mind, not now for the purpose of making it mine, but rather as a homing point for my thought-seek. And I aimed, not a coherent thought, but a signal for attention, a cry for help.

Then—I touched! It was as if I had put tip of finger to a falder leaf which had instantly coiled away from contact with my flesh. Then—it returned.

But I was racked with disappointment. With Eet mind-touch had been clear, as it had been with the Zacathan when the mutant was present. This was a jumble of a language I did not know, poured at me in a wealth of impressions too fast for me to sort and understand, forming a sickening, chaotic whirl, so that I must retreat, drop touch.

Eet was the connecting link I must have. Otherwise I could only try until that whirl of alien thought drove my brain into mindlessness. I considered the chances. I could stay prisoner here for whatever purpose Ryzk had in mind. Or I could try the Zacathan again. And it was not in me to accept the helplessness of that first choice.

So, warily, as a man might seek a path across a quaking bog ready to swallow him up in a thousand hungry mud mouths, I sent out once more the mind-seek. But this time I thought my message—slowly, impression by impression, and doggedly held to what I had to convey as the stream of the alien mind lapped over it. I did not try to tell Zilwrich anything, as I would have "talked" to Eet. I merely thought out over and over again what I would have him know, letting it lie for him to pick up as he could. Though I feared my slow channel was as unintelligible to him as his frighteningly swift flow was to me.

Once, twice, three times, a fourth, I thought through what I made as my plea. Then I could hold no longer. The pain of my body was as nothing compared to the pain now filling my mind. And I lost contact as well as consciousness, just as I had when we had snapped into hyper.

It was as if I were being pricked over and over again by the sharp point of a needle. I stirred under that torment, which was small and far away at first, and then became so much the greater, more insistent. And I fought to remain in the safety of nothingness. Prick—the summons to what I did not want continued.

"Eet?" But it was not Eet—no—

"Wait—"

Wait for what, who? I did not care. Eet? No, Eet was dead. And I would be dead. Death was not caring, not needing to care, or feel, or think—And I wanted just that—no more stirring of life, which hurt both mind and body. Eet was dead, and I was dead, or would be if the pricking would only stop and leave me in peace.

"Awake—"

Awake? I thought it was "wait." Not that it mattered. Nothing mattered—

"Awake!"

A shouting in my head. I hurt and that hurting came from outside. I turned my head from side to side, as if to shake out the voice in my mind.

"Keep awake!" screamed that order and the pain it caused me aroused me further from my stupor. I was moaning a little, whimpering through the dark a plea to be let alone, left to the death which was rest.

"Keep awake!"

Hammering inside my skull. Now I could hear my own whimpering plaint and was unable to stop. But also with the pain came an awareness which was a barrier against my slipping back into the nothingness.

"Awake—hold—"

Hold what? My rolling head? There was nothing to hold.

Then I sensed, not words echoing through my bruised mind, but something else—a stiffening, a support against which my feeble thoughts could find root and sustenance. And this continued until I stared wide-eyed into the dark, as much another person inwardly as I had been outwardly with the hallucinations born of the zero stone. For only a limited time, somehow I knew, would that support me. And during that time I must make any attempt I could to help myself.

FIFTEEN

Somehow I got to my feet, still holding Eet against me with my good arm, my other hanging uselessly by my side. I was ready to move, but where, against what—or whom? Realizing I was still helplessly caught in this pocket of dark, I was ready to slump again into a stupor.

"Wait—be ready—" There was a sense of strain in that message, as if he who sent it were making a vast effort.

Well, I was waiting and ready, but for how long? And in this dark, time seemed forever and ever, not measured by any standard I had known.

Then came sound, a small grating, and I knew a leap of heart—I was not blind after all! There was a line of light to my right. I lurched in that direction as that line grew from a slit into an opening I could squeeze through—though I was blinking against the discomfort of light.

I brought out and up against the wall of the well which was the core of the ship, too spent for a moment to turn and see who had freed me. But leaning one shoulder against the wall, I was able to face about.

Zilwrich, whom I had last seen lying on the pallet, supported himself with his two arms rigid against the floor, clearly at the end of the flutter of strength which had made him crawl to the door of my cell. He lifted his head with manifest effort.

"You—are—free—To you—the rest—"

Free but weaponless, and as near the end of my resources as the Zacathan, though not yet finished. Somehow I was able to lay Eet on the floor, get my good arm about Zilwrich, and half drag the Zacathan back to the bed he had crawled from. Then I stumbled out, picked up the mutant, and brought him back, nursed against me, though no tending would return life to that small body.

"Tell me." I used the Basic speech, glad to be able to relinquish touch with that bewildering alien mind. "What happened?"

"Ryzk"—Zilwrich spoke slowly as if each word came hard—"would go to Lylestane—return me—the treasure—"

"And turn us in," I ended, "probably as accomplices in Guild plotting."

"He—wishes—reinstatement. I did not know you had returned alive—until your mind-seek. He said—you died—when we went into hyper."

I glanced down at the limp body pressed to mine. "One of us did."

I might be free inside the ship, but that I could do anything to change the course of events I doubted. Ryzk would return us to Lylestane and we—I—would find the balance of justice heavily weighted against me. Not only were circumstances largely in the pilot's favor, but under a scanner they would have out of me all that the zero stone meant. And—the zero stone!

Eet had concealed it somewhere in the LB. As far as I knew Ryzk did not suspect it. If I could get hand on it again—I was not sure how I could use it as a weapon. But that it had possibilities of this sort there was no doubt. The LB—but Eet had hidden the stone and Eet was dead.

The bowl—if I had that I could trace the zero stone by the fire of the one inlaid in it.

"The treasure—where is it?"

"In the lock safe." Zilwrich's eyes were on me with piercing keenness, but he was ready enough with that information.

The lock safe—If Ryzk had sealed that with his own thumb, I had no chance of getting the bowl. The compartment would remain closed until he chose to release it.

"No." It would seem that like Eet the Zacathan could readily read my mind, but that did not matter. "No—it is sealed to me."

"He allowed that?"

"He had to. What is this thing you must have—that the bowl will bring you nearer to—a weapon?"

"I do not know if it can be a weapon. But it is a source of power beyond our reckoning. Eet hid it in the LB; the bowl will find it for me."

"Help me—to the lock safe."

It was a case of the lame leading the crippled. We made a hard journey of a short space. But I was able to steady the alien while he activated the thumb lock and I scooped out the bowl. He held it tightly to him as I guided and supported him back to his bed.

Before he released the bowl to me he turned it around in his hands, examining it closely. Finally one of his finger talons tapped the tiny zero stone.

"This you seek."

"We have long sought it, Eet and I." There was no use in concealing the truth any longer. We might not make the voyage we had planned, going out among the uncharted stars in search of an ancient world which was the source of the stones, but it was the here and now which mattered most—the finding of the one Eet had hidden.

"It is a map, and you hunt the treasure you believe lies at its end?"

"More than such treasure as you found in the tomb." And, as tersely as I could, I told him the story of the zero stones—the one in my father's ring, those of the caches on the unknown planet, that which Eet had secreted, and how we had used it since.

"I see. Take this then." Zilwrich held out the bowl. "Find your hidden stone. It would seem that we were on the edge of a vast discovery when we uncovered this—but one which would unleash perils such as a man thinks twice about loosing."

I held the bowl to me as I had held Eet, using my shoulder against the wall to keep erect, shambling from Zilwrich's cabin to the ladder, down which I fell rather than climbed, to reach the LB's berth. The last steps of that journey were such a drain that I could hardly take them.

Then I was back in the craft which had served us so well. I fought to keep moving, holding the bowl a little away from me now, watching the zero stone. It glimmered and then broke into vivid life. But it was hard to see how I could use it as a guide, since there seemed no variation in that light. However, I must try.

I moved jerkily, first to the tail, without any change I could detect in the degree of emanation from the bowl stone. But as I came up the right side of the small ship on return, the bowl moved in my grasp, fought my hold. I released it. As the zero stone, on its first awakening, had pulled me across space to the derelict ship where others of its kind lay, so did the bowl cross, to hang suspended against a part of the casing. I jerked and tore at the rim of the casing, hoping Eet had not been able to seal in the stone too tightly. As my nails broke and my fingers were lacerated by the sharp edging I began to despair. One-handed there was little I could do to force it.

But I continued to fight, and at last I must have touched what lock was there, for a whole section of panel fell down and I saw the brilliant blaze of the large stone within. The bowl snapped to meet it until stone touched stone, and I did not try to part them. With the bowl I began to retrace my way.

When I subsided beside Zilwrich, the bowl on the floor between us, he looked at the gems but seemed as content as I at that moment to do no more. Not only was I too weak to prod my body to more effort, but my thoughts were dulled, slow. Now that I had found the second stone, I could not see any way to make use of it against Ryzk. It seemed that, having achieved this one small success, I was finished.

Eet lay on the edge of the Zacathan's pallet and one of the alien's scaled hands rested on the mutant's head.

"This one is not dead—"

I was startled out of my lethargy. "But—"

"There is still the spark of life, very low, very dim, but there."

I was no medico, and even if I had been I would have had no knowledge to deduce the mutant's hurts. My own helplessness was an added burden. Eet would die and there was nothing I could do—

Or was there?

For a little beyond Eet's head was the bowl, the stones close-welded together. The zero stone was power. It had the power to turn us into the seeming of others and hold that seeming. And I had been able to turn Eet into a cat because I had sprung that change on him when he did not expect it. Could I will, not change, but will life itself into the mutant's body?

As long as there was a faint spark left, I must try.

I took the left hand on my limp and useless arm with my right, moved the numb palm to rest on the stones, not caring if I would be burned. At least I would not feel it. The right I put on Eet's head. I set my mind to the task, summoning, not some strange disguise for my companion, but rather the sight of him as he was alive. So did I fight my battle—with mind, with a hand which will always bear the scars, with my determination, against death itself, or what Eet's kind knew as the end of existence. And I strove with the power passing through me to find that spark Zilwrich said existed, to fan it into flame.

The stones made a fire to fill one's sight, shutting out the cabin, the Zacathan, even Eet, but I continued to hold the image of the live Eet in my mind. My eyes which had been useless in the dark of the cell were now blinded again, by light. But I held fast in spite of that in me which cringed, and cried, and tried to flee.

Nor was I truly conscious of why I fought that battle, save that it was one which I must face to the end. I was at last done, my seared hand lying palm up on my knee, the bowl and stone hidden from me by a fold of cloth. Eet no longer lay limp, with the semblance of death, but sat on his haunches, his paw-hands folded over his middle, his stance one of alert life, of complete restoration.

I caught communication, or the edge of it, between the Zacathan and my companion. But so difficult was it now for me to hold to any thought that it was more like hearing a murmur or whisper from across a room.

Eet moved with all his old agility, bringing out the aid kit, seeing to my hand, giving me also a shot to counteract the hurt in my arm. But to me this had little or no meaning. I watched the Zacathan agree to something Eet suggested and the mutant carry the bowl out of the room—into hiding again, I supposed. But all I wanted was sleep.

Hunger awoke me. I was still in the Zacathan's cabin. If Ryzk had paid him a visit during the time I slept he had not seen fit to return me to custody. But that I had slept worried me vaguely. There was much to be done and I had failed to do it.

Eet whisked in, almost as if my waking had sent him some signal. He carried in his mouth as he came two of those tubes of E-rations. And seeing them, for a second or two I forgot all else. But when I had squeezed one into my mouth and savored the first few swallows (though normally I would not have considered them appetizing) I had a question:

"Ryzk?"

"We can do nothing while in hyper," Eet reported.
"And he has found his own amusement. It seems that
this ship was not too thoroughly searched when it was
taken in as a smuggler. Somehow Ryzk uncovered a supply of vorx and is now having sweet dreams in his cabin."

Vorx was potent enough to give anyone
dreams—though whether they were sweet was another
question. It was not only an intoxicating drink, but so
acted on Terran bodies that it was also hallucinatory.
That Ryzk had been searching the ship did not surprise
me either. The boredom of space travel would set any
man immured within these walls during hyper passage
to do such to relieve his tedium. And Ryzk might have
known this was a smuggler sold after confiscation.

"He had help—" Eet commented. There was such a
bubbling renewal of well-being in him as made me envi-
ous, perhaps tired of being on the edge wash of such
energy.

"From you?"

"From our distinguished colleague." Eet nodded to
the Zacathan.

"It would seem that Ryzk's weakness is drink," Zilwrich agreed. "While it is wrong of anyone to play upon
another's weakness, there are times when such a fall
from Full Grace is necessary. I deemed that I might take
on error-load for once in this way. We need Ryzk's room
rather than his company."

"If we come out of hyper in the Lylestane system we
shall be in Patrol territory," I replied a little sourly.

"It is possible to come out and go in again before a
challenge of boarding can be delivered," Zilwrich
returned. "I have a duty to report the raid on our camp,

that is true. But I have also a duty to those who sent my party there. This map is such a find as we come upon perhaps once in a thousand years. If we can find a clue to the location of the planet it marks, then a scouting trip thither at this time means more than arousing the law as to what has happened in one raid."

"But Ryzk is pilot. He will not agree to go off known charts. And if he's made up his mind to turn us in—"

"Off the charts," repeated the Zacathan thoughtfully. "Of that we cannot be sure as yet. Look—"

He produced a tri-dee projector which I knew to be part of the equipment of the control cabin. At a push of his finger there flashed on the wall a blowup of a star chart. Being no astro-navigator, I could not read it to any real purpose, save that I could make out the position of stars and sight the coded co-ordinates for hyper jumps under each.

"This is on the edge of the dead strip," Zilwrich informed me. "To your left and third from the corner is the blasted system of Waystar. It must have been scouted three centuries ago, by your time, from the dates on this chart. This is one of the old Blue maps. Now, look upon the bowl, imagine that the dead sun of that system is a red dwarf, turn the bowl two degrees left—"

I held up the bowl and rotated it slowly, looking from it to the tri-dee chart on the wall. Though I was not taught to read such maps I could see he was right! Not only did the blasted system we had just fled appear on the bowl as one about a red-dwarf star—a dying sun—but there was a course to be traced from that to the zero stone.

"No co-ordinates for hyper," I pointed out. "It would be the most reckless kind of guesswork. And even a scout trained for exploring jumps would take chances of two comets to a star of coming out safe."

"Look at the bowl through this." It would seem that Eet must have been gathering aids from all over the ship, for what the Zacathan handed me now was my own jeweler's lens.

As I inspected the constellation engraved on the metal through the magnification of the lens I saw there were minute indentations there, though I could not translate any.

"*Their* hyper code perhaps," the Zacathan continued.

"Still no good to us."

"Of that I am not sure. We have those of the dead system—from that—"

"You can work?" Of course, he was an archaeologist and such puzzles were common to him. I lost something of my mood of depression. Perhaps because my hunger had been satisfied and I could now use my arm and hand to better advantage, I was regaining confidence not only in myself but in the knowledge and ingenuity of my companions.

When I put the bowl on the floor, open side down so that its star-specked dome was revealed, Eet squatted by it. He had taken up the lens, holding it in his paw-hands, his head bent over it as if his nose were smelling out the pictured solar systems.

"It can be done." His thought was not only clear; it was as confident as if there had been no obstructions at all between us and success. "We return to the dead system by reversing Ryzk's tape—"

"And so straight into what may be a vla-wasp nest," I commented. "But continue. Perhaps you have an answer for that also. Then what do we do, unless the Honorable

Elder"—I gave Zilwrich the proper title of formal address—"can read these co-ordinates?"

Eet did not close his mind as he had upon occasion, but I read a side flash of what might be indecision. I had never read fear in Eet's communications—awareness of danger, but not fear. But this had an aura of just that emotion.

And inspiration hit me in that same instant. "You can read these!" I had not perhaps meant it as an accusation, but it came forth that way.

His head turned on his too-long neck so that he could look at me.

"Old habits, memories, die hard," he answered obliquely, as he sometimes did. He turned the lens about, giving me the impression of uneasiness, of one wanting to escape coming to a decision.

I caught a flicker of alien mind-flow, and for a moment resented that communication I could not share. It was my guess that the alien and the mutant might be in argument about just the knowledge I accused Eet of having.

"Just so." Eet resumed touch with me. "No, I cannot read these. But they are enough like another form of record for me to guess to more purpose than the rest of you." And such was the finality of that answer that I knew better than to try to pry at how he could be familiar with any record approximating that of a Forerunner race living millenniums ago. The old problem of who—or what—Eet was crossed my mind again.

Though he made no more comment, the impression remained that any guessing he would do would be against his inclination and that he had a personal reason for disliking the situation fortune had forced upon him.

It seemed that now I was to serve as his hands. And back in the control cabin I made ready to follow his instructions to reverse the course Ryzk had set and return us, as soon as we emerged near Lylestane, to the vicinity of Waystar.

Ryzk did not appear. Apparently the smugglers' drink was of great potency. What would have happened when we came out of hyper and he was not at the controls, I do not know. Perhaps we would have aimlessly cruised the Lylestane system as a traffic hazard until some Patrol ship linked beam and dragged us in as a derelict.

I punched out the figures Eet fed me and we were wrenched back on a return course once again from Lylestane. Once more in hyper, we had plenty of time to meditate on the numerous dangers our appearance near Waystar would range against us. Certainly our successful escape with the treasure had alerted all the defenses of the pirate stronghold. They would be expecting a visit from the Patrol on one hand, now that strangers knew the co-ordinates of their hide-out, and trouble from others, perhaps even the Guild, demanding an account of how or why loot could be so summarily removed from what was believed to be an impregnable safe place.

The only answer would be that we dared not linger long enough in the dead system to be detected. Our unarmed ship had no defense against what the Jacks could easily muster. Therefore, we must follow exactly the same procedure we had on emerging near Lylestane: We must have the other course ready to punch in and spend as little time in normal space as we could.

Success in that maneuver would depend entirely on what Zilwrich and Eet could produce in the way of a new course. And since I was no help to them, the ship and Ryzk were my concern.

My most practical answer to Ryzk was to apply a force lock on his cabin. He sobered up when we were back in hyper and his struggle with the door lock led me to state through the intercom that we had taken over. More than that I did not explain, and I turned off the com thereafter, so his demands went unheard. E-rations and water went to him through the regular supply vent and I left him to consider, soberly I hoped, the folly of the immediate past in relationship to the *Wendwind* and her owners.

For the rest I tinkered in the small repair shop. The crossbows Ryzk had earlier produced I refined, making more zoran heads for their bolts. I had no mind to go exploring on an unknown planet unarmed, as I had once done in the past.

If by some miracle of fortune we did reach the world indicated by the zero stone, we would not know what we might face there. It could be a planet on which those of our kind could not live without suits; it could be inhabited by beings infinitely superior to us in every way, who would be as hostile to strangers as the Veeps of Waystar. Though the civilization the bowl represented must have ended eons past, others could have arisen from the degenerate dregs of that, and we might face such challengers as we could not even imagine. When I got to that point in my speculations, I handled my crossbows with very bleak attention to all their manifest defects.

Our first test would come when we left hyper in the dead system. As that moment approached I was tense and nervy. I saw practically nothing of Eet and Zilwrich except when I supplied them with food and drink. And I was almost tempted to let Ryzk out of his cabin in order to have someone to match fears with.

But when the alarm shattered the too-great silence of the ship, Eet was on hand in the control cabin. He curled into my lap as I settled in the pilot's seat—though he kept his mind closed, as if it were full of some precious knowledge and sharing that too soon might spill what could not be regained.

We came out of hyper and I punched the proper buttons for a reading of our present site. At least fortune had favored us to the point that we had emerged very close to that place where we had entered on our first trip, at the outer edge of the dead system.

But we were given very little time to congratulate ourselves on besting what was perhaps the smallest portion of the ordeal facing us. For there was an alarm ringing wildly through the cabin. We had been caught by a snooper and now we could expect a traction beam. My hands rested on the edge of the control board. I was ready to punch out the course Eet supplied. But would he feed me one, and could I set it quickly enough to avoid the linkage which would hold us for taking by the enemy?

SIXTEEN

Eet was ready for me, though the co-ordinates he flashed into my mind had no meaning for me. I was merely the means of putting finger tip to controls to punch them in. Only, it seemed those fingers did not move fast enough. I could feel the force of the locking beam catch at our ship.

We passed into hyper. But once the dizzy spin in my head cleared and I knew we had made the transition, I was aware that we had brought our enemy with us. Instead of snapping the lock beam in our return to hyper, we had, through some balance of force against force, dragged the source of that beam with us! We had danger locked to the ship, ready to attack as soon as we moved into normal space again.

There is no maneuvering in hyper. To do so would be to nullify the co-ordinates. And one would emerge utterly lost in space, if one were lucky, or perhaps in the very heart of a blazing sun. We were both prisoners here until we finished the voyage the Zacathan and Eet had set us. But there was this much: The enemy was as helpless as we—until we went out. And not being prepared for hyper transfer, they might be badly shaken, though they would have the length of our trip in which to pull themselves together.

"Jern!" Ryzk bawled through the ship's com. "Jern, what are you trying to do?"

It sounded very much as if the pilot not only had recovered from his drinking bout but was genuinely alarmed. Alarmed enough, I speculated, to be willing to work with us? Not that I trusted him now.

I picked up the mike. "We are in hyper—with a companion."

"We're linked!" he roared back.

"I said we had a companion. But he cannot move any better than we. We are both in hyper."

"Going where?"

"You name it!" Our momentary escape was acting on me like a shot of exult. Not that I had ever tried the stuff, but I had heard enough to judge that this must be akin to the heady feeling those addicts gained. When we snapped out of hyper we might be in grave danger, but we had now a respite and time to plan.

But his question echoed in my mind. Going where? To a planet which might or might not still exist. And if it did—what would it be like?

At that moment I felt as if I would more than anything like to be a believer in the gods of the planet-rooted. This was the time when one would prefer to kneel in some fane as did, say, the Alfandi, thrusting a god-call deep into ground already pitted with holes left by other's rods, pulling hard upon the cord which would set its top quivering to give off the faint sound meant to reach the ear—if one might grant a spiritual being an ear—of that High One, and thus alerting the Over-Intelligence to listen to one's plea. I had met with the worshippers of many gods and many demons on many worlds. And complete belief gave a man security which was denied to the onlooker. That there was a purpose behind the Galaxy I would be the first to agree. But I could not bow my head to a planet-based god.

There was one belief I had read in the old tapes, that brain and mind are not the same. That the brain is allied to the body and serves it, while the mind is able to function in more than one dimension—hence esper talents, born of the mind and not the brain.

Now when I came from the control cabin I found Zilwrich seated on his pallet, and it seemed that he tried to prove the truth of this old theory, for he held between his two hands the bowl. His eyes were closed and he was breathing in small, shallow gasps. Eet, who had preceded me at his usual speed, had taken a position which mimicked that of the Zacathan, his small hand-paws resting on the rim of the bowl, his eyes also closed. And there was an aura of esper power which even I could feel.

What they were trying to do I did not know. But I felt that my presence was an intrusion there. I backed away, closing the door behind me. But at the same time my triumph ebbed. And the fact that we had a companion locked to us began to assume the shadow of menace. If Ryzk could only be trusted! Perhaps he could as long as his own skin was in danger. The co-ordinates which had brought us here—I reclimbed the way to the control cabin. We had used a return of Ryzk's setting to take us back to the dead system. Suppose I now erased those co-ordinates from the tape. Then no move of Ryzk's could return us, only what lay in Eet's and the Zacathan's memories. Loosed in the unknown, the pilot would be no great danger, and we needed badly any knowledge he might have to help us to deal with the enemy once we returned to normal space.

I set the erase on the tape before allowing myself to have second thoughts. Then I went to unseal the pilot's cabin. He lay on his bunk but turned his head to stare at me as I stood in the doorway. I had not brought one of the crossbows. After all, I was trained in a variety of weaponless fighting methods, and I did not think we were less than evenly matched, since he had nothing save similar skills to use against me.

"What are we doing?" He had lost the anger tinged with alarm which had colored his first demand through the com.

"Heading for a point on a Forerunner chart."

"Who's linked with us?"

"Someone out of Waystar is our best guess."

"They followed us!" He was genuinely astonished.

I shook my head. "We came back to the Waystar system. It was the only recognizable point of reference on the chart."

He turned his head away, now looking to the ceiling. "So—what happens when we come out of hyper?"

"With luck we are in a system not on the charts. But—can we break linkage when we come out of hyper?"

He did not answer at once. There was a sharp frown line between his brows. And then he replied to my question with another.

"What are you after, Jern?"

"Perhaps a whole world of Forerunner artifacts. What is that worth?"

"Why ask me? Anyone knows that is not to be reckoned in credits. Is Zilwrich behind this? Or is it your gamble?"

"Both. Zilwrich and Eet together set up the co-ordinates."

He grimaced. "So we sweat out a landing, maybe to be sun-cooked or worse when we come out—"

"And if we are not, but take the others with us?" I brought him back to the one matter over which we might have some control.

He sat up. The sickly-sweet smell of the drink was strong. But to my eyes he appeared sober. Now he put his elbows on his knees and bent over to rest his head on his hands. I could no longer see his face. He sighed.

"All right. In hyper we can't switch course. So we can't try to shake them loose. We *can* set the emerge on high velocity. It will mean blacking out, maybe taking a beating. But it is the only way I know of to break the link. We will have to rig special webbing or we won't survive at all."

"And if we do break the link?"

"If we pulled them in with us, the course is only set on our ship. The break will take us out, not them. They would have to gamble on an emerge. It might land them in the same system, or somewhere else. How do I know? I say it is barely possible. I am not planning on more than one thin chance in ten thousand." And his voice said that was very optimistic odds.

"You can do it?"

"It looks as if we have no choice. Yes, I can rig it, given time enough. What are the odds if we come out still linked?"

"We are unarmed, and they can take us over. They have no use for us, only what we carry."

He sighed again. "About what I thought. You're all fools and I have to go along."

But perhaps he was not wholly convinced until we entered the control cabin and he pushed past me to read the dial above the journey setting.

"Erased!" He whirled to face me, his lips twisted into a snarl.

"No turning back." I braced myself, tensed against attack. Then I saw his eyes change and knew that if he meant me harm in the future, he was willing to wait for such a reckoning. The main interest now must be the ship and our possible manner of escape from our unseen companion.

Just as Eet and Zilwrich in their mysterious occupation with the bowl had given me no explanations, so did Ryzk keep his own counsel about the alterations he made in some wiring. But he did keep me with him as a very ignorant assistant, to hand tools, to hold this or that while he made delicate adjustments.

"This will have to be redone," he said, "before we make a return. It is only temporary. I cannot even swear it will work. We'll need heavy webs—"

We set about providing those, too. The two shock-prepared seats in the control cabin were reinforced with what we could strip off the bunks in our two cubbys. Then we descended to the section where Eet and the Zacathan were in session to provide Zilwrich with such safeguards as we could rig. Eet, I supposed, would share my seat as usual.

I tapped lightly on the door behind which I had left the two enrapt, with the bowl between them.

"Enter," called Zilwrich.

He lay now, his whole body expressive of a vast exhaustion. I could not see the bowl. Eet, too, lay there, but his head came up and he watched us almost warily.

I explained what we would do.

"This thing *is* possible?"

Again Ryzk shrugged. "I cannot swear to it on my name, if that is what you mean. It remains theoretical until we prove it one way or another. But if what you say is true, we have little choice."

"Very well," the Zacathan agreed. I waited for some comment, pro or con, from Eet. But such did not come. And that made me uneasy. But I would not press him, lest he confirm my worst doubts. It is better not to be met by pessimism when the situation already looks dark.

But Zilwrich had suggestions as to the rigging we must provide to counteract the strain on his body. And we carried out his instructions with all the skill we could summon. When we fastened the last of the improvised webbing Ryzk arose and stretched.

"I'll take cabin watch," he said as if there was no disputing that. But I did not miss the sudden flicker of eye Zilwrich made in my direction, as though he expected me to protest. However, we did not have Ryzk's experience and training in the pilot's seat. And with the erase on I did not see how he could do any harm.

He could have no reason to wish to surrender to a Waystar force. And they would give him, I was certain, no time to parlay if he tried it. He left and I said to Eet via thought-send: "The tape is on erase. He cannot send us back."

"An elementary precaution," Eet returned crushingly. "If he does not kill us all at emerge, and his theory works, we may have a small chance."

"You do not sound too sure of that." My inner uneasiness increased.

"Machines are machines and cannot be made to function too far from their norm, or they will cease to function at all. However, doubtless this is the only answer. And we shall have other matters to consider after the emerge."

"Such as what?" I was not prepared to accept vagueness now. Forewarned is always forearmed.

"We have tried psychometry," the Zacathan broke in. "I am not greatly talented in that direction, but the two of us working so—"

The term he used meant nothing to me and he must have read my ignorance, for he explained, and I was glad that it was he and not the mutant, for he did not condescend.

"One concentrates upon some object and he who has the talent can so gather information concerning its past owners. There is, of course, the belief that any object connected with high emotion in usage, say a sword used in battle, will carry the most vivid impressions to be picked up by the sensitive."

"And the bowl?"

"Unfortunately it has been a center point for the emotions of more than one individual, of more than one species even. And some of those owners must have been far removed from the norm we accept today. Thus we received a mass of emotional residue, some violent. Many impressions are overlaid, one upon another. It is as if one took a tattered skin, put over it a second, also rent but in other places, and over that a third such, then tried to see what lay beneath those unmatched rents.

"Our supposition that the bowl might be much older than the tomb in which it was found, belonging to a people different from those with whom it was buried, is right. For we have deduced, though it is very hard to define any one well, at least four overlays left by former possessors."

"And the zero stone?"

"That perhaps is the source of some of the difficulty we encountered. The force which animates it might well govern the unfortunate mixture of impressions. But this we can tell you—the map was of prime importance to those who first wrought it, though the bowl itself meant more to later possessors."

"Suppose we do find the source of the stones," I said. "What then? We cannot hope to control the traffic in them. Any man who has a monopoly on a treasure sets himself up as a target for the rest."

"A logical deduction," Zilwrich agreed. "We are four. And a secret such as this cannot remain a secret long, because of the nature of what we must exploit. Like it or not, you—we—shall have to deal with the authorities, or else live hunted men."

"We can choose the authorities with whom we deal," I replied, an idea forming in my mind.

"Logical and perhaps the best." Eet cut across my thought, picking it up in its half-formed state, following it straight to a decisive conclusion.

"And if those authorities are Zacathan—" I said it aloud.

Zilwrich eyed me. "You pay us much honor."

"By right." It gave me a small quirk of shame to have to answer so, to admit that it was the alien whom I might

trust above those of my own species. Yet that was so.
And I would hand to any one of their Council the secret
of what we found here (if we found anything worth the
title of secret) more willingly than I would to any of
my own leaders. The Zacathans have never been empire
builders, never sought colonies among the stars. They
are observers, historians, teachers at times. But they are
never swayed by the passions, desires, fanaticism which
has from the first made both great heroes and villains
among my own kind.

"And if this secret might well be one not to be
shared?" Zilwrich asked.

"That, too, I could accept," I said promptly. But I
knew that I did not speak for Eet, or for Ryzk, who must
now be included as one of our number.

"We shall see," Eet answered, his reservations plain.
Not for the first time I wondered whether Eet's dogged
insistence that the quest of the stone's source be our
main goal did not have some reason he had never shared
with me. And then, could I, myself, completely surrender
the stones, knowing what I could do with them, knowing
that perhaps there was more, much more, we might learn
from them? Supposing the Zacathans advised us to hide,
destroy, blot out all we know of the gems. Could I agree
to that with no regret?

Later I lay in my cabin thinking. Eet, lying beside me,
did not touch those thoughts. But at last, to escape a
dilemma I could not resolve until we had passed many
ifs and buts in the future, I asked the mutant:

"This reading of the past of the bowl, what did you
learn of its past?"

"As Zilwrich said, there were several pasts and they
were overlaid, mixed with one another until what we

gained was so disjointed it was difficult to read any part of it and be sure we were correct. It was not made by those who fashioned the tomb. They came, I believe, long after, finding it themselves as a treasure-trove, leaving it with some ruler to whom they wished to pay funeral honor.

"The source of the stone—" he hesitated and the thought I picked up was one of puzzlement "—was not clear. Save that we do go now, if we have read the coordinates right, to that source. And the stone was set in the chart as a guide to those to whom it was very important. But that its native planet was their world of origin—that I do not think is the truth either. However, the reading was enough to set one's mind upside down, and the less I rethink on it the better!" With that he snapped mind-touch and curled into a ball to sleep. A state I followed.

The warning that we were at the end to our journey in hyper came some time later. As the Zacathan had assured us when we rigged his protection that he could manage it by himself, I made speed to the control cabin, Eet with me. Soon I was well wrapped in my webbing, watching Ryzk, in a like cocoon at the controls, trying to relax when the final test of our drastic emerge came.

It was bad, as bad or perhaps a fraction worse than that which had hit when we had joined the ship in the LB before the other jump. Only this time we had all the protection Ryzk's experience had been able to devise, and we came out in better shape.

As soon as I was fully conscious I looked to the radar. There were points registering on it, but they marked planets, not the ship locked to us through hyper.

"We did it!" Ryzk almost shouted. At the same time Eet scrambled along my still nearly immobilized body. I aw then what he held in a forepaw against his upper belly—the zero stone.

It was blazing with a brilliance I had not seen before except when we had put it to action. Yet now it was not adding to any power of ours. The glare grew, hurting the eyes. Eet gave an exclamation of pain and dropped it. He tried to pick it up again, but it was clear he could not use his paw-hand near that spot of fire. Now I could not even look directly at it.

I wondered if it was about to eat its way through the deck by the heat it was engendering.

"Blanket it!" Eet's cry was a warning. "Think dark—black!"

The power of his own thought swept mine along with it. I bent what mental energy I could summon to thinking dark. That we were able to control the surge of energy in the stone by such means astounded me. That awful brilliance faded. However, the stone did not return to its original dull lifelessness; it continued to contain a core of light which set it above any gem I had ever known and it lay in a small hollow which its power had melted out of the substance of the deck.

"Pliers—" I did not know whether they would help, for the heat of the stone might melt any metal touching it. But we could not pick it up in bare fingers and we dared not leave it lie, maybe to eat straight through the fabric of the ship level by level.

Ryzk stared at it, unable to understand just what had happened. But I had pulled out of the cocoon of webbing and managed to reach the box of tools he had used earlier. With pliers in hand I knelt to pick up the gem, fearing I might find it welded to the floor.

But it came away, though I could still feel heat and see that a hole in the deck beneath it was nearly melted through. Once on land, once in space, once on the edge of the wreckage we had used the zero stone as a guide. Could this small gem now bring us to the final goal of its home world?

We did not need it, since the bowl chart had already located the planet for us, fourth out from the sun. And oddly enough, once placed within the bowl, the furious blaze of the loose stone subsided into a fraction of its glow, as if the bowl governed the energy.

Though we kept a watch on the radar, there was no sign that the enemy had followed us into this system. And Ryzk set course for the fourth planet.

I half expected that time would have wrought a change in the sun, that it might have gone nova, imploded into a red dwarf, even burned out. But this was not so. It tested in the same class as was indicated on the ancient chart.

We went into scan orbit, our testers questing to inform us it was truly Arth type, though we were suspicious enough to keep all indicators on alert.

What we picked up on our viewers was amazing. I knew that Terra, from which my species had come into an immeasurably ancient galaxy, had been monstrously overcrowded in the last days before general emigration to the stars began—that cities had soared skyward, tunneled into depths, eaten their way across most of the continental land masses, even swung out into the seas. I knew that, but I had never seen it. Terran by descent I am, but Terra is across the galaxy now and more than half legend. Oh, we see the old tri-dees and listen to archaic tapes which are copied over and over again. But much of what we see is meaningless and there are long arguments as to what really did or did not exist in the days before Terrans roamed the star lanes.

Now I looked upon something like the jostling, crowded—terribly crowded—erections those tri-dees had shown. This was a planet where no empty earth, no sign of vegetation showed. It was covered, on the land masses by buildings, and even across the seas by strings of large platforms which were too regular in outline to be islands. The whole gave one a terrible sensation of claustrophobia, of choking pressure, of erection against erection, or against the earth of its foundations.

We passed from day to night in our orbit. But on the dark side no light showed. If there was life below—

But how could there be? They would be smothered, pushed, wedged out of existence! I could not conceive of life here.

"There is a landing port," Ryzk said suddenly, but he had a keener eye than I, or else we had swung over and past what he had seen. To me there was no break in that infernal mass of structures.

"Can you land?" I asked, knowing that treasure or no treasure, stone or no stone, I must force myself to set foot down there.

"On deters," Ryzk said. "Orbit twice for a bearing. There are no guide beams. Probably deserted." But he looked far from happy, and I thought perhaps he might share some of my feeling about what lay below.

He began to set a course. Then we lay back in our seats, our eyes on the visa-screen, watching the dead city-world reach up—for that was what it seemed to be doing—as if its towers were ready to drag us down to the world they had completely devoured.

SEVENTEEN

It was a tribute to Ryzk's skill that our landing was three-point, exactly on fins. He rode the ship down her tail rockets as only a master pilot could do. And not for the first time I was led to wonder what had exiled him from his kind—drink alone? Then we lay in our webbing watching the visa-screen as our snooper made a complete circuit of what lay about us, reporting it within.

With that report I came to respect Ryzk's skill even more. It was as if we had been threaded into a slit between walls of towers whose assault against the sky was such that one could not immediately adjust one's thoughts to what one's eyes reported. Only now that we were in that forest of man-made giants could we see the hurts time had dealt them.

For the most part they were either gray-brown or a blue-green in color, and there was no sign of seam or join as one might sight with stone blocks or the like. But there were cracks in their once smooth sides, rents in their fabric, which were not windows or doors. We could see no indication of those.

Ryzk turned to check the atmosphere dials. "Arth type, livable," he said. But he made no move to leave his webbing, nor did I.

There was something about those crowding lines of buildings which dwarfed, threatened us, not actively, but by their being. We were as insects, unable to raise ourselves from the dust in which we crawled, confronted by men who were giants with clouds gathering about their barely seen heads. And about it all there hung a feeling that this was a place of old death. Not a decent tomb in which honor had been paid to the one who slept there through the centuries, but rather a place in which decay had reduced to a common anonymity all that had meant aught—men, learning, belief—

Nothing moved out there. No flying thing flitted among the towers. There was no sign of vegetation. It was truly a forest of bones long removed from life. We could see nothing to fear, save that feeling which grew in us, or in me (though Ryzk's actions led me to believe he must share my uneasiness), that life had no place here now.

"Let us move!" That was Eet. There was a tenseness in his small body, a feral eagerness in the way his head darted from side to side, as if he tried to focus more intently on the visa-screen—though as that continued its slow sweep I saw no change in the monotony of the towered vista.

I left the webbing, Ryzk also. The bowl with the zero stone was on the deck, with Eet crouched over it as if he were on guard above its contents. And the stone blazed, though perhaps with not the same intensity as earlier.

We climbed down to join Zilwrich. The Zacathan was on his feet, leaning against the wall. He looked to Eet and I guessed some message passed between them. I lent my shoulder to the Zacathan's support and, together with Ryzk, aided him out of the hatch, down the ramp, to the apron of the space port.

There arose a hollow moaning and the pilot slewed around in a half crouch, looking down one of the narrow passages between the towers. Save for the open pocket of the port, there was gloom unbroken in those ways, such dusk as I had seen in forests of other worlds. The moaning shrilled and then our startlement vanished as we realized it was caused by the wind. Perhaps that acted upon the rents in the buildings to produce such sounds.

But outside the *Wendwind* the vast desolation was worse even than it had seemed on the screen. And I had not the slightest desire to go exploring. In fact, I was gripped by the feeling that to venture away from the port was to enter such a maze as one could never issue from again. As to where to search—Seen from the air, this planet-wide city covered all the ground, part of the sea. We might be half, three quarters, or the world away from what we sought, and it would take days, months of searching—

"I think not!" Eet had brought the bowl with him. Now he held it out and we saw the double blaze of the point on its surface and of the jewel within. He turned his head sharply to the right. "That way!"

But whatever lay "that way" might still be leagues from the port. And Zilwrich could certainly not tramp any distance on his unsteady feet, nor would I leave any of our party with the ship this time. We had the flitter—if we could crowd two of us into its cargo space, then we could quest some distance above the surface.

We settled Zilwrich with Eet at the end of the ramp and returned to the ship. What supplies we had room for and the crossbows went into the flitter. Three of us, plus Eet, would make such a heavy load we could not gain much altitude, but it was the best we could do. The LB had been so modified it might take days to alter it again, and we had no time to waste.

Judging by the sun, it was late afternoon when we were ready. I suggested waiting until the morning, but to my surprise the Zacathan and Eet overruled me. They had been in a huddle over the bowl and seemed very sure of what must be done.

As a matter of course Eet took command after we packed ourselves into the small craft, using my hands to his service. We hovered perhaps twice my height from the ground, then headed off sharply to the right, crossing the edge of the port, turning down a dusky channel between the towers.

The dark closed about us more and more as the buildings cut out the sun. Again I wondered how men could have lived here. Away from the port there appeared aerial runways connecting the buildings at different levels, crisscrossing into a net which finally grew so thick as to shut off most of the light from the level at which we traveled. Some of the ways were broken, and the debris of their disintegration weighted those below, or had landed in a heap of remains on the surface of the break below.

We had the beamer on, and I cut the speed to hardly more than a hover lest we crash into one of those piles.

Yet Eet seemed entirely sure of our direction, sending me out of one half-filled lower way into another.

Dusk became full night. I had a growing fear we would be utterly lost, forever unable to find our way back to the comparative open of the port. There was a sameness to this level, just here and there the remains of a bridge fallen from the heights, the smooth bases of the buildings totally unbroken by any sign of an entrance.

Then the beamer picked up a flash of movement. It had been so quick that I thought my imagination had betrayed me into thinking I had seen it—until our beam trapped the thing against one of the walls. So cornered, it turned to face us, slavering defiance, or perhaps fear.

I have seen many strange beings on many worlds, so that weird defections from what is the norm to my species were not unknown to me. Yet there was something about this thing in the dark and forgotten ruins which brought an instant reaction of loathing in me. Had I been in the open, a laser in my hand, I think I would have slain it without thought or compassion.

Only for a moment did we see it so, backed against the unyielding buttress, pinned by the light. Then it was gone, with such speed as left me astounded. It had gone on two legs, then dropped to four. And the worst thing was that it looked like a man. Or what might have been a man eons ago, before time had burned out all which makes my kind more than an unthinking creature set upon survival alone.

"So it would seem that the city still has its inhabitants," Zilwrich commented.

"That thing—what was it?" The disgust in Ryzk's voice matched my own emotion. "Where did it go?"

"Turn to the left." Eet appeared unaffected by what we had seen. "In there—"

"There" was the first opening I had seen on the ground level of any building. It was too regular to be another rent. The gap was large enough to accommodate the flitter. But I had a very unpleasant suspicion that it was also where the scuttling creature had disappeared. To search further would mean leaving the craft, and to be trapped by that "thing" or others of its kind—

Yet I obeyed Eet's direction, bringing the flitter to a standing hover within the shell of chamber beyond that doorway. We were in a circular space. If there had been any furnishings, those were long since gone. But the floor was heaped with gritty, flaky stuff which perhaps had once been fittings. This was pathed, beaten solid in some places. And the paths—there were two of them—led directly to another dark opening in the floor, a well.

I moved the flitter cautiously until we nosed the lip of that descent. We could indeed lower into it in the machine. But to do this, unaware of what might lie below, was a peril I was not ready to face. If I had such fears, Eet was not concerned with them. He hung over the bowl in which the gem blazed.

"Down!" he urged. "Now down!"

I would have refused, but the Zacathan spoke.

"It is true. There is a very strong force below us. And if we go with caution—"

I certainly would not descend outside the flitter, but to go in it would give us a small measure of protection. Yet I thought it foolhardy to try at all. I fully expected a protest from Ryzk. Only when I glanced to him I saw he was as bemused by the gem in the bowl as Eet.

Moving out over the well I eased the flitter onto settle-hover, thankful that we were using a craft meant for exploration. And I kept a wary eye on the walls as we began the descent at as slow a speed as I could hold us to.

What had been the original use of this opening we could not know. Perhaps it had the same function as our grav lifts. But that it was also a passage for later users was apparent. Into the once smooth walls had been pounded or wedged a series of projections meant to serve as hand—and footholds, a very crude ladder. And the bits and pieces so used were rough, some of them surely ripped from more complex fittings. The work was very bad, its quality far beneath that of the city constructions, as if it had been done by a race who was at a primitive level.

We were descending by floors, passing dark openings in the walls of the shaft, as if that were a hub of a series of wheels whose spokes were evenly spaced passages. I counted six such levels, yet the circumference of the well did not dwindle in size as I feared it might. And though the crude ladder led to several of the cross-corridor openings, it also continued on down and down, as if it served a vast warren of burrows.

I watched the mouths of any opening the ladder served, but there was no sign of life, and our beamer could not penetrate them very far. Down and down, six levels, ten, a dozen, twenty—the wall grew no smaller. But it was a growing strain to hold the flitter on settle-hover at this slow speed. And always that ladder kept pace with us. Fifty—

"Soon, very soon now!" Eet's thought was excited, more filled with emotion than any I had ever received before. I looked to the dials. We were some miles below the surface. I cut our speed to the lowest and waited. There was a bump, and we had landed. Only a single tunnel mouth faced us now, a little to the right. And it was too small for the flitter. Any further exploration must be on foot, and I had no desire to leave the confines of the small safety offered by that craft.

My prudence was justified. There was movement at the mouth of that tunnel, though I remembered that crude ladder had ended four levels above our present position. Only what came into our beam was a machine, unlike any I had seen before. But there was enough resemblance to things I knew to suggest that the tube rising to aim at us was about to discharge something meaning no good to invaders.

When I put a finger to the rise button, both Eet and the Zacathan spoke, Eet by thought, the alien in Basic.

"Do not!"

Do not? They were crazed. We had to get out of the range of that thing, if we could, before it fired!

"Look—" That was Zilwrich. Eet was still staring at the stone in the bowl.

Look I did, expecting death to come at me from that sinister tube. What I did see was—nothing at all!

"Where—?"

"Esper impressions," Zilwrich answered. "It is known that certain things, trees, water, stones—and perhaps other objects—can hold visual impressions for many years, release them to one in the proper frame of mind for reception. The builders here may have known and used that principle. Or what we have seen may be only a report of its use at some time in the past, action which impelled such heightened emotions in those viewing it that the impression remained to be activated by us."

"We go—there—" Eet brushed aside the need for any explanation. Instead he was pushing the bowl ahead, using it as an indicator that our way led down that dark passage.

In the end he had his way. Otherwise he and the Zacathan would have set off alone. And my pride, such as it was, would not let me hold back. Because we were now a party united against the unseen perils of the unknown, I gave Ryzk one of the crossbows. So armed, we started out, Eet riding on my shoulder, where his weight was something of a problem, Zilwrich and Ryzk on my heels.

I had taken a smaller beamer from our supplies, but we did not need its ray long. Soon the gem in the bowl gave us light. And what it showed ahead for a goodly space was smooth, unbroken walling, as if we were advancing along a great tube.

Distance in the dark underground was relative. I thought we might find lack of air a danger. But apparently whatever system supplied this depths with a breathable atmosphere was still operative.

At last we came to the end of the passage and out. Not into a mine burrowing, as I had come more and more to expect, but into a room crammed with apparatus, equipment, some firmly based on the floor, the rest on tables or long counters. In the middle of this expanse was a blaze of light toward which Eet wanted to go.

A cone-shaped object, perhaps as tall as I, sat on a table by itself. And in it a transparent porthole allowed one to view an inner rack on which rested a dozen of the zero stones, vibrant with glowing life as we brought the two we carried closer to their container.

Resting beside the cone, on the table, was a second rack to which were clamped a further dozen rough, uncut stones. They were as black as lumps of carbon, yet they did not have the burned-out look of the exhausted zero stones we had found in the derelict space ship on our first trial of the power of the gems.

Eet sprang from my shoulder to the top of the table, put down the bowl, and set about prying at the porthole in the cone, trying to get at the jewels within. But something about that whole array triggered my memory.

There are many ways of cheating known to the experienced gem buyer. Stones may be so treated as to change their color, even hide flaws. Heat will transform amethyst to golden topaz. A combination of heat and chemicals skillfully used can make a near undetectable royal rovan of the best crimson hue from a pale-pink one. Heat can do—

I loosened one of the black lumps from the rack and brought out my jeweler's lens. I had no way of testing the thing I held, yet there grew in me the belief that this was the matrix, the true zero stone. They might not be natural gems at all, but manufactured—which could logically give them the power to step up energy.

The thing I held was certainly odd. Its surface was velvety to the eye, but not the touch. If it had been shaped like a seed pod—I drew a deep breath. Memory was playing a strange trick on me. Surely it had to be a trick.

Once before I had found stones, or what appeared to be stones, tumbled in a stream. To the eye, though not to the touch, they had had a velvety, almost furred surface. One of those stones had been appropriated by the ship's cat, who had licked it, swallowed it, to give birth to—Eet! These were hunks of mineral, not rounded, podlike. But their surfaces—

I looked to Eet as I weighed that lump in my hand. He had discovered the secret of the latch on the porthole, jerked it open, and was taking out the rack with the finished gems. Then, to my amazement, as the weight

of the tray was lifted from the latches which held it, I
saw the cone come to life, a light flash on in its interior.
Without thinking (further than wanting) past my desire
to prove the truth of my suspicion, I inserted the second
rack, saving out only the lump I had taken from it. My
fingers were almost trapped as the porthole snapped shut
of its own accord. And blazing light, blinding to any
direct gaze, gathered behind the view-plate.

I had my answer. "Made stones."

Zilwrich picked up one from the other rack, took from
me the black lump to compare.

"Yes, I believe you are correct. And I do not think
that this"—he indicated the black lump—"is true ore or
matrix either." He turned his bandaged head from right
to left to view the room. The light was breaking in fierce
waves from the cone, giving us a far radiance. "This was,
I am certain, a laboratory."

"Which means," Ryzk commented, "that these are the
last stones we may ever see. Unless they left records
of how—"

There was sudden horrible shrilling, hurting one's
ears, reaching into the brain. I gave one glance at the
cone and grabbed for Eet, shouldered Zilwrich back, and
cried out a warning. Then fire broke through the top of
the oven, fountained up. Somehow I hit the floor, Eet
fighting in my hold, the Zacathan's body half under mine.

Then—the light went out!

The following dark was so thick it smothered one. I
groped for the beamer at my belt, for the second time
unable to be sure whether my eyes or the light itself had
failed. But a ray answered my press of button.

I aimed at the table, or where the table had stood.
Now there was nothing at all! Nothing but a fan of clear

space, as if the power had eaten a path for itself—but away, not toward us. Only one thing still lay there, seemingly unharmed, as if it was armored for all time against destruction—the map bowl. Eet uttered a sound, one of the few he had ever made. He broke from my hold and ran for it. But before he reached it he stopped short and I cried out even louder, moved by emotion in which fear and awe were mingled.

For in the beam of the torch Eet's furred body shimmered. He reared on his hind legs as might an animal caught by a throat collar and tight leash as it reached the end of the slack allowed it.

His hand-paws flailed at the air, and from his jaws came a wail of agony. But no mind-touch. It was as if then he was only animal.

With his back stiff, high-reared on his hind legs, he began to move jerkily, in a kind of weird, manifestly painful dance, round in a circle, the center of which was the bowl. Froth gathered on his muzzle, his eyes rolled wildly, and his body continued to shimmer until he was only a misty column.

That column grew taller, larger. It might be that the atoms which had formed the substance of Eet's half-feline body were being dispersed, that he was literally being shaken into nothingness. Yet, instead of spreading out then into wisps, the mist began to coalesce again. Still the solidifying column was not as small as Eet, nor was it gathering into the same shape.

I could not move, nor did Zilwrich, nor Ryzk. The beamer had fallen from my hand, but lay so that its ray, if only by chance, held full on Eet, or what had been Eet, and the bowl.

Darker, thicker, and more solid grew the column of that shuddering thing. Eet had been as large as his foster mother, the ship's cat. This was almost as tall as I. At last it stopped growing, and its frenzied circling about the bowl became slower and slower, then finally halted.

I was still held in frozen astonishment.

I had seen Eet take three shapes by hallucinatory disguise: the pookha, the reptilian thing at Lylestane, and the hairy subhuman who had entered Waystar with me. But that he had willed this last chance I was certain was not true.

He was humanoid and—

A slender body, yet curved, with long shapely legs, a small waist, and above that—

He—no—SHE—stood very still, staring at her outstretched hands, their skin soft, with a pearly sheen to their golden hue. She bent her head as if to view that body, ran her hands up and down it, perhaps to reassure herself that this was what she now saw.

While from Zilwrich broke a single word: "Luar!"

Eet's head turned, she looked at us with large eyes, a deeper and richer golden than her skin, drew her long dark-red hair about her as a cloak. Then she stooped and picked up the bowl. Balancing it on the palm of one hand, she walked to us along the beam of the torch, as if to impress upon us her altered appearance.

"Luar?" Her lips shaped the word. "No—Thalan!"

She hesitated, her eyes not on us for a moment but looking beyond us, as if they saw what we never could. "Luar we knew, yes, and dwelt there for a space, Honorable One, so that we left traces of our passage there. But it was not our home. We are the Searchers, the Bornagain ones. Thalan, yes. And before that, others, many others."

She held out the bowl, reversed it so we could see the map. But the wink of the zero stone on it was dead, and that other stone it had held had vanished. "The treasure we sought here—it is now gone. Unless your wise ones, Honorable Elder, can read very forgotten riddles."

"Thanks to you, Jern!"

I staggered as a sudden blow against my arm threw me hard against one of the pieces of equipment based on the floor. I clung to it so as not to go down.

Eet, in one of those lightning movements which had been his—hers—as a feline mutant, snatched up the beamer from the floor. She swung the full light on Ryzk as the pilot was setting another bolt to his crossbow. And from her lips came a clear whistle.

Ryzk twisted as if his body had been caught in the shriveling discharge of a laser. His mouth opened on a scream which remained soundless. And from his now powerless hands dropped his weapon.

"Enough!" Zilwrich, moving with the dignity of his race, picked up the bow. The whistle stopped in mid-note and Ryzk stood, turning his head from side to side, as if he fought against some mind daze and tried thus to shake it away.

Gingerly I investigated my hurt by touch, since what light there was Eet had focused on Ryzk, now weaving back and forth as if his will alone kept him on his feet. I could find no cut, but the flesh was very tender, and I guessed it had been so close a miss that the shaft of the bolt had bruised me sorely.

"Enough!" the Zacathan repeated. He dropped his hand on the pilot's shoulder, steadied him as if they had been comrades-in-arms. "The treasure—the best trea-sure—still lies about us. Or"—he looked to Eet measuringly—"is now a part of us. You have what you have long wished, One Out of Time. Do not begrudge lesser prizes to others."

She spun the bowl on her hand and her lips curved in a smile. "Of a surety, Honorable Elder, at this hour I wish no hurt to any, having, as you have pointed out, achieved a certain purpose of my own. And knowledge is treasure—"

"No more stones," I said aloud, not really knowing why. "No more trouble. We are luckier without them—"

Ryzk raised his head, blinking in the light. He looked to where I leaned against my support but I think he did not really see me.

"Well enough!" Eet said almost briskly then. "The Honorable Elder is right. We have found a treasure world, which he and his kind are best fitted to exploit. Is this not so?"

"Yes." I had no doubts of that.

Ryzk shook his head once more, but not in denial. It was rather to try and clear his mind.

"The stones—" he said hoarsely.

"Were bait for too many traps," I answered. "Do you want the Guild, those of Waystar, the Patrol, always at your heels?"

He raised his hand, wiped it back and forth across his face. Then he looked to Zilwrich, keeping his eyes carefully from Eet, as if from the Zacathan alone he might expect an answer he could accept as the truth.

"Still treasure?" There was something curiously child like in that question, as if Eet's strange attack had wiped from the pilot years of suspicion and wariness.

"More than can be reckoned." Zilwrich spoke soothingly.

But treasure no longer interested me. I watched rather Eet. As mutant and trader we had been companions. But what would follow now?

Mind-touch instead of words, amusement in part but delicately so, came swiftly in answer to my chaotic thoughts. "I told you once, Murdoc Jern, we each have in us that which must depend upon the other. I needed your body in the beginning, you needed certain attributes which I possessed in the woefully limited one I acquired. We are not now independent of each other—unless you wish it—just because I have found a body better for my purposes. In fact, one which, as I remember, served my race very well thousands of years ago. But I do not declare our partnership at an end because of that. Do you?"

She came forward then, tossing from her the bowl, the torch, as if both were no longer of service to her. Then her touch was on my body, light, soothing above my bruised hurt.

I had chafed against Eet's superiority many times, sought to break his—her (I still could not quite accept the change) hold on me, that tie which fate, or Eet, had somehow spun between us since he—she—had been born on my bunk in the Free Trader.

It seemed that her touch now drew away the pain in my arm and side. And I knew that for better or worse, for ill times and good, there was no casting away of what that fate had given me. When I accepted that, all else fell into place.

"Do you—?" Her mind-touch was the faintest of whispers.

"No!" My reply was strong, clear, and I meant it with all of me.